Advance Praise

"As an author, there's a moment when noble emotions such as 'admiration' and 'respect' for a fellow scribe cross over into outright, green-eyed jealousy. And, about midway through reading Molly Elwood's page-turning novel, *Spartacus Ryan Zander and the Secrets of the Incredible*, my appreciation for her quirky, breezy style quickly gave way to wanton prose-envy of the worst kind. Elwood leads you, circuitously, to the inevitable big showdown at the Big Top. I'm a better person for every mile spent with Spartacus on his darkly comic road trip."

   - Dale E. Basye, author of the series, *Heck, Where the Bad Kids Go*

"An eccentric kidnapped mother, a malefic circus, and more evil clowns than on a clear Halloween night. *Spartacus Ryan Zander and the Secrets of the Incredible* is fast and furiously fun."

   - Gary Ghislain, author of *How I Stole Johnny Depp's Alien Girlfriend* and *The Goolz Next Door* series

"I couldn't put it down. Literally. Never pick up a book while eating a caramel apple. But if you are going to be stuck with the book for a few days, I advise you make it *Spartacus Ryan Zander and the Secrets of the Incredible*."

   - Gerry Swallow, author of *Blue in the Face: A Story of Risk, Rhyme, and Rebellion*

Copyright © 2018 by Molly Elwood

Published by
Regal House Publishing, LLC, Raleigh 27612
All rights reserved

Printed in the United States of America

ISBN -13: 978-1-947548-41-1

Cover art and design copyright © 2018 by Lafayette & Greene
lafayetteandgreene.com

Regal House Publishing, LLC
https://regalhousepublishing.com
www.fitzroybooks.com

Library of Congress Control Number: 2017959220

Spartacus Ryan Zander and the Secrets of the Incredible

Fitzroy Books

For Zachary: I wouldn't trade you
for all the rat-watching in Paris.

Prologue

There are probably hundreds of things I'm afraid of. Heights. Girls. Scorpions. Motorcycles.

My older brother.

But clowns? I'd never been scared of clowns. Not even *after* I'd heard of Bartholomew's World-Renowned Circus of The Incredible.

However.

Being chased by a mob of angry, grinning clowns? Yeah, that can change everything.

These particular clowns—they're dressed like cops. They're wearing flat-topped cop hats with blue wigs, and dark navy uniforms that blend into one another. They're waving fake billy clubs and carrying fake guns.

At least...I *hope* they're fake.

And it's not like I'm somewhere normal where I can make a break for the nearest exit. (Then again, it's not like clown cops are ever anywhere normal.) I'm in the big top at Bartholomew's Circus, a.k.a The Incredible, in front of a sold-out show. I'm perched at the tippy top of a scaffold that rises like a five-story building over the main ring—and Bartholomew's clowns are closing in.

To the left and right of me, matching clown cops swarm the scaffold, identical red smiles painted across identical white faces. I try to tell myself that they wouldn't hurt me in front of an audience. But then again, Bartholomew is crafty; maybe he could play it all off as part of the show.

"It's just fake blood, ladies and gentlemen," Bartholomew would say.

The thought makes me shiver.

I know I only have a few moments before they'll be up here with me, but I can hardly think. There's so much chaos.

The orchestra is playing a manic, galloping version of "Stars and Stripes Forever," all blatting horns and screaming piccolos. Spotlights rake the tent and drive the audience to cheer wildly. And every single performer is out and parading across the ring—mime-faced muscle men on unicycles, wiry contortionists, these creepy, spindly-legged skeleton guys.

It's like they're making a huge distraction to keep the audience from thinking about whatever *I'm* doing.

But really, I have no idea what I'm doing. It's not like this was part of my plan.

I can see only one way out: I can jump down to the diving board, ten feet below me.

Ten feet isn't that far, is it?

But that isn't a long-term solution. Even *if* I get to the diving board (because falling off is a definite possibility), I'm still *stuck on a diving board*. I'll have to get down the ladder before anyone climbs up (which seems impossible), or I'll have to jump into the diving pool. And from this height, the pool looks like a thimble of water.

And still—once I'm in that pool, it's not like I'm in the clear. Not by a long shot.

Next to the pool, in the center of it all, is the ringmaster. Bartholomew himself. He's standing silent and straight and still in his black suit and too-tall top hat. His dark-gloved hand shades his eyes from the glare of the house lights as he watches his goons clamber up the metal scaffold towards me. His half-man, half-shark sidekick is pacing beside him, gnashing his knife-sharp teeth. I have the passing thought that I might throw up.

One more glance at the advancing clowns and I know I can't stay where I am.

I drop to my stomach and swing my feet over the edge. The crowd, which has been gawking at the clowns marching across the stage like a line of ants, catches sight of me and realizes what I'm about to do.

"Ooh!" they gasp, loudly enough to be heard over the orchestra.

No kidding, I think to myself. I've never been so high off the ground before, and here I am, about to blindly lower myself off this fifty-foot high metal walkway, butt-first.

Don't look down. And don't think about death.

I scoot my torso off the edge until I'm at the point of no return, where I'm more in the air than I am on the ledge, legs hanging. I know I'm right above the diving board—all I have to do is let go, and I'll land right on it.

Just let go, I tell myself, but my hands don't listen. They keep gripping the scaffold. My fingers immediately ache.

In front of me, the clown cops emerge onto the scaffold landing. They're just a few feet away, laughing. They're so close, I swear I see one wink at me.

And that's when I panic, steal a glance down, and lose my grip.

And I fall.

For the brief moment I'm in the air, the music cuts. The audience's gasp drowns out my own.

Amazingly, I don't die. Instead, I land on the diving board to wild applause, the cymbals crashing in triumph. The wide board vibrates beneath me and I cling to it.

"Go, Spartacus, go!" someone in the audience shouts.

Morons. They're all morons.

And yet…*I'm still alive.*

The orchestra picks up again, right where it had left off.

Shaking, I scramble to my feet and look up where I'd been just a few seconds before. The clown cops are up there, shaking their oversized, fake billy clubs at me. Scowling. Taunting.

With no time to think, I lunge for the ladder. And that's the moment a new batch of clowns bursts out from behind the stage curtains.

That's when I realize: *Bartholomew always has more clowns.*

These new ones start scaling each side of the high-dive's free-standing ladder, two-by-two. I'm about to be cornered again—and this time, there's just the one way down.

No way am I jumping, I tell myself. *There has to be another way.* I turn desperately to the audience. Maybe they've figured out this isn't a game.

"Please! I'm not part of the circus!" I shout, waving my arms. "This is real!"

But the music drowns me out, and the crowd just stuffs more popcorn in their stupid mouths, loving every moment.

I peer down at the tank of water far below. I hadn't noticed before, but now I can make out a couple of small sharks in it. As if that weren't bad enough, Sharkman runs and takes a flying leap into the tank. He starts swimming around in darting circles, his dorsal fin cutting slices through the water.

I have to hand it to him: he really looks just like a shark. That, and he's blocked my last escape route.

"They've got me surrounded," I whisper. That's something I always thought would be cool to say out loud, but until this very moment, I hadn't realized that it's one thing you *never* want to say.

Desperate, I yell again: "Help me! I'm not with them!"

But it's useless. This is like a bad dream—one that's finally reached that point of weirdness where you just *know* you're going to wake up at any moment. Yet the dream keeps going.

Everyone is on their feet, cheering enthusiastically. Feeling numb, I wonder if Bartholomew planned the whole commotion.

Then, someone—probably a clown—shouts it: "Jump!"

And then another voice, from the audience: "Jump, kid!"

Are they insane?

I gape down at the tank. It may as well be a glass of water. I frantically shake my head and wave my arms in front of my body, trying to mime, "No way."

The audience loves my sheepish response and roars with encouragement. Soon the whole tent is chanting, "Jump! Jump! Jump!"

The noise is deafening.

Jumping would be crazy. I'm not my mom. I'm not invincible.

The clowns are almost to the top of the diving board ladder. When they get here, they're going to take me backstage and do who knows what. Erase me. Bump me off. Rub me out.

I'm not in a dream, and I'm not going to wake up and find myself safe in my bed. This nightmare is actually happening.

As I gulp the thick summer air, I consider everything that has led up to this moment. To what's looking more and more like the end of the line.

The fat lady singing.

The grand finale of Spartacus Ryan Zander.

Chapter One

I'm going to start right at the beginning, the day Mom left home to become The Amazing Athena, World-Famous Human Cannonball.

Sure, first there were the epic fights, the Month of Silence, and the time Dad set Mom's hula-hoops on fire. But going into all of that would just make you think Mom ran out on Dad. Trust me—none of that stuff is important.

Dad and Will (my older brother) took her departure pretty well. And by "pretty well," I mean they seemed to think we were better off without her. Will was convinced she'd left Dad for a circus performer. And Dad? Well, her absence was a touchy subject with him. The first time I blurted out how things were better when Mom was around, he didn't talk to me for days.

She went missing the same day I started sixth grade. Will and I came home to find the house looking "a little odd." (Those were Dad's exact words to Grandma: "The place looks a little odd." Personally, I think saying "The place is destroyed" would have been a better way to put it.)

Even from a block away, Will and I could tell. The windows stood open and our dark red curtains billowed out, getting tangled in the rhododendron bushes. I ran ahead, but was too nervous to open the front door, so I waited for Will while anxiously gnawing the insides of my cheeks.

The moment Will cracked the door, water poured out onto the porch. The front hall's bathroom sink was overflowing, flooding the entryway. Will slogged through the standing water to turn off the faucet while I poked my head into the living room. The couch's smoldering, smoking cushions smelled like burnt lemon custard, like they'd been lit on fire and then doused with a pitcher of lemonade. Our old box television was facedown on the floor and two sets of booted footprints, one narrow, one wide, danced up the wall.

Then there was the kitchen. The blender was running. The dining table was on its side with only three legs attached (we never did find the fourth). Six steak knives were stuck into the pantry door in a perfect vertical line. The last knife pinned a note at eye level, scrawled in handwriting that didn't quite look like my mom's.

Dear Boys,

I made it into Bartholomew's Circus of The Incredible! Sorry to leave so abruptly—and sorry about the mess. I'll be in touch soon.

Love,

Mom

XOXO

P.S.

The P.S. part of the note was torn off in a jagged line, like someone had changed their mind. I wanted to tear the note down and crumple it up, but instead I just slid to the floor and sat there staring up at it, blinking away the pressure behind my eyes.

"What are you doing?" Will, who hadn't noticed the note yet, was peering down at me. "Poop Lip—wait, are you crying?"

I scowled at his smirking face. Poop Lip. One unfortunately-placed freckle—not a mole, a *freckle*—one concentrated cluster of melanin, one overly pigmented spot just above my lip and, thanks to Will, nearly every kid at Brenville Elementary and Brenville Middle-Senior High called me *Poop Lip*. The town we live in is small and Will's reach was long—even the old man at the gas station once called me Poop Lip. I just stared at him. I couldn't think of anything to say.

I guess I was lucky that at least my dad, my teachers, and Elliott Carson (my best friend) called me Ryan, which is my middle name. I go by Ryan because my first name isn't exactly normal, but I'll get to that tragedy later.

When dealing with Will, you need to follow two simple rules.

Rule number one: Never question him. Not unless you want to walk away bruised and possibly wedgied. And rule number two: Never show weakness. Not even if your mom destroys the house and then abandons the family.

I wiped my nose before standing up. I realized I was shivering—maybe I was cold from the windows being left wide open. I pulled the note from the pantry door and handed it to Will.

"Mom left," I told him. "With the circus. She's gone."

Will skimmed Mom's note. He looked even angrier than usual. "Of course she's gone," he said, kicking a can of green beans so it skittered across the floor. "How long has she been trying to get out of here?"

Will had a point. Even though I was the only one who had known Mom was serious about joining the circus, anyone could see she wasn't happy. Brenville and her talents didn't exactly mesh. But even though I knew she wanted more excitement, I always thought that if she left, she'd take us with her.

I never thought she'd leave me behind.

Dad got home a few minutes later and the three of us just stared at the mess and the note and then—get this—no one said anything. Every time I started to speak, to ask what we were going to do, Dad glared and Will elbowed me in the armpit. Can you imagine? No, you can't, because it's not normal.

But then again, no one in my family is normal. So, instead of talking, Dad went upstairs to shower, Will called in a pizza, and then we sat and ate dinner in front of the broken TV, as if Mom trashing the house and leaving with the circus were the most normal thing in the world.

≈

It's common sense that if someone goes missing and your house looks like a tornado went through it, you call the police. Dad didn't. He made a few late-night phone calls that I couldn't quite hear through the heating vent, but he must have decided to trust what she wrote in the note and to leave it at that.

12

Maybe he was just relieved to be rid of her. Whenever he found her doing something "weird" or "crazy," he and Mom fought like stray cats. Like when he came home to find her teaching me how to throw knives. Or when she dyed her hair orange and red so that it looked like flames. Or when the neighbors called to complain that she was leaping from fence post to fence post in front of their house. Or the time, on a family hike, she somehow got on the back of a wild elk and rode it for a whole twenty yards. And that was just the stuff Dad *knew* about.

Brenville's a small town. If you stand out at all, you may as well start your own reality TV show because everyone is going to know everything about you anyway. So the neighbors talked. And Dad? Dad just wanted to be invisible.

The day after my mom disappeared, my best friend and next-door neighbor Eli Carson told me the Story of the Black Van. Eli had been home sick on the first day of school (which he's been getting away with every year since second grade) and happened to look out his window to see a black van pulling up in our driveway. An unmarked van. It definitely did *not* have Bartholomew's World-Renowned Circus of The Incredible scrawled across the side like you'd think it would if it had been there doing anything normal or official. No, it was a plain black van with tinted windows. Oh, and it didn't have license plates.

Eli kept watching because he thought the van was weird—and because he didn't have anything better to do. He said it was there for exactly forty-three minutes and that he heard banging and crashing coming from inside the house. He never saw Mom, but he *did* see two creepy men heave a big black bag into the back of the van right before it left, tires squealing down the street.

"And you didn't think to call the cops?" I asked.

"I didn't know your mom was going to be missing," he said. "Anyways, one of the guys was all pale and really tall. Like a vampire version of Conan O'Brien. The other guy was like an Incredible

Hulk, weight-lifter type. Looked like a pile of bricks. Man, I can't believe they kidnapped your mom!"

Yeah, he said it just like that. No build-up, no saying it in a Do-you-think-this-is-possible? kind of way. Just *bam*! Dropped the bomb without even thinking. Of course, he argues over who actually said it first, but this is my story and I can say with complete certainty that I am pretty sure it was Eli.

Will was dribbling his soccer ball around the lawn like nothing had happened when I ran to tell him about the Black Van. He snorted, but didn't look up. "So what you're saying," he said, dancing around the ball and breathing hard, "is that you and The Eel think she was kidnapped?"

Pow!

I jumped as Will kicked the ball hard against the fence. It always hit the same spot. He'd put one toe on it, fake left, fake right, then: *Pow!*

"Maybe," I said, trying to sound more casual than I was. Will made me nervous. But then, Will made everyone nervous. I think he even made our parents nervous.

"Why would a circus kidnap somebody?" Will asked.

"Maybe so they don't have to pay them?" I ventured.

"That's the stupidest thing I ever heard."

Pow!

I flinched again. He was kicking the ball really hard. Harder than usual. But I wasn't going to let it drop.

"What about the bag, though?" I asked. "It was big enough for a person."

"Maybe it was her makeup," he said. I worked up enough confidence to glare at him. "What? Seriously! They wear a lot of makeup in the circus," he said, before firing the ball again.

Pow!

The look on Will's face made it clear that unless I wanted him to refocus his attention from the soccer ball to me, the conversation was over. So I kept quiet for a while, but I thought about it all the time. It wasn't just the destroyed house and the Black Van and the large-enough-for-a-person bag. There was more. Much more.

A few weeks later I started getting postcards from my mom. Postcards with secret messages, saying things like "Help me" and "I'm in trouble," all hidden within seemingly happy notes. And all in her handwriting—or handwriting that was close, like she'd written them in a hurry.

No matter how ridiculous it seemed, it was true—my mom actually had been kidnapped by the circus.

Even before the postcards, Eli and I had looked into The Incredible. What we found wasn't very encouraging—in fact, it was downright sketchy.

The website for Bartholomew's World-Renowned Circus of The Incredible was kind of underwhelming. It had only a few pictures and a schedule that listed just a handful of shows. Eli and I knew from news websites, though, that the circus performed a lot more often than that. And news stories were easy to come by. Bartholomew made headlines wherever he went—and not just because people were clamoring to see his shows.

Bartholomew's Wikipedia page linked to all the legit news stories: There had been an "accident" where three trapeze artists had died (getting weird). Then there was a tiger mauling where a guy lost his tongue (getting weirder). People said the circus was cruel to its animals, that it didn't pay workers on time, but the circus got out of any legal trouble, swearing these were lies from angry ex-employees. Eli thinks Bartholomew bribed the investigators.

And all that? That's not even close to the weirdest (and worst) stuff. Wikipedia noted someone had created a forum, IHateBartholomewsCircus.com, where people shared even more stories—dark, bizarre stories. The sort of thing my dad would have yelled at me for reading. So of course Eli and I read every conversation on it. People on the forum said that Bartholomew had sold his soul to the devil. That he used dark magic to turn his audiences into zombies. That he'd helped fix the 2005 *Tour de France*. There's more, but I'll tell you about that later.

It all came down to this: I wasn't the only person who thought there was something strange about The Incredible. Okay, all the devil, weirdo-stuff sounded too stupid to believe, but if even *some* of it was true, it was bad news for my mom.

I wasn't really surprised that Dad didn't take my kidnapping theory seriously. Adults seem to lose their ability to think about anything strange or out of the ordinary. But Will, who knew evil inside and out, should have sensed that something was off.

Over the next ten months, Mom sent me twenty-five postcards, and half of them had secret codes. Each time I got a new one, I brought it immediately to Will. I've never seen anyone laugh so hard.

"How could it be more obvious?" I fumed, shoving the postcard from Last Chance, Colorado, in his face. "Read it."

"Come on," he said. "Circuses don't kidnap people. Don't be a moron."

"Just read it," I repeated. "Read it and tell me she isn't asking for help."

And so he read it out loud:

Hello Spartacus!
Everything is going well!
Lots of fun people to meat and
Places to see.
My cannonball thing is going really great.
Everyone thinks I'm the best they have ever seen!
Love,
Mom

"She's trying to get my attention," I insisted. "I mean, look how she spelled 'meet.'"

Will squinted at the card and then back at me.

"You seriously think there are hidden messages in these things, *Smarticus?*"

I wanted to think that maybe he was hiding his fear to protect me. That maybe, deep down, he saw how weird and scary the whole situation was. But when I pointed out that the first letter of each line, going from top to bottom, spelled "HELP ME," he laughed so hard, he farted.

"Why would she write that in there, huh?" I asked.

"It's a coincidence!" he exclaimed, after containing himself and wiping a tear from his eye. "Look, you know how a hundred monkeys pounding on a hundred typewriters for a hundred years—"

"Yeah, yeah. They'd write a play," I said, rolling my eyes. I hated his guts right then.

"Yeah. Everyone knows that. It's a scientific fact," Will explained. "But it doesn't mean anything. Besides, what about the other postcards? She sends you some without all the…what did you call them?"

"*Clues,*" I huffed, pulling the card out of his hand and tucking it back in an envelope with the others.

"Clues!" Will giggled. "Some don't say anything secret, though, right? Why would she do that?"

I thought about it for a minute and then shuffled through the envelope until I found one I liked, the one with the skull of a triceratops on it. It was from the Academy of Natural Sciences in Philadelphia.

Dear Spartacus,

Hello, my sweet one. Today it rained, and I thought of you. Remember last summer when we got caught in the rain in the park and we waited under a tree for it to pass? You told me about helping the pigeon with the red yarn tangled around its foot. I said I was very proud of you, yet you were sad. You asked me why such things happen. I didn't have an answer then, and I still don't have an answer now. But I do know that the world is better with you in it.

I will always think of you when it rains.
Love,
Mom

There weren't any clues on it—at least none that I could find. And it was written so much better than the others.

Why was that?

"Maybe she's being tricky, so Bart or his goons don't catch on. One normal note, one note with a clue? That's harder to figure out, right?" I suggested as Will snatched it out of my hand and began to read,

"Dear Spartacus," he began, speaking in that high lady-voice he used when he imitated Mom—or any girl, for that matter. *"You don't know how much I miss you and your lovely and generous brother Will. Will is the best brother you could—"*

"Give me that! It doesn't say that!" I lunged for the postcard, but he hopped up onto the sofa he'd been sitting on and, holding a hand over my face, jumped up and down while continuing to "read."

"The best brother you could ask for. In fact—oof! Watch it, Poop Lip!—*In fact, I've told your father to give your allowance to sweet William for the next four years and*—Ooh, Poopy, now you've done it!"

There's no reason to describe the scuffle blow for blow, so let's just cut to me, back upstairs in the safety of my room, tending my bruises and taping the postcard back together. (Will had turned it into confetti and stuffed it down my pants.)

As I taped the last piece into place, I had to admit Will had a point.

Why would only some of the cards have clues and not the others? And why would the ones without clues make it sound like she was having a great time?

But what I'd said to Will about her being tricky also made sense: she wrote and sent the normal ones to make it appear like everything was fine, just in case someone was reading them. Or maybe she even wrote them in front of others. And maybe she mixed in the other postcards—the ones with the clues—secretly. But she still put them in code, just in case.

That made total sense—right?

~

Before we get any further, I suppose I should address the whole *Spartacus* thing. Mom was pretty smart, but she seemed to have had a brain fart when naming me. I don't think it crossed her mind that growing up in a town the size of Brenville might not be easy for a kid named *Spartacus Ryan Zander*. Then again, her name was *Athena*, which is just as ridiculous, so maybe I should blame her parents— then again, we never visited her parents. Mom never told us why. It'd just always been that way.

When I asked her why Will got a normal name and I got Spartacus, she just kissed me on the head and said in her airy way, "In time, Spartacus. In time."

Whatever *that* meant.

The name didn't bother me for the most part because I'm not an idiot and I went by Ryan instead. For obvious reasons. If you're like any normal almost-thirteen-year-old, you're probably not up-to-date on how cool the *real* Spartacus actually was. So explaining to classmates how he was a gladiator who led a slave revolt? Yeah, that conversation doesn't end well (I tried to defend my name in first grade and was pummeled by a third-grader who was trying to see if I'd inherited any of the original Spartacus's gladiatorial skills. Long story short: no, no I hadn't).

So the name *Spartacus* didn't come up except when we had a substitute teacher or when it was report card time; both of these occasions reminded my classmates that I wasn't only Ryan, or Poop Lip, but also Spartacus. Sure, kids can be mean, but they're also creative ("Sparty Pooper" was one of the more popular plays on my name). I found if I ignored them, just like I ignored "Poop Lip," things weren't so bad. I mean, they kept it up, but I didn't let it get to me.

Mom, though, was the only one who called me Spartacus, at least in a serious, not-making-fun-of me way. And I never minded.

It never sounded weird when she said it. Dad, however, thought the name was just as stupid as I did. He started calling me Ryan as soon as I was born, hoping I'd "turn out normal."

Even when Mom told him that Ryan wasn't my name, he'd say "Ryan" right over the top of her "Spartacus," until they were both yelling my names back and forth over my crib. As I got older, it continued.

"Spartacus, please pass the peas."

"Ryan, pass your mother the peas."

"Phil, Spartacus *heard* me."

"Ryan. The peas. Now."

❧

I tried to talk to Dad about the postcards, but he refused to even read where they were from, let alone help me decode the secret messages. And when I tried showing him a news article about Bartholomew that I'd printed at the library? His response was—well, you know those people who can crack their knuckles without even touching them? Yeah, Dad's one of them. Two or three cracks from his fingers and that angry, hundred-mile stare and I clammed up. (That, and he marched across the room, snatched the article from me, and flushed it down the toilet—or at least tried to).

But I kept trying. I mean, this was my *mom*.

As it turns out, Dad's limit for putting up with conspiracy theories is two and a half months.

He was doing bills at the new dinner table (the old one had been tossed into the wood chipper) when he saw me standing in the doorway, postcards in hand. I was trying to get up the nerve to sit down next to him, hoping he'd finally show some interest.

He slammed his checkbook down so loudly, dust flew off the light fixture.

"No more of your stupid, silly ideas," he growled before I'd even said a word. "You hear me, Ryan? No more postcards, no more random connections, nada. If I see a map with even a pushpin in it, I will tear it up and make you eat it like cereal. Got it?"

I heard Will snicker from the family room, but I ignored him. I was just starting to think about saying something when Dad shut his eyes and sucked air in through his teeth. Then, with his eyes still closed, he pounded both his fists on the table.

"NOT."

Bang!

"ANOTHER."

Bang!

"WORD!"

Bang!

I shot out of the kitchen before he could open his eyes and light me on fire with them.

After he had shut me down, I ramped up my phone calls to the police from once a week to once a day. Then, a detective called our house and told Dad I had to stop calling them. Dad grounded me for a month. That gave me time to do some more research and draft a few letters to the FBI. But all I got back was an FBI baseball cap and a letter written from a cartoon dog.

A lot of help they were.

Nobody listens to kids.

~

Eli and I spent all winter putting a rescue plan together. But before I explain my idea, I should tell you about one of Mom's odd talents—one that would make rescuing her a snap.

One afternoon, while Dad was out of the house, I heard Mom calling for help. It took me a few minutes to trace her voice to Dad's study, but even then, I couldn't find her. The room was empty. Then I realized—her voice was coming from *inside* Dad's filing cabinet.

I opened the top drawer, thinking I was going crazy. Then I heard her say, "Lower."

She was in the very bottom drawer. A single drawer. I watched, agog, as she went from pretzel to Mom, unfolding to her full height. I mean, I wouldn't have thought it was possible if I hadn't seen it myself.

"Don't tell anyone," she said, shoveling everything back in the drawer. Like anyone would believe me. But I knew what she meant: "Don't tell Dad."

So I came up with the idea of using a suitcase the size of a small dog carrier—with wheels. I knew she could fit into that; it was bigger than the cabinet drawer. My brilliant, if simple, plan was to get to The Incredible, get backstage, and get Mom into the suitcase. Then I'd just wheel her out, hidden by the crowd. We'd go straight to the cops, Mom would tell them everything, and we'd take Bartholomew down.

Easy, right?

We planned the rescue mission for June, right after school let out. Sure, it was a long time to wait, but not skipping school just might mean the difference between being grounded for a couple of months and Dad just killing me himself. Besides, according to the Bartholomew's schedule, they had a show in June that was within traveling distance: San Francisco. It was only nine hours away.

Like I said before, we knew they performed in more places than they listed on their website, but strangely, they didn't announce them ahead of time. For all we knew, they could be performing in Brenville next weekend (okay, nothing *ever* came to Brenville, but you get what I mean). But at least with San Francisco, we could plan in advance.

And our plan was this: Eli's cousin Carl was going to drive me to Bend in his pickup. Bend is a bigger city about two hours away and that's where I'd "resurface," as Eli put it.

"You can't just get a bus from Brenville," he explained. "You have to go dark for a bit of time and pop up somewhere you don't belong. They'll never track you that way." Did I mention Eli watches a lot of old spy movies? But it made sense. So, once I was in Bend, I'd catch a ride to San Francisco. Eli would set it all up using this ride-share website he'd found.

Meanwhile, Mom's postcards got more and more desperate. The one from Imalone, Wisconsin, (which said "bring help"), made me realize that she didn't mean for me to come alone. Eli was out, though. He wasn't exactly known for his bravery—in the fourth grade, he peed his pants crossing a four-lane highway. I mulled it over and over (and over) until finally deciding Will was my only hope. After all, he's tough, she's his mom, and we're brothers. All that had to count for something, right?

And, if I'm going to be honest, I needed Will. I wasn't going to even get out the door without someone else counting on *me* to go with *them*. And I'm not exactly big. Or brave. Or a fighter. My impulse is to run away first, ask questions later—if at all. So I needed someone who wouldn't hide around the corner the moment he was needed. And I needed someone who would get fed up with me for being a wimp and stalk off angrily, someone who I'd chase after and apologize to and tell them I'd try to be braver, for their sake.

Not like I'd thought out that scene or anything.

Will was the right person. He was my opposite—and maybe he was for a reason. So we could balance each other out or whatever. Help each other. You know, if he ever stopped picking on me.

Call me an optimist.

Look, I know what you're thinking—Will would refuse to go. But I was sure that if I could just get him to really look at all the evidence (and also see that I was going with or without him), he'd have to say yes. It was just a matter of finding a good time to ask. But when your relationship is built entirely on trying to avoid getting punched in the stomach, there isn't a "good time." And so the right time still hadn't come when Will pulled the Worst Prank Ever on me.

And there have been some bad ones. Like when he used a syringe to inject my unopened yogurt with a laxative. Or the time he convinced me the house was haunted by writing messages on mirrors (and in my food) before finally putting a live squirrel in my room in the middle of the night. No. Those were just jokes. Teasers.

Child's play. They were nothing compared to what he had planned for me this time.

What I'm trying to say is that Will (and by default, Dad) left me no choice but to save my mom on my own.

Chapter Two

Brenville is just a blip on people's drives across Oregon, trips to bigger cities—cities with stop lights and things to do. We once had a place to rent movies, but it closed. There's a park with two benches and a broken water fountain, but that's it when it comes to entertainment. Other than the pool.

Brenville has a real, Olympic-sized public pool with the full ten lanes and a thirty-three-foot high dive. If you haven't seen one, try picturing a giant tower with three diving platforms. And the highest one? It's a ridiculous thirty-three feet up.

Yeah. Thirty-three feet. That means the pool has to be seventeen feet deep.

So why is this pool in Brenville? A town that doesn't have a chain restaurant or a store that sells things like shoes or hats? Well, years ago, some rich dad wanted his kid to swim in the Olympics—so he built her a pool. She lost interest, of course, and they eventually moved away and donated the pool to the town.

During the summer, pretty much every kid *lived* at the pool. As far as we were concerned, the high dive was *it*. The whole chili dog of existence.

Except, no one under eighteen was allowed off the high dive—and, face it, adults weren't interested (not even my mom, for some reason). So while everyone *talked* about going off it, only Will broke the rules and actually did. Sure, a few others did some nothing-spectacular, ho-hum cannonballs from the mid-level platforms, soaking everyone. But Will? He was an honest-to-god diver. He took his time before leaping off the platform and slicing into the water like a knife.

I didn't know how he got so good; he didn't practice that much.

I mean, really, he couldn't. He usually had to have a friend around to distract (or pin down) the lifeguard when he went up. So he didn't go up that often. Maybe he was a natural athlete, like Mom. Seeing him up there, hearing all the other kids *Oooh* and *Aahh*, was one of the few times I was proud he was my brother.

Everyone wanted to dive like Will. I'd even been up on the platform once to check it out, thinking maybe I'd try a cannonball. But thirty-three feet is high. Like stupid high. I figured you had to be kind of crazy, like Will was, to do something like that.

I must have mentioned the high dive too many times at home, though, because Dad seemed to get it in his mind that I *really* wanted to do it. (And no, Dad didn't give two finks about the age restriction.) Actually, I would have been quite happy living the rest of my life in Wimpdom. I could have grown to be an old man of forty, with kids of my own, and not have felt the least bit sad I'd never jumped off the high dive.

But, according to Dad, if I wanted it so badly, I should just do it. See, just because Dad thought Mom joining the circus was unacceptable, that doesn't mean he was against *me* doing wild things. My mom bungee-jumping off an overpass? Frowned upon. Me risking my life jumping from, like, a mile in the air? Yes, perfectly fine.

I think he was just upset that one of his sons was defective. With Will being the fearless weirdo he was, and my mom being what she was, I should have been less afraid. It's like my fear of diving represented all my shortcomings, wrapped up in one perfect, shameful package.

"So, did you go off the high dive today or what?"

Almost every summer dinner conversation began with this question. During the last week of school, while I was focused on my rescue mission, Dad focused on the high dive with even more excitement than the year before. He was like a bear trap with my foot caught in it—and he wouldn't let go. This summer would be the

Diving Summer. He actually said that: "The Diving Summer." That's when I felt I needed to speak up.

"Dad, I know the diving board is important to you," I half mumbled to both him and my plate. "But it's not important to me."

While I said this, he just shook his head in a mixture of sympathy and disgust. Mostly disgust.

"I just don't get you, Ryan," he said. "You're thirteen now, a teenager."

"I'm twelve, Dad."

"*Basically*, you're thirteen. And I mean, really, it's not that high."

I bit my tongue. Yeah, falling thirty-three feet through the air was a piece of cake. That's why there were so many Olympic high divers around.

"Besides," he continued, "you can't go through life being scared of things. When I was a kid, I was afraid of—well, I was afraid of...." Dad looked thoughtful. "Well, I could *imagine* what it would be like to be scared of, like, say, crowds or something. But I wasn't, of course. I'm just saying that I *know* what it would be like. And that I'd *get over* it already."

There was no point in telling him that I wasn't going to do it. So I kept quiet and that seemed to be the end of it, at least for that night.

But that wasn't the end of it.

The next day, Will "accidentally" ran over my binoculars while "speed mowing" the lawn. Before I got a chance to tell Dad, Will cornered me and said he felt bad about it. He said he would teach me to dive, to be just like him. He said we could sneak into the pool late at night so no one would know I was practicing.

"Let me make it up to you. You'll be famous," he said. "The girls are gonna go nuts."

First—yes. Red flags galore. Will doesn't talk to me. He doesn't do favors. He doesn't "make it up to me." Ever.

But.

But I said yes.

27

I know; this goes against everything I just said. But it was the night before the last day of school, and I was set to leave in a week. Even as I shook my head as Will tried to persuade me, I had a horrible but brilliant realization: If we bonded with the diving stuff, Will would *have* to go on the rescue mission with me.

How could he not?

And when you got down to it, I really needed Will.

Besides, I reasoned, *maybe I wouldn't even have to dive, just...you know, show up and try. Get Will to like me for me, and all that garbage.*

It was a Hail Mary, but maybe, just maybe it would work.

Okay, and if I'm being honest here, I was also *kind of* interested in the "girls going nuts" part. Well, there was actually only *one* girl I wanted to go nuts. Her name was Erika Dixon. Erika had gone to school with Eli and me since the second grade, and I could barely remember a time when I didn't have a crush on her. She was pretty and smart and popular. She also smelled like cinnamon all the time, which made no sense to me, but might have explained me liking her so much because cinnamon is my favorite spice.

Oh, and Erika never called me *Poop Lip*. Even after the time in fifth grade when I burnt her dress with Eli's homemade arc-welding science project (which he got a D on because of the danger level). So she wasn't rude to me even after I lit her on fire, which was a plus. However, when I *wasn't* burning her stuff, she didn't have two words to say to me. So, as much as I was thinking about the rescue mission, I have to admit my mind might have been on Erika a teeny bit, and the fact that she'd *have* to notice me if Will came through and taught me to dive.

Not that I was going to actually dive, because I wasn't crazy. But you know, the mind wanders a bit...

But I'm sure you've already guessed that I should have told Will *no*, right? That perhaps him teaching me was only setting the stage for the Worst Prank Ever? That I shouldn't have trusted him, shouldn't have gone to the pool, shouldn't have hoped I was on the brink of a brand-new brother?

You'd be right.

But try as I might to get a read on him, he *seemed* sincere. He *seemed* apologetic about my binoculars. He *seemed*—well, like Dad might have put him up to it. And like I said, I needed Will. So the very same night he offered, the night before the last day of school, I went with Will to the pool.

Will knew how to sneak in through a part of the fence that wasn't connected to the backside of the building. He just rolled the chain links back and we slipped in. He even knew where the light controls were. It was like he owned the place.

I stood on the cement pool deck while Will fiddled with the light for the pool. The ground was dry—it was never dry, but then again, I'd never been there after the pool closed. Crickets hummed in the dark night, but they stopped, startled, the moment the pool lit up. It was a surreal, emerald green and its surface threw wavering diamond shapes up the side of otherwise dark, ominous diving tower.

And it was terrifying. The only thing that kept me from bolting was the thought of the rescue mission. I just had to fake that I was going to dive for a little bit longer, and then I could start working on convincing him to come with me.

"You gotta get used to the height first," said Will, interrupting my thoughts.

Height. Right. I'd forgotten. I was basically here to die.

After some coaxing, I went up the steps, pretending like I was scared, even though I knew I wasn't going to jump off. All the way to the top, past the normal diving boards. Three stories into the air. A place I'd only stood once before.

But as it turned out, the only person I was kidding about not jumping was myself.

"Time to jump, Ryan," Will said, grinning.

"So, about that," I stammered, glancing down. "I really think that—"

"Point of no return, Ryan," he interrupted, taking a step toward me, making me take a step closer to the end of the board. "You know you want to do this."

"Actually, I was thinking about...not doing this?" I was officially nervous. This wasn't how I imagined it would go.

"You will be fine. I promise." He took another step toward me, forcing me back another step. I was nearing the end of the board. My heart was pounding.

"But what if—what if I'm not?" I asked in a tiny voice.

"Life is too short—"

Step.

"To be—"

Step.

"Afraid of things, little brother."

I was officially at the end of the board. Will was almost chest-to-chest with me. He lifted his chin, challenging me.

And in the end I only jumped so Will wouldn't push me in.

When I surfaced—alive!—I felt different. I felt *exhilarated.* I knew I had this. I would learn to dive. I would convince Will. And maybe I would get the girl.

You got this, Ryan.

We just did regular jumps off the high dive. More like falling off the platform, really. Pencil drops. Jack knives. Cannonballs. Once I got comfortable with those, Will took me back down to the pool deck and got me diving from there. Real diving, where I was facing straight down with my hands in front of me like a wedge. And I was pretty good. I have to say, I might even have been a natural. At first, Will thought it would take me a few days to learn, but I moved so quickly he decided I should do the high dive that night.

So we moved up to the nine-foot diving board. That came pretty easy. I just had to overcome my natural urge to chicken out and go straight back down the steps.

Then came the fifteen-foot platform, which wasn't that much scarier than the nine-foot, except there was a lot more water to swim through to get to the surface.

Then, finally, back up to the high dive again. My palms were sweaty as I looked all that way down to the tiny green pool below. Diving off was a lot different from just falling off. I mean, for one, you gotta keep your eyes open. I hesitated for a long time. Will was right beside me, though, giving me pointers. He was actually *encouraging* me.

Who was this person and what had he done with my brother?

And so I did it. I dove off the high-dive.

You know how some people are born to be good spellers or fast runners or chess masters? I was born to do the high dive. I was *that* good. I was going to go to the Olympics. I was going to be on cereal boxes.

When I surfaced this time, I was shouting.

"I DID IT! I DID IT!"

And Will just stood there at the edge of the pool, doing a slow clap.

~

"You're like Greg Louganis," Will said, shaking his head in awe as we walked home from the pool in the dark.

"Greg who?" I asked. My body felt incredibly light. I was euphoric.

Will rolled his eyes. "You know, Louganis? Like the best Olympic diver ever?"

My grin hurt my cheeks.

"Everyone is going to be talking about you after tomorrow, Ryan," Will said. "Are you ready for fame?"

Ryan? I thought. I almost tripped. What happened to Poop Lip?

"Trust me," he said, a big grin on his face. "Even Erika will remember you after tomorrow."

And then he ruffled my wet hair.

Ruffled. My. Hair.

The clues were everywhere. I should have known something was up. But just as I was about to talk to him about the rescue mission, he ducked off into the dark to go sneak a smooch with his girlfriend. I'd have to wait.

≈

The next day, after the last class on the last day of school, I stuffed everything from my locker into my backpack and raced home through the summer heat. I sort of wished Eli had been around for moral support, but he was already away at a month-long computer camp. (Dad thought that it was ridiculous that Eli got out of school early for "nerd camp.")

At home, I was scrambling to find my swim trunks when Will appeared in the door and tossed his own shorts at my head.

"Here, you can wear mine; they got a drawstring," he said with a smile on his face (or was it a smirk?). "You're gonna be awesome."

I gulped at him, standing there, looking calm as a clam, nothing like how I was feeling. Something didn't seem right. I was getting a pain in my gut.

"Maybe we should wait until another day," I said.

"Don't worry so much, Poop Lip," he said. He stopped when he saw me flinch. "I mean, Ryan. I saw you last night. You're a natural."

"Why are you being nice to me?" I blurted out, surprising both Will and me. I mean, sure, I wanted his help, but things were getting weird.

"Okay," Will said, his face suddenly serious. "I'll level with you. I'm gonna be going to college soon—"

"In three years," I added, but Will waved the comment away.

"If I don't help you grow a spine now, while I'm still here, you're going to be Poop Lip forever. That, and…"

"And?"

"…and Dad promised to get me a dirt bike if I tried to make an effort to be nicer. There, you happy?" Will crossed his arms and gave me a hard look.

"You're being nice to me for a *dirt bike*?" I sputtered. I mean, I couldn't blame him. But he actually had me thinking for a second that he was trying to be my friend.

32

"Come on!" Will exclaimed. "The bike is just a perk now. I want you to stop being so scared. I want you to be cool. And come on: we're having fun doing this, right?"

I thought about it and how—if it was somehow true—I was closer than ever to getting him to help me rescue Mom. So I nodded.

"It *is* fun," I agreed cautiously.

"Exactly," Will said, his face relaxing. "Come on, dude. Let's go impress some ladies."

≈

He kept up the pep talk and never left my side while I got ready to go. As we were walking there, he kept giving me pointers: hands out to your sides before you jump. Only pause for a moment or you'll look like you're scared. Remember to breathe until the last possible second. Don't plug your nose or close your eyes.

"And another thing, once you start the jump—"

"You have to go through with it. No matter what," I finished for him. He looked at me in surprise.

"Mom told me that, once," I said quietly. I didn't elaborate—Will thought Mom's circus stuff was dumb. He just nodded his head, kept a firm hand on my back, and, before I knew it, we were at the pool.

Thousands of kids were there. Well, maybe not thousands. But every kid from Brenville Middle-Senior High, as well as a bunch of younger kids from the elementary school.

Holy crap. I stiffened.

"I invited a few people," Will shrugged. "Don't even go into the pool first. Just dive in. Trust me, the kiddos will go crazy."

"Where's the Lifey?" I asked. The lifeguard's chair was empty.

"Probably taking a leak," answered Will, but I still didn't move. I just stood there in my brother's swim trunks that came down to my calves, suddenly shivering in the eighty-degree heat. Will finally gave me a small shove.

"Come on, Ryan. You can do it."

I stumbled forward and thought about how much I needed Will

to help me rescue Mom. If I could just survive this, I thought, then Will would take me seriously when I told him about my plan.

As I reached the ladder, the kids noticed and started whispering to each other. I saw Erika Dixon, just a few feet away. I nodded awkwardly at her, having nothing to say, as usual.

"He's gonna do it!" she hissed to her friend. She sounded impressed. It should have made me braver, more determined, but it just made my heart pound more—like in a heart-attack kind of way.

I hesitated before putting my foot on the bottom rung of the ladder. I hesitated at the top of the ladder—and again in the middle of the platform. I hesitated until there was no more room to hesitate and the platform ended. My toes curled over the edge, the sandpapery-grippy stuff cool under my feet. Standing on the brink, I thought of my mom and all the crazy things she'd done. In comparison, diving was nothing.

Kids pressed into the chain link fence and those in the pool swarmed into bunches on the floating plastic divider that roped off the deep end. All of their faces were turned up to me, mouths open. I suddenly felt very, very important. I felt, well, I felt pretty good.

Too bad I had to dive and couldn't just quit while I was ahead.

My brother looked tiny from up there, standing shoulder-to-shoulder with some older guys, blocking the restroom door. I could hear the Lifey shouting inside.

The weirdest thing, though, was that, for just a moment, I thought I saw my mom. She was standing next to the pop machine, wearing this weird red cape that billowed in a breeze that wasn't there. I shook my head to get a hold of myself and when I looked again, she was gone.

It was a sign. *Today the pool; tomorrow: The Incredible.*

I took a deep breath and did it. Really. I didn't back down. I didn't run away.

I.

Did.

It.

Chapter Three

I jumped off the platform and my body went into the shape of a perfect arrow, slicing through the air and into the deep water.

Cheers erupted as I surfaced, swam to the edge, and climbed out to take my bows. I was entirely out of the water, facing my adoring crowd when I realized something was wrong.

Everyone was suddenly quiet, for one thing. Erika was a few feet away, staring at me, eyes wide in amazement. Or was it some other emotion? She *might* have looked kind of afraid. Our eyes locked for what seemed like a minute, but was probably only a split second.

That's when a kind of group gasp came from the crowd.

That's when everybody's heads swiveled to the pool, where a wadded-up piece of red cloth was swirling just below the surface. All heads turned back to me. I could feel my eyes growing as big as pie plates as I took in the situation from wherever my inner Ryan had run to.

And that's when I looked at Will in the corner, a big, stupid grin slowly taking form on his face.

All of the town's kids, all still and quiet, watched in horror as Will's two-sizes-too-big swim trunks floated to the surface of the pool.

～

After that, I could have stayed in my room all summer. Maybe for all time.

I was in a state of permanent embarrassment, with a full-body blush radiating heat like a terrible sunburn. I could still hear the sound of the kids laughing as I ran to the shower room. I could still see Will's crooked smile.

Will. He had done it all on purpose. The diving practice, the kind words, giving me his shorts that were too big—it was all a huge set-up that I should have seen coming. It was my fault for forgetting that he was pure evil.

A dirt bike. I scoffed out loud. Dad wouldn't buy him a dirt bike to be nicer to me. But it was the perfect line to convince me. He'd known I wouldn't believe he'd be nice to me for nothing. *What a liar.*

Before this, the most embarrassing thing that had happened to me was in fourth grade when I'd spilled my lunch tray in the cafeteria and slipped on the mashed potatoes. It had been bad. Everyone had laughed at me. The next day, I'd tried to stay home sick. But *that* was nothing compared to this. How was I ever going to recover after the whole town had seen me—well, *naked?* Yes, naked. There was no other way to put it. And I didn't even like taking my shirt off at the pool!

I thought briefly about the possibility of being home-schooled. But who was going to teach me? Dad? That wasn't going to happen. Maybe I could convince Dad to send me away to boarding school? No, it was hopeless.

I was lying facedown on my bed when I heard Dad's car pull into the driveway. He was hardly through the door before I heard Will's voice filtering up the stairwell. The only things I caught were: *"Can't believe he..."* and *"Outta there so fast..."*

I thought I heard a small chuckle from Dad.

I buried my face in the pillow when Dad came up the stairs to my room.

"Hey!" he called through the door. "Big diver, you in there?"

He came in without waiting for me to answer. I kept my eyes squinched shut, still as a rock. *A Ryan Rock,* I thought. *Here I'll lie, until the end of time. Still, silent.*

"Hey, kid, you okay?" he asked, tapping the leg of the bed with his toe.

"Yep," I said, louder than I'd meant to. "Fine."

Archeologists will someday use a mallet and chisel to break me open and find a petrified boy inside, scrunched up in a ball.

"I, uh, I heard what happened at the pool today," Dad said. "Jill in Accounting told me about it. Her daughter was there."

He sat on the edge of the bed, but I said nothing. I kept hoping he'd realize that his son had fossilized and just leave.

"I'm glad you dove, Ry," he said, sounding sincere, "but maybe it's time we buy you some shorts that fit—no more of this 'room-to-grow.' I heard you gave them quite a show!"

His forced chuckle died quickly.

"Look, let me start over," he said slowly, but I interrupted him with a mumble he couldn't make out.

"Look at me, Ryan. I can't understand what you're saying."

I sat up and Dad looked surprised at my puffy eyes. "I *said,* 'They were *his* shorts.' Will did it on purpose."

"Don't be so dramatic, Ryan. You're gonna live through this. It's not the end of the world."

My fingers clawed into the bed at that line. Because, really, it kinda *was.*

"*Dad,* he planned the whole thing."

"Look, Ryan," he stood up, the amused sympathy in his voice turning to exasperation. "You're going to stop your victim stuff right now. I don't know why you think that—"

"No, Dad," I said, jumping up to face him. I'd finally had enough. I was a time bomb, seconds from exploding. I was a volcano, about to burst hot, burning lava. I was that two-liter bottle of soda that Eli and I shook for a full hour before throwing it into the street where it shot seventy-five feet into Eli's yard, barely missing Mark Twain, his cat.

"Will is—" Should I have dared? I dared. "Will is the lousiest, rottenest, scum-coated, back-stabbing, meat-brained, two-faced zit farm and I wish—"

"*Ryan!*"

"And I wish he was dead." Boy, I was on a roll and I hadn't even gotten started yet.

"*You* lose *your* own shorts in *your* messy bedroom and suddenly Will is to blame? I don't believe this."

"You never take my side, no matter what he does!" My voice rose with each word until it cracked in that way I hated. There I was, arguing like an adult and suddenly *crack!* I'm a kid again.

"You're pushing it, Ryan," Dad said in a warning tone.

"Don't you think me—*naked*—in front of every kid in town is pushing it?" I bellowed. I was an out-of-control train. I had jumped the tracks. "He *hid* my trunks so I'd have to wear—"

"Oh, he did not," he snapped back.

"Yes, he did!"

Dad scowled and looked at his feet, but I wasn't done.

"*Mom* would never take Will's—" I started, but that was the wrong way to begin a sentence.

"*Enough!*" Dad roared so loudly that I took a step back. He looked like one of those sharks you see on the nature channel, waiting to tear apart a diving cage like it was a gingerbread house. All mouth and teeth.

"Are you going to listen or what?" he growled.

My face was throbbing with anger. Nothing is worse than when a parent tells you to listen and you know whatever they're going to say won't matter one bit. But the sooner you shut your mouth and pretend like you're listening, the sooner you'll get your chance to tell them why they're wrong.

"So you finally went off the high dive!" Dad was practically shouting. "It was about time, too. I thought I was going to have to throw you off myself. And you don't even thank your brother for helping you? You can't blame everyone else whenever things go wrong. Just like your mother leaving—there's not some big *conspiracy* around it. She's accountable for her own actions, just like you are. When are you going to take responsibility for your mistakes? Poop Lip, it's time to grow up."

I was silent. He'd said It. My own father had called me Poop Lip.

38

"I'm done here," Dad said, heading for the door. "I don't want to hear from you for the rest of the night, got it?"

He slammed the door behind him.

❧

After that, I wasn't much interested in lying hopeless and ruined on my bed. I had enough anger to fuel a rocket to Neptune. I was pacing my room when Eli called me from eCamp.

"Why are you *calling* me? Is this 1995?"

"I dunno," Eli mused. "I thought using a telephone for actual talking would be kinda old-school. Anyways, I heard about the pool. That's rough."

"You *heard* about it?" I sputtered into the phone. "It just happened! And you're all the way at camp!"

"It's all over the FaceChats and SnapBooks and all that, Ryan. You're lucky; I don't know how there weren't any pictures."

"So pretty much every single person in Brenville knows—"

"And all their friends and families," Eli added helpfully.

"Right. Oh, man," I said, lying down on the floor, my face in the carpet. Maybe I wasn't done being wrecked. "I can't believe Will did this to me."

"Wait—*Will* did this to you?"

"His shorts," I said. "He rigged his shorts."

"Diabolical."

"Tell me about it."

"I think leaving now is your best bet," Eli said. "Without Will."

"Mmmph." I turned my face so I was looking into my closet, where my plans were hidden in the floorboards under my winter boots.

It was Eli who'd said we needed to keep our paper evidence hidden and to a minimum. That way, when it came time to leave, we could easily destroy it. So we couldn't be tracked. All we had was a map, a thumb drive, a notebook, and a list of disposable, single-use email addresses that we used and then crossed off, one by one. And my packing list.

Funny how back in the day, we might have had a whole tree-house fort filled with maps and atlases. Maybe a bulletin board with photos of Bartholomew and his gang, yarn connecting one person to another until we had an actual nest of villains. Yet, our evidence—I could carry it in one hand and just drop all of it into the dumpster behind the Sno-Cap on main street and it would *poof*.

Disappear.

"Come on, Ryan," Eli said. "A man can't go on living like a normal person after something like what happened at the pool. But if you rescue your mom and stop a crooked circus, nobody's going to remember how you completely self-destructed and humiliated yourself in front of all your peers. Everybody might even forget they saw your—"

"*Mmmph*," I interrupted, closing my eyes.

"Look, I can find out where she's performing now," he said. "We don't have to wait for San Francisco. You know how people scalp those tickets online. Just let me do some searching." He trailed off and we were silent for a moment. I could hear him clacking away at his computer.

"You really think we're ready?" I finally asked.

"Come on, we were ready months ago," he said. "You know, I'm kinda glad the diving board happened. Get you off your—"

"Shut it!" I exclaimed, jumping up. "Never be glad that happened to me. Ever. I'm barely alive."

"Easy, there," Eli said. "I take it back. Geez. Hey! I found it."

Please not the East Coast. Please not the East Coast.

"Not bad. They're in Albuquerque right now."

"Albuquerque? As in *Mexico*?"

"*New* Mexico, genius."

"Oh. Is that good?" I mean, sure, it was great that she wasn't in Florida or something, but *New Mexico*? I had known I was going to have to travel a bit, but this was ridiculous. That was like, what? How far?

"It's okay," Eli assured me. "It's like California. It's just twenty-three hours away by car."

"Twenty-three hours!" My jaw dropped. "That's twice as far as it was to California!"

"Hey, it's still basically on the West Coast. And really, what's the difference to you, right? What else do you have going on? You going to let a few measly hours stop you?"

"I guess not," I grumbled. He had a point. He always had a point. "When are the shows?"

"They've got one tonight and then again Friday and Saturday. You can make the Saturday show for sure."

"And what about Carl?" I asked. I'd never met Eli's older cousin Carl, but early on he promised Eli he would give me a lift to Bend, no questions asked. I just had to meet Carl in the middle of nowhere, so no one would see me get in his truck. Lucky for me, the middle of nowhere is all around us in Brenville.

"He says he's ready whenever. I just texted him and—"

"You *what?*"

"—and he'll pick you up tomorrow at five in the morning."

"Jeez, Eli," I said, covering my face with my free hand. I wasn't sure I was ready for this.

"He still doesn't want to know why you're doing this, so that's good," Eli said. That was a slight relief. We had been worried Carl would ask questions, but he insisted on us not telling him anything so he couldn't get in trouble.

"He'll drop you off in Bend at an internet café he knows about," Eli continued, "which is probably the last internet café in North America. Anyway, they have computers. Then we'll rendezvous online." He always said it like it was spelled: *ren-dez-voos.*

"Then what?" I asked. You had to press Eli or he wouldn't tell you anything.

"Then I'll find you a way to Albuquerque," he said. "Trust me."

"Right."

"Just leave it to me. I'm gonna get to work on the logistics tonight—oh, and remember your suit. You never know when you'll need a nice suit."

"Want me to pack a set of martini glasses, too?" I asked, looking out the window as the sun set. It was starting to feel less like a game now. It was beginning to feel real.

"Ha. Funny. No, seriously: pack the suit. You can be anyone in a suit."

He had a point.

॰

Talking to Eli always got me back on track. Sometimes I thought I was going crazy if I thought about the rescue mission too long on my own, but Eli always reminded me how much sense it all made. Honestly, if it hadn't been for him, I don't think I ever would have put all the pieces together.

I jumped into action. First, I pushed my dresser in front of my closed bedroom door, just in case. Then, I went to the back of my closet and pushed my boots to the side. There was a place where the carpet didn't quite meet the wall. If you knew just where to tug at it, a small square would come up, exposing a cubbyhole underneath. Mom had shown me this tiny hiding place just before she disappeared.

"Don't tell Will—or your dad," she'd whispered. "I thought that you could use a place to keep secret things. Stuff you don't want them to find."

At the time, I had thought it was a little strange that she would want me to hide things from Dad. Later, though—it became crystal clear.

I forgot to mention this earlier, but my dad? Yeah, he considered my room to be his room. My things were his things. He regularly came in and took away things he didn't like—a poster of my favorite band, The Angry Lindas. This cool silver talisman I'd secretly ordered

42

from the back of a Farmer's Almanac (Dad gave it to Will to dispose of; Will gleefully melted it down with Dad's welding torch). Dad tore up postcards I'd written to Mom where I complained about Dad's cooking. He also found where I had hidden my journal—I'd tucked it under my mattress, like an idiot—and he lectured me that "there are no secrets in our house." More important, he said, I wasn't allowed to write about "our family's dirty laundry." So my journal lived where Dad placed it—on my nightstand—and I never wrote in it again.

If only my secret cubbyhole weren't already packed to capacity with rescue mission stuff.

I got my packing list. Then I pulled out my backpack and laid it open on my bed.

First, I packed two t-shirts (both black), jeans, a blue hooded sweatshirt, and the dark suit and tie I'd worn in my cousin's wedding a month ago (I had been the oldest ring-bearer ever). Then, I packed the essentials: a heavy-duty flashlight I'd gotten at the army surplus store, a magnifying glass (for making a campfire), some rubber bands (they're just very useful), my pen with disappearing ink (for secret messages), two pairs of underwear, my camouflage paint, a stethoscope (also courtesy of Eli's dad), a ball of string, a mini-screwdriver set, all the postcards, five issues of *Captain Fantastic*, and—

I was running out of room.

Once when Will had had the flu, I had felt sorry for him, listening to him barf all night, so I brought him a stack of my comic books to keep him company. He'd looked grateful at the time, but later, he filled in every *o* and zero with colored markers and gave Captain Fantastic boobs and a mustache in every single frame.

I'm telling you this story so what I did next won't sound so terrible.

I shut my closet and shoved the dresser away from my door. After making sure the coast was clear, I snuck into Will's room (which Eli and I called the World of Fartcraft). The smell of Will's room used to be enough to keep me out, but I'd gotten one of those hospital masks from Eli's dad, who's a doctor. This let me explore the room whenever I wanted, so I knew it inside and out.

I grabbed his compass and pocketknife from his desk drawer. Then, I took his map of the U.S. from the back wall of his closet and his Boy Scout manual from his nightstand. (Who relaxes before bed by learning knots and trapping? Only masterminds in torturing brothers, that's who.)

Next on my list was Will's brand-new pair of black Air Jordans. I found them in his closet. He hadn't even worn them outside yet, just around the living room, admiring them. They were a bit too big, but I figured they'd help me blend into the dark.

Back in my room, I pushed the dresser in front of the door again and packed these new items.

Then, I prepared for the Moment of Truth. How much money had I saved?

I reached into the cubbyhole and got out the metal box where I kept my money. I'd been saving my allowance since September. Who knew how much I'd been able to stash away? A few hundred dollars—maybe more? I thought I had at least enough for a bus ticket to wherever Mom was.

Then I counted it.

Thirteen dollars and eighty-seven cents. That was it.

I hadn't been *planning* on taking Will's money. I'd *planned* on him coming with me and bringing it himself. But plans change. And I wasn't exactly feeling friendly toward my brother.

Closet door shut and dresser shoved aside once more, I was back in Will's room. On a shelf, next to his trophies, was a single book: *Shakespeare: The Collected Works.* The book didn't have any real pages, though—it just had an empty, carved out space in the middle. Will was an idiot if he thought it was a secret. I mean, he was smart, but he hated to read and everyone knew it. Inside was all the money Will bragged about saving from raking pine needles. I took it all.

Back in my room, I counted it. Seventy-four dollars.

It would have to do.

Before I closed up the secret cubby for good, two things at the bottom caught my eye: a photo of Mom in her human cannonball suit, standing proudly beside the big white cannon, and this little golden bug thing that Mom had mailed to me a few months ago. She'd called it a scarab. She said she'd seen it in Mexico and thought of me—and for some reason, she'd asked me to keep it in the cubby.

They were the only two things she'd mailed me, other than all the postcards.

It might seem kinda sappy that I brought them, but I guess it felt like I was bringing her with me for good luck. I tucked them safely into an inside pocket.

Finally, I got out the empty rolling suitcase, for Mom. It was even smaller than I'd remembered, but again, it was big enough that she could tuck herself into.

"This had better work," I muttered to myself.

That was it. I was ready.

I settled into my bedroom to wait.

And wait.

At three in the morning, I was in the pantry, silently cramming as much food as I could fit into my green backpack. I snagged a bag of chips, a six-cup pudding pack, some energy bars, a stack of fruit leather, a can of spaghetti, and three bottles of root beer. In my head, all I could hear was, *I'm gonna do it, I'm gonna do it.* My internal chant must have been too loud because I didn't hear Dad come down the stairs.

I was still in the pantry when a slice of light appeared in front of me. I froze. There, no more than three feet away, stood Dad in his underwear, swigging cranberry juice from the carton in the refrigerator light. If he turned even six inches, he would see me, and I'd be as good as toast.

I was still clutching a bag of cookies in my hand as I backed against the pantry wall. A single muscle spasm in my pinky finger would crinkle the plastic and send me straight into the depths of summer grounding and yard work.

The plastic felt damp in my hand. *Why was my hand sweating?*

I held my breath as Dad polished off the juice and tried to squash the carton with his bare hand (he failed). The suitcase and my sleeping bag lay at his feet, in the shadow of the counter.

Dead. I was dead.

Dad turned away, letting the fridge door swing open as he gazed out the window. The yellow light crept into the pantry slowly—moving as the fridge door opened further—to my toes, then up to my knees. The plastic crumpled slightly in my hand.

Dead, dead, dead, dead.

Dad whirled around and, without even a glance in my direction, slapped the fridge shut. By the time the cookies slipped from my hand (and fell harmlessly to the floor), he was already at the top of the stairs.

That was close, I thought, letting my breath out in a whoosh.

"Almost *too* close," I whispered. I'd always wanted the chance to say that out loud.

I put on my backpack and, as an afterthought, grabbed Will's black baseball cap off the table, pulling it low over my eyes. The finishing touch.

After glancing around the kitchen one last time, I finally whispered, "This is me leaving." I paused, waiting for something to stop me.

Nothing did.

I eased the door open and stepped out into the summer darkness. I stood on our back porch for a moment. I was nervous. But more than anything, I was excited. I didn't know how far I'd have to travel, but I'd get there. Nothing would stop me from coming back with Mom.

Absolutely nothing.

Three houses down I realized I'd forgotten the empty suitcase and had to run back home.

But after *that*, nothing could stop me.

Chapter Four

I knew the police would start looking for me as soon as Dad reported me gone. Dad had a weekly poker game with Officer Barton, so there might be a little more publicity than for some other runaway. Besides, the town was small—anyone running away would be a big deal.

I *could* have taken Will's cell phone. It would've made everything easier. Eli insisted I shouldn't. He watched all these detective shows and said the police would check the phone records before anything else and track me down. But at least I wasn't traveling completely blind; I had Eli in my corner. And since he was away at computer camp, he was online twenty-four/seven. And the best part? No one would be able to get to him and make him talk before Mom and I got back home, safe and sound.

Well, in theory.

In reality, Eli can't keep his trap shut, which was why I hoped he'd be untouchable at eCamp. He might be a great friend, but he's definitely a squealer. Eli's dad is always calling my dad, fuming about one thing or another, like that Eli said a curse word he said he'd learned from Will. Will would get in trouble (not for saying it, but for saying it around "that Carson kid"), and then take it out on me.

"Pay it forward," Will would say, giving me his usual Tattled-On Revenge: a dead-arm, a dead-leg, and a rug burn on some delicate body part, like my face. I didn't want Eli to feel bad, so I never told him, but *sheesh*. You'd think he'd have caught on sooner or later.

☙

I jogged lightly down the sidewalk, past all the neighbors' dark houses. Everything was quiet. I didn't hear a single car engine or a dog barking—not even a cricket.

I hurried through the main strip of town, dodging in and out of the shadows. The last thing I wanted was to be taken home by the cops only a few minutes after leaving. Luckily, I saw them before they saw me. A squad car was parked under the buzzing fluorescent light at the gas station. Officer Barton—the town's only night beat cop and Dad's best (and only?) friend—was leaning back in his seat, asleep, all slack-jawed and snoring.

It was easy to slip out of town after that. There are only about ten buildings on the main strip. Once you get past the gas station, Brenville just...stops. It doesn't dwindle off into suburbs or a park or something; it just plain *ends*. A green sign marks the city boundary with, *Next Gas: 54 mi.* After that, there's nothing. Just dirt, sagebrush, scrubby short juniper trees, and the long curve of lonely highway.

Seeing the open road ahead of me, I couldn't help but grin—I was doing it!

The plan was simple enough: be out at milepost three no later than five a.m. I walked down the right side of the county road. It felt strange being out there all alone in the dark. I still had two hours before the rendezvous with Eli's cousin Carl, which meant I had time. I didn't even need to worry about hiding from cars until then (there isn't any traffic during the day, so there definitely wouldn't be anyone out at that hour, except for Carl). And while I don't know what Eli told Carl, I hoped that I wouldn't look too suspicious to him, what with my backpack, suitcase, and sleeping bag. Maybe he'd think I was a Boy Scout, working on a survival merit badge or something like that.

Dad was always getting on me about becoming a Boy Scout, but I never wanted to do it. It was like the diving: even if I *wanted* to do it, it kind of became a bummer if Will was into it, too—and if Dad was pressuring me on top of that? I *definitely* wasn't going to do it. But Dad was always telling me I had to "take advantage of all this wilderness" and that "you'd regret it when you were older."

Dad always went on about how great the area was, but to me,

it wasn't anything special. Brenville is in something called the "high desert," which is like a desert but without the sand. It's just really brown, with these weird, scraggly trees you see on TV or in Western movies, the ones that don't look like normal trees. In the summer, it's scorching during the day and freezing at night. In the winter, it's just a frozen wasteland with snow drifting across the flatness. The one cool thing is that there are tons of animals, like lizards and scorpions and mountain lions and rattlesnakes. My favorite, though, are the coyotes, maybe because they scared Will when we were little.

As I trekked along, I heard the coyotes start up, making that *row-oooh-ooh-ooohh* sound. They kept it up a bit before fading out. In the blackness of the middle of nowhere, they sounded like ghosts.

I reached milepost three with about twenty minutes to spare. I'd originally told Eli that three miles was way too far to walk with a backpack and a suitcase, but he insisted the pick-up happen where there wasn't a chance that there could be a witness. And he was right about the place; there wasn't a car for miles.

I stepped off the road and sat down behind a large rock to drink a morning root beer. Then I heard an engine in the distance. I looked at my watch; if it was Carl, he was a bit early. I felt a pounding in my chest as I jumped to my feet.

At five a.m., it's still dark, but it's not too dark to see details. As the lights came over the horizon, I saw it. It was a truck. And as it got closer, I saw it was an old, beat-up Chevy truck hauling—what were they? I squinted in the dark. Were they *chickens*?

But the truck went on by. Coincidence? Probably. My heart slowed. I was about to sit back down when the truck lurched to a stop, maybe fifty yards past me.

So it was Carl after all? And my ride was in a *chicken* truck?

I guessed it was possible. Eli hadn't told me much about Carl, but knowing Eli, his relatives were probably capable of being chicken farmers.

As I walked in the dim light toward the truck, I let out a slow breath. This was it. The Moment of Truth.

I waited behind the truck for Carl to make his move. Greet me, open the passenger door, or something. I could see his plaid-shirted elbow in his side-mirror, but he wasn't getting out.

Strange.

That's when it hit me: *Carl was pretending to be on his phone.* I could see him in his big side mirror, under the glow of his dome light, looking in the glove compartment with his phone to his ear. If he didn't talk to me, he could say he hadn't stopped for me. He could tell the cops, "Nope, I didn't even *see* him."

Which meant he wanted me to ride in the back.

Well, it was better than walking. I lobbed my suitcase and sleeping bag into a gap between the cages, sending the chickens into an even louder fit of clucking. I had my hands on the pickup gate, getting ready to pull myself up into the truck—and that was the same moment that Carl chose to drive away.

I wasn't much of an athlete. Except for my newfound talent for diving, I couldn't really do much else in the physical activity department. I've been told I run like a wounded cow. But I *am* fast when I need to be.

Sprinting behind the chicken truck, I just barely kept my hold on the slick tailgate. Soon, the toes of Will's brand new shoes dragged along the asphalt—and we were picking up speed.

"Carl! Slow down!" I called out, but I don't think he heard me over the squawk of the chickens.

I could already see the headline about my death:

RUNAWAY DRAGGED MILES BEHIND TRUCK;
OLDER BROTHER FINISHES HIM OFF FOR
DESTROYING SHOES.

Feathers blowing in my face and legs flailing, I grabbed a bit of rope tied to the tailgate. Begging it not to snap, I used all my strength to pull myself up. I got one foot on the bumper, and then the other. The chickens sounded like they were cheering me on as I got a leg over the tailgate—and then the truck jolted like Carl had run over a tree stump.

My "oh-no-oh-no-oh-no" mixed right in with the loud clucking as I fell, headfirst, into the truck bed.

Carl drove on as I struggled to get upright. The chickens really seemed to be going nuts (but for all I knew, this was a completely normal way for chickens to act in a speeding truck). I got situated just in time for the truck to hit another big bump, which caused my sleeping bag to bounce right by me and down the road.

"No, no, no, no!" I hissed, but it was gone.

Perfect. Just perfect.

"Carl!" I tried to yell to get him to stop, but he couldn't hear me. And there were too many chicken containers in the way for me to get his attention. *What a maniac,* I thought.

I pulled myself, the suitcase, and my backpack down low between the tailgate and the chicken cages, where it wasn't as cold. At least I still had Will's hat.

Just a little tip: if you ever need to hitch a ride in the bed of a truck, a chicken truck isn't exactly the most luxurious choice. As we reached full cruising speed, the truck bed became a quaking, earsplitting, *reeking* tornado of feathers. And not just big feathers either, but little downy ones that got caught in my nose and mouth and eyes. I chose to believe that chicken crap doesn't blow in the wind, but I may have been wrong.

I got as comfortable as I could and watched the sun rise while we wound our way northwest, putting more and more miles between Brenville and me. In the back of the truck, I shivered, and it wasn't just the wind. My stomach was a lump of guilt and fear. And not just because I'd stolen from Will, though that was definitely part of it.

I was starting to realize the seriousness of what I was doing. Yes, *serious* was the word. I imagined Dad talking to me, looking very disappointed. Maybe even sad. "This is a serious thing you've done, Ryan." And it was. Look at me—I'd almost been killed already and I hadn't even been gone three hours.

But did I have a choice? I remembered the diving board incident and my cheeks reddened. I thought of the look on Erika Dixon's face as I stood in front of everyone, naked. I couldn't go back. Not now. Having Mom back would be the only thing that could make Brenville bearable now.

So I was doing it. For better or worse, I was doing it.

This was either the start of something really great, or the beginning of the end.

҂

The chickens never calmed down. I had thought they were just excited by my clumsy arrival, but apparently that's just how chickens act.

As we bumped down the road, I squinted against the feathery chaos and watched them through the crook of my arm. Some hunkered down together. Others lay on the floor of their cages like they were dead, which I guess they might have been. There was this pudgy, one-eyed hen wedged into a corner, her lumpy butt poking through the bars of the cage. Over the course of the drive, we had a few staring contests, and she won every time. Chickens can stare. I hadn't known that before, either.

After a few hours, I checked my watch and saw that we were already an hour late. I was supposed to be in Bend at eight a.m. and it was already nine. Maybe because Carl was driving so slowly. Or maybe because of all the chickens—maybe they weren't very aerodynamic. I guess it didn't matter too much. Eli would figure things out.

Finally, I felt the truck slowing. We made a few turns, went over a few bumps, and then we came to a stop. The engine shut off, and the truck door opened and then slammed shut.

I popped my head up. We were in front of a small bakery, which, I guess, is kind of like a café. I chucked the suitcase out and leaped from the back of the truck. I tried to brush the feathers off of my clothes, but they were everywhere. Inside *and* out.

I looked around for Carl. Even if he were playing it cool, maybe I could at least give him a quick wave.

"Did you just jump outta my truck?" a voice hollered and I dropped my suitcase. Carl walked toward me—or the person I had *thought* was Carl. But Carl wouldn't be surprised I was in his truck.

And Eli's cousin probably wasn't a sixty-year-old man, either.

Uh-oh.

Chapter Five

I took a step back, eyes wide. My mouth moved, but nothing came out. Nothing understandable, anyway.

"Uh, um, well, no, I was…I was just looking at your chickens," I stammered.

"You jumped outta my truck!" He strode toward me looking kind of shocked, like he didn't know what to do.

All I could think to do was snatch up my stuff and sprint.

I ran and ran. With that stupid suitcase and backpack. I ran until I was sure he wasn't following me. Out of breath, I finally stopped to look around. I was on this small-town street with buildings that had these weird western fronts. I felt like I was on the set of a cowboy movie or something. Bend didn't look like anything like this.

Well, of course this isn't Bend, I realized. The truck driver wasn't Carl, so he wouldn't be headed to Bend.

Suddenly the extra hour it had taken to get here made sense.

You're a real genius, Ryan.

I stared at my watch. It was nine-thirty. I was more than an hour late to meet up online with Eli and I was in the wrong town. Right in front of me was a big, two-story building with a plaque that read *Sisters Library.* So at least I knew where I was. I was in Sisters. I knew a little bit about that town. They had a big quilt competition every year and Mom had tried to quilt a giant tent for it. (Sadly, she ran out of fabric. Dad just said, "Thank god.")

At least the library was open. I glanced around to make sure the chicken truck guy wasn't around, and then went inside.

The library was bright and air-conditioned and mostly empty. I went straight to the computers and logged into the final secret email account I'd made for the actual rescue part of the Rescue Mission.

There was nothing from Eli and he wasn't online. I checked my watch again. Nine-thirty-five. Where was he? He was *always* online.

I sighed and looked up where Sisters was on a map (what a weird name for a town). I'd overshot Bend by about twenty-five miles.

Perfect, Ryan. Perfect.

While waiting for Eli to come online, I browsed for new information on Bartholomew. I hunted around for photos from people who went to his shows, but as usual, there weren't any. Bartholomew's Circus apparently has huge warnings about "no cameras, no phones." Anyone caught taking a photo gets their phone snapped in two by security guards. So aside from the hundreds of selfies taken in front of the tent, there wasn't ever much else to find.

I clicked over to Bartholomew's website. It looked the same as ever, like someone had made it and then forgotten all about updating it. Simple and boring—definitely not the website you'd expect for a circus as well known as Bartholomew's. It was just a single page with a couple of pictures and small white text on a black background. Eli and I found it weird that there were no fancy graphics, no way to buy tickets, no promotions, nothing. Zilch. I mean, even *I* could have made a better page. It was like they thought their name spoke for itself:

BARTHOLOMEW'S WORLD-RENOWNED CIRCUS OF THE INCREDIBLE!

See the Most Marvelous, Miraculous, Stupendous, and *Spectacular* Circus in the World!!!
See *Captivating* Contortionists!
Gasp as *Extraordinary* Tiger Tamers TAME Tigers!
(and Other Dangerous Creatures!)
Witness the *Death-Defying* and Altogether *Unbelievable* Human Cannonball!!
It's Dramatic, It's Splendid, It's Fantastic, and it's Incredible!
ALL ROLLED INTO ONE MEMORABLE NIGHT!!!

And there, at the bottom of the page: *Shows.*

I scanned it, wanting to see if there'd been any changes. The list of cities, dates, and times was the same as it had been for the past few months. I scrolled back up, and the picture of the circus tent caught my eye, as it always did.

Someone had taken the photo at night, with a full moon rising behind the huge tent. You could only see the front of it, but it looked like it was the size of a football field. The top of the tent had a tall, blue-and-red striped dome. The material looked pretty heavy-duty. I hoped Will's pocketknife would cut through it, like I'd planned.

There were two lines of people leading up to the entrance. The weird part was you couldn't see anyone's face. There must have been a hundred people in the picture, yet *nobody* was turned toward the camera. Everyone faced the circus, like they were hypnotized.

Like Bartholomew had cast some kind of magical spell on them.

The picture always gave me the chills if I sat and looked at it too long.

❧

Eli still wasn't online. I sighed so loudly that a guy near me in a cowboy hat glanced up from his magazine. I pretended I was frustrated because the mouse was broken.

Eli was going to have to find me a different ride to Albuquerque. I'd screwed it all up. I mean, *a chicken truck?* In what alternate reality would Eli's cousin be driving a chicken truck?

I tried to stop blaming myself. I mean, the guy *did* pull up and stop next to me. How many people would stop at that exact spot at five a.m.? It was just pure, bad luck. And maybe a bad sign. Well, if you believed in stuff like that.

And Eli still wasn't online to help me! Getting even more frustrated, I punched the desk. A few people looked and I reddened.

"Sometimes you have to unplug the mouse to get it started again," said the guy in the hat. I nodded and did it just to avoid looking crazy.

I turned back to the computer, drumming my fingers on my knee. *Come on, Eli.*

❧

It might be hard to believe, but a lot of people want to get into the circus. They send out these audition videos showing off their talents, hoping a circus will respond and give them a chance to apply in person.

I know this because, about a year before Mom disappeared, she showed me her own circus audition. She shared it only with me; I was the only one she trusted. She told me to keep it a secret, which I did. I never even told Eli about it until after she was gone.

The video was…well, it was incredible. I mean, over the years I'd gotten a few glimpses of what she could do. I knew she was good at gymnastics, that she could throw knives, and that she wasn't scared of wild animals. But the video was the first time I got a glimpse of *all* the stuff she was capable of.

I'd heard of people walking on hot coals before, but I'd never seen someone do it on their hands, blindfolded, while carrying a watermelon between their knees. That would have been impressive no matter who it was, but the fact that it was my mom made it totally unreal.

So I had known that my mom wanted to join the circus. But I'm sure she hadn't expected to attract the attention of someone like Bartholomew. I'm sure she hadn't expected that a black van would pull up one morning and throw her in a sack and haul her off. And I'm sure she wouldn't have gone if she'd known he'd never let her see her family.

She'd never have signed up for that.

Eli and I had heard about something called "Stockholm syndrome," which was this weird thing where people fall in love with their kidnappers. My mom was strong, so I didn't really think she could succumb to something like Stockholm syndrome, but Eli thought that could be why she sounded so happy in some of the postcards. I argued my point again, that she was probably using the happy postcards as a way to fool anyone who was watching her.

Either way, Eli cautioned me to be ready, though, just in case she was weird when I found her. I hated to admit it, but it was possible. Who knows what can happen to a person who's been trapped and stressed out for so long?

❧

I checked the email account again and saw that Eli had finally logged on. We'd agreed ahead of time: no real names. I was "Joe" (which was spy talk for a deep cover agent). Eli chose "Peter Parker" (because he loves Spiderman).

PETER.PARKER: *What happened?*
JOE: *I messed up. Got on a chicken truck.*
PETER.PARKER: *Why?*
JOE: *I thought it was Carl.*
PETER.PARKER: *Oh boy. Where are you?*
JOE: *Sisters.*
PETER.PARKER: *Oops. Close, but no cigar.*
JOE: *Can we continue with Plan A?*
PETER.PARKER: *Too late. You missed the ride.*
JOE: *Great. What now? Walk home?*
PETER.PARKER: *No. Plan B. One moment.*

A few minutes passed. Nothing from Eli. A few more minutes. I was getting impatient.

JOE: *What's Plan B?*
PETER.PARKER: *Hold your horses!*

I was rolling my eyes when the librarian walked by with a stack of papers. He taped one to the side of the nearby printer. I didn't have to squint to see that it had a picture of me on it. It was my school yearbook photo from the year before, the one with me blinking. And below that:

MISSING CHILD ALERT
FOR
GREATER OREGON AREA

RYAN ZANDER, 12 YEARS OLD
5'4" BROWN HAIR, BROWN EYES,
MOLE ON UPPER LIP
LAST SEEN IN BRENVILLE, OREGON
AT 10:00 P.M.
POSSIBLY WEARING HARRY POTTER PAJAMAS

I was angry for a split second about the whole mole thing—and embarrassed about the pajamas—then I saw that the librarian was putting the posters on every other bookshelf. A few people wandered over to look at them.

This situation was *not* good.

It was *way* too early for a missing poster. Eli and I had done the research. Odds were I should have had a full twenty-four hours before the news went out but—there it was. Dad must have found me missing right after I left last night. He must have gotten his friend Officer Barton to help him speed up the process.

I was toast.

I pulled Will's baseball hat down low on my face and stared at the computer screen. I was just a student doing research. Doing homework. But wait—school got out yesterday. Was I studying for summer school? I realized I hadn't seen any other kids in the library. Also, I had a suitcase and a backpack. That definitely wasn't helping.

I pushed my bags under the desk with my foot. Out of the corner of my eye, I thought I saw an old guy looking in my direction.

I typed quickly:

JOE: *Got it yet?*
PETER.PARKER: *One moment.*
JOE: *No time. It's getting hot in here.*
PETER.PARKER: *So take off all your clothes?*

Ha ha, Eli. Nice song lyric.

A blonde woman wandered over to a shelf of encyclopedias right behind me. She pretended to browse, but she was looking at me. I pulled the bill of my cap even lower. I could barely see out from under it.

PETER.PARKER: *1555 Northeast Hayesville Road. Go out of the library, take a right and go 2 blocks. Then make another right and go 6 blocks.*
JOE: *Then what?*
PETER.PARKER: *Wait out front, by the road. Look neat. Put on your suit. Driver will think it's your house. Getting a ride to your grandma's funeral in Boise.*
JOE: *My what? Albuquerque! Not Boise!*

What was I thinking, having Eli help me? He was crazy. Then, he read my mind:

PETER.PARKER: *You don't trust anyone, that's your problem.*
Great. A quote from an old Spiderman movie.

PETER.PARKER: Be there in ten minutes. Trust me! OVER AND OUT.

I scrawled the address and the directions on a piece of paper. The encyclopedia woman was at the front desk, talking to the librarian. The lady touched her lip, right in the same spot my freckle is, and then they both looked in my direction.

Crap, crap, crap, crap.

❧

I grabbed my bags and headed toward the front door. My luggage suddenly seemed ridiculous. I was obviously a runaway.

The encyclopedia woman and the librarian got to the door before I did. They stood shoulder-to-shoulder in front of me. I tried to act normal, but I was forced to stop right in front of them.

"Excuse me, but—" the woman began. I turned on my heel marched down an aisle of kids' books. They followed at a fast clip.

"Young man?"

"Ryan?" the man called.

I cringed. They knew my name.

I strode, head ducked, down random aisles, trying to get to the stairs leading up to the second floor. Right before I reached them, though, the librarian sprang out in front of me.

I abruptly turned to follow an aisle that ran right below the second-floor balcony. The railing was maybe ten feet up—and I could see an emergency exit up there at the end of the building.

If I could get up to the second floor, I'd be home free.

"We just want to help you!" came the man's voice behind me. He still hadn't moved from blocking the stairs. He probably figured I was trapped.

Shows what you know, I thought.

Besides letting Will teach me the high dive, destroying a library was about to be the craziest thing I'd done in my life.

At the end of the aisle, I summoned all my strength and hurled the empty suitcase up and over the second-floor railing. And then, before anyone could stop me, I climbed the bookshelf.

"Not the shelves!" the librarian shouted, running toward me. The encyclopedia woman materialized from another aisle and grabbed at me, but I was already too high. As I climbed, I kicked books off the shelf, causing the librarian to yelp.

My heart thudded, but I kept going. Once on top of the shelf, I scrambled over the railing. In my scrambling, though, my backpack knocked into a massive mobile of the solar system. Mars plummeted to the ground, where it shattered, followed by Saturn. The librarian was already bounding up the stairs, using the kind of words you never hear a librarian say under normal circumstances.

I swung over the railing, grabbed the suitcase, and raced to the fire exit door.

It said, USE ONLY IN CASE OF EMERGENCY.

I'm used to following rules, so I hesitated a second before snapping out of it. This *was* an emergency. When I punched the door open, it set off a blaring alarm.

"Stop!" bellowed the woman.

I got out onto the fire escape and slammed the door shut behind me. I was ten feet or so off the ground, and *there were no stairs!* There was just a rusty-looking ladder that I guess you were supposed to push down, but I couldn't see how.

Nice emergency exit, I thought, cursing under my breath.

I kicked at the ladder but didn't have time to figure the stupid thing out, so I threw my suitcase off the side and climbed out onto the edge of the fire escape. There was some sort of metal furnace box thing a few feet away, and when the librarian burst out onto the fire escape, I had to jump. I landed on the edge of it, but I couldn't keep my balance. I pitched off the side, landing hard on the lawn next to my suitcase.

I looked up and saw the librarian on the fire escape and a few other people looking out windows.

I didn't have any time to feel sheepish.

I sprang to my feet, snatched up the suitcase, and booked it. They were about to call the police—if they hadn't already—so I didn't stop running this time. I zigged and zagged, around western shops and through backyards and llama pastures, all while homing in on the directions Eli had given me for Hayesville Road.

Mom hadn't always wanted to be a human cannonball. According to Will (which means according to Dad), she had been basically normal before I came along. She had had a job at the mayor's office. She liked watching TV with Dad and baby William. She read. She was into baking.

But everyone knew it wasn't really me that changed her. It was the accident.

A couple months before I was born, Mom and Dad were driving back from Bend when their car was hit by a drunk driver. Dad was okay—he'd been wearing his seatbelt. For some reason, Mom wasn't. When the car hit them, Mom flew right through the front windshield like—well, like she'd been shot out of a cannon. The paramedics found her twenty feet away, stuck headfirst in a snowbank. She went into a coma and everyone thought we were both going to die. There were lots of tears and hospital visits from everyone she knew. But then, four days later, she woke up like nothing had happened.

She was different, though. Will told me that she wanted to become a human cannonball because she had liked flying through the windshield so much. But that's just ridiculous. The doctors said some medical stuff about how head traumas can have weird side effects. Like after the accident, she could never sit still. She always complained that her back and her eyes hurt. She quit her job and didn't even try to get another one. Then she got all these weird hobbies: hula-hooping, juggling, riding a unicycle. She got more excitable. More reckless. She said, according to Will, that she "needed to live a *real* life."

Dad talked about her like she'd become an entirely different person. One time, late at night, I heard him on the phone with Uncle Donald.

"It's like nothing's good enough for her. Not me, not the house, not even Brenville. I mean, how can all this open space be suffocating?"

So from everyone else's perspective, she'd changed. But for me, she'd always been weird and exciting. Okay, maybe even a little cuckoo. But that was the only version of Mom I'd ever known. And I don't think I would have changed her if I could.

I jogged down a dirt road, thinking, *How were they on to me so fast?* Eli said we'd have a day before my dad even *noticed* I was missing. And then a few more before police would look for me—and by then, I'd be on my way home.

Maybe we'd underestimated how fast Dad would catch on. Or maybe Will noticed his stuff was missing and told on me. I guess when your dad is BFFs with the local sheriff, you get prioritized. Either way, I was already a wanted man.

It wasn't even ten yet, but it was hot. My back was covered in sweat because of the backpack, and I still had feathers all over my clothes.

My clothes! I needed to have my suit on. Eli had said I was going to...*a funeral?*

I guess he'd been right about bringing the suit.

I was wondering whether I'd gone too far when I saw the street sign: Hayesville! I walked until I found the address; it didn't look like anyone was home. The mailbox said *Moe.*

Checking my watch, I saw I had five minutes to spare—five minutes until *what*, I didn't have a clue.

I ducked behind the Moes' garage and threw on my suit. I skipped the coat, though—it was way too hot. I tried to straighten myself up a bit, using the sweat in my hair to smooth it down. Gross? Yes. But effective.

As I headed back around to the front of the house, I heard a sound like a huge chainsaw chopping through a hundred trees. Just when I thought it was as loud as it could get, it got louder.

A huge-normous bearded man on a giant, black motorcycle pulled up into the drive. That's when I realized that *this* was the ride Eli had gotten for me. And that's when I felt, for maybe the tenth time that day, as if I'd made a massive mistake.

Chapter Six

Each person in my family—Mom, Will, Dad—had guts in their own weird way. A touch of bravery. A sense of adventure. Not me. For whatever reason, I had none. When the motorcycle pulled up in front of me, all I wanted to do was run and hide.

The guy cut the engine.

"Casey, right?" he said, taking off his sunglasses. He wore a leather vest and chaps over his jeans. Tattoos blackened his arms, from shoulder to knuckle. His neck was as big around as a gallon jug of orange juice.

I just stood there frozen, not even blinking. Seriously, my stomach went cold, like it was filled with ice.

"Right?" he repeated, putting the death machine's kickstand down. "You're Casey? Casey Moe?"

Casey? This guy couldn't possibly be Eli's ride. I began to back slowly away and, just as I was about to sprint down the street, he said it:

"You don't trust anyone. That's your problem."

I wavered. His eyes were black. Unreadable.

"What did you just say?" I managed.

"'You don't trust anyone. That's your problem,'" he repeated and then explained, "Your dad said you might be nervous. He said if you heard that, you'd know it was okay."

I blinked, and then nodded. *My dad? Did he mean Eli?* I couldn't piece it all together.

"Sorry about your grandma," he continued. "Dying's never a fun business."

This really was Eli's ride. This wasn't some Carl/Chicken Farmer mix-up. I rolled my eyes—well, just in my mind. Apparently Eli thought it would be just peachy to ride with this guy.

"The name's Lloyd," the man smiled, sticking out his hand. "Lloyd Lloeke." He said it like *Loy-kee*. When he smiled, his teeth shone white through his black beard. *Lloyd?* I marveled at his name as he shook my limp hand. He looked like a Rocky or a Rambo or something. I could even see him as a Mike or a Jim, but a *Lloyd Lloeke?*

"And you're Casey," he prompted. I just nodded.

Casey. Sure. That's me.

"Boise's a long trip for a funeral, but I bet your dad will be glad you're there with him," Lloyd said in a friendly way. I just kept nodding like a bobblehead, trying to think of a way to get out of going with him. Because I sure as heck wasn't getting on a motorcycle with Lloyd Lloeke. If I did, I was pretty sure we'd be going to *my* funeral in Boise.

"Here, let me get your bag."

That's when he stood up and I took in the fact that he was almost seven feet tall. Lloyd didn't notice the terror on my face—or maybe he did but was used to that. He just plucked my suitcase from the sidewalk like it was a lunchbox and strapped it to the side of his bike.

While I gawked, Lloyd brought a shiny, black, mixing-bowl of a helmet down on my head.

"You can wear mine," he said, buckling it for me.

"Thanks." Without the helmet, I could see Lloyd was bald. Very bald. His head was so bald, I imagined air molecules squeaked past it as he rode.

"You okay wearing the backpack?"

"Yep," I answered. My voice seemed very high for some reason.

"All right then," he said. "Let's get a move on!"

I wasn't sure which scared me more: Lloyd or the motorcycle. I mean, even *Mom* called motorcycles death traps. (And coming from someone who walks on high wires and shoots herself out of cannons, that's saying something.) But I willed myself not to be nervous. *Will* wouldn't be. He'd be hooting and hollering, itching to ride.

But then again, I'm not Will.

However, there was the teensy hiccup of having to rescue my mom. I wasn't going to solve anything sitting in front of a house in Cowboy Town, Oregon. If I didn't get on the bike, I might as well give up.

I took a deep breath, trying to use this thing called the "Instant Calm Breath Method" that Mom had taught me. It's supposed to help you stop the body's flight-or-fight reaction (for me, it was more a flight-or-faint reaction).

Breathe in for four counts. Hold it for four. Breathe out for four. Slow breaths...

"You okay, Casey?" Lloyd asked, looking concerned.

"Yep," I squeaked. "Fine."

ℐ

"Isn't this great?" Lloyd shouted over the roar of the Harley.

"Great!" I screamed back. I tried not to look at the road curving ahead of us. Or at the pavement zooming below me. Pavement that would rip the skin off my bones if I touched it even for a second.

Instead, I focused my eyes on Lloyd's ear lobes. They held big round earrings with hollow centers that you could *see all the way through*. I suddenly felt like an uptight nerd in my collared shirt and tie.

"Nice day!" he said over his shoulder. "Makes you glad to be alive!"

"Yeah!" I said. "Alive!"

Lloyd twisted his head to get a glimpse of me, which didn't seem very safe.

"You're not looking!" he said. "Open your eyes!"

"Okay!" And I tried to look.

"Beautiful! Sun! Air! Fantastic! Who wants a car?"

I did, for one.

"We're safe!" he said. "Completely stable!" With that, Lloyd swerved back and forth on the road.

"Don't!" I shouted.

"Sorry!" He straightened out. "Trust me! Best ride ever! Or your money back!"

So I loosened up a little. I kind of had to, or my body was going to be seized by a full-body charley horse. I took in the scenery but wasn't all that impressed. It looked kind of like home, flat and brown. But the air felt good.

"Thanks for the ride!" I shouted after a moment.

"Glad I could help you out!" he called over his shoulder.

I remembered Eli's story about the funeral. But why was I going to Idaho? I mean, the *real* me, not Casey.

"You going to Boise anyway?" I called.

"Yeah! Always go there for my lectures!"

"Lectures?" I yelled back. Lloyd, with his tattoos and tunnel earrings, gave lectures? Maybe I'd heard him wrong. Lectures? Dentures? Sweatshirts?

"Comparative anatomy lectures! Osmoregulation! Tissue structure!"

At least, that's what I thought I heard.

You can only shout so much on a motorcycle. We fell silent after that.

❧

When I was in fourth grade, Mom slid down the flagpole from the roof of Brenville's post office. Dad's co-worker's husband saw it happen and there was a lot of talk around town. Dad really chewed her out for that one.

After the yelling stopped, she said something to me that I never forgot: "It's okay when everyone else doubts you. It's when you doubt yourself that it gets hard."

Riding on the back of Lloyd's motorcycle, my own doubts about the Rescue Mission started creeping into my mind. I'd never admitted it to Eli—and barely even to myself—but I couldn't help wondering if we were wrong about this whole kidnapping business. I thought of the way Dad looked at me like I was crazy every time I brought

69

it up. I thought of how the cops completely ignored me. *What if I'd somehow misunderstood it?* I mean, *I* was the guy stupid enough to believe that Will would have taught me to dive because he'd had a change of heart. As Will put it, *Who gets kidnapped by the circus?* It was a ridiculous idea.

And it wasn't like Bartholomew was keeping Mom hidden. In the few months she'd been with Bartholomew, "The Amazing Athena" had set an honest-to-god Human Cannonball World Record for summersaults and was featured on both the local news and on the *Ripley's Believe It or Not!* website. That didn't make much sense if they were keeping her against her will.

But kidnapping was the only thing that made sense, wasn't it? Maybe she was brainwashed. The postcards with the messages, the horrible rumors about Bartholomew, the black van, the near-destruction of our house, the fact that Mom hadn't come home to visit us: there was just too much evidence. There was no way I was wrong.

But what if I was?

෨

Lloyd pulled off the main road into a gas station's gravel parking lot. Everybody stared at our roaring motorcycle as we pulled up to the gas pump. The bike shuddered to a stop and I hopped off, my stiff legs barely able to hold me up.

Lloyd stretched, his back sounding like someone shuffling a deck of cards.

"Gotta empty the pipes," he said, heading for the restroom.

After he had peed and gassed up the bike, Lloyd bought us a couple of Cokes and we went to a picnic table. It felt very, very good to be on solid, non-moving ground.

Lloyd opened his Coke with one hand while looking at me strangely.

"So, your name's Casey, right?" he asked.

"Right," I said, taking a swig. *Yup. I'm Casey. Going to a funeral in Boise.*

70

"Strange," he said. "Earlier, I called your name about five times and you didn't turn around."

Uh-oh.

"I, uh…must have been thinking about something else," I said. He nodded and let it drop.

I studied Lloyd's tattoos while he checked his phone. There was a snake in a figure eight, eating its own tail. A Rubik's cube. Something that looked like a math equation. On his left forearm was a bunch of words on a big scroll. I realized with a small shock that I knew the words—it was an old Rolling Stones song.

"I like that tattoo," I said, pointing and hoping the small talk would distract him from the whole Casey issue. "My dad likes the Stones, too." I felt even cooler because I knew to call them "the Stones" and not "the Rolling Stones."

"You know the song, 'Sympathy for the Devil'?" he asked, looking down at his arm. I nodded. Dad listened to it so much, it had grown on me.

"Reminds me to face my fears, you know?" he said, and he held out his arm so I could see the whole thing. "My dad wasn't easy to live with. He was—he was sometimes a bad guy. He died when I was seventeen. I got the tattoo then. Sympathy for my dad, I guess."

I realized what he was saying: sympathy…*for the devil,* meaning his father.

"You been to Boise a lot?" he asked, changing the subject.

"Uh, yeah," I lied hastily. "We used to visit our grandmother, Nana, in the summer."

"I like it there," he said, taking a loud slurp of his soda. "I took my mom there with me once so we could see the Boise Opera. It was pretty good."

Lectures? Opera? Maybe I'd completely misread scary Lloyd.

~

A few hours later, and just half an hour outside Boise, Lloyd stopped on the wide shoulder of the road.

"Is everything okay?" I asked nervously. Why were we stopping in the middle of nowhere?

"I think we've sprung a leak," he said, turning off the motorcycle.

"Uh-oh." I inspected the ground below the bike.

"Not the bike," he said. "Your backpack."

He pointed a giant finger over my shoulder and I looked behind us. My postcards. Somehow, my bag had popped open. Cards littered the road and the nearby field. They blew in the breeze, trailing far behind us.

I took off at a dead run.

"Casey! Watch out!"

A truck barreled by, going about a hundred miles an hour. If it'd been any closer, I'd have been flattened. I only stopped for a second, letting that fact sink in. Then I bolted again.

I snatched up a postcard from the side of the road, then another. *Minneapolis. Green Valley. Deadman Reach.* They were all I had of Mom. Not just the ones with the clues, but the others, too. And her picture! The one with her by the cannon. I'd forgotten about that, and now it was gone!

"Hey, hey," Lloyd said, coming up behind me, putting a hand on my shoulder. "You okay?"

"Yeah," I answered, wiping a palm across my cheek like I had an itch, hoping he wouldn't notice I was crying.

"Before you shoot off across that highway, you need to relax."

"I'm fine," I said, my voice cracking in the middle of the words. Another huge truck blew by, sending more postcards swirling. I made to go after them, but Lloyd's heavy mitt of a hand stayed on my shoulder, holding me in place.

"When you're cool, you can go." At first I was mad. *Who was he to tell me what to do?* But I took a few deep breaths. I felt calmer.

"All right," said Lloyd, pulling his hand back. "I'll help you. They haven't gone too far."

I nodded. We made our way down into the field, picking them up as we went. *Winnipeg. Little Hope.*

"Want to talk about it?" Lloyd asked, stooping for a card.

"Uh, well, it's just that Mom is...well, she's in the circus," I said. "These are the only letters she sends. I think, well, because she couldn't make it home for the funeral, I'm a bit...touchy."

And just like that, I discovered the secret to being an incredible liar. All you had to do was take the truth and bend it to fit. Why hadn't I ever thought of that before?

"The circus!" Lloyd exclaimed. "No way. Which circus? What does she do?"

"Bartholomew's Circus. She's the Human Cannonball." I found the picture of my mom. The one with her in her human cannonball suit. I handed it to Lloyd.

"I've heard of them! Bartholomew's Awesome Circus of the Stupendous something-or-other, right? Man, I love that kind of stuff!" he said. He looked from the picture to me, and back again. "Spitting image, you two."

I nodded, not correcting him about the name of the circus. He was so fired up, I had a hard time not smiling. I'd never heard anyone get so excited about my mom being in the circus.

I snagged another postcard, the one Will had torn up and I taped back together. *Philadelphia.*

"Man! And you're named Spartacus to boot? Crazy," he said, shaking his head.

When he caught my shocked look, he held up his hands in surrender. "Sorry, I couldn't help but see the name on the cards." He gave me the ones he'd picked up. I smiled weakly at him, then counted them. I was still missing two.

"*Audentes fortuna iuvat!*" Lloyd cried, raising his giant fist in the air. "That's Latin for 'Fortune favors the bold.' Not that it was Spartacus who said that, but still. That's a wicked name, man."

I nodded stiffly and Lloyd pursed his lips.

Another tough subject.

"I guess Casey is just easier to go by? Kids tease you?"

"Well, yeah…I mean, no," I said hastily. "I mean, *yes*, they tease me, but it's not about Spartacus. Mom's the only one who calls me that. Dad, well, he doesn't like it. He makes sure everyone knows my name is…my name is Casey."

I was so close to saying "Ryan," it wasn't funny, but Lloyd thought the pause was just me choking up again and his face fell in sympathy.

"That's rough, kid," he said. "But it *really* is a great name. The movie *Spartacus*? Phe*nom*enal. I still know parts of it word for word."

"I, uh, I've never seen it," I admitted.

"*Never seen it?* And you're the hero in the whole thing?"

"It's not on Netflix," I said lamely.

Lloyd dramatically threw his hands up in exasperation, but I just shrugged. Honestly, I was afraid watching it would just drive home how lame I really was.

"You have to see it," Lloyd continued. "I'll *send* you a copy."

"Well, I *did* read a couple books about him," I said defensively, picking up *Farewell, Arkansas*. "He was pretty cool."

"More than cool," Lloyd said. "What an excellent, courageous dude! So you know how he was born a slave, without freedom. But he didn't accept it. He inspired all these other slaves to lead a revolt against the ruling classes. There's this great line in the movie, when Spartacus is getting ready to face certain death. The guy goes, 'Are you afraid to die, Spartacus?' And Spartacus goes, 'No more than I was to be born.'"

"'No more than I was to be born,'" I echoed, thinking about what that meant. I suppose if you didn't exist before you lived, why should you be afraid of the same thing happening again?

We continued picking through the dirt in silence for a moment before I spoke up again, "I forgot; did Spartacus become a king or something? He won the war and became free?"

"Well, no." Lloyd coughed. "He got crucified. Nailed to a cross. He died a horrible death."

"Oh."

"But," Lloyd said, "the point of his story is that your freedom is worth fighting for—and even if you die trying, your effort gives others the inspiration to fight for themselves. It was true then—what was that, like 100 BC?—and it's still true now."

I paused, absorbing, before realizing what his story meant to *me*.

"But all this you've been saying, about how great he was, that's why I *should* be Casey," I said. "So no one expects too much from me."

"You have a point," he said, looking thoughtful. "It is a whole lot of name to live up to. I guess if my parents had called me Coolest Man Ever, it might cramp my style, but then again, it's still an awesome name."

Lloyd and I climbed back up the ditch to the road so we could check up there for the last missing card. As we did, I felt a small smile creeping onto my face. This big tattooed biker, maybe the coolest person I'd ever met, wasn't laughing at my name. And, even though I was pretty sure I wouldn't ever go by Spartacus...well, his enthusiasm was sort of contagious.

"You said the kids tease you—but not about Spartacus?" Lloyd asked.

"We-ell," I said, kicking bits of gravel off the road and into the dirt. "Everyone calls me...well, they call me Poop Lip. Because of the, well, the—"

"The freckle," Lloyd said, shaking his head. "Clever. But rough, nonetheless."

"My brother made it up," I explained. "He's kind of the town bully."

"And this—this bully brother calls you *Poop Lip?*"

"I don't really want to talk about it," I said, wishing I hadn't brought it up. Hearing that name again made me feel about two inches tall.

"Why don't you stand up for yourself?"

My heart sank. No one understood. I told him glumly, "You don't get it. It's not that easy."

"No, I know it can be tough. I have a rotten brother, too."

Chapter Seven

I have a guilty secret: I really enjoyed decoding the postcards Mom sent me. I know, it's terrible, considering what was happening. But Mom knew I was good at words, so it made sense that she would feel safe putting her secret messages in code. She knew I'd figure them out.

Out of all her postcards, the hardest one to decode had been the one from Fearsville, Kentucky:

Dear Spartacus:

Things are still going real good. Made friends with a bunch of clowns. Turns out, they aren't very funny. Especially one clown named Sam Eve. Sam Eve is very serious. No matter what anyone says, this isn't a joke at all.

— Mom

It took me and Eli a whole week to figure out that the clown's name was an anagram—and if you don't know, an anagram is when you rearrange all the letters up to make other words. Once we figured it out, though, it made immediate sense: *Sam Eve = Save Me.*

"Save Me is very serious. No matter what anyone says, Save Me isn't a joke at all."

It gave me the shivers.

And yet…part of me wondered why she was telling me this random stuff instead of important messages like, "Meet me in Cincinnati on the fifth." What could I do with "save me" if she didn't tell me where to go? And I couldn't even write back to ask, since she was never in the same place longer than a few days.

So many mysteries.

꙳

When we pulled up to a house on the outskirts of Boise, it was late afternoon. Dark, shiny cars filled the driveway and lined the street. The mailbox read *Geneva Moe.*

"You ready?" Lloyd asked, handing me my suitcase. It took me a minute before I understood he was asking about the funeral.

"Guess so," I answered. I had no idea what I was supposed to do next. Apparently, the Moes were *actually having a funeral.*

"Hold on," Lloyd said, pulling out a notepad and scribbling something down. He folded the paper and handed it to me.

"My phone number," he said. "Give me a call if you need help leading a revolution—or just if you need anything, okay?"

"Thanks," I said, pocketing the note, knowing I would never, ever call him. But still, the gesture was nice. "Really. Thank you." I shouldered my backpack and pressed down my hair with a shaky hand.

"You're gonna be okay, *Spartacus,*" Lloyd said, putting out his own hand. I reached out and shook it. A Rolling Stones lyric from his tattooed arm caught my eye, something about guessing his name.

Spartacus. Casey. Ryan…

A large woman in a black dress came out the front door of the house and stood there, watching us both. Lloyd waved at her in a friendly way, and I cringed. This was beyond awkward.

"Good luck, Spartacus," Lloyd said. "See you around."

I stalled. Lloyd nodded slightly toward the woman, who inched toward us with a questioning look on her face. Both of them seemed to be waiting for me to do something. With bravery I never suspected I had in me, I walked right up the sidewalk and hugged the lady.

"I'm sorry for your loss," I said into her giant, soft arm, remembering the line from a movie somewhere. She seemed to accept I was someone she knew and hugged me so tight I could hardly hear Lloyd's motorcycle as he roared away.

Eli had evidently told them that I was the deceased's paperboy. The woman immediately herded me into a crowded living room full of mourners laughing, crying, and, best of all—eating. She planted me in front of the hors d'oeuvres and I scarfed them gratefully.

Now, to contact Eli and have him get me the heck out of here.

I edged toward the back entrance and was almost in the clear when someone called out from behind me.

"Wait!"

I turned, as nervous as an imposter paperboy, my foot halfway out the door. The large woman staggered toward me under the weight of a monstrous bunch of purple and orange flowers. And I mean *monstrous*. It looked like an entire bush.

"These just arrived, you dear, sweet, young man," she exclaimed, heaving the bouquet onto the table. "Spending your paycheck on Aunt Geneva! I could kiss you." And she did. She leaned down and gave me a big, wet kiss on the cheek.

"Well, you know..." I stuttered, completely confused.

"I'll get a vase," said the woman, heading toward the kitchen. I looked at the bouquet and then realized what it was.

Eli.

Pumped up with adrenaline, I clawed through the flowers until I found the card. It was bright yellow, didn't have an envelope, and said, quite clearly:

R*emembering*
Y*ou*
A*lways.*
N*avin (your paper boy)*

Thirty seconds later, I was racing down some rural road, card in one hand, suitcase in the other. On the back of the card, Eli had had the florist write directions to a nearby intersection. There was also a time written: 6:30 p.m.

It was already 6:15.

Sometimes Eli surprises me with his cleverness. As I ran, ever weighed down by my suitcase and backpack, I took back all the bad things I'd thought about him.

By 6:20, there I was, gasping and wheezing next to a boarded-up restaurant. (For someone who hated P.E., I was doing a lot more running than I'd ever intended.) The parking lot was empty, no one in sight—which was good because I was sweating big time and wanted to change clothes. Stepping to the side of the building, I shucked off my suit and threw on a black t-shirt and jeans. It's strange how James Bond always stayed so clean, even while riding motorcycles and fighting bad guys. My white shirt already had pit stains. I flapped it around in the breeze to dry a bit before putting it back in the suitcase.

I collapsed on the curb to catch my breath. The sun was lower, glinting off passing cars. How long would I have to wait? I didn't even know what I was waiting for. A bus? A taxi to the airport? A helicopter?

Then I remembered the note from Lloyd. I pulled it out of my pocket and read:

Spartacus,
Don't forget your name:
"Maybe there is no peace in this world for anyone, but I do know as long as we live, we must be true to ourselves."
*   - Spartacus*
If you're ever in Portland, look me up!
Your friend,
Lloyd Lloeke

He'd put his phone number and email address underneath his name. I tucked the note in my pocket and then checked my watch. 6:30 on the nose.

Next stop, Albuquerque, I thought. I opened my backpack, ate one of my energy bars, and then started counting cars. I was up to a hundred and eight when a black semi rolled into the parking lot. It had orange and red flames down the sides and silver fangs on the grill. Two exhaust pipes belched black smoke, and the windows were tinted so you couldn't see who was inside. The brakes screeched as it rolled to a stop, right in front of me.

I realized I might have been too quick to forgive Eli.

Chapter Eight

I don't know who I expected to jump out of the truck cab, but it certainly wasn't a small, young woman. She was brown-eyed and brown-haired, with dirty jeans, an orange shirt, and a green trucker hat. And did I mention she was small? Like my size?

"You Brodie?" she said, yanking the bill of her hat forward on her head.

"Yeah, that's me," I said cautiously. I wished Eli had at least stuck with one fake name so I'd always know who I was supposed to be. *Brodie. Remember it: Brodie.*

"I'm Hailey," she said, putting out her hand. She was stronger than she looked; her handshake practically broke my hand. She had a brassy voice with a Southern accent.

"Pleasure to meet you," she said, though it came out more like "Play-sure to meetcha."

"H-hey," I stammered back. "Nice to, uh, nice to make your—" I couldn't speak. Something was wrong with my mouth. She was just so darn cute.

"Ready to go?" she asked.

"Yeah," I said. "You going to Albuquerque?"

"Nope, Santa Fe. Change of plans. But don't worry. You'll get there. Let's roll." She smiled at me with big teeth and then turned and vaulted into the truck.

I went to the passenger side, worrying about this "change of plans."

After struggling a bit with the handle, I got the door open. I crouched down and launched myself into the cab like I was doing a high jump.

Once inside, I gave Hailey a sideways glance. Was this *girl* going to drive me? She wasn't any bigger than I was. She had to sit on this raised platform to see over the dash—it was an adult's booster seat.

I buckled my seatbelt. The seats were soft, and the cab smelled like oranges.

"Like I said, my plans changed and I've gotta drop you off in Santa Fe," she said, putting the truck into gear. "But you'll be able to get a city bus from there to Albuquerque, no problem. I'll even give you a few bucks if you need it."

Even as I nodded, I wondered if a bus would let a kid my age ride alone—but I could only ask for so many favors. Instead, I asked, "How long is the drive?"

It was Friday, and the show was Saturday. I had to make it there by tomorrow night.

"Let's just say we've got a long night ahead of us," she said. She pulled the truck out onto the highway. "We're not stopping much, unless you have to pee."

Usually, a girl talking about peeing would have made me blush. But weirdly, I wasn't that embarrassed by it. I thought of my high dive experience. Could living through something so embarrassing make it so I'd never be embarrassed by anything again? I thought of my dad at the dinner table one night, talking about the high dive, saying, "Whatever doesn't kill you makes you stronger." Could he have been right?

"Brodie," Hailey mused. "You know, that's a terrible name to be tryin' to hide under."

"I'm not hiding," I said, a little too forcefully. "What's wrong with Brodie?"

"You should choose something plainer."

"I—"

"I ran away from home, too," she went on, interrupting me. She looked thoughtful and knit her eyebrows under her hat. "Changed my name to Jane. I was sixteen. How old are you?"

All of a sudden I was very aware of my height and Will's scuffed new sneakers. I sat up a little straighter.

"How old are *you*?" I countered.

"Twenty-two," she answered immediately.

"I'm fifteen," I countered. Hailey snorted. I tried to look offended. "What? I'm small for my age."

"I know how these lies work," Hailey said. "It's always a three-year jump. Twelve-year-olds say they're fifteen; thirteen-year-olds say they're sixteen." She rattled these numbers off like she was reciting multiplication tables, then glanced over at me with a knowing smile. "You're *twelve*, then."

"Ha!" I tried to force a laugh.

"That's a little young to be tryin' to make it on your own."

"What makes you think I ran away?" I asked.

"Whose parent would go on Craigslist to get their son a ride to the, what was it—oh yeah, the Geology Ultimate Fightin' Championships?"

I almost burst out laughing, but kept it together. "Yeah. It's—it's the finals," I managed. I couldn't believe Eli had used *that* as my story. Eli and I had once recorded classmates wrestling in Geology class and uploaded the video as the "Geology Fighting Championship"—and now Hailey thought I was competing.

Hailey just gave me an incredulous look. "It was such a stupid story, I had to pick you up, *Brodie*, but I don't believe it for a second."

"No, seriously. My team is already down there!" I insisted.

"Okay, tell me what you do at this Geology Fightin' Tournament," she said with a smirk.

"Uh, I don't like talking about it before the competition. Gotta keep my head clear."

When she laughed, it sounded like a goose honk.

"You been travelin' long?" she asked.

"A day," I said, then corrected myself. "I mean, just a few hours. I got a ride from…" Where had I come from? I didn't know what I was supposed to say. How much had Eli told her? I was getting the new story confused with the paperboy story and the story I'd had to tell Lloyd. *Navin. Brodie. Casey. Spartacus. Moe.*

82

I was in over my head.

"Did you ever go back home?" I asked her abruptly, changing the subject. "After you ran away?"

"Nope."

I thought about Hailey being out on the road, never going back. As terrible as Will and Dad were, could I do that?

"Were your parents mean or something?" I blurted out.

Hailey gave a slight, sick grin that didn't reach her eyes.

"Let me put it this way, kid," she said. "However bad you think your family is, mine was a hundred times worse."

There wasn't much I could say to that.

I watched the road fly away behind us in the side-mirror. We passed a few towns, the kind that you're practically out of before you even see the welcome sign. Patchwork fields turned into gray and black squares as the sun started to sink below the horizon.

After a while, Hailey put on a slow-paced Spanish language-learning audio book.

"*Mira el campo*," said a deep, lulling voice.

"Mira el campo," Hailey repeated, but she wasn't even trying to match the Spanish accent.

I pulled out a comic book and pretended to read, but really I was thinking about the rescue mission. Bartholomew wasn't expecting me, so I wouldn't need a disguise inside the circus. I'd just need to blend in. Maybe I should use some makeup to cover my freckle, just in case? I could probably find some at a drug store.

"*Veo una vaca.*"

"Veo una vaca."

I had a pocketknife to cut my way through the tent. Would I need rope? I don't know what I'd need it for, but it seemed like a useful thing to have. The circus would probably have some lying around if I needed it.

"*Esa es una gran cabra.*"

"Esa es una gran cabra."

My head began to feel heavy. I rested it against the cool window and watched the fields slide by.

Sleep would be really nice.

As I nodded off, thoughts of Bartholomew's Circus spun in my head.

≈

When I first discovered IHateBartholomewsCircus.com, there was maybe an entire week when I didn't sleep. I spent every free moment—lunch breaks, recess, and from after dinner until I had to go to bed—surfing the forum full of crazy stories and rumors about the circus. Or, at least, I gorged on information until Dad turned off the wi-fi. (Once, Dad caught me online at four a.m. I closed the browser window just in time and tried to pretend I'd fallen asleep while doing my homework. He didn't buy it, but luckily, he didn't know how computers worked and couldn't reopen the window.)

It was weird how all this conspiracy info was out there, yet Bartholomew was still allowed to roam the country, putting on shows and stealing people's moms. I pored over every detail, creating a chronological time line of Bartholomew's life and the history of the circus, which I'd message to Eli, with links.

Sometimes, he would reply with, "Wow. Wow. I mean. Wow."

Other times, though, it was, "GO TO SLEEP."

Bartholomew's story goes like this:

Count Csizmadia Bartholomew had lived in some country near Russia that doesn't exist anymore—one of those places that got all broken to pieces after a war or something. He had been exiled (no one knows why) and he landed in Maryland twenty-five years ago, with only the clothes on his back.

Within two days, he had landed a job mending animal cages with the The Humble Reed Family Circus. He had been the first employee who wasn't a Reed. They said he had some kind of hypnotic power over animals. That makes sense, because within two years, he was head animal trainer. He did an act where big jungle cats and bears all performed with a troupe of house cats (which I guess is hard to get them to do).

A couple years later, the owner of The Reed Circus? *Bam!* Kicked the bucket. He got cornered one night by a loose leopard, had a heart attack—and that was it. Dead. The leopard hadn't even touched him.

Then, get this: Mr. Reed left the whole circus and all its animals to Bartholomew.

I told you it was sketchy.

Bart fired all the Reeds and renamed the circus after himself. Overnight, it went from just a dozen performers to the hundred-person-strong Bartholomew's World-Renowned Circus of The Incredible—and *where* he found a hundred new performers is another unanswered question. They began traveling all over North and South America. They toured Europe and Asia—once they spent a winter in Africa.

"But where did they get the money from?" Eli always asked. "Travel is expensive. No way were they making it from admission tickets."

I didn't have an answer—and neither did anyone else.

Everywhere they went, bad news followed. The tiger mauling and the trapeze "accident" were the only tragedies that made the papers, but the rest lived on IHateBartholomewsCircus.com. Pages and pages of rumors. Some seemed real, others made up, but all were pretty scary.

For example, two guys running the spotlight went missing mid-show and were never found. There was an explosion that took out the entire exotic birds tent, singeing all the hair off the bird-keeper. And once, a group of kids found a finger in an empty field where the circus had just performed.

Just a finger.

Of course, none of these stories were proven. But still, it sounded pretty bad when you looked at it all together. And the weirdest stuff—even weirder than fingers appearing and people disappearing—was about Bartholomew.

No one could find anything about the guy. No family members, *nada*. Like he was a myth that just came into existence. Wikipedia couldn't even figure out his age. And Bartholomew didn't have *any* wrinkles on his face. Not a line when he furrowed his brow, not a crinkle when he smirked. His skin? Completely smooth.

All the pictures Eli and I found backed this up.

Everything about Bartholomew was neat and elegant in an old-timey kind of way. He was a tall, lean, pale man with a wide, smooth forehead and small, expressionless blue eyes like ball bearings. He wore his wavy red hair combed and waxed into a modest, gleaming pompadour and dressed only in slender-cut, black-and-red suits. In the few photographs of him, he held his willowy hands crossed gently over one another, as though he were patiently waiting for someone to finish speaking—before he destroyed them.

"So what, you guys think Bart has magic powers?" Will asked me and Eli once, leaning in with a mocking sneer on his face. Eli and I looked at each other, and then I snorted maybe a bit too loudly. Because when you put all the cards on the table…who knows? Who really knows?

Only Bartholomew.

They say Bartholomew kept a plastic surgeon on staff—an old doctor who used to do work for the royal family in Bart's homeland. Some people thought that was why the bird keeper who'd been burned in that explosion was able to perform just a few weeks later, without a mark on her body. And why his clowns all looked alike.

I told you Barthlowmew's story was crazy.

And even though he was the ringmaster and spoke forty-three languages, Bartholomew never spoke outside the ring to anyone who wasn't in the circus. He didn't speak in public; he didn't do interviews. Articles were written *about* him, of course; several reporters swore they'd overheard him say he hated children.

But Bart never said anything to clear the air.

And yet—despite *all* of this, crowds came in droves to watch

Bartholomew's World-Renowned Circus of The Incredible. They adored it. Even those who hated him, people who'd lost family members to strange circus accidents, admitted that Bartholomew's show was…unforgettable. It made adults feel like kids again. It made children and old people cry when it was over. Sometimes people in the audience spoke in tongues, like they were at a tent revival.

Some say that Bartholomew's fog machine pumped nitrous oxide into the tent—as in, laughing gas, the stuff the dentist gives kids that makes your body feel like a lead weight while your brain feels all fluffy and nice. Others say it's just the way Bartholomew talks to the crowd, hypnotic and trance-inducing.

When you really looked at all the information, it was overwhelming. Bartholomew and his circus were an unstoppable, dangerous riddle.

As I dozed in the truck, I dreamt my mom's kidnapping was just another rumor from IHateBartholomewsCircus.com. In my dream, I showed the story to everyone, but no one would listen. Not even Eli. I was rescuing her alone, but I couldn't find my clothes and all I had was a motorcycle to ride, and when I got there, there were fifty identical clown guards looming over me and Mom was tied up in a tiny box…

When I woke up, I had forgotten where I was until I saw Hailey sitting in the driver's seat. It was dark out and there was a puddle of drool on my arm. We were parked at a truck stop.

"What time is it?" I yawned.

"Almost one a.m.," she said. "I'm gonna pee and get some food. And caffeine. You want somethin'?"

"I'll come in with you," I answered, wanting to stretch my legs.

Inside the convenience store, bright lights buzzed and made me squint after being in the dark truck for so long. Hailey used the bathroom and then got a cup of coffee and a box of crackers. I got some Sour Patch Kids and a soda with Will's money (which felt pretty good). Then we wandered the truck stop. There were public showers, places to nap, even a few computers (though I checked and the internet wasn't working).

We were standing together, looking at the public notice board, when I saw the poster. It was partially hidden. I moved a flyer out of the way so I could see it clearly. The poster had a photo of Lloyd—big, bald Lloyd. Only the name wasn't Lloyd and he wasn't smiling. I gulped and read the details:

DAN LLOEKE, A.K.A "THE CUE"
CONSIDERED ARMED AND DANGEROUS.
WANTED IN FOUR STATES FOR BURGLARY, THEFT, ASSAULT, AND MURDER.
WANTED IN CONNECTION WITH THE DEATHS OF THREE PEOPLE.
HAS ROLLING STONES LYRICS TATTOOED ON RIGHT FOREARM.

ॐ

I wish I could tell you that I stayed calm when I saw the poster. That I took it in stride. That I bravely stared down Dan Lloeke's wanted photo and just shook my head in disappointment.

Anyway, that's what I'd *like* to tell you.

Instead, I threw up in a garbage can and slid down to the floor.

I had just become BFFs with a serial killer.

After Hailey helped me to my feet, I stood in front of the poster. The sweat on my forehead had nothing to do with the stuffy hallway.

"You gonna tell me what just happened?" Hailey said, looking between the poster and me. I told her the truth, that this guy had just given me a ride a few hours before. She hugged me tight in a way that almost made it all worth it.

Almost.

We took down the poster and headed back to her truck.

How close had I been to death? I wondered. And not an imaginary death, like dying from embarrassment after the pool incident—but *real death?*

I felt clammy.

"Should we call the cops?" I asked.

"You can once you're in Albuquerque."

"Why wait—" I was about to ask *why wait so long*, but Hailey cut me off as she kept walking.

"I don't mess with cops."

Once in the truck, I gulped my soda to get the vomit taste out of my mouth. As Hailey put the truck into gear and pulled back out on the highway, I stared at the wanted poster and thought about death.

"Look, I like you," Hailey said at last. "But I don't want to get mixed up in whatever—whatever it is you got going on. That's why I don't want to call the cops. They wouldn't just try to get that guy on the poster. They'd take you in, too. And then they'd talk to me. And I sorta don't want to be found, you know?"

I didn't know, but I nodded anyway.

"Things aren't all fun and games on the road," Hailey said. "You gotta to be real careful. When you're a runaway, you ain't got no one lookin' out for you but you."

I told her again: "I'm not a runaway."

"Mmm, okay, *Brodie*," Hailey said, mocking my name again.

I ignored her and changed the subject. "I can't believe he was a serial killer."

"Now, you know he isn't *technically* a serial killer," she said.

"What do you mean? It says it on here: 'burglary, theft, assault, and *murder*.'"

"Just because someone's a murderer doesn't make them a *serial killer*," she said. "I mean, a serial killer is doing a lot of planning, killing multiple people over time. But this guy? He's probably just takin' out people who get in his way."

I goggled at her.

"You said you guys got along fine?" she asked, and I nodded. "Then you don't have nothin' to worry about. Sure, this guy's a criminal, but he's not killin' random kids for fun."

"This all makes me feel so much better," I said, sinking lower into my seat.

"I'm just trying to give you some education about killers," she said simply. "Not tryin' to scare you."

"Look, this is a one-time thing. I'm not 'out on the road.' It was just *one ride*." My voice started to sound a bit pinched and squeaky, so I cleared my throat. "I mean, how was I supposed to know?"

Hailey paused, considering. "Did you get that sinkin' feelin' in your stomach when you saw him?" she finally asked.

I thought about my instinct to run when Lloyd pulled up.

"Well, yeah."

"Did your Mistake-o-Meter give you some sort of alarm?"

"My what?"

"You know," she said. "Your 'Mistake-o-Meter.' Everybody's got one. You gotta pay attention to it while you're 'on the road.'"

I glowered at that, but I also thought about it. She was right. I did have a Mistake-o-Meter, and I'd ignored it with Lloyd. I'd even ignored it when Will taught me to dive.

I was starting to feel a bit claustrophobic. Just thinking about my Mistake-o-Meter made it go crazy. Worse, it was telling me that what *I* was doing was crazy. *What am I doing in this truck? Who did I think I was, rescuing my mom alone?*

I started hyperventilating.

I was just a kid, and I could have died. Like, really died.

I tried my mom's Instant Calm Breath Method.

Breathe in for four counts. Hold it for four.

It didn't help.

I probably would have started crying—maybe even real, snot-dripping bawling—but luckily, Hailey saved us both. She put her small hand on my arm and gave it a little squeeze.

"Let me tell you about the tools you got," she said. "So you won't be so vulnerable."

I hated that word. *Vulnerable.* I straightened up in my chair, pretending I was okay.

"So first you got the Mistake-o-Meter—it goes up to five. If you feel a one on the meter, be ready for anything. You get a two? Map your escape plan. Three? Use that escape plan and don't look back."

"And what if it's at a four or a five?" I asked.

"You should never get yourself into a four or five unless you wake up tied to a railroad track. If you even *suspect* something's that bad? Get the heck out of there."

"He was so nice, too," I said, resting my face against the cool window. "I don't get it."

"Perfect transition to the other tool you got: Mistrust."

"Is that a good thing?" I asked.

"Yeah, when you use it right. And you should be using it a lot out here. Don't trust anyone but yourself. People will try to get you to trust them and you just mistrust them right back. Don't trust anyone until they've *earned* your trust, you see? You can trust your brothers or sisters or friends or parents, but that's it."

Maybe not brothers, I thought.

"When you're on the road," Hailey continued, "your only friend is yourself. I know it sounds cruel, but that's how you gotta do it."

"You don't trust me?" I asked.

"Not on your life." She lifted the corner of her shirt to show me a knife in a sheath on her hip.

"Whoa," I whispered.

"I just met you. Sorry, Brodie."

"It's...it's cool," I managed.

After that, we drove in silence.

It all seemed pretty clear: I was in way over my head in the deep end of a big, dark pool.

☙

As we rolled on through the night, I couldn't get back to sleep. I pulled out the golden scarab Mom had sent me. I held the little piece of metal in my hand. It sounds silly, I know, but it made me feel calmer, just having that small connection to my mom.

So I sat there and thought.

I thought about Lloyd—I mean, *Dan the Killer*—out there on the loose. I could call the number on the poster and report him, but Hailey was right. The cops would want to question me, then maybe hide me somewhere he couldn't find me. They'd probably send me off to live in Alaska in the Witness Protection Program. I'd have to change my name and always look over my shoulder and learn to sleep with a gun and—

Actually, it was starting to sound kind of cool, especially following the pool incident.

But they'd never let me go without Dad and the Jerk. I might have been down with the whole witness protection thing if I wouldn't have had to take them along.

Besides, if I called the cops, I'd never get to the circus.

I decided to write a letter to the cops after I got mom home. Then I wondered if it was selfish to wait. What if Lloyd—*Dan*— killed somebody else? Would it be my fault?

I snuck a peek at Hailey's face, barely visible in the dashboard lights. I was too afraid to ask her.

Instead, I watched the dark sky out the window. I thought about Eli, how he'd almost gotten me killed with his ride choices. He'd have to start being more careful about who he talked to online.

Eventually, I dozed.

It was morning when got to Santa Fe, New Mexico. This was the *real* desert. I'm talking cacti and houses made out of clay. Everything was so wide open and flat, you could see forever. Hailey said it hardly ever rained in New Mexico, but there were a few dark storm clouds on the horizon. The rest of the sky was a brilliant, clear blue.

"Land of Entrapment," Hailey muttered as we crossed the state line.

She dropped me off at the edge of town, where I could catch the bus to Albuquerque.

"Wish I could take you all the way there, but my boss tracks the miles I drive and I can't go over," she said, coming to a stop. "Stay by that bus stop, right over there. Should be here on the half hour."

"Thanks for the ride," I said. "And the help with Lloyd. I mean Dan."

She held out a few dollars for the bus and when I tried to turn it down, she stuffed it in my sweatshirt pocket. When she hugged me, I felt this warm glow all over. I awkwardly hugged her back.

"Don't think about him. It'll turn out okay," she said. "Listen to your heart. When things get weird, you get out of Dodge, okay?"

"Right," I said. "Mistake-o-Meter at the ready."

I jumped out of the truck with my backpack and suitcase and looked up at her.

"What's your real name?" she called down.

I thought for a second, about trust and mistrust. Hailey had earned enough for a little truth. "Spartacus," I told her, and then cringed. Why did I tell her *that* name?

But she didn't even bat an eye. "And where are you goin'?"

"To see my mom."

"Well," Hailey said. "Tell her I said 'Hey.'"

Then I blurted out the sappiest goodbye ever. I don't know what I was thinking—it just came out. "I won't forget you."

"Likewise, Spartacus. Stay cool."

I slammed the passenger side door shut and the truck lumbered off down the road. Hailey hit the horn twice, and then she was gone.

She liked me. She called me cool.

It started to sprinkle and I didn't even care.

៚

The circus was just twelve hours away. Half a day. The most dangerous part of my journey was within sight. I was pumped.

Cars blew by and I stood back away from the road under a skimpy tree. I waited for an hour, but the bus didn't come. When I finally crossed over to the bus stop sign, I saw a small sticker across the face of it.

The Santa Fe/Albuquerque bus is no longer in service. We apologize for the inconvenience.

Oh, man.

I looked down the long road, then at the speeding cars.

Oh, *man.*

I couldn't walk, but I could always hitchhike.

Eli and I had originally agreed hitchhiking was totally out of the question. It was too dangerous. But then again, look how Eli's rides had turned out.

And the show was *tonight.*

I stood there, but couldn't put my thumb out. My arm was dead at my side. I started remembering everything I'd heard about hitchhiking. All the stories I knew were about the hitchhiker being crazy, not the driver. Eli told me how his cousin's friend's dad had picked up this guy who—

Suddenly, out of nowhere, a car horn blared right behind me.

I hadn't even put my thumb out.

Chapter Nine

I turned to find a very tanned, white-haired lady behind the wheel of a white Lincoln big enough to have its own area code. In the passenger seat sat another old woman with enormous glasses and blue hair pulled back in a bun so tight she looked like she was forced to smile whether she was happy or not. Blue-Hair waved excitedly at me.

"Where you headed, young man?" White-Hair asked, leaning over Blue to speak to me.

I smiled, relieved to see that they were old. And that neither woman had a hook. Scary hitchhiking stories always start with a hook.

"Albuquerque," I answered, putting on my best smile in hopes of covering up the I-just-ran-away-from-home-to-rescue-my-mother look. It must have worked because Blue leaned back and unlocked the door behind her.

"Well, don't just stand there. Hop in before the po-po see you!"

I got in, heaved the door closed, and settled into the velvety backseat. It then struck me that what she had just said was pretty strange. *Po-po?* I'd heard Will use that word before. Was she talking about the police?

And in a place where it never rained, the sky opened up and it poured.

"Good thing we have the cover of this storm," said White. Blue grunted in agreement and I raised an eyebrow. Without looking, White pulled the boat of a car out onto the highway, causing a smaller oncoming car to slam on its brakes to avoid hitting us. Neither Blue nor White seemed to notice.

"You never know when they'll come around the corner and nab you," White muttered while Blue nodded in agreement.

"Who?" I asked, hastily putting on my seat belt.

"What?" asked Blue.

"Who?" I repeated.

"Who *what?*" asked White, looking at me in the rearview mirror.

I shut my mouth, wishing Blue had left her window down because the entire car smelled horribly of vanilla air freshener. Five yellow trees dangled from the rearview mirror alone. More hung above the back doors. I held out as long as I could, but after a silent minute, I cracked the window so I wouldn't suffocate.

"You roll that window back up, young man," White said sharply and, because I didn't know what else to do, I did. I tried to hold my breath.

"Dangerous," said Blue, shaking her head.

"I was asking who would sneak around the corner and nab me?" I asked finally.

"The pigs! The fuzz! The po-po! The law! The constabulary! The ol' black-and-white!" White croaked, her voice growing louder with each word.

"Police," chimed in Blue.

I wasn't sure what the "constabulary" was, but I thought I was getting the idea. Blue turned around in her seat to peer at me. I could only see her eyes over the headrest, her giant, thick glasses making her dark eyes look at least ten times their normal size.

"Why would the police care about me?" I asked nervously.

"You tell me," said White. "You break out of the clink?"

Blue's eyes just blinked at me.

"What?" I asked. This was getting weird.

"Bust out of the slammer? Skip bail? Fly the coop?"

"Fugitive," Blue whispered and I just stared at her.

The red arrow of my Mistake-o-Meter started to creep upward as the car drifted all over the road, cutting off cars and running red lights, windshield wipers at full speed: *thwakita-thwakita-thwakita.*

"I wasn't in jail," I managed between gasps of vanilla-scented air. I closed my eyes tight as White narrowly avoided hitting a van.

"Just as I thought!" beamed White. "On the lam!"

"Look, I don't know what you're talking about," I said, gripping the handle above my door, the air freshener flapping against my arm. I was about to tell them I'd rather *walk* to Albuquerque when White's eyes narrowed in the mirror.

"Are you packing a biscuit?" she asked coldly.

"A *what*?"

That's when we swerved into oncoming traffic to go around a car slowing for an exit.

I truly believed it was my last moment alive.

Somehow, through a commotion of red brake lights, horns, and skidding tires, we avoided unavoidable death.

"Hippies!" White cursed, shaking a veiny fist at the traffic in general.

Blue either didn't notice or didn't care that we'd nearly been flattened like a pop can.

I was starting to think that this was more than just a three on my Mistake-o-Meter—it was starting to look like a four or a five. A Flashing, Red, Bad Idea.

"A biscuit! You know, a slug-thrower. A six-shooter." White was all but shouting, gesturing with her pale, wrinkly hand. "A rod! A gat!"

"Gun," Blue whispered.

Hailey had been right. You can't trust anyone.

"Are you carrying? Strapped up? Packing heat?" White finished.

"No!" I exclaimed. "Of course not! I'm only twelve," I added for good measure.

I need to get out of this car, I need to get out of this car, I chanted to myself, desperately trying to figure out an escape.

Through the windshield, the rain was coming down hard. The road in front of us was just a blur. There was no way these old ladies could see where they were going.

"Ask him his name," White said to Blue. But before she could,

White changed her mind. "No, no, never mind. I don't think we should know it."

"My name is Ryan," I said. These crazy bats wouldn't remember what I told them anyway.

"I can't hear you!" said White, putting her fingers in her ears and letting the steering wheel spin on its own. The Lincoln immediately veered to the right.

"Steer!" screeched Blue, grabbing the wheel. She pulled too hard and we went flying toward the shoulder. I thought we were going to crash, but a curb stopped us, the hubcaps singing against the concrete. My heart thudded so hard in my throat I thought I was going to choke.

"Gimme the wheel!" White squawked, wrenching the car back to the left. "You know you can't drive," she admonished Blue before turning back to me. "She lost her license, poor thing."

"Yes," agreed Blue somewhat wistfully.

White looked at me again in the mirror. "So Randy—"

"Ryan."

"Right. Brian. We're supposed to believe you don't have a gun?"

"Wait, wait, wait," I said, holding my hands up. "I'm just a kid. I just need to get to Albuquerque. I'm not a criminal or…whatever it is you think I am. Really." I swallowed loudly.

"Sure," said White, squinting at me. "He's in disguise," she whispered to Blue out of the corner of her mouth.

"Really?" Blue mumbled back, turning to face me again, her big bug-eyes blinking.

Reality must have taken the day off.

"Check his bag," White said, and before I knew it, Blue, a creaky old lady nearing a hundred had grabbed my suitcase from my lap as easily as Will snagging my cupcake.

"Give it back!" I leaned forward, but my seatbelt locked and tightened across my lap as White slammed on the brakes.

"Chill, Rambo," she said coolly, looking over her shoulder at me.

"Please, please, just look at the road," I pleaded, covering my eyes.

And just when I thought things had spiraled completely out of control, they got worse. I uncovered my eyes to see Blue pull a pistol out of the glove compartment.

"Oh—!" I choked on my words and my blood turned to ice as Blue fiddled with the honest-to-god, reach-for-the-sky *gun*. "Lady, please!" I cried, pushing myself back into the velvet seat.

Drivers honked and swore at us silently from behind closed windows as the Lincoln hurtled past them, running some off the road. We slowed for a sharp corner and I reached for the door handle, but Blue shook her head. White glared at me in the mirror. Her voice turned quiet and sweet, as though she were offering me a cookie.

"Don't make us mad, Rufus," she said. We kept driving. *How was I going to get away?*

I decided to panic.

My mouth began sputtering anything and everything, and before I knew it, I was telling them I had to get out so I could save my mom and had to give Will his money back and make my dad proud. Telling them things I didn't even know I felt until the words came tumbling out. The only reason my lips stopped flapping was because there wasn't anything left to say.

That, and Blue slapped me. The big ruby ring she wore cut my cheek and when I reached to touch it, my hand came back with a smear of blood.

"Hush," she said sternly.

"Cool it, Ralph," White added.

Blue then proceeded to go through everything in my suitcase. She showed my rescue plan to White who made a *tsk*-ing noise. Blue then stuffed everything back in, except for the scarab, which I saw fall onto the seat.

"Spy," Blue concluded, chucking my suitcase back at me.

"What?" I squawked.

"Quiet," she growled in her tiny voice.

We left the city limits and began picking up speed, blasting down the highway at what had to be a hundred miles an hour. White threaded the car in and out of traffic like a needle.

I thought about knocking White over the head with my flashlight, but I couldn't hit someone's grandma, gun or not. I mean, they might have kidnapped me but, well...they were *old*. What can you do when they're old? Besides, if I hit her, we'd crash for sure.

"I'm not a spy," I said. I was trying to be calm, but my voice shook.

"What's with the camo paint then?" countered White. "And the disappearing ink? The—" she squinted her eyes. "Top Secret Escape Plan?"

"I'm a runaway!" I yelled, shocking both women and myself. "I have to hide and escape sometimes, don't I?" I wriggled a bit to the left, out of the direct sightline of the gun bouncing in Blue's hand as the big white Lincoln clipped a smaller car. While her finger wasn't on the trigger, Blue didn't seem fully in control of the thing and I worried it might just go off if we were jounced the wrong way.

"What should we do with him?" White asked Blue. Blue shrugged.

"You can let me out here," I said, leaning forward. "I won't say a single word about—" About what? *What was this anyway?* "Well, any of this. I promise," I finished.

"You've seen too much," said White.

"Yep," said Blue.

"No, I haven't!"

"You know everything," said White.

"Everything," repeated Blue.

"No, I don't! I don't know *anything*!" It was well beyond the time to panic. Hailey would have been so disappointed.

"You've heard all our plans."

"Plans," echoed Blue.

"What plans? I didn't hear any plans!" My face broke out in a cold sweat, making the cut on my cheek sting. Suddenly, I had an idea.

"Look out, it's the po-po!" I screamed, pointing out the windshield.

"Where?" they both shouted at once. White slammed on the brakes and the car skidded across the wet pavement. Cars screeched (and no doubt crashed) around us, but I knew what I had to do.

I threw myself and my bags out the door.

I was aiming for a cool tuck-and-roll, like something from a James Bond movie. But I probably looked more like a kid accidentally falling out of Grandma's car. I clutched my suitcase to my chest and rolled away from the Lincoln in an awkward tangle of limbs. The wet blacktop bit into my knuckles and knees, but I was free.

"No!" White wailed.

I sat for a moment in disbelief, only to be brought back to earth by a pickup swerving around me and landing in the ditch with a crunch. White and Blue appeared to argue in the car for a moment before giving up on me. They took off, tires squealing, and made a sudden right turn...

Right into a cop car.

Holy. Crapola.

I peeled myself off the road and broke into a limping sprint. Holding my backpack and suitcase, I jumped down into the ditch and tried to scramble up the other side. My fingers dug into the wet dirt, but the edge was too steep to climb.

"Easy there, boy," boomed a voice above me. I turned around to see a huge silhouette looming above me. I could just make out the police badge on his chest through the pouring rain. I closed my eyes and slumped down into the ditch.

I was done.

≈

I was sitting in an air-conditioned office at a police station somewhere in New Mexico, waiting for the police officer to come back and ask me some questions about the old ladies. The last I'd seen of Blue and White, the police had been gently handcuffing them and nudging them into the cop car. White had actually tried to spit in a cop's face, but she was too short.

Insane.

I could tell the police officers didn't know who I was. Maybe it was the dirt on my face (I'd seen my reflection and barely recognized myself) or the fake name and address I'd given them. Maybe it was the fact that they had their hands full with two little old ladies who'd created the worst traffic pile-up in state history.

For whatever reason, everyone had been really nice to me so far, but I knew I had to get out of there. I was in an office down the hall from the main lobby of the police station, which wasn't very big. There were three desks and a bunch of office equipment in the room with me, but not much in the way of escape routes—which makes sense for a police station, I guess. There was a locked door that led to the rest of the building, and a window with vertical bars on the outside. I guess they were used to keeping suspects in the room. Or at least suspicious-looking kids.

I was alone for now, but somebody was going to come back soon. They'd offer me a damp towel to clean my face, and then they'd see my freckle and—I didn't want to think about it. Not when I was this close. Plus, my bags were at my feet and I knew it was only a matter of time before they asked to search them. It just seemed like something police did.

As I waited, I eyed Mom's gold scarab, sealed in a plastic evidence bag and lying on the desk in front of me. An attached sticky note read:

Recovered at scene. Run past FBI? Interpol?
Check against known art-theft list.

It was just a silly piece of jewelry, but it was special to me and I wanted it back. I sat on my hands to keep from grabbing it. Not just yet. I'd get it on my way out—if I could find a way out. I looked around the office again. There was a chance I could squeeze through the bars in the window, but the window was painted shut. What about the air-conditioning vents? I saw one next to the window, but it was only a foot across. How did people always get away through vents in the movies?

That's when I saw the bulletin board covered with posters of the FBI's Most Wanted. And guess whose face was front and center? Lloyd—Dan—Lloeke's.

Extremely dangerous.

The letters were big enough that I could read them from across the room. I went over and looked at his face again. Honestly, he hadn't looked that terrifying in real life. He stared out of the poster with gleaming eyes and a twisted mouth. He looked so angry, you had to wonder if he'd tried to kill the camera guy right after he took his picture. I shivered, remembering how close I had been to him.

I wondered again if I should tell the cops about Lloyd, but then I remembered what Hailey said. If I did, they probably wouldn't let me out of their sight. I pushed the thought away and instead tried to memorize the faces of the other people on the list, just in case Eli sent another one to pick me up. Hailey would probably think that was a smart idea.

The guy in the poster beside Lloyd's was wanted for armed robbery, murder, and extortion. Compared to Lloyd, he looked completely boring and normal. He had neat, short hair and a polite little smile. You would never have thought he was a murderer. Like Hailey said, you couldn't tell with people. Better to mistrust them first just to be on the safe side.

The last paper on the wall was this fuzzy, black-and-white picture that must have been taken with a security camera. It showed a two-story, square-shaped adobe building at night, lit up by a few bright streetlights. I could see a man's silhouette on the roof. He had his hands on his hips and his head turned to the side and facing up, kind of like a pose you'd see a superhero make. Under the picture was written, *Georgia O'Keeffe Museum Robbery, Santa Fe*. It was dated the night before.

Georgia O'Keeffe must have been a painter. There were small, color copies of maybe seven paintings that were missing—bright close-ups of flowers and trees. And one of them had a price scrawled beneath it, circled vigorously. *$14 mil*.

Mil? As in, fourteen million?

Wow.

I didn't know people actually robbed museums. I thought stuff like that only happened in the movies. Then I thought about Lloyd. And Blue and White. They weren't exactly the normal, every-day types either.

I went back to looking around the office for a way out, but came up with nothing. There was no way out. I sent a silent apology to Mom. I had failed her. The cops were going to know I gave a fake name. I was trapped.

I sat down and felt something poke me through the lining of my jeans pocket. It was the note from Lloyd. Unfolding it, I couldn't help but feel confused. How could such a nice, kind person be a murderer? He'd been so understanding— and helpful. Maybe there'd been some sort of mistake...?

I read the quotation again:

> *Maybe there is no peace in this world for anyone, but I do know as long as we live, we must be true to ourselves.*

I looked at my name at the top of the page. *Spartacus*. Funny how Lloyd had tried to make me feel better about my name. And what was the other thing he'd said about the movie? *Freedom is worth fighting for—even if you die trying?*

I couldn't give up now. Not after having come this far. And suddenly, my real name seemed more appropriate than ever.

Think, Spartacus, think.

I looked at the barred-up window and had an idea.

❧

"So, you say one of them pulled the gun on you?" The cop was gripping the stub of a pencil in his hand, taking down my story. His nametag said *Garcia*. No officer, no rank, just Garcia.

"Yeah. The blue-haired one had the gun."

The officer jotted this down. Just then the phone on his desk rang and he picked it up, swiveling around in his chair.

"Garcia here."

I leaned forward, trying to read what he had been writing, but I couldn't make anything out.

"Yes? Yes. Really? I see…" He swiveled his chair back to look at me. "I'll call you back."

"So, Jeff," Garcia said, hanging up his phone. "Where are your parents? We tried the number you gave us and it's been disconnected."

I looked down at my hands. *All right. It's time for the plan.*

That's when I started with the waterworks.

I know, I know, it's not particularly brave, but it was always a useful skill when I was younger and Will was about to pulverize me. And if I'd figured right, it was going to come in handy here, too.

"Hey," said Garcia, looking at me with concern. "Don't do that. What's wrong?"

"It's just that…" I stopped and heaved a huge sob that made my shoulders shake.

"Hey, hey, hey," Garcia said, uncomfortably, patting my shoulder. "Hey! Do you want a soda or something?"

"Yessir," I sniffled, looking up at him with what I hoped were grateful yet watery eyes.

"All right. Just hold on one second." Garcia left the room and I almost felt guilty. He was an all-right guy.

But that didn't stop me from using his telephone to break the window.

With one swing of the ancient desk phone, the window exploded into giant, glass shards that rained down around me, tinkling off the metal bars on the outside of it. The crash was deafening—and would bring anyone within earshot running down the hall.

Knowing I only had a moment to act, I ripped off my shirt and hurled it out the broken window. It landed where could easily be seen from inside. Then I snatched Mom's scarab off Garcia's desk. For the final part of my plan, I wedged myself into the small space between the huge copy machine and the wall. There was hardly room for a cat, let alone me, but I kept letting out my breath and scrunching my way down even further. Somehow I got myself squeezed in there. If I could just get them to leave the station to look for me, I'd be able to sneak out in another direction all together.

A few seconds later, Garcia barged in. When he saw the window, he dropped the can of soda and it rolled under the desk. "Jeff!" he shouted through the bars of the window. Then he said a curse word, then, "How the heck did he…?" followed by another curse word. I was beginning to feel lightheaded from lack of air.

Garcia rushed out the door, shouting, "Renner! Renner!"

"Yep?" came a female voice from down the hall.

"Jeff bolted."

"He *what?*"

And that's when Garcia, Renner, and the person at the front desk—the only officers on duty—should have left the station.

But they didn't.

My vision was going dark around the edges from not breathing when Garcia, Renner, and a third officer came back into the office.

"He couldn't have fit. It's impossible—" Renner was saying. Just then I fell out from behind the copier.

"What the heck is going on here, Jeff?" Garcia exclaimed, seeing me shirtless on the floor. In two seconds, I was pinned to the ground with my face pressed against the white tile. And then I was handcuffed.

Really. Spartacus Ryan Zander, the kid who'd never been in any kind of trouble (apart from inadvertently exposing himself to his whole hometown) was officially a criminal. Might as well put my face up there next to Lloyd's and call it a day.

"Well, there goes the case against the two ladies!" Renner exclaimed. "No one will believe this witness now."

"Look, Jeff," Garcia said, hefting me to my feet and holding me by my cuffed hands. I hung there ashamed, like a cat held up by the nape of its neck. "I don't know what that was all about, but you've just *drastically* changed the nature of this investigation."

Renner snagged my suitcase from the recycling bin where I'd tried to hide it under the shredded papers. She followed Garcia and me down the hallway. The other officer peeled off to return to the front desk while the three of us continued down the hall, passing a whole row of closed doors and a restroom. We arrived at a room with a little plastic plaque that read *Prisoner Processing*. Renner opened the door for us.

And inside?

It was Blue and White.

❧

I felt like I'd eaten a bucket of ice cream, all cold and urpy.

The two women were sitting on a bench and were—get this— shackled together at the ankles. A metal contraption connected them at their feet, and each had a hand handcuffed to the end of the bench. They seemed completely helpless, sitting there murmuring to each other like they were discussing quilt patterns.

I shivered as Garcia pulled me into the room.

"Hello, ladies!" said Garcia.

"It's Randy!" White hissed to Blue, leaning down and fiddling with her restraint, trying to get herself free.

Free to strangle me, no doubt.

"Impossible," said Blue, shaking her head at me.

"Jeff here is going to keep you ladies company while we handle some business. Then we'll figure out what we're going to do with the three of you."

Garcia sat me down on a bench across from Blue and White. He removed my handcuffs and handed me a shirt from my backpack to put on. He then zip-tied my wrist to the arm of the bench. At least I wasn't handcuffed anymore.

"I'm sorry. I didn't mean to—" I started to plead but Garcia held up his hand.

"You're starting down a dangerous path, kid," he said before dropping his hand to my shoulder. "And if I were to let you go now, you'd stay on it. You'll thank me someday."

I was getting ready to cry. Real tears this time, not the act. But I held it back. Not now. Not in front of these crazy old women.

And with that, Garcia and Renner left, shutting the heavy door behind them. I heard them say goodbye to the officer at the front desk, and then their voices trailed off. This was bad. I noticed my bag and suitcase beside the door, just out of reach. Renner must have set them there.

I brought my free hand up and felt the scab on my cheek where Blue had slapped me with her ring during the car ride. I looked up to see Blue and White staring at me intensely. I flinched, waiting for their wrath.

"You have to get us out of here," White whispered.

She looked desperate and caught me off guard. They *didn't* want to kill me?

"I can't go back to prison. I just can't," said White.

"Can't," Blue commiserated, her eyes huge and watery and cartoonish behind her glasses. They both held their spindly, cuffed hands out to me, as though I had the key, as though I were there to save them or something. I caught a whiff of that vanilla-tree scent still lingering on them.

"Wait. Wait. I really can't help—" I stammered, but White interrupted me.

"You don't know what they do to old women like us in prison, Brandon. Poor Clementine would be shivved at Bingo by nightfall."

"Shanked," Blue corrected her.

"I—I don't have the key," I said. "And I'm basically cuffed, too!"

Not to mention the door that was undoubtedly locked.

White looked at Blue and then nodded her head. Then, to my complete disgust, Blue took out her top dentures and held them out for me.

"What are those for?" I asked, leaning back.

"Use them for your zip-tie," said White. "One of the pointy teeth has a serrated edge for stuff like this." She turned to Blue and said quietly, "You took the cyanide pill out of them, didn't you?" Blue nodded.

"What? No!" I was so grossed out at the thought that I had to close my eyes. When I opened them, White had taken them from Blue and was drying them on her sweater.

"Look, see, now they're nice and clean."

"Sparkling," Blue encouraged.

I looked from the teeth in White's hand to the plastic tie attaching my wrist to the chair. It was only part of a solution. Even if I got out of the restraint, I'd still be locked in. But I had to try, didn't I? If I had even the smallest chance, I had to try. Anyway, I was already in so much trouble, what did one more thing matter?

"Let me…just let me try for a second before I use the…the teeth, okay?" Blue smirked and leaned back, watching me with a toothless, amused look as I stretched and pulled and picked at the plastic tie. It did nothing but make my wrist raw.

I didn't have much time.

"Gimme the teeth," I sighed. White smiled and handed them over.

I won't go into detail about the teeth. Let's just say I gagged and leave it at that. But I sawed at the plastic with the sharp incisor and, in a few minutes, I was able to snap the zip-tie off.

"Genius!" I said, rubbing my wrist. I handed the teeth back to Blue.

"Yep," she said, popping them back in without wiping them off or anything. Ugh.

"Right," said White. "Now us."

My stomach sank. I'd already forgotten that part of the deal.

"Still don't have the keys," I said.

"Start yelling. When the Capo comes in, you knock her out," White said, eyes shining.

"Capo?" I asked.

"Copper," Blue said.

"When she comes in, you grab her gun," White continued. "Or, wait, you can use the leg of this bench, here." White began kicking at the wooden bench leg with her one free foot.

"Stop!" I said, putting my hand out and on her bony shoulder. "Shh! You want her to hear us? Besides, I can't do that. I'm not hitting any cops."

"What? We scratch your back and you don't scratch ours?" White's eyes flashed at me with a hint of the fire I'd seen earlier that day. "You want hush money or something?" I took a step back, shaking my head.

"I will not club a police officer," I said. "I'm grateful you helped me get free, but—"

"You a coward?"

"Yellow," muttered Blue. "Chicken." She said it in that fake quiet way people say things when they're acting like they don't want you to hear, but really they do.

"You heard her," said White, her face hardening. "You don't have the *cojones* to spring a *goomba*?"

"A *what?*" I asked, incredulous.

"Wingman! *Esé!* Comrade!" Blue supplied.

Apparently Blue could now say more than one word at a time.

"You don't care about your friends, is what you're telling us," said White.

"No, it's just that—" I had to figure out how to get out of there, not waste time talking to them. And they were being so loud.

110

Wait. What had they said about attracting the officer with noise?

"Ah, so you *are* a coward." White sat back with a triumphant smirk. It was like something Will would say.

My face went hot—she knew she'd hit a nerve.

"Milquetoast. Pantywaist," taunted Blue.

"*Pantywaist?*" I repeated and Blue nodded, sneering.

"You couldn't take the heat," White said, that slight, creepy smile on her face. "So you went belly up and turned snitch."

That's when it hit me. I knew how to get out of there—without clubbing anyone.

"You know what?" I said, leaning forward. "I am a snitch. I'm the bad guy."

"You!"

I didn't expect White to be so fast—her free hand shot out at me like an eel, her grip strong and cold on my throat, her thumb pressing into my Adam's apple.

"The heavy!" roared Blue. "The black hat!"

"Get...off...me," I choked, knocking her hand away. I backed away as they wrestled with their handcuffs. They were going crazy, despite being cuffed to the bench.

"I knew it! I knew it!" White sputtered.

"I told them everything," I bellowed back. Then I sat back down and arranged my arm like I was still zip-tied to the bench.

"Defector! Snitch!" bellowed Blue. "Stoolie!"

"You old bags are going to be in the clink a long time," I said smugly.

At this, they went berserk, jerking at the bench so hard the wood started to splinter. They yelled curse words at the top of their lungs, including some I'd never heard before.

"So help me, Brian, I will use your skull to hold my yarn balls!" White screamed.

Yep; she actually said that.

"Hey! What's going on?" It was the front desk officer, opening the door. "Keep it down in here!" She went straight over to Blue and White, not even throwing a glance my way.

Before the door could close, I sprang to my feet, grabbed my bags, and dashed into the hallway. The door slammed shut behind me, interrupting the officer's startled shout.

I could hear her fumbling with her keys, but I didn't hesitate. I shot down the hall toward the exit.

"You're gonna pay for this, Brian!" I heard White crowing. "Mark my words!"

Maybe she was right. Maybe I would pay for it someday.

But not today.

Chapter Ten

Outside, the rain was still coming down in sheets. I crouched behind a squad car and gulped air like someone who'd nearly drowned. I felt like hugging the ground. I guess spending time in the slammer can do that to you.

I was about to just run off across the scrubby desert when I saw it: My out.

It was the big white Lincoln. A tow truck was dragging Blue and White's smashed-up car out of the parking lot.

That should have been the last car I'd ever want to see, let alone get *back into*, but there it was. And this time, rather than looking like a giant white hearse, it was like some junkyard beacon of hope.

The tow truck came to a full stop at the parking lot exit, right in front of me. The driver was looking the other way.

I glanced back at the police station. No one had come out yet.

It was now or never.

I tore across the wet blacktop like the fugitive I was, and watched the driver as I opened the back door. No reaction. A fog of vanilla scent poured out of the car. Taking a last breath of clean, freedom-tinged air, I threw myself inside.

We bumped down the road. Luckily I wasn't going too far—at the first empty intersection, I bailed out and ran, bags clutched to my chest, hunched low, like I was getting out of a helicopter. I dove into a ditch beside the road, and the driver went on as if nothing had happened.

I did it. I really did it. I escaped from jail.

I lay there in the wet ditch, dizzy, laughing, snorting, kicking my feet, and generally looking like a crazy person. And when I saw the yellow vanilla air freshener snagged on my suitcase handle, I laughed even harder. I laughed until I could barely breathe. I couldn't tell what was rain and what were tears.

I'd finally done something spectacular, something reckless, and I'd come away with only cuts, bruises, and sore muscles.

Okay, so the injuries were adding up, but the point was that I'd made it out *alive*. I'd succeeded at something.

I walked a ways from the road, paralleling it. I had my eyes peeled for cops, but none came. And, while I'm not the kind of person to believe in signs and stuff like that, suddenly the sun came out. A few minutes later, it was like it had never rained at all; the ground soaked up most of the water and the air was dry and warm.

But things weren't all sunshine and jail-breaks. I had to be honest with myself: I was perhaps a fugitive and still far from Albuquerque—and on top of that, I was beyond exhausted.

It was one in the afternoon and the show was at eight.

I needed to call Eli.

⥃

"He was *what?*"

Hearing Eli's squeaky voice of disbelief was almost enough payment for nearly being killed by Lloyd. Almost.

"A killer," I repeated. I was at a rundown convenience store, talking on the last working pay phone in the country. "They call him 'The Cue.'"

"You've got to be kidding me. I have to look this up."

While Eli's fingers clacked away at his laptop, I read him a few other items from Lloyd's wanted poster. "Wanted for burglary, theft, assault, and murder. Armed and dangerous."

"Oh, man," said Eli. I knew he'd pulled up Lloyd's photo online. "And he even had the—"

"Yep, the tattoo on his right arm."

"Dude, I'm *so* sorry. Why did you even ride with him? Look at him! He's a monster!"

I closed my eyes and told myself to be patient with Eli.

"Luckily, I'm still alive," I said. "And Hailey, the girl trucker? Much better choice."

"Right! The Geology Fighting Championships."

"But she dropped me off in the wrong place."

"What? She was supposed to take you all the way there."

"You'll never believe it. She dropped me off and—" I was about to tell him everything, about Blue and White and the police station, but then I shook my head. "Never mind. It's a long story. Let's just say I'm somewhere in the middle of nowhere between Santa Fe and Albuquerque."

"Got any details?"

I looked around and saw two faded street signs.

"Looks like I'm on the corner of Foster and Acoma."

"Acoma? Oh, okay, I found you. You're near Algodones."

"Where's that?"

"You've got like thirty miles to go, but you can't walk that."

"You're telling me," I said, looking at the brown landscape. "I'm in an actual desert. I saw an honest-to-god cactus."

"Call me back in five, okay? I'll get you something." With that, Eli hung up.

I went inside the store and the guy behind the counter openly stared at me.

Okay, I thought. I bought a giant bottle of water and three hash brown wedges from the hot case. The counter dude just stood there, watching as I gulped the water and devoured the hash browns with ketchup.

"I don't think I've ever seen anyone eat those," he said.

"They're not bad," I mumbled around the last, greasy bite.

"No, I mean, I don't think anyone's ever put new ones in there since I started."

"Ha-ha, very funny."

"I think your cheek is bleeding."

In the restroom mirror, I saw he was right—I was bleeding. But that was just one of my problems.

Blue had slapped me with her ring, and the scab had cracked. But what's more, I was a mess of mud and cuts. I'd bruised my chin. Ripped my shirt. Torn a hole in the knee of my jeans.

And Will's shoes—they were done for.

Honestly, I thought I looked pretty cool. Like a twelve-year-old action hero. I wish I had a loose tooth I could spit in the sink.

Instead, I washed my face and changed my clothes. The guy at the counter nodded his head when I passed by him. Much better.

Out front, I called Eli back.

"Okay, I got it. It took some creative web searching, but I got you a ride nearby—crazy, right?"

"That's why you're the best," I said. "Lay it on me."

"So I found a blog posted by some Goth girl in Algodones. She and a group of friends are meeting up at a cemetery nearby and—"

"A cemetery?" I repeated, already not liking the sound of it.

"And then they're going to the circus," he finished.

"How do you know this?"

"People put way too much information online. Anyway, just trust me on this. The girl's name is Marianne. But she calls herself Calyxtus."

"Calyxtus?" I said.

"Yeah," said Eli. "Some Goth thing, I guess. You need to meet them there at dusk."

"When's that?" I asked.

"You know, *dusk*. It's when the sun goes down. Don't be difficult."

I looked at my watch. Plenty of time.

"They don't know you're coming," said Eli. "I couldn't get in touch with them. So you're going to have to find a way to introduce yourself and get them to give you a ride. Maybe just beg them. Or give them money."

"I hope this works," I said, sighing.

"One last little thing you might find interesting," said Eli. "They hate Bartholomew just as much as you do."

Eli told me that the cemetery was maybe an hour away. I walked through brown, scrubby shrubs, away from the road and the peach-colored houses. I had to carry my suitcase—or what was left of it—because its one remaining wheel was useless in the dirt. The fabric handle had split and was cutting into my hand. I wanted to throw it into the bushes. But I needed it for my mom, so I pushed on.

Somehow, the hash browns hadn't made a dent in my hunger; they had been like eating dust. I'd run out of the food from home, except for the can of spaghetti, which was dumb to bring without a can opener. I should have bought more food at the store. I was so hungry that my stomach felt like it was eating my esophagus. Luckily, I had more than enough water. I gulped it so I wouldn't get dehydrated, but what I wanted was food.

What I wouldn't give for one bag of chips. One peanut butter sandwich. One—

I shook myself awake. I heard you could go crazy, walking in the desert, imagining oases and sandwiches and stuff. So I started whistling, hoping it would help me focus, but the only song I could think of was a Rolling Stones song. One that, for some reason, felt like it had been playing on loop in my head since...

Yesterday.

It was the song from Lloyd's tattoo.

Wait. No, Dan's tattoo. Lloyd was a killer named Dan.

I still didn't want to believe it. And seeing as I was losing my mind in the desert, a murderer really wasn't something I wanted to focus on. But try as I might to get the song out of my head, I soon found myself humming it. Then, I was singing at the top of my lungs.

"Hey, let me introduce myself, my name's Lloyd, I've got a scary face!" I shouted. "Been riding my bike all year long, stole and killed, I'm a huge nutcase!"

I definitely couldn't remember the words, what with my brain all jumbled and slow in the heat, but my rhyme made me giggle like a madman. I stopped and pulled out the wanted poster. His eyes on either side of the paper fold were like two black buttons. Like two holes.

Like two bullet holes.

A huge nutcase was right—this man was insane! The hairs on the back of my neck stood up, and I stuffed the poster back into my pocket.

What was Lloyd's game? Why hadn't he killed me?

And what if he'd been following me ever since he dropped me off at the funeral and he showed up right now?

I spun around and found I was still alone.

The heat was really getting to me. My head was pounding.

Now, new words were replacing the lyrics to the song: a jumble of false names on repeat, in time with the beat:

Spartacus.

Casey.

Navin.

Brodie.

Brian.

Jeff.

Dan.

Lloyd.

And then I tripped and fell and scraped my palms.

I was on the verge of getting one of the potential sicknesses Eli warned me about back in our planning stage: Desert Delirium. I had to get out of the heat and get some sleep before I passed out and got eaten by wolves or whatever lived in New Mexico. Giant pythons or something.

Just a fifteen-minute snooze. Just ten. Just a minute…

I shook myself again. I knew I had more than enough time to get to the cemetery ahead of the Goth kids. I just had to get there and then I could sleep…

That's when I saw a fenced-in green park ahead, looking strangely out of place in that brown and yellow landscape. Here it is, I thought: insanity. The park will just keep moving further as I get closer. But it didn't; it stayed right where it was. I wasn't sure it was real, though, until I touched the rusty gate for myself.

It wasn't a park at all. It was the cemetery! I'd walked further than I thought. A little stream ran beside it. For a cemetery, it sure looked inviting—and as much as I didn't want to sleep in a cemetery, that's where the shade was.

The cemetery was set up with all the graves packed in tightly together in the middle and a ring of trees around the outside. Some of the headstones were ancient, just little broken-looking blocks. New ones lined the perimeter.

However, that meant there was no place to lie down that wasn't basically on top of a grave—and besides that, there was no way I was sleeping on that cemetery grass, made healthy from dead-people fertilizer.

So I looked up at the trees. There was a large one that looked promising.

I stashed my suitcase behind a bush and then hoisted myself up, one branch at a time, until I made it up to a large Y about eight feet off the ground. I threw a leg on either side of the wide branch and lay face-down against the bark, like a koala. It really wasn't too bad. Comfortable, even.

I was lost to the world the moment my eyes shut.

I was just a little kid when I first saw Mom fly.

I'd been sent home early from school for being sick, and seeing as we lived a couple blocks from the school, I'd walked home. I remember seeing this black-and-white figure standing on the roof of our two-story house, leaning forward, like one of those women on the fronts of pirate ships. It took me a few seconds to realize it was Mom. Instead of calling out to her, I ducked behind a rhododendron bush.

What *was* she doing?

There was no one else out on the street—there never was, really. And so I watched alone, in wonder. She stood there in her black swimsuit, hands on her hips, head tilted toward the sky, her toes curled over the edge of the red roof tiles. Then she turned her eyes down toward the ground. Her black hair stirred in the breeze.

Mom always did weird things, but I'd never seen her on the roof before. I shifted my weight and a twig crunched underfoot. When I glanced down at my shoe, she jumped.

I burst from the bushes, but couldn't even muster a yelp. I imagined her crumpled on the ground, like a broken doll.

Instead, there was an odd *sproing*—and then she reappeared in the air a second later, sailing from the other side of the neighbor's fence, doing three backward somersaults before landing in our yard.

She stood for a moment with her back to me, arms raised over her head. When she turned around, arms still up, she was beaming like a lighthouse—until she saw me. Then, the look of joy melted right from her face.

I stood there, frozen in time. Mom came over to me in her bare feet and knelt in front of me, her eyes searching for a sign that I was alive inside.

"You can fly," was all I could say.

"Not yet," she said softly. She leaned in closer, her voice just a whisper. "Let's not tell anybody, okay? Not William, not Daddy, not Eli. Okay?"

I nodded.

"It's our secret, Spartacus." She searched my blank face to make sure I understood, then touched her cool forehead to my feverish one. And then she took me inside and made me soup.

That afternoon in the cemetery, in the middle of the desert, I dreamt Mom crashed into a heap in the yard instead of just bouncing harmlessly off the neighbor's trampoline.

❧

120

I woke with a jolt. I couldn't remember where I was. Eli's backyard during a sleepover? No, wait. New Mexico. In a tree.

Getting ready to rescue my mom.

Adrenaline crackled down my spine

Then I remembered the kids I was supposed to meet—in a cemetery at dusk.

Is it dusk?

The sun was on the horizon and it was definitely getting dark. As I adjusted in the tree, I heard a voice.

"Shhh! You hear that?" It was a guy—and he was right below me.

"No," said a girl's voice. "Be quiet and concentrate, Puck."

"I really think I heard someone."

"If you did, then we're on the right track," said the girl. "Keep still."

There was a short silence and then they started humming—a weird droning noise.

These were the kids Eli had told me about! But I was caught off guard, being up in a tree and all—that, and Hailey's advice echoed in my mind: *mistrust everyone.*

I moved slowly, like an ant in honey, until I could see below.

Three people, all in black, right under me. They faced each other in the fading light, candles set up in a circle between them. One guy was bent over on his knees like he was bowing, his face pressed in the grass. Then he sat up into a backbend, looking straight up at me.

I almost screamed, but kept it together enough to see that he had his eyes shut. And his face? Painted dead white, like moon-white, with black stuff around his eyes and lines across his lips.

No, not like the moon. Like a skeleton.

He might have been sixteen or so, but it was hard to tell. He faced down again, lit a knotted bundle of weeds on fire, and waved the smoke around his head. He passed it to the girl next to him before putting his face to the ground again. The others did the same.

The spicy-smelling smoke rose up to me and I choked back a cough with my fist.

What *were* they doing?

"You ever wonder what it would be like to be buried alive?" said the non-skeleton-faced guy, Puck.

"*Shh!*" went the girl again.

Was this Calyxtus? It had to be.

They continued humming. I shifted in the tree, trying to see more than the tops of their heads, but my backpack made a loud rustling sound.

Their humming stopped and I flattened myself against the branch, cringing.

Nice one, Spart.

"You *had* to have heard that, Cal," said Puck. "Do you think that was him clawing at the coffin?"

Cal! It *was* Calyxtus.

"It was above us, you creep," said Calyxtus. "The coffin is under us. Anyway, stop being so morbid."

"It's not morbid," Puck said. "In fact, it's a totally scientific question."

A light went on in my head: they were having a séance. Talking to the dead. I knew all about séances; Will, Eli, and I once held one for our dead hamster, Blueberry Pie. Will, though, actually dug her up. While we were chanting, he scared Eli and me by lowering her into our séance circle using a fishing line. Rather than scary, it ended up being gross—and kind of sad.

"This isn't the right time for your questions," Calyxtus was saying. "Do you want to see Mr. Prizrak or not?"

"I *do*," huffed Puck.

"Then shut up."

I noticed that the skeleton-faced guy hadn't said anything at all. He was creepy.

Puck said, "Try the incantation one more time."

Then the girl began to speak in a low, monotone voice:

"Zacharias Prizrak, it is on this momentous evening we beseech you to join the living. We have waited for the hour of dusk to ask you to rise on this magical evening, this most auspicious evening. First, the moon is in the seventh house, just as it was the night of your murder."

"Murder," Puck repeated.

Skeleton Face rang a bell. I shivered.

"Second, as Jupiter has aligned with Mars in this, the month of June, the barrier between the world of the living and the world of the spirits has reached its weakest point. The living are but shadows lost. Only in death is peace restored to humankind."

The bell rang again.

"Third, and finally, your killers have returned tonight, as if to mock your death," Calyxtus intoned.

"We shall help you seek revenge," both Calyxtus and Puck said together.

"We shall help you seek revenge," continued Calyxtus alone, "on your killers, the despicable and evil Bartholomew and his circus."

Bartholomew? *Killers?*

And with that, I lost my grip and fell from the tree.

The phrase, "getting the wind knocked out of you," sounds a bit too mild to describe what happens to your body when you fall eight feet out of a tree. It glosses over the fact that, not only is all the air going *out* of your lungs, none of it is going back *in*. And that means no air for gasping in pain, no air for shouting curse words, and, worst of all, no air for explaining that you're not the summoned ghost of Zacharias Prizrak.

When I hit the ground, the three of them scattered. Calyxtus screamed bloody murder.

"He fell from the sky!" she yelled.

After a few seconds, though, they returned. Calyxtus leaned her pale face over me. Her hair was red—so red that in the slant of remaining daylight, it looked like it was on fire.

"Crossing over must have been so painful! Look at him." She put her many-ringed hand out and touched my face while I just writhed there, gaping like a caught fish.

"Oh my god! He's so scratched up," said a voice I recognized as Puck's. A narrow, white face with big, curly brown hair appeared in my field of vision, looking concerned. Puck wore a weird, formal-looking cape, like a vampire in an old movie. "I guess that makes sense, because he had to break through all sorts of dimensions to get here."

"*Ughhh,*" was all I could manage.

"He's so young," said the girl. "Is it really him?"

Skeleton Face came to loom over me. The other two looked up at him while he stared at me. I imagined him stomping me with his large leather boot. Instead, he just shook his head in a definitive *no* before walking away.

"He's just some kid!" said Calyxtus, jumping to her feet. "He's not a spirit, Puck! Duh!" She blew out the candles and threw them into a basket before chasing after Skeleton Face.

"He might be," said Puck, looking wounded. "He could be Prizrak in his younger form. I've heard of that."

"I'm not—" I stammered, trying again. "I want to—" The air wasn't coming yet. I wondered if I'd punctured a lung, if I were going to suffocate. Puck stood looking down at me a moment longer, doubtful.

"Yeah, this sucks," was all he said before following the others.

"*Uggghhh,*" I gasped again. I had to ask them about the circus. I had to get to the circus! It was so late—and they were my only hope.

Somehow, I picked myself up and scrambled after them. Skeleton Face sat in the driver's seat of a black, roofless Bronco while the other two shoved their séance gear into the back. I limped over, but they barely looked at me when I cleared my throat.

"Uh, hey," I finally said. "I know this is weird, but I was wondering if—"

"Get out of here, kid," said Calyxtus. She put her hands on her hips. She was in some sort of weird Victorian dress, black velvet with a string of safety pins crisscrossing the front. She must have been wearing twenty necklaces. "We've got work to do. Don't provoke us, got it?" She glared at me with icy blue eyes.

Puck stood to the side, looking bored.

"I wasn't *provoking*," I said weakly. "I was sleeping and I woke up and you were there."

"You were sleeping in a graveyard tree?" asked Puck, suddenly interested. Calyxtus didn't look impressed.

"And fell out. So sad," was all she said before stomping toward the front of the truck.

"What were you doing sleeping in the tree?" asked Puck. He looked more relaxed after she left.

"I needed a place to sleep, so I slept." I had to get Puck on my side, so I lied. "Cemeteries are so, uh, you know…peaceful. I usually sleep in them when I can. And the tree was really, uh, comfortable."

"I like the way you think," he said. "Well, we're headed out. Going to this circus thing. Sorry we woke you." He went to the front of the truck and when Skeleton Face started the engine, death metal music blared. Puck squeezed past Calyxtus to get into the back seat.

What was I doing? Was I was going to let them leave?

I ran to the open window on the driver's side and, even though Skeleton Face just looked at me with that silent stare of his, I said it. Sure, it was in a rush, and the words just poured out, but I said it.

"Could I come with you guys? I promise I'll stay out of your way." Skeleton Face's eyes narrowed, so I went on. "It would mean so much if I could get a ride. I *need* to get to The Incredible. It's a matter of life and death."

"Death?" Calyxtus asked, her face perking up.

Skeleton Face, still not speaking, stared me down. After what seemed like an eternity, he nodded.

❧

We were driving across the darkening desert in the roofless old SUV, me and Puck in the backseat, Skeleton Face and Calyxtus in the front. Puck's black cape flew behind his seat in the wind.

"I feel like I really get Rob Zombie, you know?" Puck was saying loudly over the rushing air and the blaring synthesizers. "They don't make music like this anymore."

Even though I really didn't think the music was that great, I didn't remember ever feeling so cool. And then Calyxtus turned around in her seat. "What are you, kid? Like fourteen?"

I nodded in time with the beat and she took it for a yes. Instantly, I felt even cooler.

"So, are you guys are going to watch the circus?" I asked Puck.

"Hardly!" Calyxtus forced a condescending laugh. "You know circuses are heinous, right?"

"Excuse me?" I asked, confused.

"First, they are for babies. And second, even if it wasn't Bartholomew's Circus of the Incredible, they…they're just awful. They torture animals. You think those lions and elephants and whatever else want to be there? Walk on their back legs and let people put their heads in their mouths, and stand on balls and—"

"Balls!" sniggered Puck. Calyxtus rolled her eyes.

"They're awful," she finished. "Just awful."

"So I've heard," I agreed, thinking about what I'd read online. "So if you're not going to the actual circus, what *are* you doing?"

"Holding another séance. Closer to the source—but we'll be right next to it, so you can walk there, you know, if you're a baby who watches circuses."

"I *so* thought the cemetery would be place we'd reach him," Puck said.

The séance! I'd almost forgotten about the whole Bartholomew-killed-a-guy story! Getting the wind knocked out of me had pushed it right out of my head.

Skeleton Face stopped at a stop sign and he and Calyxtus started kissing. I tried to look away and pretend I wasn't seeing them mash their faces together. Puck looked depressed.

"Zacharias Pizz-hat, right?" I asked, turning to Puck.

"Prizrak!" corrected Puck.

"Did you say the circus killed him?" I asked. I hadn't read anything about this guy on IHateBartholomewsCircus.com, but maybe they knew things the site didn't.

"Oh yeah," Puck said. "It's a well-known fact."

"What happened?" I asked, genuinely interested.

Puck looked excited to be telling the story. "See, Zacharias was a famous magician in The Incredible. He could disappear into anything—a box, a refrigerator, a small safe. He'd just bend himself up, lock himself in—and *poof!* He was gone!"

"Dark magic," Calyxtus added. She was looking at me in her sun visor's mirror, reapplying her black lipstick after the big smooch. "That's how he did it."

My mind flashed to my mom in the filing cabinet. I'm *pretty* sure she wasn't into dark magic.

"But before that," Puck was saying, "Prizrak was just a P.E. teacher here in Algodones."

"No he wasn't, you nitwit," said Calyxtus. She turned down the music.

"I'm telling the story I heard, okay?" Puck glared at her.

"Anyway," Calyxtus took over for him, "he was from Algodones—or at least, it was the last place he lived before he joined The Incredible. It's where he perfected his craft. That's why we can reach him here; it's the last place his soul was free.

"See, Zacharias was one of the greatest magicians in the world. Like, the real deal. None of this fake, camera-trick, rigged-cards kind of thing. Real spirit-realm stuff. But nobody knew about him because he was only allowed to perform with The Incredible."

"And they wouldn't let him leave," said Puck. "Bartholomew

never lets *anyone* leave. It's like the mafia—once you're in, you're in for life. The only way to leave that place is in a body bag."

I swallowed hard. I'd read a lot of Bartholomew rumors, but this one was new to me. I'd never thought about him killing people before—I mean, sure there was the severed finger, but that could just be, you know, a warning. What if my mom was afraid to leave because she knew how dangerous he was?

"How'd Prizrak get killed?" I asked cautiously.

"One night they were performing in Chicago, and Prizrak climbed into a small trunk onstage and did his disappearing act as usual. The audience cheered, expecting him to come back, but the show went on. Everybody forgot about him. The circus left and went to another town. Three days later, they found his body in an empty Wells Fargo bank vault, three blocks away."

"He was dead?" I asked, confused.

"Yeah."

"How'd he end up in the bank vault?"

"You tell me," Puck said, his eyes glinting. "A magic trick gone wrong? A setup?"

"Bartholomew couldn't control Zacharias's dark magic," said Calyxtus, turning back to face us. "It was too strong—and Bartholomew was afraid of him. So, during the show, Bartholomew used his own black magic to trap Zacharias's soul in the trunk, which had an ancient Egyptian mirror that Bartholomew had bought from Romanian gypsies. Bartholomew channeled Zacharias's material vessel, his body, into the spirit realm and then into that bank vault. At least that's what they say."

"What?" I asked. My head hurt trying to follow the way that she talked.

"He got sent into that airtight bank vault on the Friday before a three-day weekend," clarified Puck. "He suffocated in there."

"How did you learn all this?" I demanded. "Who's 'they'? Why didn't anyone call the police?"

"Algodones may be a desert, but it's hiding a river of secrets," Calyxtus answered mysteriously.

"Cal's aunt is a private detective," Puck added. "But she couldn't figure out the case and she dropped it."

Calyxtus glared at Puck, and then whipped her head around to face forward.

I swallowed hard, thinking about all of the things I knew about Bartholomew. Kidnapping, black magic, performers killed in accidents, animal abuse, and now this—whatever it was. *Murder?* Maybe. I didn't believe all the stuff about the magic, but the rest? How did a person disappear in front of a large crowd and then reappear somewhere else a couple blocks away?

There had to be some truth in it if they believed it so much.

We got into Albuquerque just before seven-thirty p.m. and it was almost dark. We stopped at a convenience store a few minutes from the circus and I sat anxiously in the car with Puck and Calyxtus while Skeleton Face (who still hadn't spoken and didn't seem to have a name) went in to buy snacks and boxed wine. He was either twenty-one or he had a fake ID. Calyxtus said we had to stay in the car or it would blow the whole deal (but she promised he would bring me some food for my poor empty stomach).

Puck and Calyxtus were saying something about auras and past lives when it hit me.

My mission was about to happen.

Time to get myself together.

My plan was to go into The Incredible with just the empty suitcase, so there would be room for my mom to contort herself into it. So I took everything from my pockets and suitcase that I didn't need and stashed it in my backpack.

"What are you doing?" Calyxtus finally asked, seeing me stuffing my backpack. I could barely zip it.

"Uh, getting ready," I said.

She scrutinized me, but I said nothing more as I changed into my suit shirt and tie from the first day, and, even though it was warm, pulled on my dark blue hoodie. I added Will's black baseball hat and then slipped his pocketknife into my right pocket and the small screwdriver and ball of string into my left.

I was putting Eli's dad's stethoscope around my neck when I saw someone familiar through the window, in the convenience store. In line in front of Skeleton Face.

It was *Mom*.

Chapter Eleven

Since my mom left, I'd kept having this dream where I'd see her in weird places. I'd dream that I was walking home after school, and she'd be walking down the other side of the street. Or I'd dream I was in class and she'd stroll by in the hall. Or in places I'd never been before. She would always be going about her own business, and never even notice me.

When dreams suddenly happen in real life, though—that's when things get weird.

❧

By the time I'd pulled the suitcase out and launched myself out of the Bronco and onto the sidewalk, Mom was already out the glass doors and walking away, her tall red boots clacking on the cement. Except for the circus-type boots, she was in street clothes, which was weird because the circus should have been starting any minute. I practically bowled her over, suitcase in tow.

She seemed stunned as I clutched her hand.

"Mom, I know it's a surprise to see me," I said, racing through my rehearsed speech. I pulled her by the arm toward the side of the building as I spoke. "There's no time to explain. You have to get in the suitcase now. I'll get you out of here."

"What are you talking about? Let go of me!" Mom yanked her hand free and shot me a look like she didn't know me. "And you're *nuts* if you think I'd fit in your stupid roller bag."

I couldn't believe this was happening. I mean, I knew it was possible, what with the whole Stockholm syndrome thing where you fall in love with your kidnapper—but still!

"I'm here for *you*, Mom," I said, slowly now, in what I hoped was a calm voice. I'd heard doctors talk this way to patients on TV. "Just get in the suitcase." I took her hand again, but this time she shook it off more violently.

"Let go of me!" she hissed. "Why do you keep calling me that?"

Now *I* was shocked. I stared at her, and she glared back, the yellow streetlight playing across her face. I realized something was wrong. I mean, *this was my mother*. It was.

But that wasn't her nose.

And there was a mole on her chin. Mom didn't have a mole. But the rest, the rest was, *it was Mom*. But it wasn't...

Just then a man's voice came from the other side of the parking lot.

"Hurry up!"

"Coming!" Mom yelled back, marching away from me.

I hesitated for just a moment before chasing after her. At that point, I was only fifty percent sure it was Mom, but I couldn't just let her go.

At the other end of the dimly lit parking lot, Mom joined a large man in a suit. Neither was even looking back in my direction as they walked toward—*gulp*—a black van! It looked just like the one in my imagination, the one Eli had described the day after Mom disappeared. Could it be that this really *was* Mom, but that the circus had disguised her for some reason?

I had to do something. I couldn't let them get away again. When the man stopped to get his keys, I swung my suitcase up blindly and hit him in the head.

I don't think he even flinched.

When he turned, unscathed and unconcerned, I saw that he wasn't a man. I mean, he was, or at least he had been at some point. But somewhere down the line, he'd turned into a shark.

Yeah, I'm talking about an honest-to-god *sharkman*.

No hair, no eyebrows, and eyeballs that were completely black. He had flaps of skin on his neck that looked like gills. He even had a dorsal fin that poked through a slit in his jacket. *How does a man have a fin?*

And I'd just hit him in the head with a suitcase.

"And you did that because…?" the sharkman asked me, speaking carefully. That's when I noticed that he had way too many teeth, teeth filed down to points.

His blank, black eyes narrowed and all my organs felt like they were shrinking at the same time. But he didn't take a step toward me. Instead, he turned to the mom look-alike.

"Come on, Charlene," he said. "Let's get this show on the road. We're late."

Mom looked at me like I was a bug to be stomped. I mean, Charlene did. Then she bent down to whisper in my ear, "I'm not who you think I am and you'd better back off with your little suitcase trick before you try it on the wrong woman. You do this again and Bartholomew will pop your head off like a dandelion. Got it?"

I nodded carefully, my head feeling only barely attached to my body. Then, the sharkman and my mom—I mean my not-mom—got into their black van and drove off into the night.

My legs shook as I walked back to the Bronco.

Who were they? What was that about? Why didn't they…? Well, honestly, I don't know what I expected them to do to me—but letting me just walk away seemed impossible.

I couldn't stop picturing that guy's teeth. And his gills.

Then I remembered that Bartholomew kept a plastic surgeon on staff. Besides making Bartholomew look young, maybe he made men look like sharks? And maybe that was why that lady looked like Mom?

Another idea hit me. Not-Mom and Sharkman were probably headed to the circus now, meaning I had *more* people to watch out for.

Ugghh.

Skeleton Face stood in front of the Bronco, waiting. Calyxtus and Puck stared from their seats with jaws agape as I heaved my suitcase in the back. I clambered into the back seat, flinching as Skeleton Face got in and slammed his door too hard.

"So, you sleep in cemeteries *and* you knock huge freaks over the head with suitcases?" Puck said finally.

I reddened. I didn't know they'd been watching me.

"You're one crazy piece of work," said Puck. Calyxtus gave a low whistle of agreement.

"This, um, this isn't just a normal day for me." Boy, was it not.

"That guy was what, a vampire?" Calyxtus asked.

"No, I think he was a shark," I said. "He had a fin."

"Circus folk," said Puck. He looked off into the distance, frowning. "They cross everyone."

But that was all they said about the strange encounter. I guess they had their own 'Incredible Weirdness' to focus on. Puck muttered under his breath about Zacharias; Calyxtus dug through her basket, manically counting candles. And, of course, Skeleton Face said nothing; he simply got us back on the road. The traffic was thick. Up ahead about a mile, searchlights crisscrossed each other in the sky.

Bartholomew's searchlights.

We were close.

~

The four of us were stuck in a line of traffic leading up to the circus. That's when I was startled by a low, gravelly voice.

"You said getting to the circus was a matter of life and death." It was Skeleton Face. Skeleton Face was actually talking. To *me*.

His black-rimmed eyes met mine in the rearview mirror for a split second before going back to concentrating on the brake lights ahead of us. Puck and Calyxtus sat with their mouths open, exchanging a look.

"Steve hasn't said a word in three weeks," Puck whispered to me.

"Life…and death," Steve repeated, making each word sound like he was weighing them in his hands. "What did you mean by that?"

I didn't answer right away. I weighed words, too: the lies I could tell. The truths. Maybe I should explain everything. I mean, they hated Bartholomew almost as much as I did. But then I remembered what Hailey had said: you don't trust people until they've earned it. I liked these guys and all, but what if they couldn't keep a secret? What if they blew my plan?

"Whose death?" Steve said. "Yours or…?"

"My family's," I answered, not meaning to say even that. It just slipped out, but when it did, I knew it was the truth. That's what I'd meant when I first said "life or death," even if I didn't realize it at the time. If I didn't get Mom back, I would blame Dad, I would blame Will, and I'd blame myself. And Will and Dad would never trust me again. No matter what happened, if I didn't get Mom back, things would never be the same in the Zander house. Ever.

Steve swung into a makeshift parking lot in someone's yard. The big, jovial guy taking our parking money saw Steve's made-up face and everyone else's weird clothes and grinned.

"Well, I see the circus *has* come to town!" the man laughed, handing Steve his change. When no one laughed, he tried again: "Send in the clowns!"

It wasn't the awkward silence alone that stripped the smile from the guy's face, but also the force of the four sets of glaring eyeballs. He was outnumbered.

"Uh, take the last spot there, by the fence," he muttered, looking sheepish.

Apparently, the stink-eye is a million times more powerful when you're in a group.

I could use a posse at home, I realized, thinking about the gas station attendant calling me Poop Lip. Some *comrades* beside me. Another Blue and White word.

We marched single-file down the side of the highway, headed toward the fairgrounds. Just before we reached the black-barred fence, Skeleton Face—I mean Steve—stopped so abruptly that Calyxtus walked right into the back of him. The crowd passed around us like we were stones in a creek, looking at us warily (I think it was Puck's cape, more than anything).

"This is where we need to leave you," Steve said. "We can't have outsiders witness the séance."

"Oh, hey, no problem," I said, honestly grateful to be losing them so I could concentrate. "Thank you for the ride. I would never have made it."

"We're happy to help a *kindergoth*," said Puck.

"Let's not get carried away," said Calyxtus, turning to him with an irritated flip of her hair. "He's no kindergoth."

"He could be. Or maybe he's a baby bat. But in a good way. Look at him! Sleeps in cemeteries, wears a tie? And look at that sunken, pale face!"

I have a sunken, pale face? The road must have been getting to me. Still, I had no clue what they were talking about. I needed to get out of there. Mom was maybe a hundred yards away, and I was just standing here.

"He might just be weird," argued Calyxtus.

"You're always so snotty!" Puck shot back.

"I'll remind you both we have a spirit to summon," Steve said through gritted teeth, like an angry parent.

I shifted from one foot to the other and then remembered something I had to do.

"Hey, before you go, would you guys mind blocking me for a second?" I asked. "Puck, could you hold your cape out?"

"It's a cloak," Puck sniffed, but he did it anyway. While the three of them stood there, I ducked behind them and pushed my backpack as far under a dumpster as I could, hopefully where no one would see it and steal it. I scrambled out to find Puck raising his caped arms high, like a giant bat. And he was hissing.

"Uh, what are you doing?" I asked.

"If they're going to stare, I might as well give them something to stare at," he answered, grinning at a little boy who looked truly afraid. Calyxtus looked annoyed, her black lip curled. I sensed another argument and headed it off.

"So, where are you headed?" I asked.

"The shadows," said Calyxtus, nodding to the east. "We're going to find a quiet place out here where we can commune with the spirits."

"And then?" I asked.

"And then it's up to Zacharias Prizrak as to how he wants to proceed."

"Ah, okay," I said awkwardly. "Well, thanks again. I have to get inside before, well, before it's too late." I hoped that sounded ominous enough for them.

"What are you going to do?"

"The less you know the better," I said. "It's too, uh, intense."

Steve nodded at this, as if it all made complete sense.

"Give them a plague of foul nature," said Puck gravely. "For all of us."

"Yeah, I, uh, will," I said, nodding. "And good luck with the whole Zacharias Prize-hat thing."

"Prizrak," muttered Calyxtus.

"May your fortune be in life—and not death," said Steve.

I didn't know what that meant, but it didn't sound very encouraging. I gave them a half-wave before stepping into the river of people headed to the circus.

Closer to the entrance, it was chaos. It was completely dark out by then, but hundreds of strings of bare lightbulbs criss-crossed above, bathing everyone in an orange light. The show hadn't started yet and organ-y circus music mixed with the noise of the crowd in a loud, crazy whoosh. People pressed against each other, all trying to get through a narrow outer gate. Kids squealed, parents shouted, trying to keep their groups together. Up ahead, ticket takers funneled people through a few lines, barking at people to pick one line and stay in it.

I was happy for the crowd—they were my camouflage—but I was also paranoid.

What if someone knew who I was?

Even in the dim light, twelve hundred miles from home, my freckled lip felt like a spotlight, a homing beacon for anyone looking for me. And then there were Sharkman and Not-Mom to look out for. They wouldn't be out here, but I had to be on my toes. At any moment, someone might recognize me and drag me off to Bartholomew. I kept my head down as I passed two uniformed guards, but they didn't look in my direction.

I was letting myself be pushed forward with the crowd when I saw the tent—just a smallish, round, red canvas tent. Lights shone through a tear in the roof.

It wasn't impressive *at all*.

Why weren't they using the fancy, red-and-blue striped dome tent from the photos on the website? It must have been more of Bartholomew's lies! I bet the pictures on his website were from a much better circus.

That's also when I saw the NO TRESPASSING sign—and nothing but darkness beyond. *That's* where I needed to be—around the side of the tent, away from the lights and the people. That's where I would make my own way in, back where the performers were.

I glanced to make sure the guards weren't looking and then ducked around the sign.

I pulled up my hood and waited a moment for my eyes to adjust. As I picked my way around the tent stakes and ropes, I rehearsed my story in my head, the if-I-get-caught story: *I'm just a local kid, I didn't have any money to see the circus, I thought I could just peek in a little. I'm really, really sorry, and it will never happen again.* It wasn't great, but I was going to stick to it.

Or run, whichever was easier.

I thought there'd be a whole swarm of trucks behind the circus tent—the trucks that carried the performers and equipment—but so far there was nothing.

I pulled my stethoscope out from under my sweatshirt and put the earpieces in. The stethoscope made me feel even more like James Bond than the suit. I crept along, running the round chest-piece along the canvas, listening for the right spot to go in. I didn't really know what the "right spot" would sound like, but I was pretty certain I'd know it when I found it.

Voices that were a roar before were crystal clear through the stethoscope. Kids whining for cotton candy. Parents telling them no. Benches squeaking. Babies squawking. I continued around the back of the tent, pausing every couple dozen feet to listen, searching for a way in. Soon, I ran into an intersection where a rectangular tent jutted off from the main circular one. Right there, at the corner where the tents met, I could hear two voices directly on the other side of the canvas. I held my breath, knowing I was just inches from them. They were whispering.

"It's the one on the right that's out. It just blew."

"Didn't I tell you to re-check them all beforehand?"

"Did you hear what I said? I said it just blew out. What was I going to do beforehand? See into the future?"

Cursing followed and I grinned, moving ahead. I'd made it past all the tourists and the commoners—I'd found the workers in the staging area.

Bartholomew was probably getting ready to go out, and there was no reason for security guards to be in back with the performers. No one would notice me once I was inside and backstage because everyone would be too busy. At least that's what I hoped.

I kept poking along, listening for a safe, silent spot. I heard things being dragged around and assembled, people giving directions, but nothing helpful. I didn't hear my mom or anyone talking about her. Finally, though, along the back wall of the rectangular tent, things were quiet. No voices, nothing moving.

This was the spot.

I took off the stethoscope and pulled out Will's pocketknife. Kneeling on the ground, I put knifepoint to canvas. This was it.

This. Was. It.

My heart pounded. My hands shook. I was moments from trespassing, from destroying property.

Moments from seeing my mom.

Come on, Spartacus, I ordered myself. *Do it.*

Somehow the name made me feel a bit braver.

I took a deep breath and plunged the knife in.

I peered under the flap I'd made in the tent and saw I'd cut my way into a bathroom. It was a small, dark space with a metal trough for a urinal, a portable sink, and a makeshift door made out of a curtain.

Perfect.

I wriggled in through the hole I'd cut, pulling the suitcase behind me.

I peeked behind the curtain door, half hoping Mom would be standing right there. But the canvas corridor was empty, no one in sight. Funny; I'd thought there would be people bustling around.

Now for the tough part. I had to walk among the circus folk— and it was only a matter of time before someone saw me and asked what I was doing there. To buy myself more time, I had to blend in.

Looking in the bathroom mirror, I expected to see someone looking more mature, like a high schooler working for the summer, but the kid staring back at me looked all of ten years old. Dirty, pale, scared. I pulled my sweatshirt off and stuffed it next to my suitcase under the small, metal washstand. Underneath, I wore my white shirt and tie, exactly the same outfit I'd worn to the funeral. I straightened the tie and flattened my hair with water from the sink. I tried to wipe a smear of dirt from my forehead and discovered it was a bruise (maybe from the car accident?). Then I tried some different facial

140

expressions, trying to capture the maturity I felt—my best was a half-scowl that kinda made me look like Will.

I decided it was good enough.

Taking a deep breath, I strode, purposeful and scowling, out from behind the curtain and toward a bundle of black and red stilts leaning against the canvas. I hefted a heavy set onto my shoulder, hoping to look like I worked there, and then kept walking, following a string of red light bulbs.

The corridor led past a series of curtained rooms. I made my way carefully, sneaking a look into each one. The first was an empty dressing room with a couple of makeup tables with those mirrors with lights all around them. The second was full of costumes: feather boas, all kinds of hats, huge pants, masks. In the third room, a lady stood with her back to the door. She had a pirate ship tattooed on her back and was pinning purple flowers into her long brown hair. I peeked into the next room. Inside, was a small, old man sitting in a child-sized lawn chair. He was smoking a cigar. And he wasn't just small—he was a *bona fide* little person, as small as a kindergartener.

I moved on to the last room. I took a deep breath, hoping to find Mom on the other side. I opened the curtain an inch—and almost screamed when I saw a headless woman propped up in a chair. I clapped my hand over my mouth at the same time as I realized it was a dummy. It was just a very, *very* realistic dummy. Cool things filled the room. There was a shrunken head on a plant stand, a birdcage stuffed with fake white doves, a bunch of chainsaws, and an umbrella stand full of swords.

I stepped back into the hallway. Well, that was all the rooms. For some reason, The Incredible wasn't that big. *Where were the sad animals Calyxtus had talked about?*

Maybe they kept them somewhere safe, like in trucks.

But I didn't see any trucks, I remembered. You'd need trucks to keep animals and equipment in, wouldn't you? You'd think they would have been out back, but there weren't any.

My thoughts were interrupted by someone running in my direction. I flattened myself against the curtains to make room as a girl about my age ran by, her black hair streaming behind her.

"Remmy?" she hissed. "Remmy!" She didn't so much as glance at me.

Whoa; that was close.

"LADIES AND GENTLEMEN," a voiced boomed from the direction of the main tent, startling me. "PLEASE SILENCE YOUR PHONES. THE SHOW WILL BEGIN MOMENTARILY."

I briefly wondered if it was Bartholomew, but realized it didn't matter. I picked up my pace. Soon, the hall ended and I found myself in pitch-black, open space, filled with people. At the far wall was a large, red-curtained doorway.

The entrance to the stage! Mom *had* to be nearby.

Everyone was too busy to notice me, so I edged into what must have been a staging room, holding the stilts upright so I could peek around them. A few people wore red headlamps and glanced at clipboards. A small group of performers hopped and stretched, like runners getting ready for a race. A few others milled about, mumbling lines to themselves.

Where were the hundreds of performers? How was it that there were all those reviews of how verifiably *incredible* The Incredible was? How it changed lives and people were so impressed?

Bartholomew's World-Renowned Circus of The Incredible was pretty pathetic. They must hide the sorry truth about their pitiful, scrimpy squad with even more lies.

That's when the noise from the audience suddenly shifted. The sound of shushing flowed through the tent walls like the sound of the ocean. What followed was a long, expectant silence.

It was starting!

For a split second—even though I'd figured out that The Incredible was probably more like The Ho-Hum—I imagined what it would be like to be on the other side at that moment, right after the lights go out but before the show begins—watching the circus like a regular kid, with Will and Mom and Dad.

Beyond the curtain, out in the main area of the tent, a strobe light began to flash, sending darting shadows into the staging room. I stayed pressed against the wall and scanned the faces around me for my mom, and for Sharkman and Not-Mom, but it was almost impossible to tell who was who. Nearly everyone wore makeup or a mask.

My eyes landed on a female mime in an old-fashioned tuxedo. Too small, too young. Then there was the woman closest to me, wearing a black leather swimsuit, with a giant, ten-foot snake draped around her shoulders. The snake could probably swallow a Labrador and still have room for dessert. The lady was letting the snake smell her face with its darting tongue. Interesting, but not my mom.

Suddenly it made sense why I hadn't seen Mom yet. Obviously, she was already out there onstage with everyone else. Up in the catwalks or under the stage, waiting to explode out of something. I relaxed a bit, knowing my chance would come, even if it meant waiting for her to return at intermission or the end.

When the introduction music started on the other side of the curtain, everyone tensed, including me.

"Ladies and gentlemen!" came the announcer's voice from onstage. My grip tightened on the stilts.

"We are charmed to entertain you on this very curious evening! The fine performers you are about to see have prepared a veritable feast for your five senses! There will be OUTSTANDING things here, in this very ring, UNUSUAL things that you may not understand—TERRIFYING things you'll wish you didn't understand—and ASTONISHING things you may never wish to see again. But I assure you, ladies and gentlemen, that you have arrived, out of sheer serendipity, at a SPECTACULAR event you'll never forget. We're sorry Bartholomew couldn't make it, but we know you're going to have more fun with us as we bring you—The World-Renowned Sideshow of Curiosities and Mayhem!"

As the performers rushed out through the curtains, my mouth hung open. I struggled to understand what I'd just heard.

Sideshow of Curiosities and Mayhem? I repeated to myself. *Wait. Had they changed their name?*

I saw the audience through a gap in the curtain. Their faces flashed orange, reflecting flames on the stage.

A *sideshow?* What's a *sideshow?* And what had the guy said about Bartholomew?

I started breathing quickly as the snare drums rat-a-tatted wildly. Now I understood why there were hardly any performers or workers. And no animals. No big trucks.

They'd left. They'd canceled their show. This wasn't Bartholomew. This was a sideshow, whatever *that* was.

Stupid tears pooled up in my stupid eyes so I could barely see. I stood there like a moron, still holding the stupid stilts.

Then the drums faded and everything went silent, like I had just dived underwater. The room was spinning—it felt like the performers were circling around me. A woman in a red tutu bumped into me as she rushed by, but it all felt so far away. I fell over much more easily than I should have, dropping the stilts and mumbling "Sorry, sorry," the whole way down to the ground.

❧

They told me later it was a nervous breakdown, but I knew it couldn't have been *that* bad.

I knew all about nervous breakdowns. Dad had one once at Will's statewide triathlon when Will's bike wheel came off. It was right at the start of the race, too, when the racers had just taken off and the crowd was cheering. Will's bike made a big snapping sound and Will went down hard while his wheel went rolling away.

Then Dad kind of made a snapping sound, too. He just lost it, flinging his hat to the ground and shouting, "RE-RIDE! RE-RIDE! RE-RIDE!"

Some other fathers came and took him away and I had to pretend

I didn't know him. He'd always taken Will's bike riding a little too seriously.

Yeah, there was no way I'd been *that* bad.

But apparently the circus people were worried the audience would hear me. As they led me out a back door in the tent, I was yelling (according to them) the whole way, "You deserve this, Poop Lip! You really, really do! You stupid idiot!"

Which is pretty ridiculous. I might have been a little upset, what with coming a thousand miles to save Mom, and finding out she'd just left town, and being a criminal and a runaway and, basically, a complete failure. Sure, I was upset. But would I really go out of my mind and forget what I was doing and start shouting? Would I call myself Poop Lip? Did I really think I deserved to fail like that?

I guess the answer in my mind was *Yes. Yes, I did.*

The next thing I knew, I was waking up, sitting on the back bumper of a parked semi.

And I don't mean waking up like you do in the morning. It was more like I just gradually faded back into my body—which was already in the process of doing stuff without me. I was sitting up in the back of the trailer with my legs hanging off the edge. Cupped in my hands was a mason jar filled with something cool. I smelled it. Lemonade.

How long had I been here, drinking lemonade? Where *was* I?

It was dark and we were outside, not too far from the circus tent. The occasional burst of music and cheers from the show interrupted the quiet.

Wait, *we*?

I did a double take. A small boy sat beside me, smoking a cigar. I could see the orange of the tip burn as he inhaled.

"Life's just like that sometimes, you know?" he was saying at a fast clip. I felt like maybe we'd been talking for a while, but I had no idea what we were talking about.

The child waved his cigar in the air. Scratch that. It was a man, a very small man, waving his cigar in the air. I remembered seeing him in the dressing room earlier. Right.

"You see that opening, that light," he continued, "and know life is about to change. You think, *Ah, I made the right choice!* And then *bam!* Just like that, you're having a nervous breakdown backstage at the wrong circus. Or, in his case, stuck, staring up at the fangs of death."

I nodded politely and then looked to where he was gesturing with his cigar.

A few feet from the trailer, a flashlight was set up on a tripod, shining down on a hula-hoop laid out flat on the ground. And in the center of the hula-hoop, half-emerged from a crack in the asphalt? A *rat*. A large, gray, squeaking rat. Its front paws scrabbled at the ground; its back end squeezed—and stuck—in the crack in the pavement. A few inches away from the rat, a dirty white cat sat very still, unblinking.

I felt like I had just woken up into a dream.

"Life imitates the circus and the circus imitates life," the old man said. And that's exactly what was in front of us: a small, bizarre, miniature circus. The hula-hoop was the circus ring. The cat was the ringmaster. The rat was—just a rat, I guess. Add in the music coming from the real circus and it was almost funny, in a sick way.

"What will happen to it?" I asked. Just watching it made me squirm, like it was me trapped there.

"If we leave it? I'd say it has three ways out." He spoke around his cigar and counted on his hand. "One, a heart attack. Two, starvation—but that would take some time and doesn't seem too likely with Lousy sitting right there, does it? And Lousy himself is the third option."

Lousy the cat hunkered down on his belly to survey the rat. He didn't seem ready to do anything anytime soon. He looked quite content just watching. At least for now.

"You're not just going to leave it in there, are you?" I asked.

146

"Why shouldn't I?" he said. "It's life. We all make choices, without knowing what the result will be. We all end up in the wrong place at the wrong time..." The child-sized old man looked up at me knowingly from under wild gray eyebrows. "What responsibility do I have to help it out?"

"'With great power comes great responsibility,'" I said, the quotation just coming into my mind. "I guess because we know we have the power to help, we should at least try."

The old man nodded, pursed his lips, and looked impressed.

"Very wise, very wise, yes," he said. "That was Winston Churchill, right?"

"Uh, no," I said. "Actually, it's from Spiderman."

"Mmmm," he said, looking back at the struggling rat. "Well, it's wise, nonetheless. What say you we get him out?"

He reached back into the trailer and pulled out what looked like a giant pair of pliers with a spring in the middle and a wide, flat spatula thing on the tip.

"Here." He handed the weird tool to me before hopping down and plodding over to the hula-hoop. He nudged the cat out of the way. "Get, Lousy!"

I got off the truck and knelt with him next to the rat. It had gone motionless, but I could see its whiskers twitching and I swear I could hear its little heart tapping away at the speed of sound.

"So, you want me to just...grab him?" I asked.

"No, no, no," he said. He indicated the tool I was holding. "These are spreaders. Put them in the crack next to him, as close as you can, and then squeeze the handles." He put his hand on the cat and held him lightly by the scruff of the neck.

I put the spreaders in the crack and squeezed, like he'd said. In a few seconds, the ground moved just enough, and the rat darted away into the darkness. The cat tried to chase it, but the little man held him for a good count.

"Give him a fighting chance, eh, Lousy?" the man said. Then

he let the cat go. Lousy took a few steps in the direction of the rat before changing his mind and rolling in the dirt instead.

"What are these for?" I asked, holding the spreaders up.

"For when the lion doesn't let you go," he said. He took them from me and used them like a cane to push himself to his feet.

"Name's Remmy," he said, putting out his hand. I shook it.

"Spartacus," I said, without thinking. I don't know why I said it. I'd never introduced myself as Spartacus before. I cringed a little bit, wondering if I'd screwed up big time. If he decided to mention me to Bartholomew, I'd be in *big* trouble.

"Spartacus? Oh, really now," Remmy said, giving me a double-take. "Now *that's* a circus name. I'd say you're ready."

While Remmy went into the tent to get us some food, I sat there wondering what to do. I could just head home. My running away would be a lesson to Dad and Will, a message that I wasn't going to put up with their crap anymore.

I imagined walking in the door, putting my bags down nonchalantly, while they sat open-mouthed in the living room. I'd wave hello, get a soda from the fridge, and when I'd come back, they'd still be sitting there, staring. Dad would finally say, "Where have you been?" and I'd just say "Out," before going up to my room.

The thought made me smile.

But, on the other hand, I could also imagine being sent to boarding school—which really wouldn't have been too bad considering my current status as The Brenville Boy Who Bared It All. But it was more likely I'd be grounded and trapped in the house with Will and Dad. Forever.

That thought didn't make me smile.

Remmy returned with two bowls of hot veggie chili. We sat in lawn chairs—him in a small one, me in a regular-sized one—and ate. As the sounds of the show continued to drift out from inside the tent—cheers, yells, organ music—Remmy talked, and I learned.

Remmy was either seventy-eight or eighty-two; he couldn't remember. Remmy's sideshow, The World-Renowned Sideshow of Curiosities and Mayhem, was the sideshow for Bartholomew's Circus. Remmy explained that the sideshow was supposed to perform *with* the circus.

"But on the side, get it?" he asked. "Sideshow?"

Remmy's team usually traveled with a lot of different circuses and carnivals and even did a few state fairs, but things had been slow, so they'd signed a three-year contract to work only with Bartholomew.

"We've always been our own company," said Remmy. "Sure, maybe this pays better than being on our own, but they don't respect us." He spat on the ground. "But then, I don't respect *him*. No ringmaster worth his salt would cancel at the last second and have the sideshow fill in. And on the last night of his run when everybody's expecting the best show? No, sir."

"So you guys perform if he doesn't show up?"

"Yep—but then we're not the sideshow anymore. Then we're just *The Show*," said Remmy, fanning out his fingers dramatically. "And it's a shame, a dirty shame, to treat customers like that. These people, they didn't come to see us. Now, I'm not saying we're not giving them a show. You ever seen our show?"

I shook my head.

"Oh, you should. I mean, we do it all. We got the knife throwing and sword eating, the Human Blockhead, Spidora, the Two-faced Man, and all the fire breathing stunts—but you'll see it all tomorrow." He took off his bowler hat to reveal a shock of white hair that went in a ring around his otherwise bald head.

Why would he think I'd be seeing the show tomorrow?

"But these people?" he continued, ignoring my confusion and gesturing at the tent with his hat. "They don't come for that. They want the trapeze, the lions, the elephants. They want Athena, the Human Cannonball. The big stuff."

My eyes widened at this. This man actually knew my mom!

"You just don't cancel like that," he went on. "And he's done this kind of thing so many times in the last year, I've lost count. Who does that?"

"I don't know," I said politely, but inside my mind was whirring: *He knows Mom!* But I couldn't say anything. Not yet.

Gotta keep up the mistrust.

"I've been in the sideshow fifty-three years now," Remmy was saying, looking miffed. "And I *never* seen no one do it like this. Bartholomew's got a good circus, I admit. But he runs it all backwards. Not professional in the slightest. Like he doesn't even care about what people think. It's not just the canceling. It's everything. They don't tell us anything until the last second. They give us our cut of the profits late. To get any info out of them is like pulling teeth."

Remmy paused for a moment. He pulled a handkerchief out of his suit pocket and blew his somewhat potato-looking nose before saying darkly, "Bartholomew seems like a real gentleman when you first meet him, too. But then you get to know him and…I'm just disgusted with him, if you want to know the truth. I think he's a no-good fink."

"Why did they cancel?" I asked.

Remmy eyed me while he folded his handkerchief back into this pocket, like he wasn't sure how much he should tell me. "Well, this time they said their lead girl had given everyone pink eye. Doesn't that just beat all? Pink eye shouldn't stop a circus. No sir, no circus with any sense of civic duty, anyway. Our kit? We could do our show with our eyes swollen *shut*." He spat on the ground again. Then he looked at me with a knowing grin.

"You looked confused earlier when I said that you'd see our show tomorrow," he said. "You thought I didn't notice. Maybe most people wouldn't. You don't get to be a showman like I am without being able to read people and keep some patter up and then come back to it."

"I *was* wondering what you meant by that," I stammered.

"Well, I assumed you'd be with us tomorrow, and not leaving our fine company, because I know that you're trying to get a job with Bartholomew."

I paused, confused. Then I nodded with a slow grin. Now *that* was a pretty good cover...

"How did you know?" I managed to ask.

Remmy winked at me and pulled a flask out of his jacket—a flask of something that smelled really strong, like something from a medicine cabinet. Lousy appeared out of nowhere, rubbing against his chair.

"Kids showing up at the circus is old hat," he said. "Bunch of kids want to get a job with Bartholomew's. But kids accidentally turning up at our little old sideshow when they think they're at Bartholomew's? That, my friend, is *new* hat."

He took a drink from his flask and then poured a little bit in the lid and set it on the ground. The cat drank it up like it was cream. Then, as if he was reading my mind faster than I could connect the dots and see the whole picture, Remmy invited me to travel with the sideshow to Bartholomew's next show in Las Vegas—just two days away.

I, Spartacus Ryan Zander, was going to go to Las Vegas!

"And we'll give you some help for your tryouts. You can't breathe fire yet, can you? Yeah, that'd be a good one for you to learn. Don't look so agog, boy, it's not flattering."

I *was* agog. I don't think I'd ever been agog before, but I was then. *Breathe fire?* I was going to learn how to breathe fire?

"Why would you help me?" I just about squeaked.

"Well, there was this man named Winston Churchill—a man who was very much like Spiderman," he said. "And this man said, 'the price of greatness is responsibility.' And since the Sideshow of Curiosities and Mayhem is great—and since Churchill is the only church I've ever attended—I feel it's my responsibility to help you out.

151

"Besides, I like your moxie. I think you deserve a chance," he added. "I may not think too highly of Bartholomew's Circus, but I can understand why you'd want to join up."

"Thank you," I said, reaching out and shaking his small hand so hard that he had to pull it away. Just thinking about getting to The Incredible gave me adrenaline again. Adrenaline and hope.

But I had to find out how safe I was, how much I should mistrust old Remmy.

"Do you guys know Bartholomew's people pretty well?" I asked, hoping it sounded like I was just trying to schmooze for the job.

"Kid, do you know what your butt crack looks like without a mirror?"

"Uh," I thought. "I don't know. I mean, it probably looks just like any butt crack. So, yes?"

"Well, you've got a good point there," said Remmy. "But what I meant was no, not really. I mean, in some ways we know them pretty well. We work with them a lot and know their performers and their acts. But Bartholomew runs a pretty tight ship. He doesn't let us in the tent when the circus is going on. And none of his people get too friendly with us. And we're only allowed to show up the day before the event—sometimes even the day of—and then we have to tear down and move on to the next place immediately after. No camaraderie. No team. It's bizarre is what it is."

This was all good news for me and The Plan. If the sideshow and Bartholomew's people weren't too close, that meant I could stay hidden from the circus. However, that also meant I might not learn very much from Remmy about Bartholomew, either.

"But," Remmy said, his round face going serious. "You have to know what you're getting into. I want you to really think about this tonight, before you do anything."

He leaned forward in his seat and I did too.

"Bartholomew's may be a circus, but it sure ain't no picnic. That circus has some mean folks in it. Like the kind of folks you wouldn't want to turn your back on unless you were wearing chainmail under your jacket, if you get what I'm saying."

I wasn't sure I did, but I nodded.

"I don't want to talk too bad against Bartholomew's, because there's a lot of good folks, too, but I think you should know."

I wasn't sure what expression I should put on for Remmy: shocked by the news or determined to join the circus despite Remmy's warnings. Inside, of course, it didn't surprise me. I already knew Bartholomew was evil.

I don't know what Remmy read in my face, but he leaned back in his chair.

"Just think about it, okay?"

I nodded, and he seemed content with that.

It turned out Remmy didn't actually perform in the sideshow—he used to be what was known as the "outside talker."

"The outside talker," Remmy said, "is the guy who stands outside the circus or fair or whatever, and talks to people outside to try to get them to come in. And I was one of the best. You should have seen me when I was at the top of my game and we had a Single-O set up on the midway," he said. "I could get any mark to pay any amount to see something."

He told me a Single-O was one of those things you see at the fair where there is just one thing inside, maybe a scary animal or a lady covered with gorilla-hair or a fake head in a jar. Sometimes the animals are taxidermied, like the alligator-man I'd seen once in Washington—a mummified alligator with a human head.

"We have a pretty great Single-O with Matilda, if I do say so myself. She's a genuine killer from Madagascar!"

"Matilda," I repeated, thinking about the spreaders from earlier. "What is she? A lion? A bear?" Or maybe he was he talking about a person.

"A killer. That's all you need to know. Here's a clue—if she looks at you and decides it's your turn to go, she'll point a finger at you.

Then it's just a matter of time before you're dead."

"Why would anyone want to see that?" I asked.

"So you believe it?"

"No, not really," I scoffed. But I hoped he wouldn't make me see her. It. Whatever It was.

"You have to see her. You'll be beating yourself up the rest of your life if you don't."

I saw that he was trying to sell me on Matilda like I was one of the people at the fair.

"Just tell me, not like I'm a, uh, what did you call them?"

"Marks? The suckers?"

"Yeah, like I'm not a mark—is it real?"

"Do your parents know where you are?" Remmy shot back. I sat back in my seat and looked away, embarrassed. I didn't answer.

"See? There are some things you can't tell people," he said. "Even if you like them."

I looked back at him and he gave me a small apologetic smile before lighting up another cigar.

He told me how he'd been with the sideshow since the 1950s. He and another performer, a younger guy named Robin Marx, had bought the sideshow a few years back. Robin was the front man inside, running the whole operation, keeping the performers comfortable and the patrons happy.

"You won't find a much better bunch than my gang," said Remmy, nodding his head. "But then, you'll be meeting them all soon. What say we get you set up for the night?"

Remmy went off to set up a bedroll for me in one of the dressing rooms. I fetched my suitcase from the makeshift bathroom and headed toward the fairgrounds entrance.

The show was still going on, but there was no one around. I wondered if my Goth friends were still around, trying to wake the dead. They'd probably figured out it was the wrong circus, though, too.

I pulled my backpack from its hiding spot under the dumpster, and started walking back, lost in thought.

Why had Bartholomew split town?

Maybe it was because his goons had spotted me in the convenience store parking lot, but Remmy said they'd canceled that morning, *before* they had seen me. Did Bartholomew get scared for some reason? Something had to have happened. Then again, Remmy said Bartholomew had done that kind of thing before. But there was something else weighing on my mind, since the police station. I had that little brain itch, the kind that tells you that you forgot something. Or were about to remember something. I knew I needed to look back at my mom's postcards and try to find the source of that itch.

I hurried back to Remmy, who was waiting for me at the back of the tent.

"I'd offer to introduce you to some of the sideshow folks," he said, "but they've still got a bit of work to do tonight—and you look dead on your feet."

"Don't you have work to do, too?"

"Didn't I mention it? I'm retired. Well, semi-retired. I'm like a figurehead. I do odd jobs here and there. Mostly I just order people around and sign things. During the shows, I get to relax. Which is what you should be doing."

I nodded, thinking about that memory itch. I had to think about things. Plan some things.

As he led me through the tent, I tried to think of some small talk, like maybe telling him how long I'd been on the road. But I couldn't even remember how long it had been. It felt like weeks, months even. I did the calculations and discovered it had only been two days.

"My parents know I'm here," I piped up, really just as a way to break the silence. "Just in case you were wondering about that."

"Don't make stuff up, kid." He didn't look at me when he said it; he just kept on walking. But he didn't sound angry, either. "I'm small, but I wasn't born yesterday. Besides, no one is going to ask any questions around here, so just keep your cool, all right?"

We passed by several performers in the hall, including a girl with dark, wild hair dressed in a suit with lightning decals. It was the same girl from before, the one who was about my age. She stared at me as we passed, but Remmy kept moving ahead. He was pretty fast for being so small and old.

When we reached my "room," he pulled back the thin curtain. There was a small oriental rug rolled out on the asphalt with a stack of folded quilts on top of it. There was a puffy pillow on one end. At first, I was like, *is that it?* But then, after another moment, it looked so cozy and comfortable, I was actually kind of touched.

"It's not much, but it'll have to do," he said. "It'll be nicer in Vegas. Breakfast will be at seven sharp. Get a good night's sleep. You're going to need it."

And with that, I was alone again. I pulled the curtain shut behind me and set my stuff down.

Remmy had put a small stool next to the bedding like a nightstand. On it was a small lamp and a drinking glass half-full of something amber-colored. What was it? I took a whiff and smelled that horrible medicinal smell from earlier, from Remmy's flask. I felt dizzy just smelling the fumes.

Uh, I think I'll save that for later.

I should have been blown away by what'd happened in the last twenty-four hours, but I didn't have time to think about any of it. Not Lloyd, nor Hailey, nor Blue and White, nor the fact that I was going to Vegas in the morning. I had to follow the questions, to get on the trail of why Bartholomew skipped town. I sat down on the quilts, emptied everything out of my backpack and pockets, postcards and all, and went to work.

It was time, as Eli would say, to "review the evidence."

In my little makeshift room behind the sideshow, I laid out the postcards, arranged by date.

I'd done this game of staring at the postcards tons of times before, always thinking something would jump out at me, some obvious connection. That's what happens in the movies. But, as always, I just sat there tapping my fingers, coming up with nothing.

It was a cold night, and the tip of my nose felt like an ice cube. On the other side of the tent, the sideshow had ended. I could hear performers pass in the hallway, but no one paused at my curtained door. It was late. I just wanted to snuggle down into the bed and think about everything tomorrow.

Snap out of it, Ryan! Focus!

I flipped the postcards over and re-read the notes Mom had written.

Eli and I had always focused on the ones with secret messages. They were all from horrible sounding towns like Crashup Mountain and Farewell. The names were real places—we'd looked them up—but they just got worse and worse over time:

Eek, Alaska
Accident, Maryland
Crashup Mountain, Arizona
Fearsville, Kentucky
Breakneck, Connecticut
Deadman Reach, Alaska
Why, Arizona
Imalone, Wisconsin
Little Hope, Pennsylvania
Last Chance, Colorado
Defeated, Tennessee
Farewell, Arkansas
Poopout Hill, California

Another mystery Eli and I couldn't solve was how erratic the postcards' locations were. For example, on September 9th, Mom had sent a postcard *without* a secret message from Nuevo León, México—I remembered it had come in a small box along with the scarab—and then the very next day she'd sent one *with* a secret message from Eek, Alaska.

"It doesn't make sense," Eli would repeat, his head in his hands. "There's no way the circus could travel that fast. And why are they hitting so many small towns? And sometimes they leave a city to go halfway across the country, only to come back to another city that is only fifty miles away from where they started?"

I sat and stared, willing something to click.

That's when Lloyd's wanted poster, which was spread out next to the postcards, caught my attention. Lloyd's grinning, madman face. The face that was so different than I remembered it being in person.

Impulsively, I separated the postcards into two rows: secret code and no secret code. When I was done sorting, I had two equally long rows. Then I rearranged each row by date.

I was close. I could feel it. But I was tired and my mind kept drifting to all the crazy things that had happened over the last few days. I couldn't stop thinking about Lloyd and my brush with death, which led me to think about Hailey. Then Blue and White. Then the police station and the two nice-ish cops, and then the story of Zacharias Prizrak and his dying inside a bank vault.

Criminals. Crime. *That* was the connection here. But was it important?

Crime.

Murder.

Kidnapping.

Robbery.

Robbery.

Puck and Calyxtus said that Bartholomew used his magic powers to trap Zacharias Prizrak in a locked bank vault. Even if Bartholemew *does* have magical powers—which I'm pretty sure he doesn't—why would he send someone into a bank vault?

…unless he was trying to rob it.

Ah! Now we were getting somewhere.

Robbery. Robbery. What had I seen about a robbery recently?

I thought a moment—and when it hit me, it came in flashes:

The poster at the police station, talking about the paintings stolen from the Georgia O'Keeffe Museum.

The security camera photo of the robber standing on the high ledge.

The weird feeling of *déjà vu* when I'd seen it.

The dream about Mom jumping off the roof.

Everything fit.

I sprang to my feet. I could hardly stand still to think through the end of one thought before getting to the other.

The poster felt so uncanny because I'd seen that exact pose before—all those years ago, Mom, standing on top of our house, just before she jumped. *That's* why the picture had caught my attention! The person in the fuzzy black and white photo had the *exact* same pose my mom made when she was about to do something crazy. Something dangerous. Like jumping off a building.

If I hadn't assumed the person in the security photo was a man, I would have noticed it *immediately.*

I didn't even have to check, but I did. I tore through my bag and yanked out the picture my mom had sent from the circus, the one of her standing in front of that big, white, cartoonish cannon.

Exactly the same. The pose was *exactly the same.*

The same as my memories. The same as that figure in the security photo.

It couldn't be a coincidence. It just couldn't. Why would Bart cancel the circus on his last night in town? Unless he was worried because something went wrong?

Like maybe Mom getting caught on camera while trying to rob a museum.

Who better than my mom to rob places? She knew how to climb and jump; she could contort herself. She was an evil villain's dream come true!

I got chills up and down my spine. Actual chills, not the adrenaline-charged chills I'd felt when I was riding with Lloyd or before jumping off the high dive for the first time. No, these were real, supernatural, premonition-type chills, like the kind you sometimes get in bed late at night when you think you see something moving in the closet. The kind of chills that happen only when you're pretty sure something very, very bad is coming.

I paced my "room"—which was all of three paces long. Was it possible I was overreacting? Maybe I was seeing things that weren't there. Maybe it was all a coincidence. Maybe I needed some sleep. I could hear my inner-Will saying, "Yeah, an evil villain using Mom as a cat burglar makes a *ton* of sense," in that sarcastic voice of his.

But then another thought struck me. I snatched up the gold scarab that Mom had sent me. It was still in the plastic police evidence bag with the note: *Recovered at scene. Run past FBI? Interpol? Also, check against known art-theft list.*

Maybe the cops had another reason for thinking it was stolen, besides the fact that it was in Blue and White's car. *Maybe*—

That's when all the lights in the tent went out, plunging me into darkness.

"Goodnight, you fantastic humans, you," called Remmy from somewhere off to my left. There was a general mumble of response from people, all around me.

Guess there wasn't much of a choice about bedtime around here.

I groped my way over to the pile of quilts and lay down. And in the dark, as the sideshow settled around me, an idea crept into my head. And even though I was exhausted and maybe not thinking straight, I was pretty sure it was spot-on. As I gradually slipped away into much-needed sleep, I tried to hold onto it.

It was very, *very* important.

Chapter Twelve

I don't know how I slept, or even *if* I slept. All I knew was suddenly there was sunlight and a weird lapping sound. I opened my eyes to see a dirty white cat drinking from a glass next to my head.

Lousy. Remmy. The Sideshow of Curiosities and Mayhem.

Call Eli!

I jumped up, startling Lousy, who knocked the whiskey glass off the stool. I don't know how I was fast enough, but I caught it before it hit the ground.

I checked my watch—a quarter after six. I had forty-five minutes to find a phone, call Eli, solve a mystery, and get back in time for my free ride to Vegas.

I packed everything except for the postcards without secret codes. These I slipped into my back pocket. I'd grab my backpack and suitcase when I got back.

Outside, a few workers were taking stakes out of the tent. No Remmy in sight. I considered asking one of the workers for a cell phone, but I didn't want anyone hearing what we were going to say. I remembered seeing pay phones just outside the fairgrounds, and took off in that direction.

❧

"Okay, Vegas," Eli was saying over the phone. Eli had seen the announcement that Bartholomew's had canceled and had already been hard at work. "I got you a ride all figured out. There's this Mormon choir bus—"

"No, no, no, I'm good for that. I got the ride all taken care of."

"You *do?*" He sounded a little disappointed.

"The sideshow is going to give me a ride on their bus."

"Now *that's* what I'm talking about!"

"I need something else, though. Listen carefully. Search for 'Monterrey, Nuevo León, Mexico.'"

"What about it?"

I looked down at the first "normal" postcard from Mom.

"Check the news from September. Robberies. Art gallery robberies, bank robberies, something like that."

"Why am I doing this?" he asked. I ignored the question and waited. "The MARCO—the Museum of Contemporary Art of Monterrey. How'd you know? They lost an entire collection by one artist. He was a gold sculptor. They said that—"

"Does it say anything about a scarab?" I interrupted.

"No...no, no scarab. Wait. Yes!" he exclaimed. "Wait, you don't think that—"

"Now search Philadelphia, for October."

"Geez, bossy much?" he asked, but I heard him typing and clicking. "Crap—again! The Academy of Natural Sciences lost their—I don't know how to say this—their *Had-ro-saurus fobla-something*. A giant dinosaur skeleton. It just went missing one night. Where are you getting this stuff?"

I leaned back against the glass in the booth, my hand to my forehead. *It was happening. It was all really happening.*

"Hello? Ryan? What's this for?"

"They aren't just stealing people," I said.

"Devil in a hang glider!" Eli cursed. "*What are you talking about?*"

"I think I figured it all out—Bartholomew is using his kidnapped circus people to rob places. It's all in the postcards. I mean, it's not *in* them. It's where they're from." I looked at my watch. Crap. It was already 6:45!

"Look, just a few more, to make sure. Here's the next: Lebanon, Ohio. November."

A pause. Then, "Warren County History Center. Some antique crap and—oh, get this, antique postcards. That's funny because—"

"Yeah, yeah I get why it's funny," I cut him off. "Springfield, Illinois. December."

"Some fine china from the Abraham Lincoln Presidential Library."

"Abe Lincoln's *china?*" I repeated. "Like plates and stuff?"

"Looks that way. But what about the other cards?" Eli asked. "The ones with the secret codes?"

"I figured it out," I said excitedly. "Remember how we said that her travel path didn't make sense?"

"Yeah."

"Her path makes sense when you remove those ones," I explained at a fast clip. "They move across the country in a straight line. Those other ones are fake."

"Like maybe she got a set of cards from places with sad names, just to help clue you in?"

"Exactly!" I said, so glad to have someone else understand so I didn't feel crazy.

Going on like this, we discovered that Bartholomew had knocked off at least five museums in the past ten months. I had twenty-five postcards (thirteen of them being the coded ones asking for help), but I knew they performed somewhere different every few days, so maybe all this was only the tip of the iceberg.

"Guess this explains why they don't put the circus dates on their website, huh?" I smirked.

"No kidding. I can't believe they made your mom steal that streetcar from the Minnesota Streetcar Museum," Eli said, his voice full of awe. "I mean, how did she even *do* it?"

"It doesn't mean it's her," I snapped. "Maybe it was Charlene."

"Who?"

"This—this lady I saw who looks just like Mom—like *exactly*. Oh, and she was with this guy who looked like a shark—"

"A *what?*"

"A shark."

"A shark?"

"Yes," I answered impatiently, looking at my watch. "A shark-

shark. I think it's the plastic surgery guy—not that he's the doctor, he just someone who—look, I know, it doesn't make sense. Google it, see what you find. I gotta get going."

"Well, if your mom is doing this—and I'm not saying she is," Eli added quickly. "But if she is—it could be that Stockholm thing. You know it even happened to Amelia Earhart?"

"I have to go," I said. "The next time I talk to you, Mom will be with me. I hope."

"Just let me know if you need anything. I'm here for you, friend."

"Sure," I said. "Hey, Eli—thanks."

"You're welcome. Good luck, Ryan."

"Thanks. See ya."

I raced back into the fairgrounds, thinking about what it all could mean. *There was no way this was all a coincidence.* I thought back to the Prizrak-bank-vault story. I should have asked Eli to check on that, too. I made a mental note to look it up later.

I came up to the fairgrounds gate and glanced at my watch: 7:02. I was just in time. I was starving and looking forward to that breakfast Remmy had promised me. I imagined all sorts of warm things like french toast or pancakes. I thought I could almost smell the food. I wondered what it would be like, eating all together, the crazy sideshow folks and me.

That's when I got close enough to see that the sideshow tent was gone. And not just the tent. Everything was gone.

There were no trucks. Nobody around.

No Remmy.

I'd only been gone, what, forty-five minutes? How could they have packed up so fast? They wouldn't just leave me, would they? Remmy had practically *promised.*

I sat down hard on the sidewalk as my heart broke in my chest. And when I realized my backpack and suitcase were also gone, it broke a second time. My heart was in fourths.

Don't panic, I willed myself. How much worse off was I really than if I'd never met Remmy? Sure, I didn't have my stuff. I didn't have the suitcase. But I could figure out another plan. A better one. I could get through this. I still had Eli on my side. I still had Will's money in my pocket.

Go back to the payphone and call Eli. My inner voice was actually being helpful, for once. I took a deep breath. I felt calmer.

All right.

I'd gone maybe twenty feet down the sidewalk when I heard the squeak of old brakes coming up behind me. I turned and saw the sideshow bus, with Remmy's grinning face sticking out the door.

"I told you 7:00 a.m. sharp, didn't I?" he called.

The moment I stepped into the bus, everyone inside greeted me with an enthusiastic, "Hello, Spartacus!" which I answered with an awkward smile and a wave. There were about twenty people, and I recognized some of them from backstage the night before.

"Where have you been?" asked Remmy. "We've been looking for you. Hurry up and take a seat." Remmy slid into the driver's seat. I realized with a start that he was actually *driving* the bus. I wondered how he could see the road, let alone reach the pedals, but I didn't want to stare.

The bus was set up all crazy, like you'd expect a circus bus to be. They had changed it so people could live in it—there were oriental rugs on the floors and across the ceiling. Some of the windows had these plastic static clings that made them look like they were stained glass. Then there were the three sets of narrow bunk beds in the back, stacked three tall. They were more like shelves, really, but the top ones had posters tacked up above them, like you'd see in a kid's bedroom. Some had curtains hanging down that made them more private.

There were so few people that most of them had their own seats. I saw my backpack and the suitcase in the seat right behind Remmy, so I sat there.

"I thought you'd left and changed your mind because of our talk last night." Remmy pulled the bus away from the fairgrounds. "But I should have known a kid like you wouldn't be scared away that easy."

He gestured back toward the guy across the aisle from me.

"Spartacus, meet my business partner, Robin Marx. We own the show together."

Robin Marx was a big, sturdy man with a thick, handlebar mustache and a black bowler hat. "Pleasure to make your acquaintance, Mr. Spartacus," he said. He had a dramatic, booming voice, and I thought I recognized it as the announcer's voice from the show last night. His mustache was mesmerizing. It was so big and thick it looked cartoonish and bounced when he spoke. "So you think you're ready for Bartholomew's?"

For a moment I thought he was talking about my rescue plan and had no idea what to say. Then I remembered they thought I was trying to join the circus.

"I hope so," I said. "I mean, I think so."

"Bartholomew's is a pretty big show for a First of May."

"A what?" I asked, thinking I'd heard him wrong.

"That's what we call a novice," he said. "A beginner. A First of May. You have some tricks ready? Some dare-devilry?"

"Uh, well—" I searched my brain. "I can throw knives." And I wasn't lying. I wasn't great at it, but it was the one thing Mom had taught me how to do.

"That's always a showstopper," said Robin. "What else?"

That wasn't enough?

I brainstormed, thinking of what was the best lie I could tell.

"I can also," I said slowly, "get out of traps. Like small suitcases and being tied up and stuff."

"Oh, we've got a regular escape artist here!" Remmy turned over and beamed at me. "We could use one of them, couldn't we, Robin?"

"Hey, stop, Remmy. There's Zeda," Robin said. He was leaning over his seat and pointing up ahead, out the windshield. A girl stood on the street corner, waving at us.

The bus lurched to a stop. I realized she—Zeda, apparently—was the girl my age that I'd seen twice last night. The bus stopped just for a second, long enough for her to jump on. She had a couple of big, white paper bags in her hands.

"Breakfast is here!" Zeda announced, holding the bags up high as the bus pulled forward. Everyone cheered. Zeda turned to me and I realized I'd been staring. I tried to make it look like I was only looking at the Rainbow Brite tattoo on her arm.

"Hey, I remember you," she said.

I didn't say what I first thought to say, which was, "I remember you, too." Because I did. Of course I did. She was…well, she was beautiful. Beautiful in a completely different way than Erika Dixon was with her carefully styled hair and shiny pink lip gloss. Different than Hailey with her trucker clothes and goofy smile. This girl had dark eyes, and her hair was crazy and tangled, but still looked somehow like a beautiful planned-out work of art.

Get a grip, Spart.

"You're the one who went crazy last night, right?" Zeda said, smiling.

I winced and reddened at the same time. *That* was why she remembered me. Of course. This was Erika Dixon and the Brenville Pool all over again. Nothing had changed.

"Yep," I said, forcing a smile. "That was me."

"You want to help me pass out these veggie breakfast burritos?"

"Sure," I answered with a lot more enthusiasm than made sense, and then I stood up too fast. She noticed both, but just smiled at me and handed me one of the bags.

I remembered why girls my own age made me so nervous. They were always so much more confident than I was—and they acted like they knew it. Oh, yeah, and they were all taller than me. Zeda was no exception on all counts.

"That's my daughter," said Robin sternly, but his eyes twinkled. "Don't get any ideas."

"*Lame*, Dad," she said, but then she laughed. I forced a small, dry laugh and then followed behind her, helping her hand out the food.

"Have you met Spartacus?" Zeda asked almost every single person.

My name made me feel uncomfortable and I wondered if maybe Zeda was making fun of me. Then again, these were circus people. Their names were all just as weird as mine was.

"Bet you're excited to meet Bartholomew," said one woman.

"Can't wait," I managed.

Inside, though, my heart was already pounding.

～

I was glad Zeda was seated in the back so she wouldn't see me devour my burrito in a few seconds like a ravenous animal.

"Gotta love that green chili, huh?" asked Robin. I looked up from the crumpled paper in my hands to see Robin still had half his burrito left.

"I was kind of hungry," I said sheepishly.

"It's okay," he said good-naturedly. "I'm going to lick the wrapper when I get done with mine, too."

"How long it is to Las Vegas?" I asked.

"At least nine hours or so," he said. "It's gonna be a grueler." With that, he settled back into his seat, pulled out a fat book, and turned to the first page.

I followed his lead and arranged my bags on the floor so I could stretch out in my seat. The rest of the bus fell into a quiet, relaxed groove. As the New Mexico scenery flew by in a brown blur, my mind automatically returned to the robberies.

It seemed pretty clear that Bartholomew was robbing places wherever the circus went. Eli had seen the evidence, too. I hadn't imagined that part of it. But I was trying to decide what it all meant.

Does it change anything?

No, not really. My mom still needed my help. I still had to get her out of there. I guess what had changed was that I wasn't breaking into just any old evil circus anymore. Now I was trying to free Mom from inside a tent of professional criminals.

I was going to need to improve my plan—and to do that, I was going to need to get some more information.

Remmy had said that the sideshow knew Bartholomew's Circus pretty well. Maybe I could get them to give me some more information without blowing my cover.

"Remmy?" I said out of the blue, startling him. Remmy looked back at me in the rearview mirror.

"What you need?"

"Uh, what's the…what's the layout of Bartholomew's tent like? Is it kind of similar to yours?"

"Not one bit."

"Oh," was all I could think to say. *Keep cool. Don't make your questions too obvious.* I tried a different approach. "I'm just curious. Where is Bartholomew's—where is his office? Inside the tent, you know. I want to know where to go to audition tonight."

I felt pretty pleased with that question.

"Don't be ridiculous," Remmy laughed. "You don't audition in his office. And not tonight, that's for sure. Do you even know your set?"

"My *set?*"

"My boy, you're as fresh as the morning dew!" Remmy chuckled. "I think you could use some tips. We can give you a little training right now."

Training? On the bus? I must have looked a little skeptical.

"Trust me," said Remmy. "Go into the back and find Nero. The skinny guy with the sideburns. Ask him to teach you something."

Okay. What could it hurt? And maybe I could press this Nero guy for more details about The Incredible.

I got up from my seat and walked down the aisle. It was funny seeing all the same people from the night before without their masks and snakes and clown faces. In the daylight, there was nothing all that freaky about them. I mean, sure, there were still tattoos and piercings and this woman whose makeup made her look like a Disney villain, but no one was doing anything crazy like hammering a nail up their nose (the Human Blockhead routine Remmy had told me about) or bending their joints backward. In fact, most people were sleeping. I saw Zeda in one of the bunk beds in the back, her tattooed arm hanging out.

Seated near the middle of the bus was a guy with dark sideburns shaped like lightning bolts. He was dressed all in black, including these black leather bracelets with shiny metal spikes. He was staring out the window as I approached, absentmindedly flipping a knife around his fingers the way Will spun pencils.

Okay, so the people were *mostly* normal.

"Hey. Are you Nero?" I asked in a soft voice, trying not to wake anyone.

"Yeah," he said, looking up kind of dazed from the window. He smiled when he saw me. "Spartacus, right?"

"Right. Cool sideburns," I said, touching my face where his lightning bolts were. It was the first time I wished I could grow facial hair.

"Thanks," he said. "They're kinda my thing."

I nodded, then said, "Remmy told me you might be able to teach me something for Bartholomew's?"

"Mmm, right," he nodded, thinking. "Let me get some stuff together and I'll meet you up front. That way we won't wake up everyone back here."

In a few minutes, Nero switched seats with Robin so he was right across from me. He had a small tackle box and a book with him.

"What do you do in the sideshow?" I asked.

"Well, my big thing is swallowing stuff—razor blades, swords, umbrellas—"

"*Umbrellas?*" I asked skeptically.

"Yeah. It's just like swallowing a sword. They're not open or anything. Right now I'm working on the world record for most swords swallowed at the same time. The record is seven, so, you know, I'm working on nine. Just to make sure no one breaks it for a while." He laughed.

"What's the trick?" I asked.

"The trick is that there *is* no trick," he said. "You're actually swallowing a sword."

"You're going to teach me to swallow swords?" I said, eyes wide. "On the *bus*?" I was terrified and thrilled. But mostly just terrified.

Zeda, who had obviously been listening to this all the way in the back, snickered and Nero grinned.

"It might take you six months to work your way up to a small dagger," he snorted. "Besides, that's the kind of cool stuff you'd get to do in the sideshow. But you're an Incredible-man, right?"

I nodded reluctantly.

"Right. No sword swallowing under the big top. Strictly the big time there. But I can teach you something that will come in handy in any circus."

I was excited. What was I going to learn? Trapeze stuff? Trick motorcycle riding? Magic? I knew we were on the bus, but maybe he was going to give me some starting-out theory.

Nero opened the tackle box, exposing tubes of paint, palettes, and little sponges.

"I'm talking," said Nero, "about face painting."

Face painting?

My eyes immediately glazed over.

"I promise you," he said. "It's not just painting horsies and rainbows."

A little more than an hour later, Nero had taught me how to paint myself in two different clown styles. I wasn't too impressed. Then I wiped it off and he showed me how to put different shades of green and brown on my face to make camouflage, like you'd see hunters wear.

"You can even put stuff under the paint, to make a big nose, or a wart or something," he explained.

He showed me how to paint my face to look like a lion, with a big, yawning mouth and sharp fangs.

"Hey, you're getting good at this," said Nero. "You're a pretty decent artist."

This *was* turning out to be kind of cool, but I still felt like I was wasting my time. I needed to gather some useful information while I was on the bus. Who knew how long I'd have after we got to Vegas?

"Have you ever seen the guy with Bartholomew's who looks kinda fishy—I mean, like an actual fish? A shark?"

"His name's Finn," he said, his lip curling in disgust. "Yeah, I know him."

"I saw him—um, I saw pictures of him online," I stammered. "Is that just paint or…"

"It's real," he said grimly. "Well, kind of. I think he started out with the gills—maybe an accident at birth or something, but then he got the fin implanted. Then he filed down his teeth and started wearing those contacts that cover his whole eye."

"The black ones. Right," I said, remembering his face. I shivered in the hot bus.

"I don't know why Bartholomew even has him in the show," said Nero. "He's not very talented—but I guess it gives the circus the scare factor that Bartholomew's looking for. Personally, I think it creeps out the kids."

"What's Sharkman—I mean, Finn—what's he like?"

Nero didn't answer right away, but then he looked at me, deadly serious. "He's bad news. I'd stay out of his way. He's not going to be your friend."

"Do you think that…well, I mean, I heard that Bartholomew has a plastic surgeon who travels with him?"

Nero furrowed his brow, looking confused. But I rushed on, "I mean, do you think they ever make, well, make performers look like other people? Maybe so a trick looks better?"

I was thinking about Not-Mom.

"No, I never heard anything like that," Nero said. "But then, there's a lot of strange stuff that goes on with them."

"Like what kind of stuff?"

I thought that Nero started to look uncomfortable.

"Well, a lot of them are cool. I don't want to say they're all bad. But, if I were you, I just wouldn't ask too many questions. They don't like that."

Of course, then I had a million more questions. About Bartholomew. About my mom. But at that moment, we slowed and pulled into a rest stop.

"Thanks for showing me all that," I said to Nero. When I went for the towel to wipe off my face paint, Nero stopped me.

"You're with a sideshow," he said. "Leave it."

❧

We'd stopped at what seemed like—to me, at least—a normal rest area. But to all the regular people who'd stopped? This might have been the highlight of their car trip. Normally, you'd see kids rolling in the grass, screaming in happiness about being free from their car. Parents standing around checking their phones. Dogs peeing where they shouldn't.

But with the sideshow bus there, everyone at the rest area who wasn't in the bathroom—four families, a young couple and an old couple, a weird heavy-set dude with two pairs of sunglasses on, a woman with a wiener dog on a leash, and five kids who seemed to be alone for some reason—crowded maybe ten feet from us, just watching us, expecting something, I dunno, weird to happen.

If my face hadn't been painted, I might have felt more comfortable hanging around with the "Normies" (as Nero called the normal folk), but as it was, I was "with" the sideshow. So I stood awkwardly next to the lady with the snake, stretching our legs in the shade, glad no one was trying to talk to me.

That's when Nero took a sword out of a storage space under the bus. And that's when he waved me over.

Nothing really prepares you to see sideshow people do their *thing*. And I'm not talking about lightning-bolt sideburns and face paint. I'm talking about seeing something impossible with your very own eyes. Like Nero said, there's no trick to swallowing a sword. It's not a prop, like a retracting sword or something. It's just sticking a sharp blade down into your guts. Well, *around* your guts.

"So, the sword goes into the mouth, then down the throat," Nero explained to me—and to the crowd of Normies who pushed closer. The sword had a gold hilt covered with jewels and was almost as long as his arm. He mimed the movement of the sword outside his body.

"Next, it passes the voice box, goes down the esophagus, and then between the lungs. Then you kind of nudge the heart to the side—"

I coughed. "Nudge? Your *heart?*" I asked, my insides squirming. The audience murmured the same thing.

"Yeah. Then you relax the lower esophagus, and you put the blade through the diaphragm, then past the liver, and down to touch the very bottom of the stomach."

"Where your *food* is?" exclaimed a young, red-headed kid with chocolate pudding on her face.

"Well, yeah. Unless you do it wrong and puncture an organ on the way there—then you're dead."

"Isn't that dangerous?" asked the wiener-dog lady, looking concerned. Meanwhile, the five kids were looking from Nero to me in awe, like they thought I was part of the show. I felt a bit taller standing with him, if you want to know the truth.

"Definitely," he said. "Hey, can I borrow that?"

"My dog?!" The woman hugged her dog to her chest.

"Ha, no, the fruit." Nero pointed to the chunky dude with the two pairs of sunglasses who was holding an apple. He gladly handed it to Nero.

Nero held it in one hand. With the other hand, he held the sword up and let it rest lightly on the apple. Without any effort from Nero, the weight of the sword pushed the blade all the way through the apple.

The wiener-dog lady looked even more distressed. Nero handed the apple back to the sunglasses man. The kids crowded around him as he showed them the hole in the apple. Nero pulled a cloth out of his pocket and wiped down the blade.

"Do people ever die doing this?" asked the old guy.

"Not if they do it right," Nero said. "Like this."

And then, without hesitating, he did it. He swallowed the sword. To the *hilt*.

All of us held our breath.

When he pulled it out again—and there wasn't a lung skewered on the end or anything—I stopped trying to look cool and applauded with everyone else as Nero took a bow.

"Oh, wow!" I said, my eyes bugging out as I shook my head. "That was awesome!"

I caught Zeda watching me with a half-smirk from across the parking lot. I stopped hooting and clapping like a regular carnival schmuck and tried to look cool—as cool as a twelve-year-old in face paint can look. At least she hadn't seen my cheeks burning red.

"Five minutes 'til lift-off!" Remmy called from the bus.

I ran to use the bathroom one more time, and washed the paint off my face while I was at it.

I was the last one back on the bus and Remmy closed the bus door behind me with a thwack. Just as I sat down in the front seat, I was lifted into the air.

"*Hey!*" I yelped.

It was Nero and Robin. *What the—?*

Nero held my arms at my sides while Robin started wrapping a thick rope around me. I struggled against them, but they were too strong and too fast.

"What are you doing?" I yelled at the top of my lungs.

"What's it look like we're doing?" grunted Nero. "We're tying you up."

Everyone on the bus was standing up in their seats, laughing and hooting as I was spun around in the narrow aisle. Even Remmy, as he drove, was laughing hysterically.

My heart thumped as I realized that I'd been tricked. I had trusted them, even after Hailey had warned me not to trust anyone. They knew who I was. They were all in on it.

They'd been working for Bartholomew all along.

☙

"You won't get away with this," I growled. This just made everyone laugh harder, which made me angrier. I fought back like an animal. I kicked Robin in the shin and he cursed. He wound the rope tightly around my legs.

"Gosh, boy, you're a fighter, aren't you?" Robin hooted. He turned to Nero. "Did you hear that? 'You won't get away with this?'"

"Classic," answered Nero.

I stood there, immobile, glowering at them. I was about to spit in Nero's grinning face, the way they do in movies (or, the way White had done), when they both took a step back.

"Now, escape," said Nero.

"You're funny," I said, glaring at him. "People will be looking for me."

"No, no, no," said Nero, shaking his head, his face stretched in a smile. "Seriously. Escape."

"*What?*"

"Yeah," said Robin. But not like a villain. Like my gym teacher encouraging me to do a pull-up. "We wanted to see your amazing escape-artist skills."

I wished my hands weren't tied up so I could have used them to cover my red, red face. That's right. I'd told them I could do stuff like that. What had I been thinking?

"Sorry about kicking you," I said to Robin in a quiet voice. I could barely look at him.

"My fault entirely," he said sincerely, his hand on his chest. "We shouldn't have jumped you like that. Seemed funny at the time."

"Uh, I'm a little bit out of practice."

"Take your shoes off for a start," Nero said. I slipped off my shoes and well, just kind of wriggled around, trying to look like I knew what I was doing. I was able to get my feet out of the ropes, but it was slow going.

"Try lying on the floor," Robin suggested. "That way you can use the ground to move the ropes for you."

With some work, I was able to get on my knees, then to the floor. It was a little easier. As I struggled, everyone else went on with what they were doing, reading magazines, playing cards—essentially not paying attention to me.

It was getting hot and the bus had become an oven, despite the open windows. It took me about fifteen sweaty minutes to finally get free. I stood up exhausted and soaked with perspiration. There was polite clapping from the other passengers who looked up from their books. I took a slight bow before falling over in my seat. Robin gave me a bottle of water while Nero wound up the rope.

"Tough, huh?" asked Robin. I nodded, gulping the water.

"Ready for the second round?"

I laughed and drank some more water.

"No, I'm serious," he said. "Stand up."

I gave him a look. "Do I have to?"

"Well, you got out. So you technically did it. But sorry to say, it wasn't impressive. It's not going to bowl anybody over, except maybe your little sister"—I bristled—"and there's no way Bartholomew would keep on watching you after the first four minutes. Come on, try again—but this time, we'll give you some tips."

I took a deep breath and stood back up.

It turns out that the most important part of escaping ropes is what you do *while* you're being tied up. Robin and Nero taught me to puff out my chest, hold my arms a bit away from my body, and flex my muscles to make myself bigger while the ropes were being wrapped around me. That meant I'd have more slack to work with. And, if you did it well, like Houdini did, no one would even know you were doing it.

The second time, with their instructions, I was out in five minutes. The next time I was out in three, the next in two.

The applause from the bus that last time was genuine and loud.

"Ready for the big time!" called someone from the back. Zeda gave me an appreciative nod. I bowed deeply and then collapsed in my seat, suddenly exhausted and peaceful. Then I slept.

❧

We arrived at an empty dirt lot on the outskirts of Las Vegas, Nevada, around four in the afternoon. I'd never been to Vegas before, and I was amazed, even at a distance. There were all sorts of crazy-looking buildings on the horizon, like a pyramid and a Ferris wheel and the Eiffel Tower, all flanked by palm trees.

"I didn't know Las Vegas was like this," I said to Remmy in awe as we climbed off the bus.

"It's Disneyland for jerks," he said, not even looking in that direction. "Come on; let's get unloaded."

I tore myself away from the sight of the skyline and got to work. Bartholomew's trucks weren't there yet, so I felt pretty safe hanging out in the open, helping everyone set up. I held stakes and pulled ropes while they put up the sideshow tent, and then I carried boxes and props inside.

A large, square container covered with gray canvas sat in the shade of the sideshow's lone truck. I was about to peek under the canvas cover when a voice spoke up from behind me.

"I wouldn't do that."

I turned to see Zeda stepping down from the running board

of the truck. She'd been putting on dark purple lipstick in the side-mirror.

"Why? What's under there?" I asked, feeling myself getting nervous again.

"*Who's* under there," she corrected me. She grinned at me when I took a step back from the box. Then she pulled a stick of gum out of her skirt pocket and popped it in her mouth before offering me a piece.

"Um, okay, *who's* under there?"

"Matilda," she said crossing over to something that resembled a wooden cutout, shaped like a person.

Matilda. I'd forgotten about her. The Single-O! The box was the right size for an animal. A lion? A tiger? I took another involuntary step away from the cage.

"Come on, Spartacus, you're braver than that," she said, laughing.

"Actually, I'm a chicken," I confessed. It felt good to finally say it.

"I don't believe it," she said.

"I am. If you don't show me what's under the canvas, I won't be able to sleep tonight."

Zeda gave me half a smile. "She isn't at her best during the daytime. She's nocturnal. Here, help me carry this thing."

Zeda and I hefted the wooden dummy across the parking lot. (Zeda said it was for my 'specialty'—knife throwing.)

"So what is she?" I asked as we worked. "Is she a big cat? A lizard?"

Zeda laughed, amused.

"Matilda is an aye-aye." She pronounced it like *eye-eye*.

"And what?" I asked.

"An aye-aye is an endangered lemur from Madagascar."

"An endangered lemur? Like, what, a monkey? A deadly, endangered monkey?"

"Sorta like that, yeah," she said, shrugging.

"What's her death trick, then?"

"It's not a trick." She blew her bangs out of her eyes. "It's all myth—and that's why she's so endangered. Some people in Madagascar think aye-ayes are some sort of death omen, so they kill them. They have this really long finger, and the myth is that if it points at you, the only way you can stay alive is by killing it. It's ridiculous. But, of course, Remmy, who is completely old-school, sees nothing wrong with promoting a stupid superstition to make some money."

"You're pretty angry about this," I said, not knowing what to say.

"Of course I am!" she said, looking at me with fiery eyes, her face flushed. "How can I feel good exploiting the very reason she's endangered?"

"You've got a good point," I said. I'd never heard anyone speak with so much feeling about a monkey—er, lemur—before. "That... sucks."

"No kidding," she said flatly, helping me set the wooden board down. "Circuses shouldn't even have animals, let alone endangered ones."

"Must make it hard dealing with Bartholomew's, huh?"

She snorted. "Tell me about it. One of these days, I'm going to open all the cages. See what they do then."

"That...that would be crazy," I replied.

"Exactly," she said. "Anyways, I'll introduce you to Matilda tonight, when she's awake. You'll see why I like her so much."

We worked side by side in silence a bit, carrying in more stuff from a truck before I spoke up again.

"Your dad is Robin, right?"

"Yeah."

"And he owns the sideshow with Remmy?"

"Something like that. Oh, set that over there."

I put down the box I was carrying before asking thoughtfully, "So does that mean you'll...inherit the sideshow someday?"

"Never." She exhaled loudly when she dropped an orange

180

sandbag into a pile of other sandbags. "No circuses for me. I'm thinking about running away to the Amazon to study aye-ayes."

"'Zeda the Adventurer' has a nice ring to it," I said shyly. Was this flirting? Was I *flirting*?

"Sadly, it just doesn't have the same ring as Spartacus," she responded, giving me a sly look as we walked back to the truck.

I cringed. *Here come the jokes.*

She saw my face and elbowed me, giving me a genuine smile. "Come on; it's actually a cool name. Is it real?"

"Unfortunately," I answered, but inside I was marveling. She thought it was *cool*?

"Are you kidding? It's awesome."

"Well, not if you don't live in a sideshow," I said and then felt bad, like maybe I'd insulted her. I changed the subject quickly. "That's a cool Rainbow Brite tattoo."

"It isn't real, you know," she said. "You can't get a tattoo until you're eighteen without a parent signing off."

"Yeah, that blows," I said, acting like I already knew that. "Well, it *looks* real. What is it? Permanent marker?"

"Yeah," she said, looking at it admiringly. "I've retraced it every day for over a year now to prove to Dad that I wouldn't regret having it as a tattoo. He's still saying no."

I thought about all the stupid stuff I'd get tattooed on me that I'd probably regret after a few months. I bet Lloyd/Dan even regretted his tattoo—especially because it made him easier to identify.

"I'll give you one, too. That is, um, if you'd like," she said.

"Yeah. That'd be cool," I managed, but inside I was like, *Wow.*

"I'll think up a good one for you in the next day or so, one that suits you," she explained. "Then you could retrace it until you're ready to get it done for real."

"Awesome," I said. And I meant it—except that I knew I didn't have the next day or so to hang out with Zeda or the sideshow. Bartholomew was going to be there that night or early the next morning. And then what? How was I going to go back to being *incognito* after the circus came? And what if one of the sideshow people told Bartholomew's people I was there, waiting to try out?

Why did you give them your real name, buttface? Will's voice had returned to make me feel stupid—and it was working. I was lost in thought when Zeda spoke up.

"Hey, Spartacus," she said. "Wanna learn something cool?"

❧

Letting a girl I hardly knew talk me into breathing fire might be one of the stupidest things I'd ever done.

"I'm going to do it a few times, and you're going to watch," she said, gathering up a box that said *Zeda Marx* on it. "And then I'll teach you."

"You're going to teach me to breathe fire?" I asked, my voice cracking halfway through the question.

"Shh!" she hissed, putting her hand to her lips. "I'm not supposed to show you. Dad said it was too dangerous for a novice, but I think you'd be great. Unless, of course, you don't want to," she added, her dark eyes daring me to say *No.*

"No, sounds good," I managed. She told me to fill a bucket of water from the spigot and meet her around the side of one of the buildings where nobody would see us.

It turns out that, like sword swallowing, there is no trick to fire breathing. There's lighter fluid, a torch, and a flame, and then—*bam!*—fire is flying from your lips!

I'd had crushes on girls before. There were a couple of girls besides Erika Dixon in Brenville that I'd liked at some point. Of course, I'd never really talked to them or told anyone I liked them—or even admitted it to myself. When you start liking girls, you have to be ready for rejection. I had already had enough of that in my life.

But after seeing Zeda do her fire-breathing act, I knew there would never be another girl for me. Zeda was *it*.

"And you do this in the show?" I asked, watching her put the torch out with a wet towel.

"Yeah, that's my thing," she said. She gargled green mouthwash and then spat it on the cement. "I do a whole fire routine you can see tomorrow."

I shook my head in amazement. "Aren't you, like, my age?"

"I'm an old soul," she said, preparing her tools again. "I met a fortune teller at a show once who told me I'd been breathing fire for thousands of years."

"And you believed that?" I asked. I'd meant it as a real question; I was really curious if she believed it, but I think she thought I was judging her.

"I mean, I'm not saying I *for sure* believe it," she said huffily. "But I think anything's possible."

I shrugged, not wanting to upset her.

"Are you ready?" she asked.

"I don't know." And I didn't. If Robin didn't think I was ready for this, should I trust his daughter to say I was? My Mistake-o-Meter was flashing a blazing red three. But when I looked at her holding the torches out to me, her pretty face expectant and encouraging, I couldn't say *No*.

Some things are just out of our control.

For the record, I did it right the first three times.

It was the fourth time, when I tried to show off, that the wind changed and blew the flames back in my face.

"Oh, no!" Zeda shrieked. With zero hesitation, she grabbed the water bucket and tossed it on me. One moment I was breathing fire, acting cocky—and the next I was soaked to the bone, torch still smoking. I stood motionless, bewildered.

"Uh—what?" was all I managed.

"Oh, Spartacus, I'm so sorry!" She grabbed me in a hug, even though I was drenched. She sounded like she was about to cry.

"What, uh, what happened?" I asked, dazed, hugging her. I patted her on the back because she was patting mine.

"The wind shifted and…" She pulled away and touched my face, inspecting, looking for something. "Nothing. There's…nothing?"

She looked confused.

"What?" I asked, thinking I'd missed something.

"Well—honestly, your hair should be singed and your eyebrows should probably be burnt off, but…" She stepped back, looking at me like I was a strange specimen. "You're a fire-breathing miracle."

⮞

I went and changed into my holey jeans and my last black t-shirt. Then I joined Zeda and the others on some picnic tables, where we all ate pizza.

I sat there, knowing I should be thinking about what my plan was, but it was hard to stay focused. I mean, how often do you get to hang out with a sideshow and a cool, fire-breathing girl? And they were *all* cool. Nero entertained us with more of his tricks, and the woman with the huge snake came out and did a belly-dancing routine. Zeda told me about what it was like for her living on the road.

So yeah, I was a bit distracted from my mission. But I had the vague idea that I could just make myself scarce when Bartholomew's people started showing up. Maybe I could tell Remmy and Robin to keep my presence a secret, because I wanted to surprise Bartholomew when I was ready.

Zeda had come up with an idea for my tattoo a lot sooner than she'd thought she would. She told me not to look while she drew on my bicep with permanent markers. I was kinda hoping it would take a long time to finish.

"Now she's got *you* wanting a tattoo?" Robin asked, walking up.

"I don't know yet," I said.

"You'll want one when you see how cool this is going to be," Zeda said. Robin laughed and sat down to apply wax to his mustache. I couldn't decide which was cooler—Nero's lightning-bolt sideburns or Robin's handlebar mustache.

"Do you go to school?" I asked Zeda, watching Remmy feed tomato slices to Lousy.

"I do it online. I'm going to graduate early, though. I'm already taking classes through one of those online universities."

I turned to look at her in surprise and she turned my face away.

"Don't look yet!" she giggled. But the moment her dad walked away, she pulled me nearer. "I need to tell you something." She spoke quietly, so only I could hear. I scooted closer. "Joining The Incredible isn't... it isn't a good idea."

"Oh?" I asked, trying to sound nonchalant.

Come on, Zeda. Gimme some dirt on Bart.

"I'm only telling you this because now that I know you...well, I like you."

"You like me?" I blurted out in my normal voice, my face going hot immediately.

"Shh, dumbo. Keep it down," she hissed. "Yeah, I like you. But this is about Bartholomew. You have to listen to me. He can't be trusted. I mean, animals aside. He's a maniac."

The hair on the back of my neck prickled at this. "What do you mean, exactly?"

"Did you hear—"

But she didn't get the chance to finish. A big truck rolled up toward us. It was a normal-looking brown delivery truck, except it didn't have a company name or anything on it. And it was driving pretty fast. Everyone in our camp went quiet, watching it get nearer. I had an instinct to run, thinking it might be Bartholomew. Then the truck stopped short, maybe ten feet from us.

"Not again," Robin said. He put on his bowler hat and stood up.

Remmy stood up on the bench, squinting at the truck before cursing, like he knew who it was.

"Walk over with me, Robin," he said, his lips barely moving. "Keep me from tearing the messenger's fool head off."

❧

185

I didn't know it, but over the past three days, I'd been mastering the ability to handle disappointment. It was the little letdowns—like Lloyd being a murderer and the museum theft stuff—that helped get me ready. Oh, and the circus not being in Albuquerque—that sure was a big blow.

The old me, the *not*-Spartacus me, might have started crying or something.

The old me would have screamed and shouted and stomped and knocked something over. Who was I kidding? The old me would have just given up and gone home.

Well.

The *new* me didn't do any of those things when the next letdown came, when Bartholomew cancelled. Again.

What was the point? It was just toughening me up for future letdowns, right?

~

I listened as Remmy and Robin talked to the truck driver, my nails biting into the wood of the bench. The bench was my cool and I was hanging onto it for dear life. I didn't dare think about what my new plan was going to be. That would have sent me over the edge.

Remmy's constant stream of curse words made it kind of hard to gather the exact details of the conversation, but the basic gist was this: Bartholomew had changed his plans (again) and had, instead, booked a two-day gig in Portland, Oregon, starting tomorrow.

Yep.

Oregon.

Not too far from where I'd started this whole journey.

So I sat very still, hoping to either a) avoid another nervous breakdown, or b) at least get around the corner and away from Zeda before shouting, "You deserve this, Poop Lip! You really, really do!" once again.

"Unbelievable," Robin was saying as they walked back to the tables. Everyone in the sideshow watched them carefully, except

186

Zeda. She was still drawing, pressing the pen so hard on my arm that it hurt. She was, however, the first one to speak up.

"So, I suppose they want us to perform tomorrow and then go to them?"

"Of course they do," Remmy fumed. He spat on the ground.

"This is just so stupid," Zeda muttered under her breath. Only I heard her.

"Well," said Robin, stepping in. He took off his hat and examined its brim. "In lieu of going, Remmy and I could send a message back with the delivery guy—that is, if it's all right with all of you."

Everyone blinked at one another for a moment before Nero stood up.

"I think we should be done with Bartholomew," he said. "I wouldn't care if he *doubled* our pay."

"Me neither!" said the snake lady, standing up.

"Well, if that's how you all feel, let's put it to a vote. Yea or nay?"

There were so many *yeas* that I swore there were fifty people and not just the twenty. Remmy grinned at Robin.

"Then that's it," Robin said. "We're free."

"Tell Bartholomew to find himself a new sideshow!" Remmy shouted to the truck driver, who didn't look like he cared all that much.

"Whatever," he muttered, looking at a clipboard.

Meanwhile, everyone at the tables cheered. Well, except me. I was still willing myself to stay sane.

"We're our own show again! Who needs 'em?" Zeda exclaimed. She jumped up from her seat and hugged Nero, her dad, and then Remmy.

"You'd be better off with us, if you wanted to stay," Nero said to me. "I'm sure Remmy wouldn't mind."

"You *should* stay," Zeda exclaimed, coming over to me. "You'd learn so much more with us. And," she added under her breath, "we're not maniacs." She was still looking at me, grinning, when the driver yelled out:

"What about that animal? You gonna help me load it up or what?"

"Bartholomew is paying you, isn't he?" Remmy bellowed. "You got two arms—use 'em!"

"W-what?!" Zeda sputtered, looking from Remmy to Robin. Her dad just shook his head sadly at her.

"What's happening?" I asked Zeda.

"Bartholomew is going to take Matilda back," she thundered. "That piece of absolute *garbage*." She punched the table. It looked like it hurt.

"What? I thought she was yours?" I said.

"No. She belongs to Bartholomew. But we've always taken care of her. That moron doesn't know how to take care of her. They kept her in this tiny cage and she was all dirty and had fleas and—"

She stopped abruptly and waved her hand. She was too angry to speak.

It almost made me forget all about my problems.

Almost.

Zeda was just about to stomp off, but I grabbed her arm and whispered, "I need to talk to you."

I took her away from the group, where no one could overhear us.

"What's the plan?" she asked, looking hopeful. Even that teeny smile was like a hundred heavy-duty flashlights and I wanted to melt.

No time for melting, Spartacus.

"I need to get on that truck," I said.

"Oh, I thought this was about Matilda," she said, her face falling. "I meant what I was trying to tell you about Bartholomew. He is dangerous. I don't have time to tell you everything he's done, but look—you don't need to get into Bartholomew's. We'll teach you so much more than—"

"I don't want to join the circus," I blurted out. "My mom is with

The Incredible and I think…I think she's there against her will. I'm trying to get her out."

"Your *mom*?" She took a step back. "Who's your mom?"

"Athena," I said. "The—"

"The Human Cannonball!" she gasped, covering her mouth. "Right! Oh my god, you look just like her! She's amazing!" Zeda's face darkened suddenly. "Wait. You're saying she was kidnapped or something?"

"Yeah," I said. "I know it sounds crazy. But trust me. She told me herself."

"Oh, I believe you," she assured me. "It doesn't seem crazy to me. I *know* Bartholomew is a bad guy. I have so much to tell you about him—I just thought we had more time. But you're not just going to be able to waltz in there and get her back."

"I know it's not going to be easy," I said. "But I have a plan."

I told her about how my mom is a contortionist and about my suitcase and cutting into the side of the tent.

"That's all well and good," she said, "But what if you get caught? Bartholomew's insane. Those people are always doing odd things. And they're violent. One time, Finn almost put Nero in the hospital just because he was looking around backstage. My dad thinks they're in a crime ring, but he can't prove it."

"I think he might be right," I said. "And just yesterday, I ran into this woman who looked just like my mom—"

"No way—the *doubles!*" she exclaimed, actually hitting me in the shoulder with her excitement. "I read about that but didn't think it was real! Have you ever seen a website called IHateBartholomewsCircus. com?"

"Of course!" I blurted out. "My friend and I basically memorized it. But that's weird. We never saw any posts about doubles…?"

"It was just up on the site for maybe an hour. I happened to see it pop up and I read it. When I went back to find it, it was gone."

"Like someone deleted it?"

She shrugged. "I assumed it was deleted because it wasn't true."

"And you think the rest of it is?"

"I'm telling you, that circus is *dangerous*. I was about to tell you earlier—once you work for him, you're never allowed to work anywhere else. You're in it for life."

"Like Prizrak," I said in a whisper, remembering what Puck had said.

"You know about him?" Zeda said.

"Yeah, the magician. In the bank vault."

"No, no," said Zeda. "Prizrak was some kind of genius animal trainer, like a lion whisperer or something. It was about five years ago, in Chicago. They found him dead in some rich guy's mansion, in his private safe. He was trying to make friends with some guard dogs, but it didn't work. They tore him to shreds. Everyone knew Bartholomew must have been involved, but nobody could prove it."

I swallowed hard.

Which parts of this story were true? Zeda's version sounded a lot more realistic than the Goth kids' story.

At that moment, Bartholomew's truck driver went walking by us, rolling Matilda's canvas-covered cage behind him.

"Oh, right," she said softly. "Matilda."

We fell silent, watching him. Her eyes started to fill with tears and she looked down, scuffing her foot on the ground.

I had to do something. I just had to.

"Zeda," I said, "if you help me get in that truck, I promise I'll bring Matilda back to you."

"You'd do that?" Zeda asked, her mouth open in shock.

Inside I was thinking, *Uh-oh. What did I just do?*

"Yes," I found myself saying in a voice that didn't sound at all like my own. "I won't let her be another one of Bartholomew's—" I searched for a word—"slaves."

"You're really a hero," she said, and my face got all hot.

She started firing off tips for handling Matilda, but it wasn't until she started saying stuff like "just keep her under your sweatshirt" that I fully understood what I'd promised.

When would I have time to take Matilda back to Zeda? How would I keep track of a lemur when I was doing everything else?

But looking at Zeda looking at me, I didn't even try to take it back. I remembered once Dad told me that girls were trouble, and now I was beginning to think I knew what he meant.

"All right. I'll help you get on the truck if you promise me one more thing," she said.

Uh-oh.

"Promise me that, if you get the chance, you'll take down The Incredible."

"I promise."

And then she kissed me. Like we were in some kind of movie.

It was pretty ridiculous—and pretty incredible.

I was in a daze while I got my backpack and the suitcase. I hadn't wiped off my lips; I was just letting her kiss evaporate into the desert air.

I felt like a poet when I realized that's what I was doing.

Concentrate, Poop Lip. Don't be any more of a twit. It was Will's voice again, and for once I was grateful.

I watched from around the corner of the tent while Zeda got Nero and her dad to help load Matilda's cage into the back of the truck. Then Zeda pretended to cry.

"Please make sure they take care of her," Zeda sobbed, collapsing into the stunned driver. "She's not strong enough for the circus life."

"Hey," said the driver, looking around him for some help. Robin and Nero just looked at him like, *What did you expect?*

Zeda took the driver's arm and dragged him over to Remmy at the tables—*away* from the truck. The coast was clear.

It was my chance.

I tore across the pavement to the truck and jumped in. The narrow opening between the cage and the wall was barely wide enough for my suitcase, but I wedged it in there and crammed myself in after it.

All they had to do was close the back door and I'd be as good as in Portland.

"But she's *endangered!*" I heard Zeda cry out. I wasn't sure if she was acting then or not. I heard something skitter under the canvas and I flinched. Matilda! I still had no clue what she looked like.

Come on, Zeda, you can stop acting now. Let him shut the truck and get me on the road!

Then I heard Zeda's voice, closer now, saying, "No, no. I'll get the back door. I need to tell her good-bye."

I peeked out. Zeda stood at the truck's back door, silhouetted against the fading daylight. She slid a small box across the truck floor toward me.

"Good luck, Spartacus," she whispered, right before slamming the door shut, leaving me in darkness.

Chapter Thirteen

I don't know how I fell asleep wedged in behind the cage, but I must have, because I dreamt I was a kid again, riding in the back of our red wagon. It was one turn, one jolt after another. A dip in the road thumped my head against the wall and I woke up, thinking Will had just pulled my wagon off into a ditch.

I pulled myself out from behind the cage and stood in the dark of the truck, my legs stiff, rubbing the sore spot above my ear where I'd also banged my head against the cage. Headlight beams bounced through the cracks in the door. I didn't have a clue how long I'd been asleep, but when I thought about the distance between Nevada and Oregon, I knew I had a lot longer to go. I pushed a button on my watch and saw it was almost ten at night. We'd been on the road for about two hours.

I groped around in my backpack and found my flashlight. Turning it on, I could see the compartment was rectangular. And it was pretty much empty. The cage stood covered on one end, against the cab of the truck. The small box Zeda had pushed in was on the other end, next to the door.

Zeda!

My heart pounded.

I almost tripped over myself to get to the box. I plopped down on the cold metal floor next to it and tore the box lid off. Inside were a bunch of granola bars, a can of nuts, a bottle of water, a face-painting kit, a book about breathing fire (*Doug the Dragon's Official Guide to Fire Breathing [Without Loss of Life]*), and a compact torch with a small bottle of paraffin (for fire breathing). Finally, there was a small key, a couple of bananas, a large mason jar of cut fruit, and a plastic container filled with—*ew, grubs!* Each was labeled "Matilda."

I'd almost forgotten—I wasn't alone.

The cage waited for me at the other end of the truck, nylon ropes securing it in place. I hadn't noticed before, but the air had that thick, farm-like smell of animal.

Gulp.

I guess I had no choice but to meet Matilda.

I went over to the cage and propped up the flashlight. Then, slowly, I lifted the canvas off one side. I couldn't see anything at first.

"Hey, Matilda," I whispered, getting closer. "It's okay, girl. I've got some fruit." I took a banana out of the box, and held it between the bars.

"Here, Matilda. Looky what I have here…"

I knew that Matilda was a lemur, but I guess I was still picturing a monkey. And when you think about monkeys, you usually think of those cute ones with the long arms, or maybe, if you don't know the difference, you might think about a chimp or a gorilla.

Never, in your strangest dreams, would you expect Matilda.

I'm ashamed to say it, but I actually let out a terrified "AYIEEE!" when she came into the light. Matilda was *not* a chimp or a cuddly monkey. Matilda was this black and gray gremlin-like thing the size of a large cat. She had the pale, whitish face of a blunt-nosed possum, the tail of a squirrel, the ears of a bat, and sparse fur like—I don't know, like a cheap stuffed animal. But her eyes! *My god*, her giant eyes were practically glowing yellow.

"Matilda?" I squeaked. She didn't seem at all alarmed by me—or my scream. She probably got that all the time. In fact, she padded over on four legs before pulling herself up the cage wall until she was eye-level with me. She reached through the bars with a long, slender arm—and I saw it. The finger of death. It was longer than all the rest, as thin as a twig…

And she pointed it right at me.

"She'll point a finger at you and then it's just a matter of time before you're dead," Remmy had said.

I looked at Matilda, who was still pointing at me and twitching her huge ears and her possum nose. Then I realized the truth of what Remmy had said. It was a fact: I would die eventually. But hopefully not for a while.

Besides, she wasn't pointing at me. She was pointing at the banana.

ઍ

It took me a while to go from just tossing the fruit to Matilda to actually handing it to her. I had to get used to her, though—I was going to have to carry her out of the truck.

"Under your sweatshirt," Zeda had said. I shivered. At least she seemed tame enough.

"You're going to be fine—right, Matilda?" I shined the flashlight in her cage and watched her amble back toward the corner, where there was a small log. She tapped at it with her long finger, like she was looking for something. Then she just sat there, looking kind of pathetic. I understood why Zeda felt so bad for her.

I took out the book on fire breathing and read sitting next to the cage. I read it through twice before checking my watch. Nearly midnight. I had no clue when we'd get to Portland, but I figured I had time to get some sleep.

I put the canvas back the way it had been in case the driver looked in while I was sleeping. Then I ate a granola bar and drank some water. I hate to say it, but I relieved myself in the corner of the truck near the door. I didn't have much of a choice. At least the pee seemed to trickle out the back door.

I set the box off to the side and wedged myself back behind the cage. I wished I knew how long the drive would take, but all I could figure was that it took nine hours to get from Albuquerque to Las Vegas, and Portland had to be at least twice as far.

ઍ

I'd burrowed into the canvas next to the cage and must have

slept for eight hours straight before I woke up with a jolt. We weren't moving, but there was no way we were there yet, either. The driver was talking on his phone, right outside the back of the truck. "Keith? Yeah, it's me. Just crossed into Oregon. This drive is killing me. Yeah, I'm busting my balls to get there. This is such a waste of my time. They should have just bought the stupid animal a plane ticket."

There was a pause. Then,

"How big is it? It's, well, it's huge. Looks like a tall goat."

Like a goat? I frowned.

"*Oh*, the cage. Let me go measure it."

My blood ran cold. He was going to find me. I felt completely exposed, even from my spot behind the cage. I pressed myself further into the corner as the door trundled up, letting the morning light shine in.

"Yeah, yeah, I'm getting out my tape measure. *Geez*, it smells back here."

I held my breath, waiting for the sound of him climbing in the back, but it didn't come. I did hear the measuring tape hitting the ground outside.

"Yeah, I'd say it's…five feet by…four feet…by four feet."

What? Was he just making it up?

I didn't dare look—and apparently, he didn't either. At Matilda, that is.

He was scared of Matilda, so he was just making it up!

"You got that? Good. Well, *yeah*, she was pointing her stupid hoof at me the whole time, but I don't give a crap. So, I'll be about five more hours…Yeah, this should be a cinch compared to last time. Silverware's a lot easier to haul than paintings, that's for sure."

What had he said? *Silverware's a lot easier to haul than…? Paintings!*

"Well, Bart's gotta do some of his own legwork. It was too close last time. Yeah, well that's a bunch of bull—" The slam of the truck door cut off the rest.

I would have bet *anything* that they were talking about the

Georgia O'Keeffe paintings they had stolen in Santa Fe. If I hadn't had enough proof already, this conversation sure sealed the deal. I wasn't imagining it all. But what was that about silverware?

The truck came to life and started moving again.

I leaned back on my backpack, and, try as I might to think about the robberies, I began thinking about the sideshow.

Okay, I thought about Zeda.

She actually kissed me.

That's when I remembered the tattoo she'd been drawing—I hadn't even had a chance to look at it! I got out the flashlight, shined it on my arm, and grinned. She'd drawn a lion, shouldering his way through flames, with *Spartacus* written on a waving banner beneath it. I sighed just looking at it. It really was cool.

After I'd stared at the tattoo long enough, I started to get my stuff together. I emptied out my backpack and separated the things I'd need from the stuff I could get rid of. I couldn't believe I'd packed so much useless—and heavy—junk. Will's scout handbook, for example. Sure, it explained how to make knots and eat off the land and store water, but why did I think I was going to need that?

Sure, just steal my stuff, Poopy. It was Will's voice, threatening me. *I'll get even sooner or later.*

Maybe I *did* need to learn something from the book. Like, how to barricade a bedroom door.

As I thumbed through it, a thick piece of paper came loose and fell into my lap.

It was a blank postcard.

&

I shook Will's book, and five more blank postcards slipped out. They were all from different places, places with weird names. Dynamite, Washington; Stop, Arkansas; Asylum, Pennsylvania; Covert, New York; Murder Bay, D.C.; Hazard, Nebraska.

No. It wasn't possible.

I flipped the cards over, scanning them quickly. On the back of one card, dated ahead for mid-July, there was this message:

Hello, Spartacus!
Wwell! Everythhing is going greeat out herre on thee roaad. Had a grreeat crowd on the fourth of Julyy—so many peoople! Tell Will hi and give youur dad a hug, ok??
Love,
Mom

It was a really simple code. All you had to do was read the doubled letters to spell, "Where are you?" As in, why haven't I come to rescue her yet, I guess.

But the messages didn't matter anymore. I stared at the cards. There was only one explanation for them: Will had sent me the postcards—the ones I thought Mom was sending to ask for help.

No. No. No.

"No!" I finally growled through gritted teeth.

I was beyond seething. Beyond rage. Those words don't begin to describe what I felt. Even "seething, white-hot rage" doesn't cut it. I was so angry, *I was seeing through time.*

Mom hadn't been kidnapped at all! And Will was—well, Will was the most hateful, rotten, arrogant, gutless, goat-faced, moronic, maggot-infested garbage pile to ever ooze across the face of the earth.

Sometimes I wished there were better words.

It was probably a good thing I was trapped in the back of that truck. If I'd had any room to move or stuff to throw, I would have started destroying things—like my fists, trying to punch a building over.

"*Where are you?*" I spat out, repeating Will's secret postcard message. *Oh, Will, just you wait. I'll be there soon enough.*

In my mind, I was already home and in Will's room destroying every single trophy in the World of Fartcraft with a sledgehammer. I was shredding the sports posters that plastered his walls. I was ripping his mattress apart with my bare hands. See a common theme here? Destruction. I wasn't Poop Lip anymore. I wasn't Ryan. I wasn't even Spartacus. I was The Destroyer.

Yeah, "seething rage" doesn't quite cover all that.

I stomped around in the back of the truck, making up new curse words and fantasizing about which of Will's prized possessions I'd break first. When I added it all up, the day-to-day crap, the swimming pool trick, and now *this*? I mean, what was *wrong* with him?

I took a deep breath. Then another. Trying to clear my head. Trying to think.

Breathe. Instant Calm Breath Method.

Breathe in for four counts. Hold it for four. Breathe out for four…

Forget about Will for a minute, Spartacus. Just think about what this means for the plan.

⤳

I already talked about how my mom was always doing odd things. There was the jumping off the roof, of course. And the time I found her karate-chopping boards in half in the garage. And the time she practiced kickboxing with a mannequin she got from the mall.

It wasn't until after she showed me her audition video, about a year before she disappeared, that she opened up to me. One day I came home to find her throwing knives at a dartboard in the backyard. She was going to stop, but I convinced her not just to keep going, but to teach me as well.

We spent the next few hours throwing knives. She showed me how to hold them so I wouldn't hurt myself, how to feel the weight of the knife, how to fling it with just the right amount of spin. Then Will and Dad got home. Dad discovered us in the yard and hollered at Mom and we had to stop. That's how a lot of our time together ended.

I wasn't good at knife throwing that day, but despite Dad forbidding it, I practiced on my own in secret and got a lot better. I decided to surprise her, to show her I had a crazy side, too. I got a couple of library books on it and read about it online. Then, I practiced using our steak knives and the side of the shed. After a few months of chucking knives, I finally felt ready to show Mom what I could do.

And I've already explained how Mom could be weird sometimes. But there was more than knife-throwing weird or elk-riding weird; those was okay with me. But weird like—well, let me explain.

Ever since the accident, she had these headaches that kept her in bed for days. Other times, she wouldn't sleep at all. Sometimes, she said, the ringing in her ears was too loud to hear anything. When she was having one of these "spells," Mom was irritated and just wanted to be alone.

She was smack dab in the middle of one of these episodes when I said I wanted to show her something. I don't know why I asked her then—maybe I thought it would cheer her up. She had a migraine, but still agreed to come out back with me.

Mom stood there in her robe with her arms crossed while I pinned my target to the shed—a shark photo from National Geographic (which is funny, when I think about it now). I stepped ten paces away from it. Then I did Mom's Instant Calm Breath Method to ready myself for the throw. I pulled back the knife, aimed, and let it fly.

It stuck right in the shark's forehead.

"Splendid spin," she breathed. "Impressive."

I'd definitely chosen the wrong time to show her, because that's *all* she said. Then, she patted me on the back, and turned to go inside. But I couldn't let her just go back in. I needed to ask her something. I felt like I'd *earned* the right to ask her this—maybe that's why I'd been working on the knife throwing all along.

"What happens if you get into the circus?" I blurted out, my words almost running together.

She turned back to me and smiled weakly.

"Well, it's not easy to get in. It's a long shot for me to make it. I don't think I'm ready yet."

She didn't get what I was asking, so I said what I meant: "Will we get to see you?"'"

Her eyes went bright for that moment, like she was really there with me and not thinking about her bed.

"Of course you'd get to see me, Spartacus," she said, looking at me. Her voice was soft, but clear. "You'd see me a lot. And I'd come and see you. We'd still be together. I promise."

She even put her hand on my shoulder and squeezed it before turning to go back inside.

But that's what she said: "I promise."

And she had never broken a promise.

What I'm trying to say is this: My mom was bizarre. That's pretty clear by now, I guess. Maybe it was because of the car accident. Maybe it was a midlife crisis. Maybe she'd always been that way. Who knows? But whatever she was, she cared about me. And she wasn't a liar. Something must have been really wrong for her to break her promise.

So *that's* why I had to keep going, no matter what.

Even if Mom hadn't been asking for my help. Even if the postcards weren't true. Even if there had been no destroyed house, no Black Van, no Not-Mom. Even if Bartholomew *hadn't* been involved in robbing museums. I knew, beyond a shadow of a doubt, that Mom would have visited me and Will if she could.

So what did Will's prank with the postcards change?

Absolutely nothing.

I still had to make sure my mom was okay.

When I was calm again, I lifted the canvas on the cage and fed Matilda some grubs (all I can say is *Ewwww*). After she finished eating, she lay down against the bars with her body warm against my thigh. I sat there and petted her surprisingly soft fur, trying to clear my mind. As mad as I was, I couldn't afford to spend all my energy plotting against Will. I needed to focus on what was coming up, what

I was about to face in Portland. Bartholomew was today. Will could wait until tomorrow.

So there in the dark, I tried my best to sit still and meditate like a monk. As I concentrated, my plan began evolving, improving. When the final idea came, though, it gave me a rush of chills. I was almost too scared to even think about it, but as I tentatively turned the thought over and over again in my mind, I realized it was fairly airtight. That, and it meshed perfectly with my reckless mood.

It was good. This new plan just might work.

&

By four in the afternoon, it was time to put my plan into action—and I was more than ready to get out of that hot, stinking truck. We might arrive in Portland at any time, and when I got out of the truck, I'd have to hit the ground running. Literally.

With that in mind, I decided to leave the suitcase behind. It would just slow me down and make me look even more suspicious—besides, I had another way to get Mom out.

The first thing I had to do was use Nero's face paint to cover the freckle on my lip. It wasn't a "disguise," but it would help. Next, I gathered everything I was going to keep with me and stuffed it into the side pockets of my backpack. I left the main part empty so there would be a nice, big-ish place for Matilda.

Yep, I thought to myself with self-loathing. *Just gonna carry a wild animal in my backpack. Brilliant, Poopy.*

Apparently, in my darkest moments, I still thought of myself as Poop Lip.

Okay, this *wasn't* the best plan. First of all, Matilda was an endangered species. How many aye-ayes did Zeda say were even left? Like, a thousand? What if I squished her in the bag or something? But with how she looked—patchy fur and giant yellow eyes—well, I couldn't just carry her around in public.

"I bet you have a great personality, though," I said. Matilda blinked shyly, the flashlight's beam making her delicate, crinkly black ears glow pinkish. She reached out with her long finger and touched the door latch, her whiskers quivering.

Think about Zeda. You're doing this for Zeda.

Before I lost my nerve, I fished Zeda's key out of my pocket and flung open the cage door. Matilda didn't hesitate either—she scrambled right up my pant leg and into my arms.

I cringed as she sniffed my face with her damp, pug nose. "You're—you're just like a slow-moving cat, aren't you?" I said, trying to make myself feel better.

After that, Matilda and I sat in the dark, the backpack open in front of us. I ate the last two granola bars and gave some water to Matilda, who slurped it straight from the bottle.

That's when the truck started to slow down. I put a mildly annoyed Matilda in the backpack (after distracting her with some more grubs), and got into position.

Chapter Fourteen

The look on the driver's face when I burst out from the truck, screaming, "*Yahhhh!*"?

Priceless.

I streaked off like a madman through a parking lot filled with midnight blue trucks. Printed on each of them, in red, curvy letters, was *Bartholomew's World-Renowned Circus of The Incredible.*

There was no mistake—I was *finally* in the right place!

But I didn't slow down. I ran and ran. I ran until the circus was out of sight. When I finally ran out of gas, I was in a park next to a river.

"*Yesss!*" I whispered out loud. I was so proud of myself. I was panting and slowed to a speed walk, feeling more than a little cocky. That is, until I saw a poster with my face on it, stuck to a lamppost. Then another one.

Not good.

I immediately tore down the Missing Child fliers and stuffed them in a trashcan.

I don't know how the fact that I was still a missing kid had slipped my mind—I'd only been worried about Bartholomew catching me— how was I going to do this if everyone *else* was looking for me, too? All my nervousness came flooding back. I yanked Will's baseball hat further down on my head and looked away from people as we passed.

I saw another Missing sign, this one inside a shop window. Guilt washed over me. I'd probably messed up Dad's whole week—and yes, even worried him—but I had to push that feeling away. If everything played out according to plan, I'd be forgiven in just a few hours. Mom would be home and Bartholomew's secret would be uncovered for everyone to see. I took in a shaky breath and kept going.

The park curved with the river and I walked until I could look back and see the circus. It was set up right at the edge of the park, with the sprawling blue and red tent backed up against the water. It looked just like the picture from Bartholomew's website.

It's funny; I knew I would catch up to the circus at some point, but I didn't imagine how it would feel, seeing it in real life. I thought I'd feel a little bit of amazement, but all I could feel was anger.

I couldn't watch very long, though—by now, the guy from the truck must have told everyone about the screaming kid jumping out at him, not to mention the missing animal. I needed to get out of the area for a bit.

As if reading my mind, Matilda started scritching around inside the backpack. I reached back and absentmindedly patted the bag, hoping she wasn't getting too rattled around in there. But my mind was racing. Would Bartholomew's people connect me with Matilda? Maybe, if Not-Mom and Sharkman had told Bartholomew about our run-in in Albuquerque.

Don't think about it, I told myself. *You can't change what Bartholomew might or might not know. Not now.*

But I still didn't have a good grasp on what I was going to do with Matilda once I was inside the circus—not to mention during the rescue.

And why did you promise this again?

Well, I knew why. Zeda. Now I had to deal with it. Sure, Matilda was a small hiccup in The Plan—a tiny, balding wildcard. But the rest? I had the rest figured out.

&

Portland is five hours away from Brenville—and they are about as different as they could be. Portland has skyscrapers and green parks and seems to sprawl forever. Will and I had been to Portland a few times with Mom. Dad hated the city and never went, but Mom loved it. She would take us to these hole-in-the-wall places to eat noodles, to renovated warehouses to buy stacks of used books, or to outdoor markets to hunt down bargain hula-hoops and old trunks and other used junk.

"Treasures," Mom would always correct me.

The park was downtown and ran along the river that went right through the city—in fact, Mom, Will, and I had gone to a carnival in this same park the year before. The carnival hadn't been anything big like Bartholomew's, just a few rides and live music and fair food. Will and I had shared an elephant ear and I threw up on The Zipper.

That was the last time we took a trip together—and the last time we'd left Brenville since Mom disappeared. I sighed. Dad must have been pretty depressed with Mom gone. He hadn't done much of anything since she left—we didn't even get a Christmas tree.

I thought I remembered Mom taking us to a big library downtown. I was in luck—I found a huge tourist map mounted on a lamppost and it showed the Central Library only a few blocks away. I made my way down the busy streets to the huge brick building with an arched entryway, and not one person recognized me from the posters.

Once inside, I found a computer that someone hadn't logged off of and sat down, propping the backpack gingerly at my feet. Matilda was still calm as a clam in there, moving around a little bit, but not making any noise. I hoped she'd stay that way. I didn't want this library trip to end the way the last one had.

I checked my email and saw that Eli wasn't online. There were two emails from him, though. I opened the newest one first. It was from that morning. A small wave of panic came over me when I read it.

Joe: They got to me. They only know about Las Vegas. Don't contact me—I can't blab what I don't know. Sorry and good luck.
– Peter Parker

I resisted the urge to email him back. Eli was right. If he didn't know where I was, he couldn't spill the beans. But poor Eli! I felt terrible. Helping me run away was pretty much the worst thing he'd ever done, and his parents weren't the type to punish with grounding or no TV or something. Instead, they might make him do something horrible like read some old, seven-hundred-page novel and write a report on it. His summer was basically ruined.

But I couldn't dwell on it there in the library. Sure, not having a moment of silence or something felt cruel, but James Bond wouldn't abandon the mission over something like this. Eli was what James Bond would call *collateral damage*. Eli would be okay—but I'd have to be extra nice to him when I got back. And besides—once it ended, we'd be heroes.

At least they didn't know I was in Portland.

Except...

Except if Eli told them I was following the circus, it wouldn't be too hard to track me down. Even though Bart's website didn't have the Portland performance listed, it would just take a quick internet search to bring it up, the way Eli had.

That's when it hit me: it was tonight or never.

My heart pounded as I opened the second message from Eli.

Joe: Probable cause to abort mission. Open forwarded email.

– Peter Parker

I scrolled down and found an email from Will attached. It was from yesterday.

Dear Eli,

I know you're at camp but I'm sure you know Ryan went missing on Friday night. I know you think I'm a jerk, but I need to ask you if you're helping Ryan. If you're in touch with him, please let him know that I wrote all the postcards from Mom, saying she was kidnapped. I didn't know I'd gone too far until he was gone. Please tell him I'm sorry and ask him to come home.

– Will

The first thing that came to mind was, *Wow, he must feel terrible.*

The second was, *Good.*

I hadn't run away to make Will sorry, but maybe an *eensy* bit of me hoped he would be—and that was even before I found out about

207

the postcards. Then an evil smile spread across my face, wide and bright. Man, he was going to be in *so* much trouble when Dad found out.

Now *that* was something to look forward to.

Next, I did a search for "Portland Bartholomew Incredible" and found a news blurb about it right away. The show started at eight p.m. That was just two hours away. Then I remembered what Bartholomew's truck's driver had said about silverware. I typed in "Portland Oregon silverware museum." The first result: The Portland Art Museum. I clicked on it. Oldest art museum in the area, blah, blah, blah...and...*Ah-ha!*

Bingo.

Just a month ago, the museum had received a gift from an anonymous donor—an extensive collection of European silverware from the 1500s.

One of the few collections of its kind. Sounded like a pretty boring thing to steal—not nearly as impressive as the streetcar or the dinosaur bones. But it did sound like it would be worth a lot of money. Not only that, the museum was only a few blocks away—within easy reach of the circus.

This is *it*, I thought. I'd found Bartholomew's target.

I scrolled through the pictures of the silverware collection, feeling weird—guilty, even—for looking, knowing it was about to be stolen. It wasn't hard to imagine Mom rappelling down from the roof and swinging through one of the windows.

I stopped, mid-thought, and shook my head. Nothing was going to be stolen. Mom would be there with *me*. And Bartholomew would be at the police station.

Anyway, it was time for the next part of The Plan. The dangerous part.

I carefully shouldered my backpack and then hurried over to the payphone I'd spotted in the library lobby. I pulled a slip of paper out of my pocket, pumped a couple quarters in the slot, took a deep breath, and dialed the number on it.

"Be brave," I told myself, even though my hand had already started sweating.

It rang twice—and then came the answer.

"Lloyd here."

ॐ

I opened my mouth and nothing came out. Just hearing Lloyd's voice made my heart race and my hands go clammy.

Remember. He's not a *serial* killer—just a *regular* killer.

Somehow Hailey's words of wisdom didn't relax me.

He spoke again, "Hello?"

Say something!

"Hey, Lloyd! It's…it's Ry—it's, uh, it's Spartacus," I finally forced out. I couldn't even remember which fake name Eli had given him.

"Spartacus!" he roared (happily?). "How are you?"

"Okay. Well, uh," I stammered before saying all in a rush, "I remembered you said you lived in Portland. Well, uh, my mom's show—I mean, The Incredible is in town tonight and I—"

"No way!" he whooped into the phone. "You didn't tell me that before."

"Well, yeah," I said, picking at a taxi advertisement sticker on the wall. I didn't know what to say. "They change their plans a lot. It's hard to tell where they're going next."

Half lie, half truth.

"That's good news," Lloyd said. "You seemed kinda down before. I hope everything's okay."

I nodded into the phone. "Oh, yeah, everything's fine. I wanted to—well, I wanted to see if, well…" I trailed off. This was worse than asking a girl out. Not that I'd ever actually done that. "Would you want to go? I mean, you said you really liked the circus."

All true, so it was easy to say. So far so good.

"Well, absolutely! Did you want to meet up for dinner beforehand?" he asked.

"Uh, no! No, this is kind of last minute. It actually starts pretty soon—at eight p.m. I'll just meet you in front, huh?"

I put my hand up to my face. My voice was almost shaking as we confirmed the details—we were going to meet at the ticket booth at seven forty-five.

Okay, so you probably want to know why I invited Lloyd the Killer to the circus.

The way I saw it, I couldn't just sneak Mom out like I'd originally planned. I'd left behind the suitcase, and The Incredible was too big, too organized for that kind of child's play, anyway. Plus, they might know I was coming. What I needed was chaos. What I needed was a diversion—a big, bald, scary diversion.

That's where Lloyd came in.

My plan went like this:

First off, if Bartholomew was looking for me, he'd be looking for a kid who was alone, so I'd use Lloyd to help me blend in—and maybe even use him as muscle, just in case. If Lloyd turned on anyone, I wanted to believe he might protect me from Bartholomew. It was kind of like having a wild dog on a leash.

I'd sit with Lloyd for the first half of the show, then slip away to call the cops at intermission—apparently, kidnapped mothers weren't enough to get attention, but maybe an FBI's most-wanted murderer *was*. Most importantly, I wanted them to arrive before the end of the show. As the ringmaster, Bartholomew would be so busy, he wouldn't see it coming—and he couldn't slip away.

After calling, I'd sneak backstage to find Mom and let her know that cops were coming—maybe even the SWAT team (Lloyd was an incredibly dangerous fugitive, after all). So as the cops closed in on Lloyd, I predicted that Bartholomew would think they were coming for him, and chaos would break loose. With cops all over the place, Mom and I could escape with one of them to safety. Once out of harm's way, Mom could tell the cops about Bartholomew—the kidnapping, the stolen artwork, and whatever else he's been up to.

The cops would arrest Bartholomew, and throw him into the back of a squad car, right beside Lloyd.

Simple, really.

Okay, so maybe it wasn't *ideal*. Everything had to go just right—and I had to explain the lemur in my backpack to the wanted felon I was about to betray—and explaining the lemur was going to be the easiest part.

So, yeah, I wouldn't say that the plan was *flawless*. I'd said such things before and been very wrong. But even though I was terrified by all the dangerous wheels I was setting into motion, it was what I had to do.

And besides, what had Lloyd said before? *Fortune favors the bold?*

If anything, my plan was bold.

❧

Before leaving the library, I ducked into an empty bathroom—luckily it was private, with its own room and door.

I opened the backpack to let Matilda out for a minute—but she just yawned and then winked sleepily at me from the bottom of the bag.

"Come on, lazy," I said, nudging her. "It's a rest stop." I even tried coaxing her with a piece of watermelon, but she only sniffed it and then closed her eyes again.

"Suit yourself," I said, giving her a light pat. I just hoped she'd stay this calm once we were inside the circus. If she started making noises or moving around too much, she could blow my whole plan. But Zeda *had* said she was nocturnal. Maybe that would help me out.

Next, I changed into my dark suit and tie. When Eli and I had planned this out, he'd thought I'd blend in better backstage if I dressed nicely. I'd initially thought it was stupid, but I'd seen it work when I sneaked into the sideshow.

Next, I put my pocketknife and screwdriver set in one jacket pocket, and the small torch and bottle of paraffin in the other. Finally, I touched up my freckle with beige face paint. It was funny

211

how much that freckle made me who I was—without it, I didn't look like me at all. I could have been anybody.

As I buttoned my cuffs, smoothed my hair, and straightened my clip-on tie in the mirror, I felt very James Bond. Very Secret Agent Man.

I practiced my scowl in the mirror.

Not bad, Spartacus. A few more bruises and cuts and you'll look like an action hero.

I checked inside the bag, where Matilda was snoozing. She was even making a little nose whistle, and she didn't seem to notice me zipping the bag closed on her.

"It'll just be a few hours," I whispered. "I promise."

ॐ

I wanted a chance to case the joint and plot all the major escape routes, so I got to the circus about an hour before I had to meet Lloyd. It was buzzing with activity, with the action spilling out into the park. Kids were everywhere. Most of them were trying to get a look beyond the waist-high fence that kept them back.

I hoped I would blend in, but I was older than all of them and taller by a foot—that, and I was wearing a suit. That was starting to seem like a bad idea. The suit might help me blend in when I got backstage, but it wasn't helping me out front. I even saw a lady nudge her friend and secretly point at me.

Just stay confident, I told myself. *They don't know who you are. Maybe you're the kid of some rich family.*

So I kept staring straight ahead, ignoring everyone. Inside the fence, men and women in dark blue shirts bustled in and out of booths stocked with food and souvenirs and kids' stuff, like face-painting and balloon animals. I wondered if they were in on the robberies too, or just a few chosen henchmen. I studied them for a bit, but no one looked particularly sinister. Then I walked the length of the tent, hoping to get a glimpse of the side that faced the river.

I'd just reached the far end of the low fence when I saw them: Bartholomew's giant tour buses, just rolling in.

"No way," I said, under my breath.

I mean, I knew Bartholomew was an upscale circus, but *tour buses?* They looked like something movie stars would travel in. They were painted with giant, vibrant murals of tumblers, trapeze artists, magicians, tightrope walkers, contortionists, lions, tigers, elephants— all in shades of bright green, red, and orange, and all larger than life.

As the buses pulled in beside the tent, a flood of cheering kids surrounded me, chattering excitedly and pointing. I stood there, heads above them all, scowling, knowing how Bart paid for those buses. Dirty money. And what if what Puck and Zeda said was true, that the performers were stuck in the circus for life? There were probably bars behind those painted windows.

I snorted and shook my head at the horribleness of it all. Three girls, a little bit younger than me, stood beside me watching the vans. One turned when I snorted.

"It's all fake," I blurted out to them. She and her friends giggled, and I looked back at the buses, my face burning red. They didn't care if the circus was evil or not—they just wanted to be entertained. It wasn't their fault.

That's when the last bus pulled in. I knew it was hers, without even reading the side of it. But there it was, in scrolling red letters: *The Amazing Athena.*

The mural was a close-up of her face. They'd painted her to look like a superhero, in deep blues and reds and a crown of stars, with her black hair changing into rolling hills, and camels and elephants walking along her dark locks. When the bus turned, I saw the other side. She stood next to a white cannon, a helmet under her arm and a wall of flames behind her.

"Holy moly," I said under my breath.

I hate to admit it, but it's true: there was the teeniest grin on my face. Even though Bartholomew's was a front for a crime ring, even though my mom and all her fellow performers were basically kidnapped—Mom was still the star. I knew she was amazing. She'd be able to leave Bartholomew's and find a better circus. She had all the potential in the world—if she could only get free.

We're almost there, Mom.

I heard the girls beside me whispering. I turned to see them staring at me. Wide-eyed.

"Um, your backpack is moving," said one of them.

Matilda!

And it was. I could feel the lemur digging into the canvas like she was trying to escape.

"Oh," was all I said before turning on my heel and speeding back toward the park.

"Hang in there, Matilda," I said, reaching back and patting the side of the bag. The pressure of my hand seemed to calm her and I slowed down.

I checked my watch. I had thirty more minutes until I had to meet Lloyd. I felt that familiar panic rising in my chest.

Breathe, Spartacus.

Lloyd wasn't going to kill me. Not in front of all these people. All these people who kept glancing over at me. People who had seen the Missing Child posters...

As I watched the ticket line form, my fear flip-flopped between Lloyd and Bartholomew and being a runaway. I started to feel extremely—well, conspicuous. Could I really get inside the circus without Bartholomew's people or anyone else recognizing me?

If only I had a mask...

That's when I got the idea.

৵

It wasn't hard to find a port-o-potty. Taking a deep breath, I went inside. It was hot and smelly, but it would have to do. When I opened the backpack, Matilda darted out and clung to my waist, suddenly looking a lot more alert—and nervous—than she'd been before.

"Easy, Matilda," I said, handing over a banana and then petting her, which seemed to calm her—but she didn't climb down. So, with Matilda hanging on me, I put the toilet seat down and got out my face painting kit. Using the plastic mirror on the port-o-potty door, I painted my entire face with flames. It wasn't perfect, but it was good enough. I stepped back and admired my work in the mirror.

Not too shabby.

And it wasn't. Not only would I blend in a bit more with all of the rest of the kids (suit aside, of course), but no one would recognize me as Ryan the Runaway, or Spartacus, Son of Athena. I hardly recognized myself in the scratched-up mirror.

"Pleased to meet you," I said stoically to my reflection before laughing. I didn't know how to introduce myself anymore.

I'm Ryan. Poop Lip. Spartacus. Guess my name.

I continued thinking about Lloyd as I put Matilda back in the bag (and she was not as easygoing this time). What was that movie quotation Lloyd had told me again? Someone asks Spartacus if he is afraid to die, and he says something like, *Not any more than I was afraid to be born.*

Sure, freeing some circus folk wasn't exactly the same as leading a slave revolt or anything, but I was still afraid. As I straightened up, I checked my face paint in the mirror one last time.

"How about it, Spartacus? Are you afraid to die?" I asked myself. And suddenly, saying the name out loud, I felt it. I mean, I really felt that name *meant* something. I looked myself in the eyes, trying to decide how it felt to be Spartacus.

Was I still scared? Yes.

"But no more than I was to be born," I quoted. And I meant it. I think.

❧

When I stepped out of the stinky, hot port-o-potty, it was seven-forty.

Here we go.

The park was now crawling with families and the ticket line snaked all the way down the street. Babies cried and kids played in the grass. A clown on stilts stood by the road, holding a sign upside down that said *Circus Tonight!* Some kids threw dandelions at him.

I knew I'd made a good choice with the face paint—almost every face under ten years old had been painted like some sort of animal or other. My flames were by far the coolest, which helped make up for the fact that I was obviously too old for face paint.

I hadn't ventured very far into the crowd when I felt Matilda moving again. Like before, only more frantic.

Uh-oh.

Suddenly, my hope that Matilda would stay calm during the show seemed incredibly stupid. I mean, the success of my entire plan depended on the mood of a monkey-thing. If she gave me away, I was toast. As if to illustrate my point, she chose that very moment to release a series of short, unhappy screeches. And people definitely noticed. Two little kids stared, mouths open. A man, lugging a whining toddler, paused to listen to the noise.

Crap. Crap. Crap.

I ducked behind a funnel-cake stand, away from the people. Despite the crowds, our little spot was out of sight. Retreating as far behind the booth as I could, I shrugged off the backpack, hoping Matilda was just bored and not, well, angry. I got out an apple slice, hoping it would calm her down.

"Hey, Lemur, what's happening—"

I never got to the last part of that question.

I'd unzipped the pack the tiniest fraction of an inch when she burst out like she'd been shot out of a cannon. In two seconds, she'd raced up my arm, leaped off my head, and scrambled up the funnel cake stand.

Oh, man. I smacked my forehead. She was so quick, I never saw it coming!

I watched as she scampered up a wooden pole, about twenty feet above me. She'd been so slow and calm before! I never even thought about what to do if she tried to escape. Why hadn't Zeda warned me? *Just carry her in your sweatshirt!* Great idea.

"Matilda!" I hissed, but she didn't even blink.

How was I going to get Matilda back to Zeda now? I was crazy to have made that promise. I'd probably just doomed Matilda to her death, being loose in this park in the city.

"Matilda!" I spoke louder. Still no reaction. She just looked down at me, serene as can be.

I held out the apple, hoping to tempt her, but nothing. The thought of calling Zeda, and how her voice would sound when I told her what happened...well, the thought actually hurt.

"Matilda!" I finally shouted. Matilda tapped the wooden pole, then casually licked a bug off her finger.

I stood there, panicked. I was already late to meet Lloyd. I didn't know what to do. Then I remembered Mom pressing her forehead to mine. I had to go.

"I'm so sorry, Matilda," I whispered, deciding. "I'll come back. I promise. I won't leave you for too long."

I put apple slices on the grass and wondered if she would stay where she was or if she would accidentally scramble out into traffic before I could come back?

I had no idea. I sighed heavily.

Coming out from behind the booth, I made a mental note where I was. After the circus. Maybe she'll still be here after the circus...

I was still looking up at her when I heard it.

"Spartacus!"

I turned to see who was calling my name, even though I knew who it had to be. There he was, looking twice as big as I'd remembered. Lloyd Lloeke (a.k.a. Dan Lloeke, a.k.a. "The Cue") strode directly toward me.

Chapter Fifteen

Spartacus!" Lloyd's voice boomed over the squawking children. "Whatcha looking at up there? A squirrel?"

"Oh, hi," I said, surprised again just by the sheer size of him. I turned away from the funnel cake stand, hoping he wouldn't keep looking up there. "Uh, yeah, big squirrel up there."

"Huh. Well! It's good to see you again!" he said, giving me a hearty pat on my back. "Great face paint. And that suit again. Very dapper."

"Er, thanks." He must have mistaken the look of terror on my face for simple surprise, because he kept grinning.

"Mom, this is the boy I was telling you about. Spartacus, this is my mother, Beverly." He was gesturing to an elderly woman standing beside him and my throat tightened.

His mother? Why did he bring his mother?

"Nice to meet you," said the small, elegant woman, offering me a bejeweled hand. I shook it, trying to hide my shock behind a nervous smile.

"We were about to head to a movie when you called," Lloyd explained.

I nodded, but it didn't answer my larger question: Could I still use him as a diversion in front of his mother? Have him arrested in front of his pink-cheeked, smiley, elderly mother?

Without hesitation, I knew the answer. *Yes. Yes I could.*

I was a horrible person.

"So..." I said, trying to smile a real smile. "How's everything? How was Boise?"

"Good, yes. The lecture went well. But, more importantly, how are *you?* I mean, after the funeral and all?" He seemed so genuine—

218

not at all what you'd expect from a murderous fugitive. I wondered if his mom knew he was a killer?

"Doing good," I answered shakily. We got in line and Lloyd looked around us in a searching way. Was he looking for cops?

"You here with your dad and that bully older brother you told me about?"

"Nah, they couldn't make it," I shook my head. "I mean, they're coming late," I added. I didn't want him to think I was here by myself. "We had some…some family stuff, you know, come up."

"Nothing bad, I hope," Beverly said.

"No, no, nothing bad," I said. We'd reached the ticket booth and as I reached for my wallet, Lloyd pushed in ahead of me.

"Hey, don't worry, I got it," he said, handing money over my shoulder to the ticket seller, who had tattoos of spiders on her face. I don't know if I imagined it, but it seemed like she was staring at me as she pushed us our tickets.

"Be sure to switch your phones off and place them in your pocket or purse before entering the tent," she said sternly. "Any phones seen inside the show will be confiscated and they will not be returned."

So that *explains why there aren't any photos from inside the tent.*

"How will I live Tweet this without my phone?" Lloyd joked, fiddling with his phone.

"Enjoy the show, folks," she said blankly, ignoring Lloyd.

"Thanks for the ticket," I said to Lloyd.

"No problem," he said, gesturing to his mom and me to go in ahead of him. *He really doesn't seem like a murderer,* I thought for the umpteenth time. He was just so…*nice.* Not that that's any reason to trust someone. But still.

"Lloyd tells me he gave you a ride on his bike from Sisters to Boise. Is that right?" Beverly asked. We were walking up a long, curving ramp in a dark hallway that led around the outside ring of the tent. Red glowing markers on the floor pointed the way. "Is that where you're from?"

"Yeah," I said absentmindedly, trying to concentrate on how the tent was laid out. There were more concession stands all along the front area—popcorn, corndogs, nachos.

"I love Sisters," she was saying. "Lloyd took me there once—it was such a treat!"

"You go hiking often?" Lloyd was asking.

"What? Oh, sure. The whole family does," I said. I didn't know what I was talking about.

We followed the curved enclosure for a little way before finding our entrance. At the top of a short flight of metal stairs, we met the big top.

It was like stepping into a kaleidoscope: bright red, indigo, and grass-green curtains draped the walls while hidden, pulsating lights made all the colors swirl together before my eyes. A strange, pink fog rolled across the stage in waves, drifting into the front rows. A light in the rafters made stars circle above us. Even though there was music swelling and the audience was bubbling with chatter, it all felt so silent in my head that I held my breath.

I had arrived. I was really there.

"This is impressive," Lloyd said.

He didn't have to tell me.

Bartholomew had turned the inside of the tent into an exotic place. Most circuses I'd seen in movies had a middle area surrounded on all sides by the audience. Bartholomew's was set up differently, though, with the three rings near the back of the tent, and the audience seated in a half-circle, facing the rings. That meant there was a whole backstage area we couldn't see—which is exactly where I needed to go when intermission arrived.

The tent must have had room for a thousand people, at least. Maybe two thousand. I'd been expecting some bleachers on the grass, more like how the sideshow had been set up.

Checking our ticket stubs, an attendant in a red sports coat led us to seats that were only five rows or so back from the stage. We were so close we'd probably be able to smell the animals.

So close that Bartholomew might be able to recognize me. Great. I wished I had my hat with me. I hadn't worn it because I thought it wouldn't go with the suit and would draw attention to me.

Says the guy in the suit and the fire face paint, Will would have snorted.

All around us, families filed in. Parents were laughing and pointing out interesting things while clowns wandered through the audience, riling up kids with balloon animals and tripping over people's feet. Lloyd flagged down a vendor and bought cotton candy for us. The fluffy pink goodness turned to grainy sugar on my tongue. I had to admit that, despite everything that was about to happen, eating cotton candy made me feel a little better.

"Nice seats," said Lloyd and his mother nodded in agreement.

"Amazing," I chimed in, trying to sound normal. I was worried. What if the lady gave us these seats on purpose? So Bartholomew could keep an eye on me?

"Spartacus? Are you okay?" Lloyd asked.

"Hmm?" I said, but I panicked, thinking maybe he'd been talking and I'd missed something he'd said. Was that suspicion or concern in his eyes? He was still looking at me, waiting for an answer.

"Yeah. I guess I'm just really anxious to see my mom," I said, remembering how easy it was to lie by telling the truth.

"What does she do again?" asked Beverly.

"She's the Human Cannonball," said Lloyd. "The Amazing Athena."

I cringed, hoping no one around was hearing this.

"We saw her bus outside!" she exclaimed, nudging Lloyd. "I bet you never get tired of seeing her perform."

"Actually," I admitted. "This will be the first time."

"You've never seen her perform?" she exclaimed.

"She hasn't been in the circus that long—just since the end of last summer, so this will be the first time."

And hopefully the last.

I put some more cotton candy in my mouth so I wouldn't have to say anything more.

Lloyd smiled gently at me. "That's gotta be rough, never seeing your mom," he said sympathetically.

I nodded, feeling a twinge of guilt at Lloyd's words. He was a killer, sure—but he was also, in a way, my friend. And I was going to get him arrested by the SWAT team right in front of his own mother. Could I betray the guy who'd encouraged me to stand up for myself and told me it was okay to embrace my ridiculous name?

The lights began to dim, as if to say that these questions didn't matter anymore.

There was no turning back.

౭

"Ladies and gentlemen, boys and girls, friends and animals of all ages!" a voice boomed in the blue darkness. "You are about to experience the most marvelous, prodigious, miraculous, stupendous show to ever visit the Pacific Northwest. Welcome to Bartholomew's World-Renowned Circus of the Incredible!"

The audience burst into wild applause and a live orchestra at the front of the stage started playing. At the same time, there was a loud *BOOM* and the spotlight appeared, shining on a cloud of red smoke. A tall, slender, and elegant man in a red suit and a black top hat stepped out from the fog, a cane raised over his head. I narrowed my eyes.

Bartholomew.

I was sitting so close I could see his pale, smooth skin and the light glinting off his red hair. My blood began to boil, just seeing him looking all smug and important. And to see the audience respond to him like they thought he was so great! They had no idea what he really was. The Count from who-knows-where who forced people to perform against their will, who stole from museums, who may have sold his soul to the devil so he could do black magic…

Okay, so that last stuff was a long shot, but still.

Boy, they wouldn't be applauding him for long.

What followed was a huge fanfare of performers around him. He stood still in the middle of it, directing it all while a line of animals and a whole slew of clowns and performers marched and jumped around the ring.

"Clowns freak me out," Lloyd leaned over and whispered. "You can never tell what they're feeling."

I nodded. *Same with murderers*, I thought.

I scanned the performers for my mom, but didn't see her. At the end of the little parade, Bartholomew pointed his cane at a box on the stage and flames suddenly shot out of it, followed by four tumblers.

"Behold, the phenomenal, sensational, spectacular, and wholly singular magic of the human body!" his voice boomed, filling every corner of the tent.

We watched what looked like nine-year-old quadruplet contortionists twist their bodies into knots while balancing on chairs and each other.

After that, we "beheld the magic of the flame" while a man breathed fire (*snore*), and watched "the magic of gravity" while a woman juggled while using a trampoline to run up a makeshift wall. After each performance, clowns came out and did funny skits for the little kids.

Mom still hadn't come out.

The scariest was Sharkman's routine, which was just before intermission. Even though I'd seen him before (and yes, hit him over the head), him being there really freaked me out.

They introduced him as a *bizarre, baffling, bewildering, perplexing, and peculiar fluke of nature*. But I remembered what Nero had said about him—it was mostly plastic surgery. He was muscular in a shiny gray bodysuit, his dorsal fin sticking out and his gills flexing with each breath. They'd somehow attached a fake shark nosepiece to his face. Even though I knew he was just a man in a permanent costume, knowing he might be backstage when I was trying to find my mom was *terrifying*.

223

His stunt was diving. There was a large, clear tank of water with a couple of small sharks, and a ladder and high dive above it. Just seeing the high dive gave me horrible flashbacks.

"That guy's a real piece of work," Lloyd whispered to me, interrupting my thoughts. I nodded and we clapped politely as Sharkman did some okay dives from really high up, like the stuff you see at the Olympics. The sharks in the tank didn't seem to care whether he was in there or not.

But honestly, Will could probably do better.

&

As the first half wound down and the circus broke for intermission, my heart thumped like a drum. It was time to make the phone call. Time to ditch Lloyd and his mom. Time to get the real show on the road.

"Some circus, eh?" Lloyd said loudly, leading us through the noisy crowd to the concessions.

"Yeah," I agreed. "It's really good."

"I especially like the tumblers," Beverly was saying as we got to the front. "Say, when is your mom—?"

"I waited way too long to pee," I blurted out. "Gotta find the restroom!" Without saying anything more, I dove into the crush of people before Lloyd or his mom could follow.

Let's do this, I told myself, trying to psych myself up as I shouldered my way to the entrance.

The sun had gone down since the circus started and I left the grounds under the cover of…well, I guess Eli wouldn't call it dusk. It was too late at night for that. Twilight, maybe.

I went to the phone booth I'd staked out earlier, just across the street a ways. I looked over my shoulder, making sure Lloyd hadn't followed, that he wasn't going to eavesdrop on the call…

…and take out a knife from his jacket and…

I shook my head. Couldn't think about that. Must not think about that. I let out a shaky breath, picked up the receiver, and dialed.

224

"Nine-one-one, what's your emergency?"

I hesitated for a long moment before I spoke. Once I did this, it couldn't be undone.

"I want to make an anonymous tip," I finally said. "I just saw this guy—the murderer from the wanted posters. Lloyd—I mean *Dan* Lloeke. He's at the circus tonight."

There was some clacking on the keyboard. "And how sure are you that it's him?" the man asked.

"One hundred percent," I said with confidence. "He has the Rolling Stones tattoo, right forearm."

"Where are you located?" he asked.

"Bartholomew's Circus of the Incredible, near the park downtown. The intermission is ending, so you should probably get here fast." And with that, I hung up the phone.

My body felt heavy. I'd done it. It was out of my hands. Things were going to start happening now. I could feel it.

Better hope this works, Spartacus.

With this cloud hanging over me, I raced back to the circus. I stopped at the edge of the concessions, spying on the place where I'd last seen Lloyd. Luckily, there was no one left there except for the concessions people. No Lloyd. No Beverly. They must've gone back to their seats.

So far so good.

The popcorn lady saw me and called out, "It's about to start—hurry up!"

"Oh, no!" I yelped, faking concern as I sprinted by her and down the hall.

But I wasn't going back to my seat. It was time to find Mom, and then wait for the fireworks.

❧

I rushed along the curving hallway. This time, all the audience entrances had curtains drawn across them—and oddly, there wasn't a soul in sight. The music had begun and Bartholomew was announcing the next act.

I got to the end of the corridor and skidded to a stop in front of a swinging door marked:

STAY OUT! CIRCUS PERSONNEL ONLY.

I'd planned on slicing through the canvas again, but—here was a door, completely unguarded.

Is it a trap? Is it—

I didn't have time to think about it, though, because I heard someone coming from behind me.

Here goes everything, I thought, barreling through the door.

I found myself in an even darker corridor, and right next to me—was a security guard. Her face was glowing green in the light of her phone screen.

"How's it going?" she asked, not looking up from the text she was writing.

Don't hesitate, Spart. Don't stutter.

"Great," I grunted, not missing a beat, not slowing my walk.

"Break a leg," she murmured as I sped away from her. And that was it. I was in.

How am I in? Is my suit actually working? Or do the security guards not know what they're guarding? Either way, I couldn't believe my luck; finally, something was going right!

Inside, the floor was a steel ramp that spiraled up and around the side of the tent, back behind the stage. At first, I could hear the circus going on to my left, the audience laughing and *oohing* and *ahhing* as the music rose and fell. But the ramp jigged and jogged; I went up one set of metal stairs and down another. It wasn't long before I was all disoriented.

I was about to lose my nerve, but I stopped and took a deep breath.

Don't panic, I told myself. *You can do this.*

Finally, I heard people ahead. I crept along the curve to see a stage entrance on my left. Clowns and performers bustled up and down a ramp to my right. Some were changing costumes as they raced down the hall; others had on headsets and were cuing entrances and lights and effects.

It would have been pretty cool to watch—any other time, that is.

I could have turned back to find another path, but I already knew what was back there: nothing. If I wanted to find my mom, I would have go through them and find out where the people were coming from—and go through like I belonged there. But standing at the edge of the activity, I felt a nauseating wave of *déjà vu*. My forehead broke out in sweat under its face paint.

It's just like sneaking into the sideshow, I reminded myself. *I have nothing to worry about. There are a hundred performers here.* The sideshow had only had twenty and I'd blended in. If I just acted like I was supposed to be there... Besides, with my face painted, even if they discovered me, they wouldn't know I was *me*.

So I closed my eyes and counted to three. When I opened them and saw the first gap in the foot traffic, I merged into the chaos.

Just keep moving. Just keep moving.

What with the circus music and jostling amongst the performers and the tech people, the moment felt surreal—it was like I didn't exist. Everyone was so focused on the show that I didn't even get a glance as I hustled past the stage entrance. I caught a fleeting glimpse of Bartholomew in front of the audience, but I immediately ducked my head and pushed on.

Then, in what felt like a few seconds, everyone suddenly thinned out. It was like I'd just swum through a school of fish and they'd all darted away. I looked around in alarm, only to see the performers had scrambled to take their places onstage—some were even climbing the scaffolding above. A giant security guard leaned against the wall, but he simply nodded back as I went by.

My plan is working! Thank goodness he couldn't hear my heart pounding over the music.

As I sped down the ramp on the other side, I met a couple stragglers straightening their green tutus as they hustled for the stage, but neither even glanced in my direction. The ramp curved down until I was walking on grass, in another long corridor of canvas. With all the performers hurrying from this side of the tent, I knew I didn't have far to go.

The sides of the corridor were lined with colorful doors a few feet from the ground, metal stairs leading up to them. I scratched my head for a second before I figured out that they were entrances to the tour buses arranged around the outside of tent.

The performers' buses.

I was almost there!

I tried not to run as I passed by them, looking at the names next to the doors. I saw one labeled DR. HEISLER. The plastic surgeon maybe? Scary. I hurried past.

The fourth door I passed said BARTHOLOMEW in big gold letters. And the very next one said ATHENA.

Mom.

Heart pounding, I glanced around to make sure I was still alone. Then, I knocked on the door.

I waited for all of about three seconds before pulling it open and throwing myself inside.

∽

I hate to admit I cried when I saw her, so I won't.

"Mom, I know it's a surprise to see me—" I began, but Mom jumped up from a chair before I could even close the door behind me, smothering me in a hug.

"Oh my god! Spartacus!" she said into the top of my head, squeezing me tight. I think I was as shocked as she was.

"What are you *doing* here?" she exclaimed, pulling back to look at me. Relieved, I saw immediately that this *was* Mom and not Charlene. She looked at the orange and red makeup smudges I'd left on her black shirt. "What's that stuff on your face?"

"I had to see you," I said, forgetting my speech and suddenly so overwhelmed that my voice was trembling. I couldn't believe I'd made it. She was *there*. She was *real*. She was all right. She wasn't handcuffed or beaten up or anything.

"Oh, come here, my baby," she said, pulling me back and holding me again, not seeming to mind the paint.

After a minute she let me go and walked me over to a big, sleek black couch—I almost forgot we were on a bus. We both sat down and I looked around. It was awesome, with a kitchen and a bedroom. There was even a large walk-in closet, stuffed with colorful costumes.

"Look at you in that suit," she said in that adoring way that had always embarrassed me. Hearing her now made me realize how much I missed it. "You're growing into such a young man, and it's only been a few months."

"It's been *ten* months," I murmured, not looking at her.

"Has it?"

I was looking at the closed door that must have led to a bathroom when Mom gently turned my face toward her.

"Spartacus," she said, pausing to breathe and then starting again. "Your dad got a message to me, telling me you'd run away and I didn't know what to think. I—well, I was afraid you'd been kidnapped."

I almost laughed out loud, but instead I just sputtered.

"You were afraid *I'd* been kidnapped?" I said, maybe too loudly. But she didn't know about Will, about the postcards. I didn't even know if she knew about the museums—maybe she wasn't involved at all. But Mom interrupted my thoughts.

"How could you have done this?" She looked at me with her dark eyes in that way that always made me feel like I'd done something wrong.

"I'm sorry, Mom, I didn't mean—" I started to explain, but she cut me off.

"Spart, if you wanted to come see me so much, we could have

planned it out," she said, scolding me. "You and Will could have come up to see me together."

"How could we have planned something when nobody could get in touch with you?" I asked.

"Your dad could have reached out to me any time he wanted," she said. "He just…honey, I think he's still hurting. That's why we never talked. He won't take my calls."

I stared at her, blank-faced.

Any time he wanted. Dad could have—

Then I shook my head. This was no time to play the role of the angry child. I leaned in close to her so that no one could hear through the door or the walls.

"I came here to get you out," I whispered. "I know *you're* the one who was kidnapped."

"Me?" she said, and then she was laughing.

"*Shh!*" I said. "With the house the way you left it, and Will sending, well, sending these postcards—" I paused. This was going to take too long. I changed my angle, telling her everything in a flood. "Look, I know Bartholomew won't let anyone leave once they're in the circus. I know that he's stealing from museums."

"What are you talking about?" Mom said in her normal-volume voice, pulling away. "The mess at the house was obviously from my audition. I didn't get a chance to—"

"Keep your voice down," I flinched. "I know about Santa Fe. I know about Prizrak and how he got locked in a safe and died in Chicago. I know about the streetcar and Abraham Lincoln's china."

Mom stood up, eyes widening, and shaking her head. "Who told you this? How about we get that makeup off you and—"

"I figured it out. Mom—I know about everything. You don't have to pretend with me."

She crossed over to her vanity, pulled out some wet wipes, and sat back down next to me. She looked nervous, with that crazy kind of smile she'd sometimes get when Dad would go on one of his angry rants. Maybe these were the signs of Stockholm syndrome? Maybe she was afraid to admit that she needed help.

"Pretend?" Her laugh was thin and tight, as she tried to wipe my face. "Let's stop talking like this and—"

"Mom!" I interrupted, pushing her hand away. "Look, maybe you don't know about it. Maybe they're doing the jobs without you."

"*Doing the jobs!*" she exclaimed. "You—you are so *nutty*. Whoa, look at this bruise, honey. What happened?" I pulled the wipe out of her hand and threw it on the floor.

"Mom, you have to come with me. *Now*." I was so angry I was shaking. "Even if you don't believe me. Just trust me."

I got to my feet, slow and determined and held out my trembling hand. Frustrated tears welled up in my eyes. I'd known it was going to be hard, but I was totally unprepared for finding her like *this*. Why wasn't she listening to me? She was just sitting there, shaking her head, mouthing the word *no* over and over again.

"I don't know what's wrong with you, but please just trust me." I took hold of her hand and tried an encouraging voice. "Maybe you're scared. But you don't have to be. I've called the police. They're going to show up and then you can tell them what you know."

"The police?" she said in a low, low voice.

"Yeah. I told them everything." It was a little white lie that I thought would help. If she *did* have Stockholm syndrome, this might help her feel safer.

"What do you mean, *everything*?" came a man's voice from inside the room.

My heart sank as a tall, pale man stepped out of the bathroom. In his hands was a large top hat.

Bartholomew.

Bartholomew stood a moment in the narrow hallway, letting his presence—and what that meant—sink in.

He'd been there the whole time.

But wasn't he just onstage? Somehow he'd snuck into the bus before I'd found it!

Bartholomew came over and stood right next to my mom. She didn't shudder, didn't shrink away. In fact, she didn't even seem to be scared at all...

"I, I—uh," I had no words. I was dumbfounded. I was speechless.

Bartholomew up close was much scarier than Bartholomew in the ring. He really did have a smooth face, like they said. Smooth, shiny, and ageless, pulled tight like a fish. I couldn't even guess how old he was. He could have been twenty. He could have been as old as my grandparents.

"Pleasure to meet you, Spartacus," said Bartholomew, with a half bow and now a wide, easy smile on his face. But it was a clown's smile, almost like he'd painted it on. I didn't think for a second that it was real—it didn't reach his eyes. And his accent was different than his performing voice. It was a strange accent I'd never heard before. "I've heard a lot about you."

I stayed quiet. Bartholomew leaned down, studying me closely.

"Tell me," he said in a calm voice. "Did you honestly call the police, Spartacus?"

"Yeah, I did. They'll be here any minute."

"What *exactly* did you tell them?"

I stared him in the eye, trying my hardest to look confident, like someone who had just called the police and had nothing to worry about. Then Bart stood up and looked at my mom.

"No," he said to her, shaking his head. "He didn't."

I thought I saw my mom relax and let out a big breath. Then Bartholomew laughed a big laugh, with my mom laughing a smaller one.

"Spartacus, I remember what it was like to have so much imagination," he said in his deep, melodic voice. "I truly do. When you're young, it seems like everything is big and mysterious and everyone's plotting something, doesn't it? But Spartacus, we're not stealing anything and nobody was kidnapped and nobody in my circus is trapped. Your mom is staying here because she wants to be here. She's an amazing performer and we're glad to have her. There's nothing more to it than that."

I glared at him.

"Sweetie," said Mom. "It's true. I shouldn't have run off without talking to you first. I'm sorry, I was impulsive. But no one is trapped. No one's holding me against my will. I can leave anytime I want."

"Fine," I said. She was either completely in the dark about the museum stuff or else she was too afraid to say anything in front of Bartholomew. But I couldn't stop my stupid mouth. "What about him stealing museum art? Did he tell you about that?"

"What *are* you talking about?" asked Bartholomew, that painted-on smile back on his face.

"You know. The Georgia O'Keeffe Museum. And all of the other places. The streetcar? Abraham Lincoln's china? That dinosaur skeleton?" And then, just to see if there was any reaction, "The gold scarab from Mexico?"

Mom blanched, but Bartholomew laughed. "I heard about the O'Keeffe museum. I don't know the other ones. But what makes you think we were involved with any of that?"

"Every time you visit a city, something gets stolen."

"Trust me, Spartacus; we haven't stolen anything," he said. The tone of his voice sounded so reasonable that I blushed. "You're over-reacting. Things get stolen in big cities all the time and you never hear anything about it. Just because we've been to some cities and they've had a few things go missing isn't proof of anything."

I knew I should just keep quiet, but I couldn't help talking back to him. "But what about the woman who looks just like Mom?" There was no way he could explain that. "I saw her in Albuquerque."

"Albuquerque? You mean Charlene? We do look alike," Mom said, her eyes and voice soft. "But maybe you just wanted her to be me so badly that you imagined we looked more alike than we really do."

233

Was it possible I'd made a mistake about that? There was no way. She'd looked just like Mom. *Hadn't* she?

"But what about Zacharias Prizrak?"

"You know how rumors are, Spartacus," he said. "Prizrak used to work for me. But he was a criminal. He got in trouble and, yes, he had an accident while he was committing a crime. I know people have blown that out of proportion. But trust me that it was entirely his doing, not mine. I can't be blamed for the actions of everyone who works for me."

Bartholomew had a way of looking at you that made it hard to look away. Those small, blue eyes set in that pale face were almost… mesmerizing.

I shook my head and took a step back. "Mom, they say he's violent. He's vicious. He stole the circus. He even fixed the *Tour de France!*" I practically shouted this out, just releasing all my suspicions in one stupid rush.

Bartholomew smiled like he felt sorry for me. "Have you been visiting IHateBartholomewsCircus.com?" He didn't wait for me to respond, he just nodded and smiled. "That's a fun website, isn't it? Would it surprise you to know that I put that website up myself? Would it surprise you to know that we make those rumors up? For some reason, people like to believe in mysterious, dark things. And that's what our circus is all about. Giving people what they want."

"It's true, Spartacus," said my mom. "That's just a thing to get people interested in the circus and make it all seem more mysterious than it is."

I felt like I was sinking slowly, slowly into quicksand. Not that I'd ever been in quicksand, but that's exactly how I thought it would feel.

Bartholomew looked at his watch, then glanced at Mom. "We do have to get onstage in a second, so we'll have to continue this conversation after the show." He and Mom exchanged a strange look. I couldn't tell what they were thinking.

"And surely, Spartacus," Bartholomew continued in a calm voice, calm as a clam, "you have to admit it all does seem a bit strange, doesn't it? You have to admit that maybe you've been a little immature about all of this, Spartacus. We all want to have a big adventure once in a while, but surely, Spartacus, the world isn't as big a place as you think it is. It's a calmer place. It's a much more boring place, really. It's a much more peaceful place, really, Spartacus."

There was something about the way he talked. I couldn't put my finger on it. He kept saying my name over and over and his voice had a weird, lulling quality that made me think of my mom when she used to read to me in bed.

That was it. His voice made me tired. Or maybe I was already tired. I had been awake a long time and I suddenly felt all of those hours I'd been up.

My mom started to say something—"I'm really happy here, Spartacus, you have to—" but Bartholomew shushed her gently.

"Maybe you need a nap, Spartacus," said Bartholomew. "A nap would truly be good for you. After all you've done. All you've traveled. A nap in this comfortable place that your mom finds very comfortable, too. When we get back, we'll talk about this a little more, but right now I imagine sleep sounds very good, don't you agree?"

Yes, I did. He was right. I wasn't sure why I'd been so angry and upset a few minutes ago. Taking a nap seemed like a reasonable idea. I would wait for them to get back and we could figure things out then. It was silly to get so upset.

I stretched out on the couch and closed my eyes. My head was swimming. How could Bartholomew and the circus be doing all the stuff I thought they were? It didn't make any sense, did it? I'd gotten it all wrong from the start. Will had written the coded postcards, not Mom. Mom had wanted to come here. She was happy here. I had been so stupid to think she needed rescuing. I'd been very silly the whole time.

But then Zeda's face floated into my mind. Like one of those real-life pictures that you get in your head right before you drift off to sleep. Zeda's pretty face. Telling me that nobody trusted Bartholomew. Zeda and Nero and Remmy and Zeda's dad—they all hated Bartholomew, didn't they?

Zeda. I promised Zeda I'd help Matilda. Matilda. Where was she again?

My mind wasn't working right. I didn't know why, but I knew I needed to snap out of it. I did something that always worked in the movies. I hauled off and gave myself a big cracking slap across the face.

"Aaah!" I cried out, sitting up. That did the trick. I was fully awake.

What the heck had happened?

Mom and Bartholomew were gone. I didn't even remember them leaving. One second I was standing there, listening to Bartholomew defend himself, and the next I was waking up on the couch.

Strange. I went to Mom's vanity and wiped the rest of the paint off my face, thinking about absolutely nothing at all—until the roar of the audience outside brought me back.

Did Bartholomew hypnotize me?

I stared at my bruised and scratched face in the mirror and felt the remaining fuzziness disappear. I'd read rumors online that Bartholomew had the power to do that to people—but that was on the IHateBartholomew website, which he and Mom insisted was fake.

I shook my head, my brain feeling thick and slow. I put my head in my hands, rubbing my temples. I didn't know what to believe right then. It really did seem absurd that a circus would be involved in the museum robberies.

But all those places had stuff stolen while The Incredible was in town. That was too big of a coincidence, wasn't it? And the scarab. Eli and I knew the scarab was stolen. Mom had even looked funny when I mentioned it.

Another cheer from the audience.

Time was passing and the circus was still going—but for how much longer? Lloyd and his mother were still watching, probably wondering where I was, if I was okay. And the cops would be here any moment to arrest Lloyd.

I only had one choice. I had to get to the police and tell them everything I knew about the museums and Bartholomew. If it wasn't true and I *had* been wrong about everything, they could sort it out. If it was true, they could help me save my mom.

When I went to the door, though, it was locked.

I shook the handle, fiddled with the lock, and tried the handle again. It wouldn't budge. I should have been able to open it from the inside—I mean, it was a bus door. But it was stuck shut, which meant they had locked me in from the outside. If they were innocent, why would they lock me in?

They?

Yes. They.

I could just barely remember it, but right before they left, I'd caught a glimpse of Bartholomew taking Mom's hand to lead her out. Bartholomew and my mom, as thick as thieves.

I barely made it to the toilet before I threw up.

I felt cold and clammy as I paced the length of the bus like a caged animal, trying to find a way out. There wasn't a mobile phone anywhere to be found. It wasn't long before I picked up the chair and tried to break the windows. They didn't break, though, just as I'd thought. It's like they were made of shatterproof glass. Maybe bulletproof? Figures a criminal mastermind would have those in his girlfriend's tour bus—just in case she snapped out of it and got the idea to leave him.

Girlfriend. That's what the situation was, wasn't it? Bartholomew and my mom were a couple. Together. "An item." She was with him and knew all about everything. But then again, there was also that trick with the hypnotizing. I was breathing hard through my nose.

There was still that teeny chance, that last shred of hope, that Mom wasn't a criminal. That she had been hypnotized by him. That she was still my mom, the one I remembered.

I shouted loudly in frustration and kicked the wall. *What now?* I thought. *What's left? Just wait until Bartholomew comes back and puts me in a bank vault? Wait until—*

Just then the door swung open silently. I had just enough time to dive in the bathroom to hide, thinking it was Bartholomew again, or maybe Sharkman. No one came inside, though. A few seconds later I heard—

"Ryan?"

Chapter Sixteen

The voice sounded familiar. I peeked out over the couch.

It was Will!

"You got the door open!" I exclaimed.

"Ryan!" he blubbered, running to me and collapsing like a giant, stubbly, after-shave-soaked baby. "Ryan, I thought you were *dead!* I thought that I'd killed you."

"Thank goodness you're here," I exclaimed, patting him on the back. "We've got to get out of here." I tried to pull away, but he just kept hugging, kept sobbing.

"I did it. I sent the postcards. It was just a joke—I never thought you really believed it."

"I know all this," I pleaded, pushing him away so he'd look at me. "I figured it out forever ago. But you *have* to believe me. We need to get out now!"

But he just kept talking.

"I saw this morning that the circus was in Portland and thought this was my only chance to get to you. I sold my iPhone to get bus fare and—"

He wasn't stopping. And, in an instant, all the anger about the postcards and the pool and his general awfulness boiled up inside me. I knew it wasn't the right time, but I couldn't help myself. Mid-sentence, as he burbled away, I hauled off and slugged him right in the mouth.

Even though it felt good, one look at his shocked, sad, crying face and I knew that this was all the revenge I would ever need.

"I'm sorry," I mumbled, rubbing my stinging fist.

"I deserve it," he said, calm now, putting his hand to his jaw. "I deserve much worse. Pretty good punch. Wait... *why* were you locked in here? And why are you wearing your suit?"

239

"I'll tell you all about it—but first, we have to get out of here, okay?"

I ran down the bus steps, Will right behind me. Will showed me the "lock," which was a large crowbar they'd jammed into the doorframe.

I shivered.

Nobody normal uses crowbars. People only use them when they're serious about breaking something—or hurting someone.

I was done playing around. It was time to get out of this funhouse hall of mirrors. Mom didn't want to come with me. I wasn't going to save her. Not tonight. I had to make it to the cops and tell them what I knew.

We headed for the back of the circus.

"So where's Mom?" Will asked, huffing beside me. "I was looking for her when I found you. Why were you locked in? And why are we running away?"

"No time for that," I panted. "Just know that you can't trust anyone here. They all—"

But I didn't get a chance to explain.

Two dudes wearing security guard shirts stepped out of the shadows, directly in front of us. I was a few steps behind Will, but Will didn't have time to stop.

"*Oof!*" Will bounced right off them and fell on his back, confused. Will was a big guy, but these guys were much, much bigger. One guard immediately pinned Will down.

"Hey, get off me! My mom works here!" Will yawped, surprised.

That won't help at all, I thought grimly.

The other guard took a few steps toward me. I had no choice but to run.

"I'll get help!" I shouted as I took off.

The security guard was right behind me, breathing hard, coming at me like a freight train.

I raced past the buses again, sprinting toward the curtain and a group of performers standing in a huddle. They were getting ready to go onstage—and in the middle of them was Sharkman.

The performers' eyes widened—while Sharkman's narrowed—as I barreled toward them at full speed, the guard right on my heels. No one dared shout out in alarm, seeing how close we were to the stage. Instead, they crouched for impact.

"Stop him!" hissed the guard.

Sharkman lunged, but I zoomed to the right, just out of his reach. I was running alongside the heavy red curtain—the one that bordered the stage. I tried going back the way I had come, parallel to the stage, but there was a bunch of metal scaffolding in my way. I spun around and saw the security guard and Sharkman inching toward me.

"Don't worry, we're not going to hurt you," Sharkman said—which I did not believe for a second.

I was officially cornered.

I didn't have any choice.

With my heart pounding in my ears, I got down on the floor and rolled right under the curtain—and onto the stage.

Other than the spotlight centered on Bartholomew, who was sitting astride a big white cannon a few feet away, the stage was dark. I recognized the cannon immediately as the one my mom used in her act.

Bart glanced at me and he froze for all of one-sixteenth of a second—it was so quick that no one else noticed, but I sure did. I didn't dare back up because I could hear Sharkman cursing right behind me, on the other side of the curtain.

I froze. My breath stuck in my throat.

This wasn't good.

I didn't think anybody in the audience had seen me yet, since I was on the very edge of the spotlight. All the focus was on Bartholomew, who continued to speak as though I weren't there.

"I would like to present to you the most awe-inspiring, stupefying, petrifying, horrifying, electrifying, and death-defying event of the evening. This act will amaze, astound, and astonish you. You're about to behold an unbelievable, unimaginable, unutterable, miraculous, spectaculous, and all around cracktaculous feat of wonder!"

Are those even words? I thought. But I sensed that Bartholomew was stalling, giving me the chance to go back under the curtain. But I wasn't going anywhere, not with what was waiting for me on the other side.

That's when I noticed something a few feet away. It was a small, orange megaphone, the kind you could yell through to make your voice boom. It must have just been for show, though, because Bartholomew had a microphone.

That's when I got an idea. And if you can't go back…you might as well march ahead.

೫

I stepped deliberately forward into the circle of light, toward the megaphone and the middle of the ring. I could sense the audience notice me, but I couldn't see them because of the lights in my eyes.

I could see Bartholomew, though.

He looked down at me from his perch on the cannon and fear flickered in his eyes. Just that tiny flash made me feel more comfortable. If I hadn't seen it, I'm not sure I would have been brave enough to face him like I did.

I picked up the megaphone and then planted my feet, glaring up at him.

"I say," boomed Bartholomew. "If it isn't the newest member of our performance troupe—and the son of our own Human Cannonball, Athena! Young Sir Spartacus. Let's have a round of applause for him, shall we?"

The crowd clapped politely.

They all thought that this was part of the show! *Wow.* Bart didn't miss a beat, did he?

"Were you scared for your mom?" Bartholomew asked, still playing his role. "It's only two hundred feet. I promise, on my honor, you will not become an orphan!"

The crowd tittered at this.

"What do you say—should we bring out the Flying Athena?"

The crowd began to cheer, and that's when I put the megaphone to my lips. I didn't even know what I was going to say.

"Excuse me. Before you start," I said, my amplified voice making me jump. I turned toward the audience. "I'd like to tell everybody what kind of things Bartholomew does in his free time."

"Oh, dear, now, child, don't... uh—don't go sharing *that* information," he said, scrambling off the cannon and moving a few feet toward me. But I was ready. I dropped the megaphone and pulled out the paraffin and torch from my pocket. When Bart took another step forward, I lit the torch and then blew a huge fireball toward him. I thought it might have burnt his eyebrows, it was so big. Zeda would have been proud.

The audience cheered and Bartholomew balked and ducked back behind the cannon.

"Is this the roast of Bartholomew?" he quipped.

The audience laughed.

That infuriated me. My torch was still burning as I grabbed the megaphone again.

"No, it...it's a game," I stumbled.

"I like games," he said, peeking from behind the cannon. "Can we play hide and seek? You can hide first."

"No. We're—we're going to play Truth or Dare."

"Is this family friendly?" he asked, and everyone laughed again.

"Depends," I said, speaking slowly and loudly through the megaphone. I had to make sure everyone heard this. "Do you think stealing from museums is 'family friendly'? How about hypnotizing people? Or locking kids up in buses?"

There was scattered, confused applause from the audience and one person shouted out, "I hate Bartholomew's Circus!" Others chuckled.

These idiots! They thought this was part of the show! What could I possibly say to make them believe me? It all sounded so ridiculous when you said it out loud.

But Bartholomew's eyes blazed.

"I think somebody's broken out of the loony bin," he said pointedly.

"Truth or dare?" I shouted.

There were some snickers from the audience. I happened to look out and catch Lloyd's eye, in the fifth row. He didn't seem to be laughing. He was leaning forward in his seat, like he was watching a very close tennis match that he had money on.

"Oh, dare, I guess," said Bartholomew after hesitating.

"I dare you to come out from behind that cannon," I said, my torch's flame still flickering.

"Truth be told, I'm afraid you'll toast me like a marshmallow."

"No, I won't do that. Not if you stay away from me."

I caught movement out of the corner of my eye and saw that there were police officers in the audience. There were four of them in navy blue suits and flat-topped caps, edging up the aisles.

They'd actually come for Lloyd!

As long as they were around, nobody could hurt me or Will. This might work out after all.

I looked back to Bartholomew as he stepped out from behind the cannon and faced me from ten feet away. The orchestra gave a large *ta-da!* that made the audience clap.

"That was an easy dare," he said. "Now your turn. Before they come and take you away. Truth or dare?"

What was he talking about? Take me away?

He was still stalling, trying to distract me. The cops had already passed by Lloyd's row, though—and were moving toward the stage. Maybe they had seen the security guards grab Will and were coming to intervene.

"That's not how *my* game works!" I said, with renewed confidence. "True or false—you stole Abraham Lincoln's china?"

"What on earth are you talking about?" he laughed, looking nervously at the cops. "Are we playing *Clue* now, too? You have the rules all wrong."

I sniggered a little myself. He was trapped and he didn't even know it.

"What about a dinosaur from Philadelphia?" I shouted. Even though my knees were shaking, I took a few steps toward him. "Did you take that, too?"

Now that I was closer, something about him looked a bit odd. His hair wasn't as red as I remembered. And his eyes—his eyes didn't have that same hypnotic effect that they had in the tour bus. I thought about Not-Mom and something clicked.

"You seem to have lost your steam, child," he said, eyeing me as I eyed him. "Have the voices in your head turned off for a second?"

"No. It's just—I don't think you're the real Bartholomew," I said. Because he wasn't. This man was a good six inches shorter. There were wrinkles around his eyes. His skin wasn't as smooth as it had been in Mom's bus.

"You know what happens when you stop believing in Bartholomew," he said and, with a snap of his fingers, the band started to play a distorted version of "Stars and Stripes Forever" and the cops sprinted up onstage.

But they were after *me*.

One glance was all it took for me to see that these weren't real cops after all—their mime-painted faces and green hair proved it.

I dropped the megaphone and moved away from them. Three more clown cops joined the original four, creating a dark wall of blue between the audience and me. But I didn't hesitate. I got my paraffin and torch ready. Then the clowns rushed me. I found myself running around the stage, blowing fireballs at them while the orchestra blared zany marching music. Every time I tripped or a cop ducked, a cymbal crashed.

It was total madness. Not-Bartholomew had turned me into part of the show. No one in the audience had believed a single thing I'd said.

I couldn't tell if the clown cops were really trying to get me or if they were just putting on a goofy act. But I knew if I got caught, they'd just drag me backstage. And Bartholomew wouldn't be too happy about all of this.

When my torch's flame went out, I chucked it at one of the clowns. It caught him square in the neck and he cursed under his breath.

"You'll pay for that," he growled under his breath while flashing a lunatic, red-lipped smile

"All right, coppers!" shouted Bartholomew through the megaphone I'd dropped. "Enough puttering! Let's take him away!"

The cops formed a semicircle and cornered me near the back of the stage. They crept toward me, making little fake grabs as they closed in, gnashing teeth.

There was nowhere to go except up.

The scaffold behind me stretched up to the rafters. Maybe if I could get up there, I could stall until someone figured out that I wasn't part of the show. Or until the real cops came for Lloyd.

I made a grab for the scaffold ladder as the clown cops rushed me—but they were too late. They missed me by a hair.

As I scrambled up, my heart thudded—*this is crazy, this is crazy, this is crazy*—and the music picked up speed, sounding as tense as I felt. Everyone in the audience *ooohed* and *aahed*.

Bunch of dumb sheep!

The clown cops started up after me, but I climbed faster. Soon, I was on top of the scaffold, high above the stage. I tried shouting, but no one could hear me above the crowd and the music.

I didn't see how this could end well at all.

Chapter Seventeen

But here I am, at the beginning again.

Well, the beginning of the end. There was even a fat lady singing—literally. She'd come out with the rush of performers who'd stormed the stage, adding to the confusion. She was warbling along with the orchestra's "Stars and Stripes Forever," but she was the least of the chaos.

Strobe lights flashed, tumblers tumbled and jugglers juggled and unicyclists unicycled. A fog machine belched purple smoke. The tech people above let loose some paper birds on strings that began swooping through the audience, dropping confetti. Kids squealed, adults guffawed. Everyone was so entertained, they forgot all about the kid in trouble. They'd never seen such an apparently well-organized mess.

Then again, neither had I. Maybe I was missing the hilarity, though, seeing as I was too busy escaping a mob of deranged clown cops.

So, to refresh your memory: after climbing a fifty-foot scaffold and then falling ten feet to Sharkman's diving board, I was officially cornered—again. Clown cops above, below, and climbing. Sharkman in his tank with his little sharks. My mom and *real* Bartholomew were nowhere to be seen—maybe they'd escaped. Maybe he'd kidnapped her for real this time.

The audience was my only hope, but my throat was sore from shouting and I was only getting harder to hear. But it didn't really matter. Nothing in the world would have shushed that mass. They thought this was all just part of the show and, by the grin on Not-Bart's face, he knew it, too.

His grin got even wider when the first person in the audience shouted, "Jump!"

They call it *déjà vu*, but for me it was more like *déjà vomit*. Suddenly I was back in Brenville all over again, reliving that horrible nightmare at the pool.

What is it with me and diving boards?

At least this time I had my clothes on. Even in the serious situation I was in, my face reddened thinking about how everyone had stared at me when I got up out of the Brenville Pool. When everyone saw what had happened and they went silent as death.

The clowns were about ten feet below the diving board and gaining. I edged further down the high dive. They would be up to me in seconds, and then they would grab me and haul me backstage and that would be all she wrote. No one would ever hear from the Zander brothers again.

What is it that you do when you're being kidnapped? I racked my brain. *If…if you're getting kidnapped, you throw a fit. You make a lot of noise. That's what they told us when we were young.*

"You let anyone nearby know that something strange is happening," Dad had said. "Even if they can't stop them, they'll remember. They'll remember what happened, and maybe it'll help find you."

But I couldn't make noise! I'd tried that and no one could hear me.

I looked down and could make out Lloyd standing up, looking at me. He was the only one who looked like he wasn't fooled—but he also looked boxed in by the swarming crowd. But even if Lloyd could read my lips, it didn't help having an about-to-be-arrested murderer on your side. Speaking of which: *Where were the cops?*

Behind me, the first clown had reached the top of the diving board ladder. Maybe it was just his makeup, but his grin was terrifying.

If everybody would just shut up, I could tell them that none of this was an act!

Then everything fell into place. In one second, I knew what I had to do.

I took a deep breath and did it. Really. I didn't back down, I didn't give up.

I.

Did.

It.

&

In one swift move, I dropped my pants—and my boxers.

Spartacus Ryan Zander, once again, naked for the world to see.

The gasp from the crowd felt endless. Hands flew up in front of kids' eyes. Old ladies swooned. Jaws fell open and little girls giggled. The music screeched to a halt, ending in an oboe squeak, but then that was it.

The whole circus had fallen into silent, gaping, motionless horror as I stood there, my suit pants around my ankles, my button-up shirt barely covering my rear end, a red blush covering my entire body. Yes, my entire body.

But.

But.

But the clowns on the ladder backed off. Sharkman stopped swimming. Not-Bartholomew's eyes bulged from his fake Bartholomew face. He looked like he might have been even redder than me. The stage was mine.

"I'm sorry," I shouted into the silence. I pulled up my pants and secured my belt as I spoke. "I don't want to offend you all, but I need to say something and I need you to listen. What I said was true. The Incredible has been stealing from museums. Tonight I think Bartholomew's planning on taking silverware from the Portland Art Museum. He locked me in a tour bus, but I got out. He's even got my brother backstage. Bartholomew is evil—and it's not just made-up stuff on some website. Please—call the police!"

The silence was so thick I thought I was going to choke on it.

And, because I couldn't think of anything else to do, I launched myself off the diving board in an Olympic-worthy half gainer into the water tank below. After being naked in front of a thousand strangers, it didn't even seem that difficult.

The first thing I saw when I surfaced was the angry face of Sharkman, glaring at me with his black eyes from across the tank. Luckily, he stayed on his side with his small sharks.

"You stole my act, kid," he whispered. "Get out of my pool before I eat your face."

I didn't wait to see if he was just talking tough or if he meant it. My suit made it hard to swim, but I got up the ladder and pulled myself out, dripping, onto the stage. The whole tent was so quiet you could hear the water sloshing in the pool and the dripping of my suit. I stood in front of the spotlights, not sure what was going to happen, when the music gave a large *ta-da!*

"How about that?" boomed Not-Bartholomew, his voice cutting through the awkward silence. He looked at me like I was some vile thing he wanted to stomp, but he also held his arm out to me like I was his son. I felt myself being nudged over there by one of the clowns and I stumbled forward. I tried not to flinch as he put his arm around me.

"That was a little experimental entertainment we're working on," said Not-Bartholomew, his hand pinching the back of my neck so hard I thought he was trying to do some sort of Spock move on me to make me pass out. "He's wearing a body suit, though, folks, so don't worry! We wouldn't really... Crazy stuff, huh?" Not-Bartholomew kind of faded off, finally at a loss for words.

The crowd was still uncertain and quiet. Then Not-Bart leaned down and whispered in my ear, "Look to your right. Offstage." Instinctively, I looked.

It was Will. The two security guards were holding him where the audience couldn't see him. Will looked at me with scared eyes. He looked like he'd been crying.

"If you ever want to see your brother again," Not-Bart hissed down to me, "you will take a bow. And you will smile. Like you mean it."

I was *so close*. So close to exposing Bartholomew. So close to getting Mom back. All I had to do was say a few more words to the audience and everyone would believe me.

But I couldn't let them hurt Will. Even if he was the worst brother in the world, he was still my brother. I glanced offstage again, but the guards had already dragged him away. I felt my eyes welling up.

And so I took a bow. And I smiled. Like I meant it. At that, the crowd laughed awkwardly and clapped politely, but there was no cheering. Not like before. I thought I saw someone pull out a cell phone and start to dial, but I wasn't sure—it might have been a trick of the light.

Within a few seconds, the circus music started up again and a few of the clowns play-fought with me as they led me backstage, into the dark.

↾

They barely had a chance to push me behind the curtains before I was tackled to the ground. Clowns, fake cops, Sharkman—the gang was all there. It was like, suddenly, I was not just one scrawny kid, but some kind of superhero that required massive strength to contain.

"Please, don't do—*mmmph*," I was about to say "this" when someone shoved a scarf in my mouth. The scarf tasted like face paint, making me gag.

This was not good. Will and I could both be dead before the cops arrived. Or we might simply "vanish." Maybe the plastic surgeon would make a double of me and they'd be able to play off everything I'd done as part of their routine.

I turned my head and saw Will through the wall of clown cops surrounding me. He had a security guard on either side of him and had already been gagged. I took a little pride in the fact that Bart's people thought I was a bigger threat than Will, who was twice as big as me and ten times as mean. Then I noticed another clown—how many clowns does one circus need, anyway?—pull out a length of rope. Were they going to hang me? String me up?

But no, they just started wrapping me in it.

I'd never been more relieved to be tied up in my life. *You won't get away with this*, I thought, remembering the exact phrase I'd used when Nero and Robin had tied me up on the bus. I remembered what Nero and Robin had taught me: puff yourself up, push your arms out. I did that secretly as the cops spun me around, wrapping me with so much rope you could have made a rope bridge out of it.

I'd be out of that rope the moment they left us alone.

But then again…

If they put Will and me in one of those buses, we'd never get away. My mind began racing with all the horrible possibilities. Being locked in an airtight safe. Being dumped in the river…

My blood went cold as Sharkman leaned over me.

"You know, Bartholomew might have something to say about all of this," he uttered in a cold voice.

They dragged me over to where Will was. Sharkman looked at us both for a beat before turning away to the others.

"Take them somewhere and lock them up," he ordered. Then he smiled at us coldly, exposing his razor-sharp teeth. "Or maybe we should just feed 'em to the animals." Will's eyes darted around frantically, and Sharkman laughed.

"Everyone else, back to your places—we've got a show to finish."

Chapter Eighteen

Four clown cops carried me and half-pushed/half-dragged Will down a set of metal steps, around a corner, and into some kind of dimly lit animal staging area. Beside me, Will was doing his best to fight back. It's hard to do much damage when your hands are tied.

Each pen was separated by a short wall of canvas to keep the animals from seeing each other. As we approached the tiger pen (they appeared to be asleep, but even so, they were huge and absolutely terrifying), a feeling of dread settled over me. They weren't really going to feed us to the tigers, were they? I relaxed a tad when we continued past the tigers and then tensed again as I saw a giant, floor-to-ceiling cage with two slow-looking elephants.

"You like our rubber cows?" one of the clowns said, jabbing Will, who grunted in response. "Maybe we'll let you feed one, later."

"Feed you *to* one!" Another clown laughed.

But we kept going until we reached the last cage in the row, half-draped in canvas. It was empty—and I recognized it: it was Matilda's.

I was shoved in first, Will second.

"Mmmph!" Will grunted as he tripped over the lip of the cage and landed on his knees. It was a tight fit, but there was just enough room for the two of us.

"Might as well put this to use," said one of them. "I hate to think of where that crazy animal is, though. Just running around somewhere?"

"Yeah, gives me the creeps, too," agreed another.

Funny how I had freed Matilda and now I was locked in her cage. I hoped her escape had been more successful than ours.

The tallest clown shut the door and locked it. That's when I remembered: *I had the cage key in my pocket.*

I could not believe my luck.

What with the ropes and that key, we'd be out of there the moment they left!

"Hey, honestly, kiddos," said the tall clown, looking serious. "We were kidding about feeding you to the animals. Finn just wanted us to scare you. This is just until the show's over. Then I'm sure Bart'll have a nice long talk with you and send you on your way."

"Or something like that," said a shorter one. The tall one shot him a dirty look. But with that, they pulled the canvas down over the cage, and then the four clowns were gone.

It was dark in the cage, but not pitch black. Will immediately started rolling around, trying to get untied. I counted to thirty before moving, just in case the clowns were still around. After that, I wriggled into action just like the sideshow had taught me. I slipped my shoes off and—well, I don't mean to brag, but I was out of that rope in, at most, two minutes.

I staggered to my feet, sweating, aching, rope burned—but free. I pulled the wadded scarf out of my mouth and spat on the floor a few times, trying to get the taste of clown paint off my tongue. Then I knelt down and pulled off Will's gag.

"Ryan?" he asked, coughing. "How'd you do that?"

I grinned at him in the dim light. "It wasn't *that* much rope."

I started patting down my damp suit pockets but couldn't find my pocketknife—or the screwdriver—anywhere. Maybe I lost it when I dove into the tank...?

"Seriously, Ryan," Will was saying. "You got out of that so quick!" He seemed to be waiting for an explanation.

I sighed. "Well, I met a bunch of sideshow performers in Albuquerque and—"

Will just stared at me in shock. "Wait—Albuquerque?"

"Yeah, Albuquerque," I said.

I helped him to his knees so I could start working on his knots—which was no easy task. He must have struggled quite a bit when they were tying him up because the knots felt like rocks under my fingers.

"Spartacus!" Will exclaimed. *"What is going on?"*

He looked so confused I had to laugh. When I thought about it from his perspective, the whole thing must have made zero sense. Him finding me locked up, him being grabbed by security, me getting naked and jumping off the high dive. It would look like lunacy.

"I'll tell you everything once we get out of this cage," I said. Even if Will was still tied up, we could still run out the back of the circus.

I started digging through my suit pockets while Will just stared at me like I was crazy.

"What are you doing now?" he asked.

"I have the key to this cage, somewhere," I explained. "Zeda gave the key to me so I could break out Matilda—she's a lemur. It's like a monkey. This is her cage—"

"What the heck are you talking about now? *Keys? Monkeys?*" But he was looking expectantly at me while I checked my jacket pockets again. "Well? Where is it?"

But then I remembered. The key was in my *jeans*—which were in my backpack.

Which was with Lloyd.

I slapped my forehead. "The key is with the murderer. In my bag."

"The *murderer?*" Will practically shouted. *"What are you talking about?"* All this was obviously getting to him.

I put my hands on the bars of Matilda's cage and shook them as hard as I could. They didn't budge. We weren't going anywhere. I slumped down next to Will and sighed.

"I've got a lot to tell you," I said. "And I guess we have the time for it now."

Then I dumped everything on him—the places the circus had been, the museums that had been broken into and robbed, the picture of the person breaking into the art museum and how it had looked like Mom. I told him about Mom's double and Sharkman, and how Bart had hypnotized me and how he and Mom had left holding hands.

"And then they locked me in that tour bus and that's where you came in," I finished. It was a relief to tell someone everything. I'd kept it all in my head for so long, it had started driving me a little crazy.

"Wow," he said, dumbstruck. "I just…I can't believe you did all that alone. Geez, Ryan!"

"Well, I *tried* to get you to come with me, but then you pulled that swimming pool joke and—"

"Wait," Will said, turning to look at me. "You really thought I did that on *purpose?*"

"Well, *didn't* you?" I scoffed, glaring back.

"I would *never* do something like that to you," he said, and he looked so upset, I felt like *I* was the jerk. "I mean, I might play a lot of jokes on you, but I'd *never* do that. That goes against all the rules of being a dude. You don't ever do that to your little brother. Maybe I shouldn't have given you those big shorts, but I swear I didn't know they'd come off like that. You gotta to believe me."

Seriously? Will didn't do that?

I just sat there, stunned, turning it over in my mind. With all the other stuff he'd done, it had seemed like a given.

"But I guess I can't blame you thinking that," he went on, as though he was reading my thoughts. "I haven't…uh—" he coughed and looked at his feet. "I haven't been the nicest person to you. And…and the postcards were super over the line. Like, too, too much. I'm really sorry. About all of it."

We sat in silence for a few moments more when I realized what was bothering me about the whole fake postcards thing.

"*About* the postcards," I said and Will sighed guiltily. "Eli and I studied every inch of them and they looked real. How did you get them postmarked from all those places?"

There was a long silence. Then, "I joined a postmark club."

"*A what?*"

"I joined a postmark collectors' club," he repeated. "I learned that you can send a stamped postcard in an envelope to a post office, and they'll stamp it and return it."

"That must have taken forever."

"It did."

"Why would you put so much effort into that?"

"Because you're fun when you're all riled up," he mumbled, staring at his feet. "I liked messing with you because you'd come to me looking for answers and… Look, like I said, I wouldn't blame you for hating me. But I'll say it again—I'm sorry. I wish I could take it all back."

I couldn't handle Will being so serious like this. I stood up and tried Will's ropes again. Even though he was apologizing, seeing him so pathetic made me uncomfortable.

"I don't *hate* you," I managed. "Just, if we get out of here, can you stop being such a—"

"Garbage pile?" he supplied.

"Yeah. That."

"I can try," he said, then, "I mean, I will. Believe me." He strained to turn his head to look back at me, like he wanted to make sure I got that last part. This was the most serious talk we'd ever had.

And it was too much.

"You know what I *can't* believe?" I asked. "How you got caught so fast by that guard. What happened back there?"

"You know what *I* can't believe?" Will asked, catching my tone. "*I* can't believe you dropped your pants again—but this time on purpose! Seriously. Who does that? You're a maniac. That took, well…there's no other way to put it. That took serious *balls*."

"Let's just never bring it up again, okay?" I asked.

Will snorted.

"Agreed."

❧

We'd fallen into a comfortable silence (well, as comfortable as you can be crammed into a dark cage, waiting for certain doom), when we heard what could only be described as the voice of an angel.

"*Spartacus?*"

I shot to my feet.

"Hello!" I shouted back. *Had I imagined it?*

When she called out a second time, I found myself falling in love all over again with Zeda Marx.

"*Spartacus?*"

"Zeda!" I exclaimed. "At the end! Under the canvas!" I couldn't believe it!

"Are they friendlies?" Will whispered, like we were in a spy movie.

"Friends of mine. From the sideshow."

We heard two sets of feet, rushing toward us. They yanked the canvas up and I found myself I was face to face with Zeda, her cheeks flushed. Nero was at her side, looking grim.

"I *knew* you were in trouble," Zeda said. Then she saw Will. "Who's that?"

"That's my brother, Will. Will, these are Zeda and Nero."

"Whassup," Will said, for some reason trying to look cool, even though he was still tied up.

Glad to know he's still an idiot.

"*So* good to see you guys!" I whooped, turning back to Zeda. "What are you doing here? How did you find us?"

"Lucky, I guess," said Nero. "You lose the key?"

"I don't have it; it's in my bag," I said.

Zeda nodded and pulled a large ring of keys from her backpack and began trying one after another.

"Who put you in here?" demanded Nero.

"A bunch of clown cops," Will answered bitterly as I helped him get to his feet. "Tied us up—Ryan got out of it like a pro, though."

I beamed at the compliment, but Nero's face stayed a dark cloud.

"I'll admit it. I didn't believe you, Zeda. I really didn't. But seeing you guys in here…" he trailed off for a moment, as he closed his eyes in thought. Then he set his jaw and nodded. "We'll put an end to this. I promise. Zeda, you sure you got the key?"

"Positive. Just, well, gotta find the right one." She tried another, but it still didn't turn.

"We have to hurry," said Nero. "They're getting to the end of the show. Here, turn around, put your hands through the bars." Will did as he asked and Nero took a long razor blade from his pocket and began slicing through the ropes.

"How long have you guys been here?" I asked, suddenly nervous about my appearance onstage. I hoped they hadn't seen my…well. My thing.

"We just got here," said Zeda, continuing to sort through the keys. (I inwardly breathed a sigh of relief.)

"We heard them playing 'Stars and Stripes' from across the lot," she went on. "Circuses only do that when there's trouble and they want to create a diversion."

"No kidding," I said, remembering everyone rushing out from backstage.

"I made Nero come with me and—" Zeda paused, looking up from the keys. "Where did you stash Matilda?"

"Oh, Matilda. About that. She—"

But before I could break her heart, Nero put his hand up, shushing me.

"We've got visitors," he whispered.

"Who's back here?" a voice bellowed.

Will and I cringed, but Nero actually smiled.

"I'll be right back," he said. "Stay here."

I wanted to stop him, but Nero tiptoed out of view. Zeda looked unconcerned and kept trying keys. She saw the look on my face, though and tried to assure me under her breath.

"Nero's not a very big guy, but he knows aikido. He can fight anyone."

Suddenly, we heard a scuffle: some *oofs* and *thwacks* and panting.

"Got it!" Zeda whispered, as the key in her hand clicked in the lock.

Will and I burst out of the cage, ready to help Nero (or run), but at that moment he came back around the corner, rubbing his hand. We peeked around the corner and saw two clown cops on the ground.

"Are they *dead?*" I squeaked. Nero smiled.

"Unconscious," he said.

"That was—what?—like twenty seconds?" Will asked, his eyes round. "For *two guys?*"

"What can I say?" said Nero, smirking. "Security is lax around here."

We were all about to head down the corridor when Nero's hand went up again.

"Get back," he whispered urgently. "Out of sight."

Will, Zeda, and I ducked behind the cage again. We went silent, listening as footsteps stopped just a few feet away.

"Well, if it isn't Nimrod," said a man's voice. Even though I couldn't see him, my blood went as cold as the Brenville Pool in January.

It was Sharkman.

Zeda's face went pale.

"They *hate* each other," she murmured, her eyes widening. "This won't turn out well."

She moved the canvas so we could peek.

"*What is that?*" Will whispered, horrified, seeing Sharkman clearly for the first time.

"That's Finn," I said darkly.

"What are you doing here, Sword Boy?" Sharkman was asking Nero.

"I don't want trouble," Nero said calmly, his hands outstretched. "Just came to gather up a few things that belong to us and then I'll be out of your…well, I was going to say hair, but…"

"Can't let you do that," said Sharkman, ignoring Nero's insult and taking a step toward him. "The boy isn't your concern."

Will's grip tightened on my shoulder.

"So, how long have you been snatching kids? I don't think the sideshow got the memo that that was the new gig."

"I *said*, this doesn't concern you," Sharkman repeated, stepping forward again.

"I'm not leaving without him," said Nero.

"You're not leaving *period*."

And with that, Sharkman lunged at Nero.

There, in front of our eyes, the two wrestled and fought on the ground.

I'd never seen a real fight before. And I definitely didn't want to see one again. Especially a fight where one guy is half-shark.

"Piece of ocean trash," Nero growled, punching him in the stomach, but Sharkman got the upper hand, biting Nero on the arm. Nero cried out in pain.

Will and I found ourselves struggling with Zeda, who was trying to get to Nero.

"Please," I pleaded softly as she flailed at Will and I. "You can't go."

Then we heard a dull crash and someone running away. We peered around the canvas. Nero lay motionless on the ground.

Sharkman was gone.

"Nero!" Zeda cried out in a small voice, dashing for him. Will and I went after her and my heart pounded in my ears.

Was he dead? What if he's dead?

When we got to Nero, a wave of relief spread over me. He was breathing. But there was a shovel on the ground next to him, a rising goose egg on his forehead.

"That *monster!*" Zeda shrieked, jumping to her feet.

Before we even saw it happening, she was sprinting down the corridor after Sharkman.

"Go stop her!" Will commanded, already pressing on the bite wound on Nero's arm. "I'll make sure he's okay—and Ryan?"

"Yeah?"

"Be…be careful, okay?"

I nodded. "You, too. And watch out for clowns."

Will nodded back grimly.

And with that, I took off after Zeda.

Chapter Nineteen

As I raced after Zeda, I could hear Bartholomew's booming voice finally announcing Mom's human cannonball act.

The grand finale.

His voice rumbled through the tent.

"The Incredible is proud to present the unbelievable, unmatchable, phenomenal, and the world's only female cannonball—Flying Aaaa-theee-naaa!"

But of course, I knew it wasn't Bartholomew—it was his double. Not that it mattered at that point.

Zeda was fast, but I was faster. I caught up to her as she rounded a corner. Sharkman was silhouetted just ten feet in front her—and she was barreling toward him at a dead sprint.

I had no choice. I tackled her.

We hit the ground behind a support post hard, rolling over a few times. Against all odds, she hadn't shrieked when I hit her. She glared at me while I tried to send telepathic signals to Sharkman.

Don't turn around. Don't turn around.

Luckily, Not-Bartholomew covered up any noises we'd made.

"You are about to witness the most exceptionally-extraordinary, impressively-inconceivable, death-defying act to appear in any circus, anywhere in the world!"

I peered out from behind the post. Sharkman was crouching, maybe ten feet away, shining a flashlight into...

What is that, a hole? No, wait.

It wasn't a hole.

Was it...was it the sewer?

Sharkman was only there a second before my mom's head appeared, coming up from below. I was aghast.

"Isn't she onstage?" Zeda asked in the tiniest whisper. I shook my head. I knew that *this* was my Mom.

"Her double is onstage," I whispered back.

But if Not-Bart and Not-Mom were onstage, what were the real ones doing?

In a flash, it all made sense. The doubles. The museums. The circus. It was all one big alibi. One big front. If their doubles were onstage, that meant they couldn't be considered suspects. It also meant that Bart and Mom went out—*during the show*—to loot the museums. It was genius. It was diabolical. And it made sense. Every bit.

Zeda saw the realization on my face, but there was no time to tell her what I'd figured out—Sharkman was pushing my mom back into the hole.

"Move it," Sharkman snarled at her. "Your son's ruined everything."

She started to say something, but he put his hand on her head and shoved her underground.

I paused a beat before bolting to my feet. This time, Zeda was pulling on *my* arm, protesting, but I shook her off and crept over to the hole. I was certain it was the sewer—there was a manhole cover right next to me. We stood over it, searching the darkness.

If only I had my flashlight!

But I couldn't wait. Of all the possible reasons I could come up with for Sharkman shoving Mom back down, not one of them was good. He'd sounded mad.

Really mad.

I started to go for the ladder, but Zeda seized my shoulder.

"You're not going down there without me."

"I am," I said, standing firm. "You need make sure Nero is okay and then go get help. Just tell them where I've gone."

"No way!" she argued, shoving me a bit. She sounded mad, but her eyes were large and scared. "I won't let you go alone. You need me."

"Look, if I don't go now, it might be too late. Don't follow me!"

I said resolutely. I mean, really resolutely. I don't think I'd ever been more resolute in my life.

Zeda even took a step back.

Mom needed my help. That was all I knew. That was why I'd gone through all of this. If I didn't help her now, or at least make sure she was all right, what would be the point of me even coming?

I gave Zeda one last look before climbing down into the sewer.

☙

It was dark as a sealed bank vault at the bottom of the ladder. It smelled musty, but not like, well, not like poop, like I'd imagined it would.

Every direction seemed to be an even darker dark. I couldn't see, but you know how you sometimes have a sense of space, even when you're in the dark? It felt more like a tunnel than a room. I put my hand out and found a brick wall. I didn't dare leave that wall, so I stood there, straining my ears and eyes for *something*. My chest felt desperate and tight as I willed something to happen.

But there was nothing.

Don't panic, Spart—they didn't just disappear. Just give it a second.

I felt blind and deaf. It was like I was struggling to use senses I didn't have.

But then…to my left.

Something, in the blackness. It was a sound. Something heavy being dragged—and then, something, like a *jingling*.

I took three slow, deep breaths and then inched along the wall. The jingling grew louder, and then there was a buzzing sound.

No, not a buzzing. *Voices.*

Sticking flat to the wall, I edged along. Soon, I could make out a dim glow. As I got closer, I saw a little more light. I *was* in a tunnel. A short way ahead, the tunnel turned to the left. And someone was just around that corner, with a light.

As I got closer, I started to make out the words.

"...falling apart up there...so stupid!" That was Sharkman's voice.

"Let's use our civilized-people words." That was Bartholomew— I'd recognize his calm, low voice anywhere.

The jingling, tinkling sound made me imagine they were setting a table or doing the dishes.

"...knows everything. And then I found Nero snooping around in the back—I took care of him, but not before he took out Ed and Louie. I think the place is crawling with—"

"Nero?" Bart interrupted. "Why does that name sound familiar?"

"From the freak show. I think they—"

"Finn, I hate be clichéd, but I don't pay you to think," Bart said. "That being said, did you also *think* it was a good idea to use *cloth sacks* to hold silverware? As in actual, honest-to-goodness, sharp knives?"

Silverware. They'd done it! They'd stolen the silverware from the Portland Art Museum, just like I'd guessed!

It took all my willpower not to peek around the corner. But as my eyes adjusted, I could see the shadows of three people on the far wall, people picking stuff up from the ground.

"Well no, I didn't think about it," Sharkman said in his rough growl. I heard more clinking. "I'd just assumed that the stuff was old and wouldn't be that sharp."

"Your assumptions have led to mint-condition, fifteenth-century Elizabethan silver to be spread all over the ground. This—this scratched sauce boat is essentially worthless now."

Ah! They were picking up the silverware!

"It doesn't matter," said Sharkman. "It's over. We need to just leave it and go."

"You're always so quick to tuck your little fin and run," said Mom.

Mom said that? I couldn't believe what I was hearing.

"Think we have enough time to return it?" Mom asked.

"We don't have a choice," answered Bartholomew with a sigh. "If your son's strip show happened as Finn said it did—that's going to make people remember what he said about the museum—shine a light over here, Finn. But if they don't find the silverware missing, they've got nothing on us. Except Spartacus's story and a bunch of circumstantial evidence. And that's if they even decide to look into it."

There was silence and the clinking of silverware, when Mom spoke up again. "The streetcar was easier than this."

"We didn't have to *return* the streetcar, did we?" said Sharkman. "And all because of your kid."

"Lay off, okay?" she retorted. "You think I wanted him to show up? Think I invited him?"

I turned away from the corner and pressed my head to the wall.

I know it sounds naïve and stupid, but up until then, I'd still been clinging to the idea that Mom was an unwilling party in all of this. That Bartholomew had hypnotized her or threatened her to get her to stay. I hadn't prepared myself for the possibility that she was really, truly a thief herself. I was trying to come up with something, some idea to explain away what I'd heard. But as if to drive it home, Mom went on.

"After we return the silverware, we'll entertain Spartacus. There's nothing we can't explain away. He'll end up doubting himself. He'll go home. Then we'll only have to lie low for a few months, and everything will blow over. It'll be like it never happened."

I felt sick listening to her talk to these maniacs like she was one of them.

"Indeed," Bart agreed. "I think that's our only option at the moment. And dear, your most inconvenient child aside, I do have to hand it to you. This space. These—what are they? These Chinese Tunnels?"

"Shanghai Tunnels," Mom corrected him.

I squeezed my eyes shut.

This isn't happening. This isn't happening.

"They are quite a bit nicer—and cleaner—than the sewer. Good find."

"They cross the whole downtown," Mom said. "We'll have to come back to Portland and try this again."

She couldn't be in on this. *But she was.* And now that I knew it, did I want to take her down, right along with Bartholomew? Now that I saw she was every bit as guilty as he was?

No.

I was done.

I was officially done chasing after my mom.

This was, without a doubt, no longer a rescue mission.

I had to get out of there, while I still had a chance to save Will and Zeda and Nero and myself. Bartholomew couldn't find out I'd heard everything they'd just said. That would mean they'd *really* have to get rid of me.

"I think this is the last piece," Sharkman was saying. Then—a noise, coming from the dark, to my right. A rat maybe? Or was it the scrape of a shoe?

"Hey, what was that?" asked Sharkman. I held my breath and shrank back.

Then, even though I couldn't see Bartholomew and the others, I saw their flashlights swivel in my direction. And that's when I saw another shadow—a smaller one—appear on the wall.

It was Zeda.

She'd run right past me, and right into the middle of them.

≈

"Who is this now?" I heard Sharkman exclaim. "Kids are friggin' everywhere!"

Why did she follow me? I panicked. *Why couldn't she stay put?*

"It *is* a circus," Bartholomew said pointedly to Sharkman. "But please, miss, you are...?"

"I—I was looking for someone," she answered in a small voice. "I'll just...um, be going."

She'll be okay, I told myself. I still couldn't see what was happening, but Mom was there. She wouldn't let anything happen to her.

"No, no, by all means, stay," snapped Sharkman.

"Hey! Let go of me!" Zeda cried out.

"Finn!" Mom exclaimed.

I couldn't just listen and imagine what was happening any longer.

I peeked around the corner and there they were: Mom and Bart, dressed all in black with three large duffel bags at their feet—and Sharkman, holding Zeda by the arm. He'd apparently lost one of his black contacts in the scuffle with Nero, which made his eyes look all lopsided and even more terrifying.

As I watched, Bart stepped forward and Sharkman took a tiny, unconscious step backwards.

"This," Bartholomew said through clenched teeth, "is not how we do things."

I breathed a sigh of relief as Sharkman let go of Zeda's arm. Her face was white and unreadable as Bart put his arm around her thin shoulders.

"Besides, it's not necessary, is it?" Bart said, as much to Zeda as to Sharkman. "She's just a girl, Finn. We'll just keep her with us until we find out what's going on. Sometimes it's good to have a little bargaining chip."

Then Bart took out what looked like a walkie-talkie and began fiddling with it.

"Hey, I recognize you," said my mom, crossing over to Zeda. She actually reached out and raised Zeda's face so she could see it better, like an evil villain. "Right! You're from the sideshow, too. You're the fire-breathing girl, right?"

"Nice to meet you, too, Athena," Zeda said icily. Mom dropped her hand away, while Zeda rubbed her face. "We always knew you people were doing something funny."

I cringed. *Why would Zeda say that?*

But she wasn't done.

"I can't believe you're really Spartacus's mom. What kind of mother—"

"You know Spartacus?" my mom asked. She returned to Zeda, looking her in the eye. "What do you know about my son?"

"I know he took on all sorts of danger to try to help you," Zeda said, and I blushed. "And you sure don't look like you're doing him any favors."

"I love my son. You don't know anything about Spartacus or me."

"Both of you—shut up," said Sharkman. "I don't want to hear that kid's stupid name anymore."

"Shhh! All of you," Bart said before speaking into the walkie-talkie: "What's happening up there?"

There was a static-filled pause before the crackling answer came.

"Everything has gone down the toilet. Grand finale went off without a hitch, but for some reason that sideshow is out front, performing—so now the audience isn't leaving, they're just milling around. And we lost the two kids—door was just wide open. I thought—"

But Bart turned off the walkie-talkie with a snap. "Oookay," said Bartholomew coolly to Zeda. "I believe a certain line of civility has officially been crossed. Trespassing. Breaking and entering. *Et cetera.* Finn—as you were."

There was a slight nod to Sharkman and he lunged immediately at Zeda, grabbing her by the throat. This time, he had a gun in his hands.

"Ow!" Zeda cried out in pain and fear.

Oh-no-oh-no-oh-no.

"All right, fire breather," Sharkman said. Still holding Zeda's neck, he put the gun to her stomach. "You tell me every single thing you know, right this instant."

"He's bound to get a fair bit angrier," Bartholomew said to Zeda. "So I would start talking if I were you."

Why did I bring her into this? Why didn't I just go get help with her and leave Mom? My fingernails dug into my palms, my mind racing.

That's when Mom stepped forward, looking concerned.

"This isn't right," she said to Bartholomew.

I breathed a small sigh of relief—she wasn't completely rotten to the core. Bart just shook his head slightly at her, though, like everything was under control.

"I don't know anything!" Zeda shrieked as Sharkman smiled, all his pointy teeth inches from her face.

I'd never felt more helpless in my life. *Think, Spartacus! What should I do? What* can *I do?*

I was about to just jump out and pummel someone (a lot of good that would've done) when my eye caught something shiny on the ground.

It was a fork. A large, heavy-looking fork.

I had only trained with knives, but what was the difference when you got right down to it? Without a moment of hesitation, I stepped out, snatched up the fork, and flung it as hard as I could. It landed square in the middle of Sharkman's back—where it stuck.

"Argh!" he cried out, his hands going to his back, dropping the gun. Zeda was in shock and didn't move a muscle, staring at the three of them in horror.

"Who threw that?" Sharkman demanded. *"Who threw that?"*

Bartholomew picked up the gun—and the flashlight.

"I believe I can answer that," he said, shining the light in my face. "Here's our young hero now. Nice aim with that fork. I might have an opening for you after all."

I squinted back at him, trying to look taller and braver than I was.

"Spartacus!" Mom and Zeda both exclaimed. Zeda rushed over to me and almost crushed my arm in her grip. She was shaking like a leaf. Then again, so was I.

"You're going to pay for that, kid," Sharkman sneered at me, throwing the fork to the ground. Bart looked at him and then at the fork. Sharkman scowled before picking the fork back up and putting it in his duffle bag.

"So you two know each other," Bart said, gesturing wanly with the gun at Zeda and me. It was them versus us, facing off in the tunnel. "Certainly making some interesting friends on this trip, eh, Spartacus?"

I glowered at him. When Mom tried to take a step toward me, Bartholomew held out his arm and stopped her, sighing heavily.

"You don't quit, do you Spartacus?" he asked. "I normally like that quality in a person."

"You can't keep getting away with this," I said, but I was only talking to my mom. I had to reason with her. "Everyone knows about the robberies now."

Zeda nodded in agreement, but otherwise remained silent. My mom started to answer, but Bartholomew interrupted.

"Spartacus, I must correct your language. You keep using the word 'robbery.' These are not *robberies*. *Robbery* is when you take something by force or threaten to harm someone to gain what you want. The word you are looking for is *burglary*. Or even *theft*. But we never hurt people."

"Could have fooled me," I said, glaring at Sharkman, who glared right back.

"There's an exception to every rule," Bart sighed. "Finn is who we use when there is, well—an exception."

"I guess that includes putting me and Will in a cage?" I demanded.

"Will?" Mom asked, looking bewildered. "He's here, too? What cage?"

Sharkman scowled at her. "Your other son showed up. We had to put them both in the monkey cage to keep them out of the way."

Mom shot an angry look at Bartholomew. "What did I say about my kids? I said, *Be gentle with them*."

He held up his hands innocently. "I swear to you, Athena. I knew nothing of this."

After a long moment, Mom's shoulders relaxed, and she nodded. I shook my head in a mixture of disbelief and anger.

"Really, Mom? Cages? You're okay with that?"

"I'm sure the cage was just for a little while. To keep you both safe," she said.

"What kind of mother are you?" Zeda interjected.

"You have a mouth on you," Mom answered in a warning tone.

I stepped between the two of them. *So much for her liking my first girlfriend.*

"*Why* are you doing this?" I asked in desperation. "How can you work with these people? This isn't you!"

"You don't understand, sweetie," she said. "It *is* me." She wanted to say more, but I interrupted, trying to bargain with her.

"Look, if we could get all the silverware returned, like you said, the police wouldn't know you robbed—I mean stole stuff. You could come back home, like it never happened, right?"

She shook her head, not like a "no" to the question, but like in a "you'll-never-understand" way. It was the expression she wore when she was breaking bad news—the type of bad news that wasn't going to change.

"Spartacus," Bartholomew said, looking at his watch. "I'm sorry to say, but the time for returning the thieved items has come and gone." He pulled the walkie-talkie out again, keeping the gun trained on us. "Our other show, on the other hand, must go on."

"How is it up there?" he spoke into the radio.

"It's crazy. People everywhere," came the fuzzy answer.

"We can deal with that. Any boys in blue?" he asked.

I realized he meant the police.

"Not yet," came the answer.

Geez, what does it take to get a couple of cops to show up around here? With accusations of theft and kidnapping, a sighting of a wanted killer, and a display of (very) public indecency, you'd think at least a couple of officers would be kind of curious!

"Perfect. We're going to leave everything in the back yard, and go with Plan S. Copy? Plan S as in Sam."

"Copy that. We have her up and running; meet at point W, as planned."

Was that his escape car? I was confused. He was speaking in some weird code. Zeda looked just as puzzled as Bart put the radio away. He smiled his plastic smile at us.

"Sorry kids, but the intermission is over."

He directed us toward a metal ladder conveniently located just a few feet away. "If I've guessed our location correctly—and I'm quite sure that I have—this exit ought to put us in the perfect position."

Sharkman went up the ladder to remove a manhole cover.

"After you, children." Bartholomew stood aside and waved us up with the gun.

❧

Zeda climbed up ahead of me, glancing down as I followed. Bartholomew and my mom brought up the rear.

I heard Bart speaking to my mom as we climbed.

"I have to say, I'm very sorry to lose the circus—if even for a short time. The children will be so disappointed. I admit, I will be, too."

What did it mean?

When we got to the top, I saw that we were in the empty main tent. The lights were mostly out, except for one of the spotlights. Mom's cannon sat in the ring, but the audience was gone.

There was no one up there except Sharkman, looming over us.

No one to see us; no one to save us.

Zeda's eyes met mine. *What are they going to do?* she seemed to ask.

I shook my head. I didn't have a clue.

Bart and Mom emerged from below, and Zeda took my hand and squeezed it.

I can't believe I got her into this! I glanced around for a way to escape, but all the exits were too far away. Seemed like, even with my mom there, Zeda and I were both in danger—and for once, there was nothing I could do.

And then—something strange happened.

Bartholomew tucked the gun into his jacket pocket.

"Your little burlesque routine on the high dive was—" He paused, pursing his lips. "Well, it was something else. I cannot imagine any other way you could have gotten yourself out of that situation."

I stood there, not understanding.

Bart continued: "You have a lot of gifts, Spartacus. You're cunning. You're astute and quick-witted. You're tenacious. Your aim is...impeccable."

My mind was spinning. *Where was he going with this?*

"You would be an asset in my organization," he said. "I don't offer this lightly. Would you like to join us? I do believe your mother would approve."

My mom looked at me expectantly. Sharkman glowered. Zeda scoffed.

But I just stood there, mouth agape. My whole life came at me in a flash. Will, and Eli, and my dad. Brenville and the pool and my normal, boring life as Spartacus Ryan Poop Lip Zander.

And even though they were thieves and criminals, my mind tried to picture what life with Bartholomew's circus—I mean, his *organization*—would mean. And I couldn't grasp any of it. It was a fuzzy, unimaginable life. All I knew of it was my mom—and when I looked at her, waiting for me to answer, I realized that I didn't know her at all.

"No," was all I could manage.

"Very well," Bartholomew said abruptly. "I rescind my offer. Athena, Finn. Shall we?"

"You're letting us go?" Zeda blurted out.

"Regrettably, yes. And Spartacus," Bartholomew said, bending that smooth, horrifying face close enough to whisper in my ear. "Never forget this: Freedom isn't something I've offered to anyone. Ever. Don't make me regret it."

A chill went down my spine as I nodded.

Then Bartholomew turned to my mom, touching her cheek.

Mom reached up and held his hand while I silently gagged.

"You have five minutes," he said tenderly. "That's all I can wait. I'll meet you in the middle."

❧

Bartholomew and Sharkman strode off through the curtains, leaving Zeda and my mom and me in the empty tent.

I turned to Zeda. "Wait here?"

She nodded.

Mom put her hand out to me. I took it, confused about what this meant, what was happening. We walked toward the stage.

"I'm a bad mother," she said in a shaky voice. I wanted to comfort her, and say she wasn't, but it would have been a lie, and I didn't have any energy left for lies.

It didn't matter that I didn't say anything, though, because she went on.

"I do love you, but I've also got some issues, bigger than you or your father or brother. Problems in my head."

I started to protest, but she put her hand up.

"You have to let me speak," she said softly. "I know how you feel about me. You love me. I know that. But you don't really know me. To you I've always been just *Mom*. But that's not who I am. I mean, that's not all I am. I stayed as long as I could. And when I got the chance to join Bartholomew—well, I didn't know *this* was the kind of adventure I wanted. But now that I have it, I wouldn't trade it. Not for the world."

Then I asked the obvious question. Call me naïve.

"Not even for Will and me?"

She shook her head and I looked away, tears blurring my own eyes now. I rubbed them away with my suit sleeve.

"I know you'll both grow up to be clever and brave young men," she said. "I've always known that. You especially."

I didn't like her talking like this. It sounded like a goodbye. The kind of goodbye that means never going back to the way things were, ever.

I didn't want to hear the rest.

I wanted to run away from her, even after I'd worked so hard to find her.

"You can't just *go*," I whispered.

"I can. And I will miss you, baby, but you have to stay with your family." Mom tried to put her arms around me, but I pushed her away.

"My *family*?" I cried out. I couldn't help it. I was shaking. "You're leaving me with Will and Dad—'*my family*?' They don't understand me, and I don't need them! Will makes my life awful and Dad—Dad doesn't even care. Did I tell you that Will made me think you were *kidnapped*? What kind of rotten family is that?"

"But they *are* your family," she said, tears in her eyes, too. "And you won't get another one. You'll have friends and adventures, but you'll only have one family that's your own blood."

"But it's okay for *you* to throw your family away? How could something so important be so easy to walk away from?"

"It's different—*I'm* the one who doesn't deserve *you*."

I turned away from her and stared at the cannon while she spoke in her low, breaking voice.

"Your dad was there for you when I wasn't. Even when I was home, you can't lie to yourself and say I was a good mother then. Your dad and your brother, they love you, in their own way. That's your family, like it or not. I'm only me, and I left. And while I was there, what did I do for you except give you a name?"

"Great name, too," I muttered to myself.

"I gave you that name for a reason, Spartacus. Because when I was pregnant with you, I had a feeling that your life wasn't going to be normal. Or easy. I wanted you to be strong—a lot stronger than I felt. And look at you now. You are. In every way. You've become stronger than I ever hoped you'd be."

I turned back to face her. We stood looking at each other for a moment before she put her arms out again. I fell into them.

"You were the only thing that made it good," I whispered into her shoulder. "And now you're leaving me again."

"I'm sorry," she whispered, rocking me. "I'm so sorry. I do love you. Remember that."

She was still holding me like that when we heard the crash of doors flying open all around us. I flinched, but Mom just squeezed me tighter.

There were cops—real cops this time—posted at every entrance.

"Time to go," she said, pulling away.

I couldn't tell if they were police, FBI, SWAT, National Guard, or what, but they were closing in. Zeda, who was on the other end of the tent, ducked down behind the seats.

"Put your hands where we can see them!" a man barked. He was actually wearing a bulletproof vest and a helmet.

I threw my hands in the air, but Mom—well, Mom didn't listen.

In an instant, she had scrambled up the backside of the scaffolding next to us and then, like she was some sort of ninja, she leaped at the canvas tent and slid down it, using a knife to slice a hole as she went. Cold air immediately came rushing inside.

Wow. She still impressed me.

"Get on the ground, lady! Get on the ground!"

They moved in closer, but still, she ignored them.

I watched helplessly as she wheeled the cannon to face the hole she'd made.

"Ma'am? Ma'am! I said, don't move!"

She plucked up the helmet from the ground and pulled it on her head, then popped herself into the barrel. Then her head reappeared. "A little help, Spartacus?" she asked, as casually as if she were asking me to help her zip up her dress. But her eyes were pleading.

"Lady, do not—do not do whatever it is you're about to do."

It was funny. She still kind of looked like Mom in there, the mom that made me green-dyed pancakes and who taught me how to play Gin Rummy. She *was* my mom, and when it came down to it, I'd rather have her free somewhere in the world than locked up like an animal in a cage.

"What do I do?" I asked.

"Just turn the key there, and press the button," she said. Then, "You make me very proud, Spartacus."

I didn't know if she meant I *had* made her proud or I *should* make her proud, but I didn't have time to ask.

She dropped down inside and I turned the key and hit the button.

In reality, a circus cannon makes very little noise. Without the fake fuse, fireworks, and explosion, there's nothing really to it. There was just a pause and then the hollow *thwack* of compressed air. We all watched as she shot through the hole in the tent.

It was the first and last time I ever saw my mother perform.

Chapter Twenty

After Mom had blasted off, the cops stared for a second at the hole in the tent, in amazement. Then they cursed and took off for the front of the tent.

Zeda and I raced out after them.

There was a chaotic crowd outside facing the river—it was like the whole audience was still there. Zeda and I shoved our way to the front, scanning the water for my mom.

Where was she?

We could see strange lights on the water. I squinted to make it out—it was like some kind of low, black boat. Then I saw it: the silhouette of someone on top of it, helping my mother out of the river.

"Meet you in the middle," he'd said to her. He'd meant the middle of the river!

"Do you see that?" exclaimed a cop.

"I do, but I don't believe it. What *is* that?" answered another.

"I think...I mean, it *looks* like the submarine," said the first cop.

"From the museum across the way?"

"Yeah—but that thing doesn't work, does it?"

"Got it up and running," Bartholomew had said on the radio. *"Plan S."*

We all watched in disbelief as the two silhouettes climbed into the hatch, closed the door, and then the lights submerged.

Kids clapped. Parents gasped. A helicopter swept over the area, its spotlight showing nothing but bubbles.

"I gotta say," murmured one of the cops. "She makes one heck of an exit."

"You might even say—an *incredible* one?" added a dad standing next to him. His kids groaned.

Zeda rolled her eyes at me, making a gagging face.

"And *I* have to say," said Zeda, turning to me. "That your mom may be the most terrifying and—honestly?—the worst mom I've ever met."

"No kidding," was all I could manage. I was still in shock. But not in enough shock to not realize that some kids—and adults, too, let's be honest—were goggling at me, recognizing me from earlier. I felt heat rising instantly to my face.

"Spartacus Zander?"

I turned. It was one of the SWAT-looking guys who'd been in the tent.

"Yeah?" I answered sheepishly.

"Come with me," he commanded. I didn't even argue.

He took me by the arm and led me to a park bench. Zeda followed.

"Don't move a muscle," he said as I sat down. "Just stay right there, okay?"

I don't know why he trusted me, but I knew I was done running.

So Zeda and I sat there, looking at the craziness around us. The place was absolutely crawling with people. The sideshow had done its job, keeping everyone there. Their bus was across the way, strung with lights, but there were too many people to actually see what was going on.

But in the foreground, there were police cars, fire engines, and ambulances. It was what I'd been hoping for all along. They'd finally come—too late, I guess. But at least everyone would finally know the truth. We watched as the police rounded up the performers and tech people Bartholomew had left behind. Some were just being questioned; a few had blankets thrown over their shoulders while they cried. I saw quite a few clown cops being loaded into waiting squad cars.

"Pardon the phrase," Zeda said, "but what a circus."

I wasn't sure if she meant Bartholomew's circus or all the

confusion. But I didn't care. Instead, I turned to her and abruptly asked, "Why did you follow me?"

"I couldn't let you go down there alone," she answered, exasperated. "You shouldn't have run off after them in the first place."

"No, no," I answered. "Not in the tunnels. I mean to Portland. Why are you here? *How* are you here?"

Zeda gave me an awkward smile. "I talked the sideshow into coming and performing after the show. The people always linger when there's a second show. I assumed it would create too much chaos for Bartholomew to really try anything."

"So everyone in the sideshow knew what I was trying to do?" I asked.

"Well, I told them what you said—I don't know how many of them believed me. You heard Nero. Even he thought it was crazy until he saw Will and you in the cage. But the rest, no matter what they thought, wanted the chance to stick it to Bartholomew. The sideshow always annoyed him—what? Why are you looking at me like that?"

I guess I was grinning a bit too widely at her. But I couldn't help it.

"You did that for me? Why?"

Zeda's cheeks flushed.

"Well, I couldn't let you do all that yourself," she said. "I mean, we're friends, right?"

I think we were about to have some big romantic, mushy scene, but my dumb brother chose to interrupt at that exact moment.

"Ryan!" he gasped, running across the grass toward us. Zeda and I jumped back from each other, embarrassed. He sat down next to me, oblivious to the perfect moment he'd just ruined, his face shining with excitement. "You guys okay?"

"Yeah. You?"

"Fine. I'm fine. Nero is fine, too," he told Zeda, pointing over to an ambulance out in the street.

282

"Nero! I need to see him," Zeda said, jumping up. She and I exchanged an awkward look. "I'll see you in a bit, okay?"

I just nodded and watched her disappear in the crowd, in utter disbelief.

She likes *me. Sure, she'd kissed me before, but that was just about—*

Then Will interrupted again, this time snapping his fingers in my face.

"Hey, Casanova!" He was giving me a sick grin. "What was all that about, eh? Did I interrupt something?"

"Shut up," I said, but I couldn't keep the corners of my mouth down. Luckily, a paramedic arrived to check on us, so he changed the subject.

"Was that Mom who blasted out through the tent? Into the river?"

I nodded. The paramedic was trying to be professional, but I could tell she was listening. She gave me an ice pack to hold against my knee.

"Where's she going?" Will asked.

"All I know is that it's not Brenville," I glowered. Will stared at the river with a weird expression. Sadness, maybe? Or longing? I'd never really thought that Will even missed Mom, but the look on his face pretty much proved that he did. I could tell he wanted to say something, but he must have pushed it down, because he stayed quiet.

"What happened after we left?" I asked, trying to get him talking again.

"Oh, yeah, I forgot to say, thanks *so* much for coming back to help," he said sarcastically. "I had to carry Nero outside to the sideshow, but by then all the cops and ambulances were arriving. Hey—*are those my shoes?*"

I was about to explain when I heard a familiar, booming voice.

"Got another one for you!" It was Lloyd, coming up from the riverbank—and he was dragging a thrashing, but pretty much defeated, Sharkman behind him. I couldn't believe my eyes.

What was Lloyd doing?

I tried to slouch down so neither of them could see me, but the paramedic squeezed my wrist.

"Try to sit still, please," she said while dressing a cut on my arm.

By the looks of both Lloyd and Sharkman, there had been another epic battle—one that Lloyd had apparently won. Sharkman had a bloody nose and it looked like his fin was crooked. Two police officers rushed over and handcuffed him. As they heaved him past us, though, he saw me on the bench. The look he gave me chilled me to the bone. Even the paramedic flinched when she turned and saw him.

"You don't know how many people you've crossed, you little rat," Sharkman snarled. "This is bigger than Bartholomew now! *Way* bigger!"

One of the cops was about to say something when Will stood up, his chest thrust out.

"Shut your friggin' fish hole!" Will hollered. "No one threatens my brother, you got it?"

And before Sharkman could say anything else, the cops threw him in the back of a squad car. He was still yelling in there, but I couldn't hear anything.

I turned to stare at Will like I'd never seen him before.

"What?" he said sheepishly.

Then he saw my expression change.

"What?" he asked again, only this time it was nervous.

There was no time to explain to Will about Lloyd—but he was approaching us fast.

∾

Lloyd strode over to us, shaking his head, a grin on his face.

What was he doing here? A killer surrounded by cops and not batting an eyelash—it's ridiculous!

"Never thought I'd get bitten by a shark on dry land!" Lloyd joked, limping toward us and dropping on the bench next to me.

"H-hey, Lloyd," I stuttered, watching him pull up his pant leg to show a bite mark on his calf.

"You got any antiseptic for this?" he asked the paramedic.

Oh, god, don't leave us alone with him, I pleaded with my eyes, but the paramedic nodded and jogged over to one of the ambulances.

"Guess Bartholomew had had enough of his fish friend," he said. "I heard him on the bank of the river, shouting for them to come back."

"So you fought him?" Will asked.

"Let's call it a citizen's arrest," he winked, before putting out his hand. "I'm Lloyd, Spartacus's friend. I gave him a ride from Bend to Boise a few days ago, for the funeral."

"Right. The funeral…" Will said slowly, shaking Lloyd's hand, but looking at me. "I'm his brother, Will."

"I think he told me about you," Lloyd said. Will looked confused.

"Where's—uh, where's your mom?" I asked Lloyd, struggling to act natural.

"I sent her home in a cab when I realized things were getting too out of control." There was a long pause before he said it. "That was some mess you were in, Spartacus."

"No kidding," I managed. I mean, there wasn't anything I could really say about it at that point, was there? It was exactly that: a mess.

"I kinda knew you were in trouble, even before you called about seeing the circus," Lloyd continued. "Something just seemed *off*. And when you didn't come back after the intermission? And then, of course, there was your *performance*."

My face went red again, just at the thought of what I'd done in front of…oh god, thousands of people. I'd probably relive that moment in nightmares for the rest of my life.

"It wasn't supposed to turn out like that," I mumbled.

"I wouldn't think that would be part of your plan," Lloyd said wryly. "That's what made me call the cops."

285

"You?" I asked, incredulous. *"You* called them?"

"Who wouldn't?" he countered. "You laid it all out on the line. And I mean *all* of it."

It didn't make any sense. *Why would he...? He'd put his own freedom at risk for me?*

At that moment, two younger performers from the circus approached us, a guy and a girl. Behind them was a tired-looking cop, gripping a notepad.

"Hey kid," said the cop. "They got something to say to you."

I gulped.

The performers looked shyly at me; I recognized that they were the contortionists from the beginning of the show.

"We just wanted to thank you," said the guy, surprising me.

"All of us thank you," added the girl. "I didn't think we'd ever get to go home."

It took me a second to realize what they were saying. They *had* been trapped. The rumors about The Incredible were true! My heart pounded as I looked back to the crowd of performers. Those that weren't arrested were hugging one another. Dancing. Crying. Laughing.

My mouth fell open.

"You mean that—" I started, but the cop corralled them away before I could finish.

Lloyd, Will, and I exchanged amazed looks. We didn't get the chance to say anything because, waiting patiently behind them, was a small man in a brown suit.

I thought he was also there for me, but he spoke to Lloyd instead.

"Dan Lloeke?" he asked. One hand showed a badge and the other was on the butt of his gun. My stomach dropped and Will's mouth gaped open. It was the last piece of my plan, falling into place—too little, too late. I felt guilty and my gaze dropped to my lap.

"Oh, hey, Jerome," said Lloyd easily. "Nope. I'm still Lloyd. Busy night, huh?"

What? I looked up and saw Lloyd holding out his arm with the tattoo while the guy with the badge inspected it with a penlight.

I watched, completely confused.

"You have no idea," answered the officer, putting the penlight away. "I'm glad I'm only here to see you—the rest of this looks like a nightmare of paperwork."

"No doubt," Lloyd chuckled.

"Sorry to bother you again," said the officer. "Have a good night." He turned away and disappeared into the crowd.

"What was that?" I ventured.

"We-ell, since you've shared your family secrets," Lloyd said. "I might as well share mine. Remember when you said you had a rotten brother?"

Will shot me a dirty look, but Lloyd went on.

"And I told you I have one, too. Dan Lloeke is my brother—my twin brother. And Dan...well, let's just say he's done some awful things that we're all paying for."

"Your twin," I repeated slowly.

"Yep," Lloyd said, looking at me thoughtfully. "Jerome"—he waved in the general direction of where the man had disappeared in the crowd—"and I do this pretty regularly."

Oh god. I knew I was giving myself away, but I didn't care.

"But the shaved head—" I stuttered.

"We both went bald in our twenties."

"And the tattoo—"

"Same band, different songs."

"And...and the face."

"Twins," he said again. "Identical."

Will just sat there in disbelief, trying to sort everything out from the pieces he was hearing.

I was quiet for a few moments before I confessed.

"I called the police. I thought—"

Lloyd waved his hand dismissively, before I could apologize.

"I understand, Spartacus," he said, looking me in the eye. "You did everything you could. I would have done the same thing."

As he said my name—my *real* name—I felt like I finally understood who I was.

ॐ

After Lloyd drifted off and Will went to fetch my backpack, I had my first moment alone.

I felt like I'd been going at a hundred miles an hour since, well, since forever. I saw Zeda and the sideshow through the thinning crowd and she waved at me. I was smiling, waving back, when I remembered. I'd been going a hundred miles an hour *since I lost Matilda.*

Matilda.

I couldn't believe I'd forgotten about her.

I am the worst pseudo-boyfriend ever.

Ignoring what the SWAT guy had said about staying on the bench, I raced over to the first firefighter I saw.

"I need a ladder. My—well, my pet is up in a tree and she's... she's really important."

Zeda jogged over to me while the firewoman fetched a ladder.

"What are you doing off your bench?" Zeda teased.

"I didn't get the chance to tell you earlier," I began, my shoulders slumped. "Matilda—well, she got out."

"Oh, no!" Zeda clapped her hand over her mouth. "I forgot about her!"

"She might still be in the last place I saw her, though," I said trying to sound hopeful, but I couldn't hide how dejected I felt. "I'm so sorry."

"It's not your fault," she said softly, surprising me by pulling me into a tight hug. When I pulled away, I saw she was crying.

Will appeared with Remmy and Robin and we all walked along with a panicked Zeda as I led three firefighters over to the funnel-cake stand.

288

"That old girl has got enough sense to survive anywhere." Remmy was trying to comfort Zeda. Then he turned to me. "And don't look so glum, kid. That Great Responsibility we talked about doesn't mean you have to be a superhero and save everyone."

"But it was just one lemur," I sighed. "How could I not hold onto a single, tiny lemur?"

"Spiderman, as far as I know, never had to babysit an aye-aye," Remmy said. "And, lemur or no, I sure think you've done more than your fair share of the hero work in the past few days."

"I agree," said Robin.

"Me, too," sniffled Zeda, squeezing my hand again.

"Ditto," said Will.

I looked around at the tired but hopeful faces and felt a bit of relief. There was nothing I could say. I was with friends—and they understood.

The firefighters leaned a ladder against the booth and Zeda called out: "Matiiiilda! Matilda? Here, girl!" She was wringing her hands so tight it was hard to watch.

I really, really hoped she was still up there. It was so dark and everything had been so crazy and loud. She had to be scared, being in a strange place, away from Zeda and the sideshow. They were the only family she had. She just had to be up there.

Will, seeing my shining eyes, reached out and put a heavy hand on my shoulder. I nodded back at him.

Then the five of us just stood there, looking up into the dark tree branches, listening as the firefighters rustled about. And then one of them let out a frightened yell:

"AAAAYEEE!"

Zeda clapped her hands, jumped up and down shouting, "Matilda! Matilda! Matilda!"

We all cheered. Zeda grabbed me in a bear hug. Relieved, I looked over Zeda's shoulder at Will, who was giving me the thumbs-up.

Funny how it all turned out, this reuniting-families business.

Zeda got Matilda…and I got Will.

Will was pretending to make out with his hand.

I snorted.

At least it was something.

Epilogue

After the police were through talking with us, the sideshow offered to give Will and me a ride to Brenville. I won't ever forget the look on Dad's face when he saw us getting out of that crazy sideshow bus. At first, he was angry with everyone. He yelled at me and Will and even Remmy and Robin. But he calmed down after they explained to him how I'd pretty much single-handedly brought down Bartholomew's World-Renowned Circus of The Incredible and International Crime Ring.

Then I couldn't get Dad to shut up about it.

It was embarrassing. It didn't help that the story was all over the Oregon news. It even made the national news. By the end of the first week, everyone in town had heard, and I couldn't avoid the whispers of people saying, "Did you hear what Spartacus did?"

The Sideshow of Curiosities and Mayhem stuck around Brenville for a few days—they even did a few performances in the pool parking lot. It seemed like the whole town came to watch them at least twice.

The show was every bit as amazing as Remmy had said it was. I definitely thought Zeda's fire-breathing routine was the best part.

But even though I was something of a hero, Dad didn't think that completely made up for my running away. Will came up with a deal, though, where he'd share in my grounding. That way I'd only be grounded for the rest of the summer—and not the rest of my life.

It was pretty nice of him.

But then, it was pretty nice of *me* not to bring up the whole Will-sending-me-postcards story to Dad. But after all we'd been through together, we had a newfound respect for each other.

It took maybe two weeks of transition, but Will never called me Poop Lip again. Neither did anyone else—except for the guy at the gas station, but he'd always been weird. And, strangely enough, everyone thought the logical replacement for *Poop Lip* was *Spartacus*. It was like, over a week, I'd become someone else.

And not a single person brought up the pool incident—to my face at least, which was all I could hope for.

As for Eli, he was grounded for even longer than *I* was. Then again, it was because he took forever to read James Joyce's *Ulysses* and write his book report for his parents.

"Eight hundred pages!" he'd exclaimed to me. "Eight *hundred!*"

I figured I was going to owe him for a long time to come, but he never complained or blamed me. In fact, when Dad sent me over to apologize to his parents, Eli greeted me with a triumphant smile and a couple of enthusiastic high-fives.

"We *totally* brought him down," he said, and I grinned back.

Then his parents sent him up to his room. He gave me a thumbs-up as he slowly and comically backed out of the room. His parents just shook their heads.

And if his parents weren't happy with him, they wanted to *strangle* me. I had to sit at the Carson dining room table and get chewed out by his father *and* mother, each of them speaking over the other in their rush to call me "reckless" and "irresponsible" and "out of control."

It was a strange summer, to say the least.

I hadn't been home long when I read the news online about Blue and White. They were let out on bail, but disappeared before their trial. Two crazy bats, out on the lam. I honestly wasn't too worried about White coming after my skull to hold her yarn balls, like she'd threatened. But…even a whiff of vanillaroma air freshener made me jumpy.

I never heard from Hailey again. I tried to find her online, but she wasn't anywhere to be found. I wished I could find out if she ever went home, or if she found someone to trust. For a while, every time I saw a semi-truck, I craned my neck to see if she was driving.

Eli and I weren't allowed to talk until school started. We *did*, of course, we just had to be sneaky. We met at the fence a lot that summer, me slipping comic books and candy to him from the "outside."

We also emailed each other strange new posts we found on IHateBartholomewsCircus.com. Someone was still updating the site. The posts had gotten more and more outrageous, including ridiculous stories about The Incredible's temporary hiatus and exile to Asia. Even though we were fairly certain Bartholomew was the one updating the site as part of his evil plans, I couldn't help checking it. It was as addictive as ever. And it made me feel like I was staying connected to Mom.

Mom.

I heard from Mom less than before, but it's not hard to understand why. Her postcards came from places like Shanghai and Seoul. She said they were still "performing" (whatever that might have meant), but she never mentioned where. I guess with Interpol after you, you couldn't be too precise in your postcards. And I'm sure they were all being read before they got to me, anyway.

It's kind of hard facing the fact that the world is sometimes *nothing* like you think it is. I could make a mile-long list of things I'd gotten wrong—everything is so much easier to see in retrospect. Sure, it's easy to say I made mistakes because I was just a kid who didn't know any better. But if I learned anything from the whole experience with Bartholomew and my mom, it's that you can't ever be too sure about anything.

Just look at Will. I thought he was evil, without one redeeming quality. But after he realized what a crappy brother he'd been… everything changed. Will became, well, actually *cool*. We even started having fun together.

And then there was Dad. I'd always looked at him as the enemy, the one who practically drove Mom off. But what Mom had told me was the truth. He *had* stayed with us after she'd taken off. Sure, he was a big grump for a long time after she left, but, looking back on everything, I couldn't really blame him. Dad was someone who'd loved and lost, but he was dealing with it the best he could. He loved Will and me, though. And he was trying. Especially after I came back, I could see he was trying. So I tried. And when he suggested I join the swim team in the fall, I humored him.

And my mom? Well, she wasn't the person I thought she was. To say the least.

For a long time, lots of people would ask me about her. Teachers, kids, Eli, Zeda. Especially Zeda; she always grilled me for details. Whenever we saw each other (which was never enough), or talked on the phone (which was as often as we could), she had a hundred different questions for me.

"Do you hate her? Do you love her and hate her at the same time? Can you ever forgive her? What would you do if you saw her again?" Tough questions like that.

But it's complicated.

I always think about what Lloyd told me on the phone once, when I asked him what it was like having such a messed-up brother.

He said, "You can hate what your family does, but you always have the choice to still love them like family."

I guess that's how I feel about Mom. I don't like what she's doing, but I don't have a say in how she leads her life, do I? If I could stop her, I would. Honestly, just thinking about her and Bartholomew out there, together, makes me so mad sometimes. But I know that I still love her, and I always will. And I still haven't given up hope that she might get tired of her dangerous life and come home someday. If she does, well, I'd take her back, no questions asked. (Though I can't say the same thing about the cops or Dad.) Even after all she's put me through, she's still my mom.

And I love her.

And that's one of the only things I am sure about.